LILAC

Braxton

Houston

Loren

Rich

B.B. REID

Lilac by B.B. Reid

ISBN: 9798570567030

Chief Editor: Rogena Mitchell-Jones of RMJ Manuscript Service LLC
Co-editor: Colleen Snibson of Colleen Snibson Editing

Cover Design by Amanda Simpson of Pixel Mischief Design
Interior Design/Formatting by Champagne Book Design

For Tijuana Turner.

She dragged me kicking and screaming to the finish line.

She had not known the weight until she felt the freedom.

—Nathaniel Hawthorne, *The Scarlet Letter*

ALSO BY B.B. REID

Broken Love Series

Fear Me

Fear You

Fear Us

Breaking Love

Fearless

Stolen Duet

The Bandit

The Knight

When Rivals Play Series

The Peer and the Puppet

The Moth and the Flame

Evermore (novella)

The Punk and the Plaything

The Prince and the Pawn

Standalones

Lilac

PLAYLIST

Lose Yourself—Eminem

Monsters—Shinedown

Dear God—XTC

Down with the Sickness—Disturbed

Love and War—Fleurie

Headstrong—Trapt

I Want It That Way—Backstreet Boys

Sober—Tool

Angels Fall—Breaking Benjamin

Black is the Soul—Korn

Polyamorous—Breaking Benjamin

Best Thing I Never Had—Beyoncé

Bed of Lies—Nicki Minaj ft Skylar Grey

Apologize—Timbaland ft OneRepublic

Spastik—Plastikman

Basiel—Amelie Lens

Oh Bondage! Up Yours!—X Ray Spex

Open Your Eyes—Disturbed

Bring Me to Life—Evanescence

So What—Pink

Light My Fire—The Doors

THE WORLD MOURNS A TRAGIC LOSS
October 20 2017
America's Daily News

Calvin Everill, the lead guitarist of Bound, was found dead yesterday morning from a drug overdose. At twenty-seven, the not-yet proclaimed legend is survived by his bandmates who could not be reached for a statement. While mourning, fans are anxious to learn about the fate of the upcoming world tour and who Bound's front man, rumored to be meticulous, will deem worthy of filling Everill's shoes.

ONE

Braxton

THE NEWS WAS REPORTING THE SAME STORY.

No one would suspect the government had shut down, and parts of the country were still suffering from last year's hurricanes. There had been ten mass shootings this month alone, but reports had taken a back seat for one tragedy in particular.

Every channel and their avid audiences were tuned in to the death of Calvin Everill.

After three months, there was nothing new to report, no suspicion of foul play.

The rock star had simply overdosed on cocaine.

My gaze remained glued to the screen of the mounted TV across from me while the smell of brine filled my nose. I couldn't stop my leg from bouncing or the umpteenth shift in the hard plastic chair. The receptionist who'd greeted me when I arrived was oblivious to my distress as her desk phone rang nonstop.

The offices of Savant Records were thirty floors up with the Los Angeles sun shining through the windows and highlighting the modern industrial space. More phones were ringing somewhere, accompanied by the clicking of computer keys and the hurried footsteps of a low-level employee and confident stride of an executive.

Everyone seemed to be in a frenzy today, which meant something big must be happening while I awaited my fate.

I blamed myself for arriving late even though my sister had

puked all over my clothes, leaving me no choice but to borrow something from her closet. Each choice had been more god-awful than the last.

With shaking hands, I smoothed down the dress I'd chosen, a corduroy ankle-length tarp with wide shoulder straps. Since it was January, I'd paired it with a white long-sleeve shirt. The only things I wore that were mine were my thong, second-hand Docs, and the black choker around my neck with a gold crescent moon hanging from the center.

No, this one was all on me.

I'd known going home before the most important meeting of my life was irresponsible. It's just that Amelia Fawn, nearly six hundred miles away, still ruled me with an iron fist.

When the news story changed, my interest in what was airing became very real. I couldn't look away. Like the rest of the world, I was hoping for a glimpse of them—Houston Morrow, Loren James, and Jericho Noble.

The remaining members of Bound.

Most celebrities would have tweeted how sad they were by now. In the age of social media, you weren't angry or grieving unless you posted about it online. Our instincts dictated we run to strangers on the internet the moment we experience pain, to tell the world how deeply gutted we are over the loss of our loved ones—as if the multitude of absentminded apologies and offers of prayers would actually mend the rip. Calvin Everill's bandmates, on the other hand, had no comment.

Not a single goddamn word.

And so the world forgot their grief for intrigue.

Just like that.

The once adoring fans' favorite target of the three was Bound's front man and lead vocalist. The latest asinine theory was that Houston Morrow murdered his guitarist.

Even I had to admit that it wasn't *entirely* baseless.

Morrow and Everill had kept the voracious blogs busy for the past year with their open hatred for one another. The world was now divided between people who believed Morrow murdered

Everill and those who couldn't care less for the same reason the talented guitarist had gotten away with being a junkie.

Houston Morrow was revered.

Even more so than Calvin. While the guitarist had been on the road to legendary, Houston had already blazed that trail.

A clip of the band's last performance together flashed across the screen as they played one of their biggest hits, "Fatal Fever."

Hearing the lyrics, I was more anxious than ever. It was impossible that Bound had written them specifically for me, but that's what it felt like. Even though I'd shown up for this meeting and filled my lungs with hope, I was still pretending to be normal, still pretending I wanted to be cured.

Sweeping the red strands of my hair off my nape, I piled them high into as neat a bun as I could manage without pins or a mirror and only my black, almond-shaped nails. It was hardly professional, but neither was sweating profusely.

I tasted the syrupy sweetness of cherries on my tongue, even though I hadn't eaten since last night, as I watched Houston Morrow shift between crooning and screaming into the microphone he clutched as if it had personally wronged him. The camera zoomed in on the raging storm and the thick strands of dark brown hair and his eyes, which reminded me of evergreens—an entire forest of them. Each droplet of his sweat seemed perfectly timed with the arousal pooling between my thighs. I didn't bother pressing them together. I already knew it wouldn't help.

Neither would soothing the ache—unless he had all night.

On cue, the camera moved to the most ostentatious display of arrogance and sex. Loren James stood on the stage behind Morrow, but he performed as if he were front and center. My hands clutching the arms of the chair and the rest of me clinging to control had two distinct reactions. As one grip tightened, the other loosened. The stage lights bounced off the silver medallion hanging from the bassist's neck. The chain swayed over pectorals exposed underneath his unbuttoned black shirt while the glinting metal of the trinket called attention to his nipples. His shirt was so dark and delicate that the material made his tan skin and elaborate coif of dark-blond hair appear pale. He flirted with the crowd, the music, and the camera with a smile I could feel in my *bones*.

I sighed with want for something I could never have just as the camera panned again. Furthest from the front of the stage, but still somehow a relentless beacon, sat Jericho Noble. The true heart of Bound. He drove the beat and tempo that kept the crowd on their feet and their hands in the air as he hammered the drum kit and kept time. He always looked as if he'd been caught in the rain with his inky black hair falling over his eyes and curling around his ears as he twisted and bounced his head in perfect rhythm. I knew that when he inevitably looked up to tease the crowd, I'd find silver eyes flecked with gold and a black spiral piercing at the corner of his bottom lip.

At last, the camera settled on the scruffy beard and shoulder-length blond hair of Calvin Everill as he provided Houston with backup vocals. I felt the heat warming my freckled cheeks fade as sorrow took hold. Despite his shady personal life, he had a gift no one could replicate, though I'd been his pupil for years. Eventually, I learned to trust myself as a guitarist and even preferred my own style.

Still, there was this stirring in my gut that began the moment I learned of his death, and it wouldn't abate. Conceitedly, it felt like the weight of the world had settled on my shoulders. I was trapped inside a well of confusion, wondering why I couldn't shake the feeling that I was all that remained of Calvin Everill's legacy.

Like all the times before, I brushed aside what was undoubtedly a fantasy rather than a warning of destiny. I was pretty certain every guitarist who fancied themselves a student of Calvin's felt the same. Besides, there had been nothing admirable or worth idolizing about Everill beyond his skill with a guitar—or any of Bound's surviving members.

Was it coincidence or fate being cheeky that Morrow, James, and Noble were the ones who'd founded Bound and were now the only ones left?

"There you are!"

I finally tore my gaze away from the television just as some girl with brown braided pigtails and a colorfully striped sweater rushed into the waiting area. She had stars in her eyes, and I wondered who put them there. I stared at her, making sure I was who she was looking for even though no one besides the receptionist and me was around.

"Sorry, I'm late," I greeted while standing and holding out my hand. "Braxton."

"Casey. I'm Oni's assistant. If you'll just follow me. Everyone's already waiting in the conference room. I'm afraid the meeting started without you."

I inwardly cringed.

That meant all eyes would be on me when I walked into the room, and I wouldn't be able to hide or play off my tardiness.

Casey rushed off, and I tried to keep up while thinking of an excuse to give Oni. The artists and repertoire rep wasn't known for her welcoming personality. She was a bit of a hard-ass, but I'd been raised by the worst of them, so I told myself I could handle anything she threw at me.

I just hoped it wasn't the door.

I wasn't like the other musicians who'd clawed and scraped for this moment, this once-in-a-lifetime opportunity. Did I earn it? Yes. But it had never been my intention. Now, I couldn't blow it, and it wasn't because Oni had made it clear this would be my only shot.

I almost groaned out loud when "Lose Yourself" by Eminem began playing in my head.

Great.

I didn't pay much attention to my surroundings as Casey led me to a conference room, but I couldn't ignore the drastic change in atmosphere when I stepped inside the large room.

My gaze fell on Oni Sridhar first.

Brown skin, black hair, and even darker expression, the A&R rep looked understandably pissed as she sat at the long conference table. The apology I rehearsed was on the tip of my tongue when my nervous gaze shifted to the other occupants in the room.

Genuine surprise tasted tart like ripe, green apples—crisp,

sour, sometimes sweet, and while mostly refreshing, this wasn't one of those times.

The power running my brain flickered uncontrollably until blinking out completely—a total fucking blackout. When the backup generator finally kicked in, my first thought was that Casey had made a huge mistake. This was the wrong room, the wrong meeting.

It had to be.

And there wasn't just one reason.

There were *three*.

The first leaned against the floor-to-ceiling windows. Bundled in a white hoodie with long arms folded, his gray gaze shone like silver, and the gold in them rivaled the center of our solar system beaming through the windows behind him. As that sun touched his black hair, I was tempted to run my fingers through the messy strands. His hair was so dark that the white cotton of his hoodie appeared starker than freshly fallen snow, his pierced lips a tempting pink like strawberry icing on a cupcake.

God, I wanted a taste.

The second lounged carelessly in a high-backed chair, his blond hair gelled and pushed off his forehead and tucked behind his ears. While he lazily chewed a stick of gum, I ran my gaze over his torso, unsurprised that the dress shirt he wore was splayed open, despite him being in the middle of a business meeting. He flaunted and seduced as if it were second nature. The strong column of his neck even sported the medallion he never seemed to be without. I'd never been close enough to see what was on it, but I was told it was his family's crest. He'd been the only one of the three to come from money.

The final earth-shattering reason stood at the head of the conference table. His gray T-shirt was fitted enough to show off his impressive chest without making it obvious he wanted everyone else to notice too.

You know the type.

I admired his arms and the corded veins until my gaze reached his large hands planted on the table surface. When his finger tapped the wood impatiently, my gaze shot up to his styled brown hair, though not as thoroughly as his bassist, before finally meeting his gaze. Instantly, I was drowning in a forest of green. Instantly, he hated me.

Hester, give me strength.

My eyes had to be deceiving me.

What was unfolding…couldn't possibly be.

The only flaw in my logic was that no one could ever mistake Houston Morrow, Loren James, and Jericho Noble.

It was them.

Bound.

TWO

Houston

Time stood still when she walked through the door.

Wearing a burlap sack and red hair like living fire, her brown eyes seemed to stretch wider than humanly possible when she realized who occupied the room. I was genuinely surprised she recognized us. I would even have been flattered if I weren't so pissed. She looked like she'd come straight off the prairie. That hideous dress she wore covered her from neck to ankle. Her too-big eyes and lips made her look weird as fuck. And unpredictably stunning.

I couldn't look away from the beautiful paradox, and there were a few reasons why.

The first was because she'd rudely interrupted me. I was in the middle of telling Carl Cole and his flunkies exactly how I liked my dick sucked when she barged in. Now I couldn't think of anything other than enlightening her. Those lips of hers looked perfect for the job—even if the rest of her wasn't up to the task. No way she wasn't a virgin—not that she'd say no.

The seconds ticked by, too many of them, and she still hadn't spoken. Her only reaction was her full lips parting. They were red and swollen like she'd been kissed to within an inch of her life. Even as my jealousy struggled to surface, I wondered if they were natural. My dick told me they were. My gut was too busy tying itself into an endless knot.

"Are you lost?" Loren inquired, always the first to be an asshole. "Or did you lose your voice in that ugly-ass dress?"

There were snickers drowned out by a throat clearing.

Carl.

The dick who owned this shady label, and now he was intervening before the fire rising in the girl's eyes turned Loren to ash.

Shame. I would have enjoyed watching her try.

"Casey, can we help you?"

The intern looked ready to shit a brick when she realized her obvious mistake. "I'm sorry, sir. You told me to bring Ms. Fawn right away when she arrived."

The room fell so quiet I wondered if they heard my nuts retracting back inside my body.

No.

Hell. No.

This could not be Braxton Fawn. To start, I assumed he'd be a dude. Even worse than Fawn being a woman was the fact that I wanted her.

As if only now remembering that she was responsible for this mess, Oni Sridhar shot to her feet. When the pain-in-the-ass A&R rep didn't immediately dismiss the intruder, I stood up straight, catching the prairie girl's reaction to my height.

Give me a break.

"Yes," Oni confirmed as she strutted with too much confidence for my liking toward the door where her intern and the imposter stood. "This is the promising up-and-comer I was telling you about. I think Braxton is just what Bound needs to take it to the next level."

"The next level?" Rich spat as he straightened from his position near the windows. It took a lot to anger him since he was supposed to be the nice one. Right now, he was *pissed* and rightly so. We'd given the world everything, and it still wasn't enough. It never was. "Who's your mom's favorite band? Pink Floyd? I bet if Nick Mason gave her a million to suck his dick, she'd still suck mine for free."

Oni whirled on her fuck-me pumps to face my drummer. Fucking her was what I should have done when I had half the chance. Now she couldn't stand me, or any of us for that matter, and I hated whenever we breathed the same air. "Perhaps she would if my mom were still alive and Nick wasn't over seventy years old. *Are you done*?"

I saw the regret in Rich's eyes, but he didn't offer an apology. Oni had already turned away. Before she could continue with her ludicrous pitch, Loren took his turn exploding.

"Please tell me you're joking. This is Braxton? *She's* our new guitarist?" My bassist didn't move from his slouched position in the chair, but the vicious sneer he shot Braxton did the trick. "This chick looks like she just came from choir practice."

Slowly, little Miss Fawn's head turned. We weren't prepared for the force of her full attention. The awe in her gaze when she'd stepped into the room was gone. Her doe eyes had sharpened and cut us down before she spoke.

"Actually, it was Bible study."

Loren jerked as if someone had run an electric bolt through his heart before remembering he had the upper hand. "I don't give a fuck if it was Bible *camp*. Get lost."

Disappointment ripped through my chest when Oni cut in before Braxton could retort. I had no intention of letting some blushing virgin join Bound, so I was more than eager to have my fun with her while I could. Loren would eat her insolent ass alive, and I'd savor every second of it.

"You had your chance to find a replacement and knew what would happen if you didn't. The tour starts in *three months*. You barely have any time left to rehearse."

"We know the material," Rich reminded her dryly. "We wrote it."

"*Braxton*," Oni said, emphasizing her name, "doesn't."

"Hello? Is anyone at home in there?" Lo inquired, tapping his own skull. "Or are you secretly blonde?"

"So, the pot calls the kettle."

He ignored that. "If she doesn't know our music, what makes you think she's a good fit for our band?"

"You can teach her."

Rich's nostrils flared.

Loren rolled his eyes. "Not interested."

"They don't have to teach me," Braxton announced. She'd found her damn tongue. A moment later, we all learned a valuable lesson.

It was sharper than razor blades.

"I know the material." Her gaze found Loren's, and I was sure he had stopped breathing. He sat so very still. "Probably better than you since I caught your last performance. You missed three notes and were behind your drummer half the show." She tipped her head in Rich's direction, her red mane shimmering under the natural light. The very sun seemed to serve as her personal spotlight.

For a moment, I allowed myself the vision of pulling on her hair while I punished her pussy from behind. From her looks, she had no idea what a dick looked like, much less how to handle one. I shoved the pointless fantasy away.

Loren, miraculously, had nothing to say. I'd already ripped into him for those very mistakes. I didn't miss his surprise and fury at being called out by an amateur, but my focus was now on Carl, who was stroking his weak chin thoughtfully.

I took that as my cue to end this.

The label had every reason to ruin us, and Braxton Fawn would undoubtedly deliver.

Moving away from the table, I took slow steps toward Oni and her pet project. It wasn't my intention to put them at ease—quite the opposite. I wanted to rattle the troublemakers, give them time to regret their mistake.

Oni squared her shoulders, standing tall beside Braxton. She probably thought she could stop me if I decided to choke the life out of Bambi.

Closer now, I could see the freckles peppering Braxton's nose and cheeks. It almost worked in concealing her blush at my proximity. Annoyingly, there wasn't a single thing I wasn't noticing about this girl. She smelled rich and sinful like forbidden fruit and wore no bra. Her nipples were hard enough to make themselves known through the thick material of her dress. I wondered if the sweat beading her pale skin was from fear of me finding out. Braxton was too damn young, her eyes appearing even bigger up close. She couldn't be much older than eighteen.

Which meant I was nearly a decade older.

"Though I can't say the same for you, my time is valuable, so let's drop the dramatics." The fact that these were my first words to her tore at something inside of me. Something I had every intention of avoiding. "I'm sure you think you play well to your soundproof ears, but Bound isn't looking for a reunion with amateur hour. Run back to your mom's garage or whatever hole-in-the-wall club Sridhar found you. We're not interested."

"Aren't you, though?" For some reason, my fingers and toes curled. She acted as if I couldn't and wouldn't break her in half and sleep like a baby tonight. "If you were half the artist you think you are, you wouldn't feel so threatened by an *amateur*. You wouldn't be shaking in your big boy boots. My God, I could hear your poor knees knocking thirty floors down." Lips pursed, her gaze boldly drifted down. I could have sworn she'd zeroed in on the exact spot where my dick slowly grew against my thigh. *Not a virgin, after all.* "I'm surprised you haven't pissed your pants yet, Morrow. Don't tell me you have stage fright."

My eyebrow rose when she finished her little rant. It was cute at best. I swallowed my yawn.

"So that's your plan? You're going to appeal to what you assume is a fragile ego? I'm *confident* I'll trample you, your childish dreams, and that chip on your shoulder if you don't get the hell out of my sight." When she didn't immediately run away, I felt blood rush to my groin. The fact that I was in danger of pitching a tent pissed me off even more. "Why can I still see you?"

"I didn't hear you say please."

Silence descended over the room.

Neither Braxton nor I looked away from one another. I wondered who would break first when a masculine chuckle interrupted my plotting.

I knew without confirming that it hadn't come from Loren

or Rich. I couldn't remember a time we weren't on the same wavelength. Whatever I felt, they felt, and vice versa. Right now, I could feel them both as eager to get our latest stroke of bad luck the hell out of the room.

There was clapping as the laughter continued, and then Carl spoke. "I have to admit that I wasn't sold when Ms. Sridhar pitched a female member of Bound." My fists balled because clearly Bound had been the only one kept in the dark about Braxton. Carl continued speaking, unaware that his life was in danger. "I was even less convinced when this young woman walked through the door, but she's managed to spark my interest at the very least." To Braxton, who I wouldn't allow him to see since I still stood in front of her, he added, "Young lady, you've done the impossible. You tied Houston's tongue. That's not a feat easily accomplished, even for me."

I smirked even though that piece of shit was trying to threaten me. He didn't want to risk tipping Braxton off that he was as crooked as they come. Carl was nothing without us, but he held on to the delusion that it was the other way around.

"Stay awhile," Carl invited, making my heart drop into my stomach. Braxton looked like she'd disembowel me if I made a wrong move. If she did, my heart would undoubtedly fall at her feet. "We have much to discuss."

My fingertips dug into my palms as I sat across from Carl in his high-rise office with Los Angeles bustling on the streets below.

"Find someone else."

An hour ago, I would have been too proud to beg. I just couldn't stop recalling the glow in Braxton's eyes, along with excitement and wariness, as she signed her name on the dotted line. She was too goddamn eager, too unaware of what she'd done.

"Anyone else."

It was pointless asking him to cancel or postpone the tour since he'd already refused. Carl had a bigger stake in this tour. It was also his last chance to squeeze us. We'd wised up a long time ago, and now his mission was to make us pay for it.

Behind his desk, Carl smugly sat back in his chair. The bastard knew this was a terrible fucking idea. It was the exact reason he'd signed off on it. I felt the ice growing at my fingertips and slowly crawling its way up my limbs.

This was not happening.

Braxton Fawn could *not* be our new guitarist.

"Why would I do that? She's perfect."

"You haven't even heard her play," I pushed through gritted teeth.

"I trust Oni. She found *you*."

And I've regretted it every single fucking day. I kept those thoughts to myself because it was pointless to voice them when Carl already knew. He delighted in our misery. For five fucking years, he slept like a baby, knowing he had us under his thumb. We should never have signed that bullshit contract. I should never have been so weak.

Only one year to go.

The end of our world tour marked Bound's hard-won freedom. After three albums and too much lost, the knowledge should have filled me with joy.

There was only one problem.

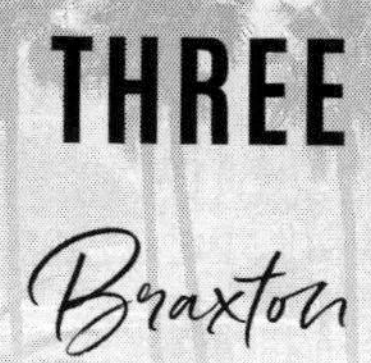

THREE

Braxton

THAT COULD HAVE GONE BETTER.

Despite the shitshow the meeting had turned into, I felt like I was walking on a cloud. I expected to walk through those doors with only a handful of empty promises. Instead, I was Bound's new guitarist.

Bound.

Bound.

BOUND.

My arm throbbed where I'd pinched it the entire elevator ride down. I was expecting to wake up any moment now. I was trapped in an endless dream and wasn't sure I *wanted* to leave. There was only one problem: America's sweethearts turned out to be real douchebags.

I made it to my car parked in the building's garage just as my phone vibrated, and a text appeared in a banner at the top of the screen.

Poison. 9 p.m. We need to talk.
—Oni

Groaning because this day was starting to feel like it would never end, I threw myself into my hooptie and headed straight home. Home was a cheap three-bedroom apartment in Mid-City, where I found my best friend and roommate sitting crossed-legged on our couch.

Griffin Sinclair reminded me of Nicola Peltz with her blonde hair, green eyes, and perpetual soul-searing gaze. Only with longer legs. Maeko, our other roommate and bestie, was nowhere to be found. Maeko had moved to Los Angeles with the dreams of becoming an actress, so I was hoping her absence meant she was at another audition. Unfortunately, with her Japanese-American heritage and the lack of diversity in Hollywood's starring roles, she'd yet to land more than a small part, but she wasn't giving up. Griffin and I wouldn't let her.

"Back so soon?" Griff quipped. Her green gaze was assessing as she watched me instead of the show playing on TV. "Why am I not surprised?" She then wrinkled her button nose at my sister's dress. It really was hideous. "What are you wearing?"

I paused, debating telling Griffin about my new gig before deciding against it—at least for now. Griffin, who worked part-time as a paralegal while studying law, was a bloodhound for secrets. It was nearly impossible to keep anything from her. However, the biggest reason was that my blooming music career rested on my surviving a world tour with three egomaniacs. Carl Cole's words replayed in my head as if on cue.

"Learn the words, survive the tour, and then we'll talk. In the meantime, sign this."

The paper he'd shoved at me had been a short-term contract that lasted until the end of the tour. It basically ensured that I couldn't quit for any reason without serious financial repercussions.

Translation: He'd sue the fuck out of me.

I still wondered how the agreement could be considered short-term since standard recording contracts only lasted a year. Even I knew that it was career suicide to sign with a label for longer than twelve months at a time. There could be differences in vision between the label and artist too vast to overcome, a lack of funding and influence causing stagnant careers, or corrupt labels who demanded too much and gave almost nothing in return.

"You're not surprised because you know me well," I answered my friend.

"That I do. So what happened with your folks?" she asked,

referring to my impromptu trip home. It was maybe my third in the four years since I left home.

"Rosalie's dating an atheist," I blurted unceremoniously.

Griffin winced before shaking her head. "Poor baby sis."

"Indeed."

I shuffled into the living room barely large enough to fit our second-hand coffee table, armchair, and dilapidated couch. The furniture was a little masculine, but none of us minded since we were too poor to be picky, and we'd taken it off a neighbor's hands for free. His asking price had been two hundred dollars, but Griff worked her magic. Men had a tough time saying no to her, which was ironic since they weren't her type.

My bones ached from unknown exertion as I flopped next to Griffin on the couch. I then settled onto my side before laying my head in her lap. Staring at the TV but not watching whatever was playing, I replayed the meeting with Bound and Savant Records over and over in my head.

Bound's reaction to me, *a stranger*, had been almost violent. I hadn't done anything to earn it. My only crime was being fashionably late, but they seemed prepared to hate me either way. Curiosity and a little disappointment that my idols turned out to be jerks had me wondering why.

Feeling my head begin to ache, I decided I didn't care. I had an agenda that was bigger than me, and three overgrown toddlers weren't going to get in my way.

My mind was a whirlpool of jumbled thoughts and emotions, and any moment, I'd drown. Ever the mind reader, Griffin's fingers began gliding through my hair, and it took no time at all before my eyes began to close.

"Wake me in a few hours," I sleepily managed to get out. "I'm meeting someone tonight."

I felt her fingers pause in my hair, but I was asleep before she could interrogate me.

A quarter past nine, I was rushing through Poison's doors.

Since the night was young, it was easy to spot Oni sitting at a table furthest from the dance floor. She was sipping the bar's most lethal drink with the look of someone who'd fucked up royally. It was a far cry from the confidence she'd displayed earlier, but I didn't take it personally. Witnessing her uncertainty only assured me that I was doing the right thing.

Houston, Loren, and Jericho had been right.

It was their delivery that sucked.

I had no business breathing Bound's air, much less sharing a stage. I could predict each minute change in Houston's pitch, the pluck of Loren's pick, and the pattern of Jericho's strikes as if I'd choreographed them myself.

It. Wasn't. Enough.

I didn't know *them*. There was a reason they played so beautifully together. The answer was in the name they'd chosen. Houston, Loren, and Jericho were bound, which meant I was trespassing on destiny.

No wonder they hated me.

I powered ahead, pushing through the thin crowd. Spotting me before I could reach her, the hopelessness vanished from Oni's eyes as she watched me closely. When I finally reached the table, my lips parted, but she quickly held up her hand.

I was silenced before I could even get a syllable out.

"Whatever sad spiel you're about to give me to try to pull out of this deal, save it. You're doing the tour."

"This was a huge mistake," I admitted anyway. There was no use pretending she hadn't known exactly what I was thinking. She'd at least saved me from trying to find the right words.

"Probably," Oni agreed with a shrug. "But it doesn't matter now, so let me give you a warning that I hope you'll heed." She paused to make sure I was listening before continuing. "The *last* thing you want to do is bare your belly to those assholes. They won't show you mercy."

"Thanks." I dragged myself onto the high stool before snagging her drink and taking a large gulp. I barely knew her, but since we were about to walk through hell holding hands, I figured swapping cooties was the least of our worries. "Speaking of warnings, I could have used one *before* walking into that room."

"I wanted to see what you would do when your back was against the wall. Get used to it because what happened today was just the start, and when you're on the road, there will be no one to play the mediator. I needed to know you could hold your own."

"Sure." I still wasn't happy about being ambushed, but what could I do other than let it go? No one else was beating down my door to give me an opportunity like this. I wanted to make some noise, and now I had my chance. Touring with Bound would reach all corners of the world.

I could take that to the fucking bank.

"Now, for the reason I called you down here."

"You mean scaring the shit out of me wasn't the reason?"

"Not even close."

"Fuck."

She looked away, toying with a dark curl as she sunk deep in thought. I took the time to check out the band walking on stage now and realized I'd never heard them play before. I wondered if they knew who sat in the audience tonight. Oni was one of many A&R reps at Savant Records, but she was obviously willing to think outside the box, and what she managed to pull off this afternoon was huge. I'm not sure how many strings she pulled behind the scenes, but it seemed so effortless from where I sat. If I weren't so desperate, I'd be suspicious, but I couldn't afford to look a gift horse in the mouth.

"Did I ever mention I was the one who discovered them?" she asked after several minutes had passed in silence.

I felt my brows dip as I turned away from the five-piece on stage. "Who?" Surely, she couldn't mean—

"Bound."

My eyebrows kissed my hairline. I swore I could feel the strands touching. "Really?"

"Try not to look so surprised," she tossed back.

"Sorry, it's just…I had no idea." I would never have guessed, considering the words they exchanged at the meeting. "They don't seem very grateful."

Oni snorted before rolling her eyes. "They're not. They hate me, themselves, and each other. In my case, the feeling is mutual."

"But why? Without you—"

"Savant would have never found them," she finished for me. "They were a lot like you. They weren't looking for fame. Fame found them. Although they weren't as hard to convince."

Oni gave me a pointed look, a reminder of the months she spent wooing me with the promise of a record deal until one day, I simply gave in. I was fine letting her believe that since I preferred my cards close to my chest.

Clearing her throat, Oni looked away, and I had a feeling we'd finally arrived at the real reason we were meeting in secret. "There's something I'd like you to do for me."

I should have been ready to do anything for her. I should have been grateful, but the graveness in her tone kept me wary. "Okay…" I drew out instead.

Reaching over the round table, she grabbed my hand and squeezed. My spine was ramrod straight from the unexpected touch and the warmth that, until now, Oni hadn't shown toward me…or anyone. Oni Sridhar was all business, all the time. "Find a way to keep them together."

"Keep who together?" Her nostrils flared with impatience, and I realized I was starting to sound like a parrot who'd been crossbred with an owl.

"Bound." Seeing the question in my eyes, she went on. "When I met them, they were finishing each other's sentences, and now they can barely stand to be in the same room together."

"They seemed fine to me," I mumbled. I couldn't forget how they had circled and preyed on me the moment I stepped into that room.

"Because you saw what they wanted you to see. The only time they're united is when they've set their sights on the same game."

"Meaning me." She gave an apologetic nod in confirmation. *Splendid.* "So what am I supposed to do? Put an apple on my head so they hate each other a little less?"

"Nothing quite so dramatic," she replied with a tip of her red-painted lips.

"Then what?"

"In short? Find what's broken and fix it. If you can't, at the very least, keep them from killing each other. I don't care how as long as it gets you all home in one piece."

"I'm confused," I said as my gaze narrowed. "Am I playing for Bound or babysitting Bound?"

"You're securing your future," she vehemently shot back. "I know those assholes *seemed* like a unified front in there, but they're one bad argument from breaking up, and they've all been best friends since their first boner."

"How is that my problem?"

Sitting back in her seat, she studied me, searching for a weakness. Obviously, she found it because she finally answered, "No Bound, no deal."

My eyes were mere slits now as I regarded the cutthroat businesswoman lurking underneath that angelic face. "I'm starting to see why they don't like you."

I was also getting that it was hard to rattle Oni Sridhar when she shrugged. "It's this business. It brings out the worst in everyone." She tipped a head full of dark curls toward me. "Including you."

My stomach turned as cold dread replaced the warm blood in my veins. God, I hoped not. I'd seen me at my worst, and it wasn't just ugly. It was catastrophic. The casualties were endless.

I found myself staring a little too closely at Oni's lips as she bounced her head in time to the music, completely unaware of my focus or interest.

"Anything else?" I demanded curtly. I needed a distraction before I hit on the A&R rep. There was no reason for me to sleep my way to the top. I was already there, and I still didn't understand how.

"In a few days, you should hear from a man named Xavier Gray." I didn't miss the way her lips flattened at the name. Another fan of hers, I supposed. "He's Bound's manager, and he won't like this any more than they do. Luckily, he's a professional, and he's good at his job, so you shouldn't have too much trouble from him."

I felt my heart quicken. "Why wasn't he there this afternoon? Couldn't he have done something?"

"No," she said as she stood from the stool. I guess our clandestine meeting was over. "And they blame me for that too." She walked away without saying goodbye, and I watched her disappear before finally exhaling.

Fantastic.

It's been two weeks since I became Bound's guitarist and not a peep from Xavier or my new bandmates. I knew Oni had given them my contact information. I also knew they weren't occupied with anything pressing. Just last night, a blog had reported spotting them walking inside a Las Vegas casino.

I felt like I was in high school again, except instead of waiting for one boy to call, I was waiting for three. Four if I counted the manager who'd despised and discarded me already. I wasn't even afforded the pleasure of giving them a reason to hate me first.

Bummer.

Oni, on the other hand, didn't seem surprised when she called to check on things. However, in typical Oni fashion, the conversation abruptly ended once I informed her that I hadn't heard a peep. That was close to forty-eight hours ago, and now she'd disappeared too. I wasn't sure how much of this was in her job description, but since she was the only one in my corner, I didn't ask questions.

Pounding on my bedroom door jolted me to the here and now.

"Yo, Brax, let's go!" Griff demanded. "We're going to hit traffic."

"It's L.A.!" I shouted back even after glancing at the time on my phone and cursing. "There's always traffic," I muttered more to myself since she was already gone.

I stood from my bed and began stuffing last-minute shit into my rucksack. My sleeping bag took up most of the space, but my dad had shown me a few tricks since my sister and I spent our summers camping with the church growing up.

This weekend was the Indies in Indio Festival, and my name was on the lineup. I was glad the guys I usually played with talked me into it since I had spent the last two weeks of my spare time rehearsing rather than waiting by the phone.

I'd invited Oni, who only offered a maybe.

Now I was starting to think it would be best if she didn't show. The crowd wouldn't be more than I was used to, but somehow, I was more nervous than I'd ever been. What if I floundered tonight and ended up on the internet as a source of ridicule only to later be discovered as Bound's newest member?

Holy fuck, I really knew how to stir a pot full of steaming shit, didn't I?

Wearing only a thong, I quickly squeezed my ass into my tightest pair of blue jeans. I then paired it with a cropped black corset that pushed my tits up to my chin.

Perfect.

If only those assholes could see me now.

Bound's first impression of me hadn't been exactly accurate. They'd been too quick to judge me by my cover while ignoring the pages inside.

As I shoved my feet into a pair of thigh-high boots with fake crystals and silver spikes adorning the black straps running the entire length, I considered biting the bullet and calling *them*. I wasn't a fan of the self-involved who assumed communication was only found from one end, so if the three of them couldn't be mature about this, I would.

Perhaps it would be for the best.

Houston, Loren, and Jericho were undoubtedly expecting me to cower. If Oni was right and Bound was splintering, a new threat *would* force them together. I just wasn't thrilled at the idea of turning myself into a target. It wasn't quite what Oni had asked me to do, but I didn't see any other way.

Carrying my ruck and guitar case into the living room, I found my backing band in the living room pregaming with my roommates. I'd met Liam, Mason, and Abe two years ago in a dive bar. Liam had hit on me first, followed by his brother, who somehow thought he had a better chance after I'd turned down his twin, who was identical in every way.

It wasn't their fault they had no shot. The night we met, I was a skittish kitten still adjusting to my surroundings even though I'd been in L.A. for two years. Once upon a time, their blond hair, blue eyes, and the boy-next-door charm would have won me over. I turned them down because I knew what they were inviting into their bed while they had no clue.

Abe, their equally hot but too shy roommate, hadn't bothered trying after watching his friends get shut down. Apparently, rejection had never happened to the Miller brothers before. I was grateful that at least one of the trio could take a hint since Liam and Mason, usually when alcohol was involved, hadn't entirely given up on getting down.

They might not have been able to weaken my resolve, but they had convinced me to let them back me on stage since I was more adept at scoring gigs, and they needed the extra cash.

Tonight was one of those nights.

The guys were decent musicians with Liam on lead guitar and backup vocals, Abe on bass, and Mason on drums while I doubled up on vocals and rhythm. It's just that their hearts belonged elsewhere. The twins were both studying to be doctors and Abe an engineer. Music was just their side bitch.

"You ready for this?" Liam greeted after pouring a shot and handing it to me. He studied me so intently that paranoia had me fearing he knew my secret. I hadn't told anyone, not a single soul, that I was Bound's new guitarist, so I knew it wasn't possible. I doubted anyone would believe me even with my tour contract bearing Savant's letterhead along with Houston's angry scrawl, Loren's practiced one, and Jericho's lazy loops beneath my effeminate signature.

Stupidly, I'd stared at our names for hours that night, and it wasn't awe over my fast road to stardom that made me do so. It was seeing my name mixed among theirs. The strangest part was how right it all seemed—like lost pieces connecting at last.

Nodding at Liam, I took the shot glass, tossed it back, and decided as liquid courage burned its way down my throat that Bound's time was up. I'd give them until morning before I broke down the walls they'd built and stormed my way into their lives once again.

FOUR

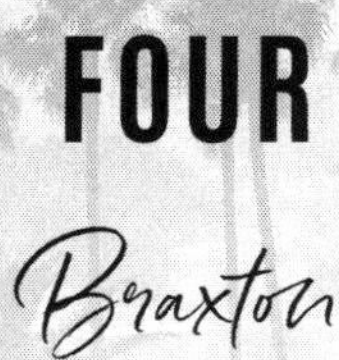

Braxton

"Aren't you cold?"

Bundled in a magenta winter coat with a fur hood, Maeko peered up at me through dark eyes while waiting for my answer. Despite it being winter, it was seventy degrees today and wouldn't get cold until much later. I'd give it another hour before Maeko gave in and peeled off those unneeded layers.

Griffin, the most daring of us, wore even less than I did. Her entire ensemble was red—faux-leather skater skirt and sheer, long-sleeved crop top. She didn't leave much room for guessing, even though the stares she caught lasted an uncomfortable length of time. She'd turned down every single advance as she kept a tight grip on Maeko's hand. They were thick as thieves, and when they were together, no one else existed.

Sometimes not even me.

"Nope." The truth was, I was burning. *Always burning.*

The guys and I had just returned from checking in backstage, dropping off equipment, and confirming our input list and stage plan one last time with the festival's sound crew while Maeko and Griff set up our tents.

Now that it was done, the six of us wasted no time jumping into the fray. The festival was already well underway, and I needed the distraction. The massive stage and the flashing colorful lights were more intimidating than usual even though nothing was special about the setup.

I wasn't sure if five minutes had passed before Liam, Mason, and Abe ditched us. Their chances were better at finding girls to take the edge off if they weren't mistaken as taken.

We shouted our agreement to meet backstage in a couple of hours before the crowd swallowed them. Left alone with Griffin and Maeko, who were already on their way to being wasted, I sighed. Fear of tumbling off stage kept me sober. I'd save getting wrecked for after the show so I could quickly forget if I made a fool of myself.

The winter music festival was amateur hour. Half the acts were booed off the stage, but it brought the people out in droves. Really, any excuse to get drunk and have something new to post on Instagram would bring them out. If I never read another *living my best life* hashtag, I will have lived *my* best life.

Before I knew it, after ducking wandering hands from anonymous culprits, eating overpriced food from the food stalls, window shopping at the clothing vendors, flirting free drinks out of guys, and warming up by random bonfires, two hours had come and gone. I now had only fifteen minutes before our changeover time.

The last festival we played only allowed ten minutes to get one band offstage and the next ready to perform. We were allotted fifteen minutes, which was doable, considering only the headlining act would be given the luxury of a soundcheck. Twenty minutes for setting up would have been ideal, but the festival had booked plenty acts for the weekend. In addition to selling more tickets, it kept the crowd pacified if too many of the performances stunk up the place.

"Are you nervous?" Maeko shouted so loud I wouldn't be surprised if she'd gone hoarse. We'd been slowly forcing our way through the drunken, half-dressed assemblage, and now that the stage was mere feet away, the music had become deafening.

I knew what put that worried look in Maeko's eyes. I'd been too quiet for too long. Because I liked to be in my head where I felt at home amongst my own chaos.

A nod was all I offered since my tongue felt too thick, and the smell of brine made me feel as if I were in the middle of the ocean rather than the desert. If I swallowed, I was afraid I would choke.

"You're dynamite, babe," Griffin assured me as she rubbed my back in a soothing motion. Sure, Griffin looked like the popular cheerleader, but she had the personality of a nursemaid. "You've got this."

At least one of us could say it with a straight face. With my friends sticking close, I approached the line of guards keeping backstage separate from the crowd and the short, overweight man wearing a full beard and a headset.

Before I could give my name, he spoke. "Hey, are you, Brandy?" he asked even as he glanced at his clipboard where my name was printed clearly.

"Braxton."

"Backup's already here," he announced, making me sigh in relief. The guys getting hammered or caught up chasing ass had been on my mounting list of worries these last couple of hours. "Get backstage. You're up next." Headset guy then started shouting at one of the crew members without acknowledging his mistake.

What if there was a Brandy waiting to perform, and I took her spot? I knew I was overthinking things considering the organizer had emailed the running order, but that didn't stop my pits from perspiring. The lights and constant need to vomit would keep me warm if the temperature dropped, so at least I had that. Freezing on stage wasn't what terrified me anyway.

Reluctantly, I waved goodbye to my friends, who held each other as if I were going off to war, and passed through the metal gate one of the guards held open for me. Once I cleared it, I debated calling Oni to see if she'd been able to make it.

And that was when I heard them.

Helicopter blades.

My attention shot toward the sky along with everyone around me. Chances were that it was just one of the local channels reporting the festival. It took a few minutes to realize that it wasn't just approaching or flying overhead.

It was *landing*.

Even though we were in a desert valley, a collection of horrified gasps rang out since the pilot had chosen to land within a stone's throw of the stage. A gust of wind threatened to knock over any equipment not tied down along with everyone backstage when it hovered twenty feet off the ground before executing a smooth landing.

There was a moment of hesitation before the asshole with the clipboard rushed toward the chopper as its blades still circled. He was yelling something into his headset. Whatever was said in return, there was too much happening for me to overhear. Four more guards materialized on the heels of the headset guy as they rushed for the bird.

With my arm up, I shielded my face as best I could from the strong gust the blades stirred. I guess they couldn't be bothered to cut the goddamn engine. Maybe they weren't staying.

As if hearing my thoughts and purposely crushing my hopes, the engine died, and the blades slowed. One of the doors had barely opened before someone started screaming. There were no words of warning—just a long, piercing shrill.

And then…pandemonium.

The backstage crew, volunteers, groupies, and musicians blocked my view as they dropped what they were doing to rush for whatever had caused them all to lose their minds. Different smells and tastes assaulted me all at once until I was close to gagging. Whoever had stepped from that helicopter, I'd only managed to glimpse blond hair gelled to perfection. I didn't even know if they were alone.

The screams, shouts, and stampeding feet baffled me. There was no one on the lineup who could have sparked such an explosive reaction.

I turned since I was still lingering by the gate, hoping to get answers from the guards, only to see they were occupied with keeping twenty thousand people on the other side of those gates. Word had managed to spread without ever reaching my ears. I wasn't convinced ten guards could control a hysteric crowd that large. Even now, there were more barreling through to help them.

Holy shit.

I was standing in the middle of chaos and the only one without a goddamn clue. I was Mark Wahlberg in *The Happening*. Everyone around me had lost their minds, running toward danger instead of away from it.

Not willing to be left that way, I moved toward the short metal stairs leading to the stage and climbed until I reached the top.

It didn't help.

A moment later, I didn't need it to.

The screams heightened just before the last of the maniacs who were backstage were shoved aside by the hulking security guards, and then…

My living nightmare walked through.

A smorgasbord of smells and tastes fought for dominance as my emotions unleashed themselves. My stomach clenched tight. I felt like I would never breathe again.

So I watched them instead.

They moved as one in perfect symmetry.

Houston Morrow was at the helm. Loren James was a step behind and flanking his left. The final piece, Jericho Noble, walked in perfect line with Loren on Houston's right. Together, they formed a pyramid.

Towering, impenetrable, and utterly beautiful.

I wondered if they'd rehearsed it and for how long.

Houston's gorgeous brown hair was free to be caressed by the wind. He wore a T-shirt that read *Not Someone Who Cares*, distressed blue jeans, and a matching denim jacket.

Loren looked succulent in his red dress shirt, which, as usual, was splayed open despite it being winter. Seriously, how had he never caught pneumonia? With each step Loren took, I could see his hard nipples peeking through the edges of his shirt and the silver medallion gleaming against his skin.

Jericho, swaddled in a navy blue hoodie and toying with his lip ring as his dark hair pressed against his forehead and brushed his ears, brought back all the teenage angst that made my stomach ache and my toes curl.

When I felt my feet itching to carry me forward, I wrapped my hands around the cold metal of the railing as if it were a life raft in the middle of the sea. I didn't have much, but I still had my dignity, thank you. I wouldn't run to them as everyone else had.

Spotting me at once and seemingly hearing my thoughts, the guys stopped only a foot away from the stairs. I could see the command in their eyes for me to come to them. Loren wore his perpetual smirk while Jericho eyed me warily, and Houston scowled.

What the hell were they doing here?

"Pretty fucking rude of you not to invite us to your show," Loren accused.

The first chance I got, I'd find out why he always insisted on being the first to speak. Was it to fool everyone into thinking that he was the one in charge? My gaze drifted to Houston, the silent but undisputed alpha of the pack—oh, how it must have twisted Loren's knickers. I filed that away for later, though I was sure Oni would disapprove. My mission was to salvage, not sabotage.

So much for my *actual* mission. With each encounter, I began to wonder if succeeding was worth putting up with their crap.

Of course, it is, Fawn. Keep it together.

Houston, Loren, and Jericho were obstacles, and while they might seem impenetrable, I wouldn't let them get in my way. Crossing my arms, I went for indifference. It was quickly becoming a familiar ruse.

"You're here, aren't you?"

The only questions were how and why. The only person who could have tipped them off was—

Oni.

Through vigorous effort, I moved my gaze away from the stunning trio and searched the eager crowd behind them. The festival's security helped the ones Bound came with to keep them at bay, but it didn't seem like it would be enough.

Where is she?

"Sridhar isn't here," Jericho informed me.

I couldn't tell if it was out of kindness or cruelty. It didn't matter when I realized they were his first words to me and how easily I lost myself in his attention. The finest silver had nothing on the pureness and beauty of Jericho Noble's gaze. But that wasn't what called to me.

It was the sadness.

I willingly submerged myself.

Just when I thought I might never find my way back to the surface, the commanding drawl of Houston's voice yanked me out. It was no wonder he could captivate a crowd.

"It's not like Sridhar could help you if she were," Morrow taunted in the blandest tone he could muster.

With one threat, he'd reminded me that they, for now—or always—were my enemy. Getting lost in their beautiful gazes was unequivocally out of the question.

"Bold of you to assume I'd need it," I heard myself say. "It's three against *me*, Moe, Curly, and Larry."

I delighted in the subtle shift of their eyes and the quiet agony over which Stooge I'd associated them with. They wouldn't let themselves ask, and I wouldn't enlighten them. Instead, I let them decide and hoped it destroyed them.

"And when we get you alone?" Houston challenged. He started up the stairs, and I backed up a step before catching myself and staying put.

They could crowd my space, but it would still belong to me. They could make my belly ache with want, but I'd still hold all the power.

Their control was a fallacy.

An image of them surrounding me, clothes discarded, and souls bared, invaded my thoughts in vivid fucking clarity—a warning of what would happen if they ever let go.

Waiting for the taste of cherries to dissipate, I glanced at the crowd again, wondering how much they could hear. They hadn't grown bored or lost their determination to reach the rock gods yet. Some women had resorted to lifting their shirts and baring their tits in the hope of capturing Bound's attention. If the guys noticed, they didn't let on.

They were used to it.

I didn't linger on how much that annoyed me.

"I'm curious," I pondered out loud. "How did you plan on getting me alone when you've been running scared of little ole me for two weeks?"

Before they could respond, the band I was supposed to replace on stage at that very moment pushed through the curtains.

Shit.

I looked around but didn't see Liam, Mason, or Abe. I just hoped they were busy plugging in for the show and not one of the eager ones behind Bound straining to reach them. Our only saving grace was that the festival supplied a surprisingly good backline, so we didn't have a ton of equipment we needed to prep for stage. The rolling riser we'd rented for Mason to set up his drums beforehand was a godsend.

No one else seemed to notice that the festival had come to a halt. I didn't doubt that every breath held out there was for Bound. No doubt, I'd be booed off stage simply for not being their idols.

Crazed Nuts—*what a name choice*—stood with their mouths agape and eyes wide as they realized who stood ten feet away from them. Once their shock cleared, they inched closer, eager for a chance to mingle with legends. The amateur band didn't make it two steps before more security appeared from thin air and carted them toward the stairs, stage right. It was only then that it occurred to me—no one had bothered to shoo me away. It's not as if the world knew that I was Bound's newest addition, so why—

My lips formed a curse since there was only one other explanation.

Everyone thought I was their goddamn groupie.

My gaze returned to Bound. The matching feral grins the trio wore told me they'd read my mind and came to the same conclusion.

"Fuck you," I blurted unapologetically.

"You might as well," Loren retorted with a shrug and a snort. "Everyone already thinks you are. Congratulations, groupie. *Now* you're a part of the band."

My lids lowered until my eyes formed slits. "I'm going to offer you the same advice you gave me two weeks ago. *Get out of my sight and get lost.*"

Jericho spoke first, and Loren followed up.

"No can do."

"We came to enjoy the show."

Fuck.

My stomach twisted, wringing free my tumultuous emotions. Bound watching me perform was even more nerve-wracking than twenty thousand pairs of eyes. I didn't stand a chance. Not when the alternative was *them*.

A light bulb went off before I could finish losing my shit.

"I've got a better idea," I announced with a confidence I didn't feel. "Why don't you go in my place? They're all expecting you anyway, o' great ones."

I mocked them with a curtsy.

When I tried to push past the wall they'd formed with their bodies, Houston caught my wrist. The warmth of his skin and the strength behind his grip was not something I'd been prepared to face. He could easily break me in two with half the effort. Our height difference, even in my heels, was daunting enough. Loren matched his height, with Jericho standing a couple of inches shorter. All three dwarfed me, but that didn't give them permission to make me feel small.

"All that lip and you have the nerve to run and hide?" Houston spat.

"No pun intended," Loren added through a fake cough. I blinked in surprise before catching myself. Yes, I had full lips, but I didn't think they'd noticed. Why would I, considering how they treated me.

"I'm *walking* away from a situation that doesn't interest me," I corrected Houston. "If you'll excuse me." I tried to free my hand, but he tightened his hold. "Let go of me."

"Or what?"

I'd never forgive myself if I let Houston know he was getting to me, so I steeled my spine and dug in my feet. "Do you really want your adoring fans seeing you get kicked in the balls? It's not a pretty sight on anyone."

"Do you really think you'd make it through them if you tried?"

No.

Dammit, he was right. I wouldn't.

Some of the women looked ready to kill me just for allowing Houston to touch me. Some looked willing to lay on train tracks if he told them to. Only a few seemed envious but not entirely threatening.

"You go, girl!" someone shouted, proving my theory. More shouting followed, each more alarming than the last.

"Jericho, I love you!"

"Can I please suck your dick, Houston?"

"I'm having your baby, Loren. Call me!"

My gaze darted to Loren, who didn't even blink. I guess having babies pinned on him wasn't anything new. I snorted, surprised I could find anything about this situation humorous.

Ignoring the shouting, Houston held me tighter. "Get your ass on stage and play for me."

"So that's why you're here? To assert your dominance and put me in my place?"

His lips curled as he leaned forward and something akin to a growl sent a shiver down my spine. "Don't test me, Fawn. I'm much better at *inserting* my dominance." He finally let me go, blatantly confident in the knowledge that I wasn't going anywhere. I was too busy picturing him making good on his threat.

He didn't seem to notice as his gaze moved over my shoulder toward the curtain dividing a crowd of thousands and us before finding mine again. "You're out of time. Stop stalling and show us what you're made of."

"You aren't ready for what I'm made of, Houston." Liking the sound of his name on my lips a little too much, I let my attention wander to his cronies, standing closely behind him. "None of you are."

Jericho yawned, his gaze staying blank. Loren blew a large, blue bubble of the gum he was chewing in response. Houston's only reaction was to stare down at me in silent contemplation. There was reluctant curiosity there—the insatiable need to test those waters and submerge himself within my depths.

Why did that sound so deliciously debauched? I hadn't meant it to sound that way.

"If I do this, will you cut the macho bullshit and be professional?"

Before he could answer, Loren spoke, his voice an ingratiating mumble, "We don't negotiate with terrorists."

Jericho snickered, and I realized with the daunting awareness of someone up shit creek without a paddle that I'd attached myself to silly boys parading as grown men.

Ignoring the consequences, I centered myself between them. They didn't miss a beat, surrounding me as if we'd done this before and many times.

My most remarkable feat, while breathing the same air, was pretending the sensation of them pressing in close didn't smell sweet and spicy like freshly-ground cinnamon. While I've been excited before, the feeling had never been quite this sharp. I couldn't see anyone or anything but them. Even though they kept me on edge, I felt safer within the circle they created than I did out there. It felt like no one could touch me.

Only them.

"Come now, Loren. We both know I was talking to Houston." I turned to face him, putting Houston and the wall of heat and menace he created behind me while Jericho stood just within my peripheral. I could feel that torturously beautiful gaze of his roving over every inch of me while he thought I was distracted. "He is the one calling the shots, right?"

The sweet smile I gave Loren made his eyes flash with something dark and unreadable. Whatever it was, I secretly wanted in.

"For now," he admitted readily, blowing another bubble of his gum.

My smile became genuine, hearing the warning growl from Houston behind me. I'd ventured into dangerous waters, and I was only getting started. Loren had blatantly challenged his authority, and Houston was ready to accept. The thrill of what they might do to one another tiptoed down my spine.

Without thinking, I reached up and stabbed the bubble protruding between Loren's sinful lips. The gum popped and deflated, leaving a sticky, blue mess. Those pools of ink he called eyes widened in shock even as the irises gleamed with retribution.

The last thing I expected was for him to press forward, place his nose against my hair and inhale. He was *smelling* me and didn't care if I noticed. I found myself doing the same, breathing in the mint on his breath and bergamot in his expensive cologne.

Fuck me.

"When you least expect it, baby fawn, you're going to hurt for that."

Don't make promises you can't keep.

I forced myself to step away before crossing my arms. I may have a great poker face, but the rest of me was a different story. Loren's punishment, coming sooner than later, smelled like cinnamon rolls fresh out of the oven. I sensed the thrill stirring in other places too. Apparently, I was a masochist, among other secret things.

"Do you understand what a tautology is?" I waited for his answer, and he didn't disappoint.

"As unquestionably as your nipples are hard right now."

Fuck.

I dropped my arms, but to his credit and my relief, Loren's gaze didn't stray from my face to confirm.

He knew.

"It's the middle of winter," I found myself explaining.

"Oh, is it?"

A moment later, I heard the beginnings of a chant. With each second, the voices grew louder, the crowd's demand clear.

Bound.

The crowd expected Houston, Loren, and Jericho to take the stage next, and they knew it. They were sending me to the slaughter. I wasn't who the people wanted to set their souls on fire. It was three assholes entitled to nothing but given everything.

I met each of their gazes—green, silver, and opaque.

I wasn't the only one hiding.

If Bound expected me to beg for mercy, they were in for a rude awakening well overdue. Without another word, I turned on my heel and pushed through Jericho and Houston. I felt three pairs of eyes on me and squared my shoulders as I headed for the curtains. I should have been relieved to see Liam, Mason, and Abe waiting for me, but the questions in their eyes told me I had a long night ahead of me.

"One of the crew said that *Bound* was here," Mason spoke first. "He was shitting me, right?"

"Afraid not." Their frowns deepened at the apparent fact that I was unhappy about it. "I'll explain later."

Gazing at the black curtain and now knowing Bound was on the other side, the guys were too star-struck to do more than nod. Liam eventually handed over my second-hand blue and white Fender Strat, tuned and ready to go.

Why couldn't they have something to prove? Why couldn't they lie and claim they hated Bound's music? At least then, I wouldn't be subjected to the fanboying I knew would come later.

I let the guys enter the stage ahead of me and cringed when they rounded the massive LED screen and were immediately greeted with a chorus of boos louder than anyone had been subjected to thus far.

Great. Just…great.

Gripping my guitar, I pushed through the curtain without a second thought. This was the hand dealt me, so I'd just have to bluff my way through. If I allowed myself to stop and think…my heart skipped a beat before falling and crashing into the pit of my stomach. No, I couldn't allow that.

"Pssst!"

Without thinking, I spun on my fabulously wicked heels to find Loren poking his gorgeously infuriating head through the curtain. "Make it good," he threatened. His gaze seemed endless as he held me with it. "We'll be watching every second."

True to his word, I could see Houston and Jericho flanking him through the small opening above his head. I offered him a smile that suspiciously felt real. Like the flip of a switch, I was anxious to get out there.

"Eat your heart out, dick bag."

FIVE

Loren

THAT ASS. MY GOD, THAT *ASS*.

I couldn't remember a time I'd beheld something so… perky. I could feel Houston and Rich behind me, straining to get a peek. Now that Braxton wasn't looking, they didn't bother with pretending. They were interested, and so was I.

Like an only child, I hogged the view. I never liked sharing anyway.

This new toy of ours was fucking magnificent.

Exciting, sexy…a menace.

She was the only thing my mind and dick could agree on in a long time. I wasn't too excited about that, though. I didn't need Braxton Fawn in my head—just in my bed.

I was so wrapped up in the curve of her ass in those skin-tight jeans that it took me a second longer than my bandmates to notice the boos and jeers.

"Do you think we should have sent her out there?" Jericho asked, always the first to backtrack. No matter how hard he tried, he couldn't commit to being an asshole, though he tried, bless his heart.

"No one made her go out there," Houston remarked. Unlike Rich, being an asshole came naturally to him. "She's the one who decided she had something to prove."

As if she could.

We would never accept her, which made us even bigger dicks

for making her think that we would. If she wanted this gig, she must roll with the punches, and because we always got our way, there would be many.

Houston damn sure would make sure of it, and Jericho didn't have a mind of his own. He was a follower and would do whatever Houston said. As for my reasons…well, life had gotten boring. This was my chance to have a little fun.

While a decent size, the stage still swallowed her up whole as she stood in the center of the blinding lights. I couldn't wait to see how she'd fare with even bigger crowds. I was patiently waiting for her to tuck tail and run when she opened that beautiful, insolent mouth.

"I know," she spoke to the crowd through the mic. "I'm not what you were expecting, right?" The crowd answered with a resounding *no* before chanting our name again.

Unable to help myself, I pushed through the curtain but made sure to stay hidden behind the equipment. It wouldn't be the first time someone rushed the stage. I could feel Houston and Rich flanking me but paid them no mind.

I was too fascinated by *her*.

"Recently, I made some new friends. I think you know who I mean." I was at the perfect angle to see Braxton's conspiratorial wink. Slowly, the crowd grew silent as confusion and curiosity rippled through them.

Fuck.

She had their attention. I didn't know how to feel about that.

"They're watching right now." Without warning, she began with a novice pattern of chords. My mind tracked them even as I held onto every word she spoke.

"They want to know what I'm made of." She peeked over her shoulder, and I held my breath until I realized her attention was on her bassist and drummer. It was my first time even noticing them. I wondered if they knew she was ours now.

Evil intent spread through me, but just as quickly, it was vanquished by the unexpected might of Braxton's voice.

Open your lips
Say you want me
I won't ask you if you're sure (God ends here)

You came alive; then you set me on fire
I'm burning, burning within
Insatiable, undeniable, you have no idea what's in store
Strip me, fill me, and then kill me
I'll never not want more
I'm a slave to the mania; you're the truth I can't deny

Until then, I'll hide in plain sight
Until then, I'll die a little inside
Until then, I'll drown in this endless, black tide

My heart is a well
Watch me fill it with pain
My body is a garden (I'm Eden)
Watch them pillage and plunder
Watch me sate the hunger
There's no sleep for the wicked
There's no saving the damned
There's no prayer to be had
You're already ensnared, my little lambs

Open your eyes
Look deep inside
I'll ask you what you see (God ends here)

Find what you love and let it kill you
If I'm what you love, you're already dead
Wanting the taste of you, craving the feel of you
I'll drain you to the very last drop
If I'm toxic, you're poison
You say you want more
If I'm a monster, you're the darkness

If I'm addicted, you're the drug

Fuck it, stay awhile
We're already in too deep

Open your mind
Say your darkest desires
You'll never want to leave (God's not here)

Incredible, unforgettable
You have no idea what's in store
Strip me, fill me, just don't turn away
I'll never not want more
I'm a slave to the mania; you're the truth I can't deny
There's no reason left to run
There's no reason left to fear
There's no reason left to hide
God's not here

The roar that erupted from the twenty thousand that only minutes ago had booed her shook me to my very core.

Standing on my right, red bloomed on Rich's cheeks as his lips formed an *O*. I looked to my left, already knowing what I'd find. Houston's jaw was locked tight, his gaze burning as his nostrils flared. There was fury, wonder, and the need to devour as well as to destroy. It was the same internal war waging inside of me.

She told me to eat my heart out, and that's exactly what I'd done. Braxton looked like an angel, but she played like a demon—one not even Satan would dare cross. There was no way now that we wouldn't make her ours. She was Bound.

Braxton performed two more numbers before she pranced her happy ass off stage, but still, the crowd wasn't sated. I didn't like that she'd forgotten all about us as she laughed and celebrated with her *former* bandmates, but then Houston stepped into her path, blocking her from leaving. The light left her eyes, and it felt like someone had yanked a magic carpet from underneath me, and now I was plummeting back to earth.

Her bandmates didn't move a muscle, and neither did she as Houston invaded her space before holding up a small white card. I already knew what he'd scribbled on it.

Wordlessly, he slipped it inside the décolletage of her corset, right between the fleshy mounds of her breasts spilling from the top. I didn't miss the unnecessary brush of his finger against her skin, either.

Bastard.

Why hadn't I thought of that?

Unmoved by her anger at his violation, he spoke his parting words to her before turning away. "Don't make me wait."

Jericho trailed after him, but I was a little slower to follow. I didn't *want* to leave. The dark look Braxton wore shifted to me when she noticed I was still standing there. I watched one of her perfectly arched brows rise in question. I wanted to stay, but she wanted me gone.

Needing to save face, I shoved aside my fascination. The shit was embarrassing, not to mention nauseating. "See you later, Amy Lee."

I heard choked laughter from the three who'd backed her before it ended abruptly. I guess she had them by the balls, but we wouldn't make it so easy for her. Looking over my shoulder one last time, I smirked when I caught her watching me go.

The seventy-two hours that followed were the longest fucking three days ever.

SIX

Braxton

"How could you not tell us you knew them!" Griffin shouted as she tossed her camping bag on the floor next to our front door.

"Or that she's one of them," Maeko reminded our already peeved roommate.

I'd been getting the third degree since my performance last night, which surpassed even my expectations. I never dreamed I'd feel so alive and refused to give Bound's presence credit.

Griff, Maeko, and I had to leave the festival a day early when the heat that came down on me turned into a wildfire. My affiliation with Bound and what it entailed was now a hot topic. Clearly, I hadn't thought it through before I announced to the world that I knew them just to get under Bound's skin.

I wasn't sure how much I was at liberty to say, so I kept my mouth shut. It didn't stop anyone from speculating, though. Candid photos of me at the festival started appearing online, and it wasn't long before the blogs caught wind. Even those fan pages dedicated to every move Bound made, including whenever one of them scratched their ass, were now reposting old selfies of me stolen from my page.

After only a brief period of deliberation, the consensus was unanimous.

I, Braxton Fawn, was just another groupie.

"How did this happen?" Griff woefully demanded.

"It's just a job," I mumbled as I moved to sit on our ratty couch. "It's not a death sentence." Maeko perched next to me on the arm of the couch, a silent show of support as Griffin angrily paced the floor in front of us.

"But your life will never be the same again. Can't you see that? I thought you didn't want to be famous."

"I didn't. I don't," I quickly corrected. "I told you why I'm doing this, Griff."

"But what if it doesn't work?"

Shit.

Perhaps I hadn't considered all the possibilities, but there was nothing I could do about it now. Bitching out would be even worse than failing since it was the only guarantee I wouldn't succeed.

"I have to try."

"Can't you just be happy for her?" Maeko snapped at Griff. "This is amazing, and if anyone deserves it, Brax does."

Like always, Griff melted at Maeko's ire until she slumped defeated onto the couch next to me and took my hand in hers. "I am happy for you, Brax. I'm sorry if it didn't seem that way. I'm just…worried."

Join the club. "It'll be fine."

"Do you really know for sure, though?"

"No. But I also don't know if I won't be hit by a bus the next time I walk outside. I can't let an unknown tomorrow stop me from living today."

Griff nodded reluctantly before a wide grin spread her lips. "So when do I get to tell the world that my best friend is a rock star?"

I thought about the card in my pocket. The one with an address, date, and time scribbled in Houston's angry handwriting. Did this mean Bound had finally accepted me as one of their own? I shouldn't care whether they did, but I had a lot on the line, so it was easier said than done.

"I'm not sure, but we start rehearsing for the tour in a couple of days."

"Can we come?" Pink tinted Maeko's round cheeks, excitement taking over her soft features.

I considered how nice it would be to have backup of my own until I remembered the two words Houston had written beneath the address. *Come alone.*

"Not this time," I answered Maeko. And maybe it was for the best. Maybe Bound would finally understand that I wasn't going to cower any more than I would worship. "I need to do this one alone."

Late that night, as I impatiently waited for sleep to steal me away, my phone chimed yet again. Resolved to stay awake and stare at the ceiling all night, I fumbled around for my phone lost in my sheets. I didn't want to look, knowing that it could only be trouble at two in the morning, but I was a glutton for punishment.

All day, I'd been getting tagged on social media by people I didn't know from Adam. The last one I dared to look at was some asshole on Twitter theorizing that I must give good head with lips like mine because why else would Bound make a special appearance to my show.

Before that, a fan page had photoshopped a stolen picture of me with each of Bound's members and then took a poll on which pairing made the better-looking couple.

Baffled, but keeping it real, I found myself staring at those pictures for longer than I cared to admit. I couldn't decide any more than the hundreds who'd flooded the comments, so my roommates and I drank two bottles of wine to banish the thoughts.

Staring at my phone screen and the most recent Instagram notification, I realized I had a direct message from someone but not just anyone.

[thebassistLo]: good show, baby fawn

Before I could think of what to say, though a simple thank-you would have been the most appropriate, Loren messaged again.

[thebassistLo]: But are you a vocalist, or are you a guitarist?

Growling as if he could hear me, I quickly typed a response even as my heart pounded, my skin flushed with heat, and cinnamon filled my nose. Thanks to the electricity buzzing through my body, it took me longer than usual to type a coherent response.

[BraxtheFawn]: I thought you were watching? I'm both.

[thebassistLo]: But you performed like you couldn't decide.

Once again, another message from him came through before I could respond.

[thebassistLo]: What color panties are you wearing?

My ears burned, and my nostrils flared as the smell of something burning filled them. I read the message and then again—three more times.

I was shaking with a different emotion this time.

Anger.

Who the hell asked for his opinion? Why did I care even though I hadn't? I was mortified and disappointed, which pissed me off even more.

[BraxtheFawn]: Get fucked, you narcissistic, fragile, small-dick debutante! I didn't ask—

Inhaling deeply, I erased what I'd typed before starting again and hitting send. Loren wanted to get under my skin, and I'd cut my own arm off before I let him.

[BraxtheFawn]: Thx. I'll work on that. See you Monday.

The asshole responded with a smirking emoji.

SEVEN

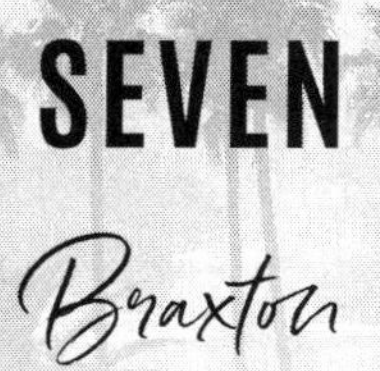

MONDAY CAME TOO QUICKLY.

Even after having my jalopy break down yesterday and the shop quoting my kidney to fix it, the last twenty-four hours seemed to fly by, giving me no chance to reconcile with my fate. By the time dawn broke, I'd gone through seven outfit changes. They were all either too bold or blatantly underdone. Either way, Bound would see right through me.

With less than five minutes to spare, I decided to keep it genuine with a gray Guns N' Roses T-shirt just long enough to wear as a dress and black fishnet stocking. For accessories I wore two chokers, one studded and the other black, and my usual ten rings stacked on three of my left fingers. I then slipped my feet into black thigh-high boots with heels even though I'd be on my feet for hours. I never wore sneakers. When I wanted to be comfortable, I wore combat boots, even in summer.

Today it wouldn't matter what kind of shoes I wore. Bound would be judging me on how well I played.

Grabbing my guitar case, I headed out. Since my car and my cash flow were both out of commission and neither Maeko nor Griff had a car, I'd have to take the bus instead of an Uber.

I used the walk to the bus stop to clear my head and find the nerve to be alone with three of the most notorious men in the world. I desperately wanted to channel the same energy from Friday night if only I could pinpoint the source.

Two buses and forty-five minutes later, I was standing on Sunset Boulevard, a mile downhill from the Beverly Hills address. I guess public transportation wasn't allowed near the rich and fabulous.

Fantastic.

I'd only been to Beverly Hills once out of curiosity when I first arrived in the city and haven't been back. Why would I when any check I wrote would bounce?

Forcing my shoulders to square and the pep in my step, I started the trek, feeling like Julie Andrews in *The Sound of Music*.

The only difference was that she hadn't been wearing high heels. I imagined doing this every day for the next three months, and by the time I reached the halfway point, I was seriously considering investing in a new car. Or at least a pair of decent sneakers. I couldn't afford either.

I was limping by the time I arrived, and to make matters worse, no one had notified the guard at the gate that I was coming. Convinced that I was just a crazed fan, it took me ten minutes to convince him to call one of the assholes inside. I was forced to stand on my blistered feet, my freshly styled hair plastered to my head from sweating, and my thighs burning from the winding walk uphill while the guard tried several times before someone picked up.

"I'm sorry to disturb you, Mr. Noble. I have a Braxton Fawn here claiming to have an appointment." He then looked me over before deciding I wasn't anything of note. "Should I send her away?" I glared at the guard's profile while he listened to whatever Jericho was saying on the other end. "My apologies. Right away." Hanging up, he pressed a button, and when the gate slid open, he immediately went back to Friday night's game and his bowl of Fruit Loops.

"The 76ers won by six points," I told him, making the spoon fall from his lips. I then swung my hips as I walked through the gate with a smile on my face. Okay, it was a bitchy thing to do, but seriously, fuck that guy.

Somehow, I made it up the short drive and to the front door

without falling on my face. Knocking, I waited, half expecting to be waylaid by a butler or housekeeper this time but was surprised when the door opened and Houston stood there.

"You're late."

Of all the greetings, like "hi" or "good morning," *that* was the one he'd chosen.

"Good morning," I returned pointedly.

He squinted back at me. "I warned you not to make me wait."

My fists balled at my side, thinking he'd look good with a black eye. "Maybe if you'd bothered to tell your guard that I was coming, I wouldn't be late since it's only two minutes past eight." I didn't mention that I would have been early had it not been for my treacherous hike in these heels. My feet throbbed at the reminder while Houston simply stared down at me. "Are you going to let me in or not?"

He pretended to mull it over before finally stepping aside and letting me in. I swallowed my whimper when I stepped over the threshold. I needed these shoes off *now*.

Jericho and Loren appeared in the foyer, hair mussed and eyes still glazed over from sleep. Houston moved past me, and I realized he was the only one remotely ready for the day.

"Why did you have me come so early if it wasn't a good time?"

"Who says it's not a good time?" Houston shot back. He didn't wait for my answer before disappearing.

Was I supposed to follow him? I scoffed while staying put. Only dogs trailed their master when they moved.

I tucked my lips to hide my smirk when Loren and Jericho left the room behind Houston.

Entering the first room on my left, I found the dining room, which led to the kitchen. Helping myself to one of the Fiji bottles I found in the fridge, I guzzled the water down while kicking off my heels.

I stopped caring about decorum the moment they left me to fend for myself. Hearing my stomach growl, I found the walk-in pantry, spotted a box of granola bars, and tore it open. I devoured two before Loren found me.

Taking in the crumbs dotting my lips and chin, his eyebrows rose as he held up my discarded heels with his forefinger. "You sure made yourself comfortable quick."

Shrugging, I swallowed the last bite of my breakfast. "None of you seemed interested in playing host."

"Among other things," he agreed. His gaze dropped to my chest, and then he groaned. I was about to punch him for ogling when he spoke. "If I didn't before, I definitely hate you now. Let me guess, you had a thing for Axl."

"What?"

Wordlessly, he nodded to my dress and the Guns N' Roses print on the front.

Oh.

"Dictators aren't really my type."

Loren peered at me curiously before plucking the box of granola from my hands and returning it to the shelf. He then pulled me from the pantry, and I tried to ignore the burning sensation of having his hand on me. Sure, it was only my elbow, but I was hard up. Sue me.

"Do you have any coffee?"

He dumped my heels unceremoniously on the floor before nodding toward a fancy-looking machine that I had no clue how to work. Jericho walked in before I could ask Loren to show me. When he beelined for me, my guard shot up even higher.

"I'm calling a redo," he announced, thrusting out his large hand. "I think we can all agree that we got off to a bad start." I was shocked, to say the least, and when he smiled…I'd never witnessed anything more magnificent. Jericho had perfect pearl teeth and plush pink lips, but it was more than that. It was the sheer honesty behind the gesture that made it even more breathtaking. "I'm Jericho. My friends call me Rich."

Shaking his hand, I returned his smile. "Brax."

"Brax?" Loren mocked, wiping the smile from my face. His back was to me, but I could hear the sneer he undoubtedly wore as he fiddled with the coffee maker. It was all he seemed to do whenever I was in the room. "Is that supposed to make you sound cool?" Sensing that he'd won my attention, he peeked over his shoulder, and the look I gave him made him snort.

I decided right then and there.

I hated him the most.

"*You* can call me Braxton."

His stormy gaze, the color of a starless sea, held mine. For a while, it seemed we were both caught in the whirlwind.

Unfortunately, he broke free of the spell first, and I cursed him for beating me to it.

"How about I call you brat instead?"

"I'll up the ante—don't talk to me at all." Deliberately giving him my back, I faced the drummer with the genuine smile. "So, your name is *Rich Noble*?"

"Yup," Loren answered despite me dismissing him. "He's a pretentious little shit, isn't he?"

I inhaled deeply, ready to give him a piece of mind when it occurred to me that Loren wasn't being rude to be cruel. The wild thoughts flitting through my mind were my most insane yet—worthy of a trip to the looney bin. Still, they couldn't be helped.

Was Loren trying to steal my attention from his friend? That would imply they were in competition and—

No. I wouldn't go there.

Without turning around, I spoke to Loren while staring at Rich. "I thought we established that you and I had nothing more to say to each other?"

He didn't respond right away. Instead, he prowled on silent feet. By the time I realized he was on the move, it was already too late. Loren had me pinned between himself and Rich. "Bothered, *Brax*?"

The cool mint on his breath from his toothpaste wafted over my nape like a cool breeze. The small hairs stood on end while goose bumps spread over my skin. He was too damn close. It was all I could do not to drive my elbow into those abs he loved to flaunt. I bet he oiled them since he thought he was too pretty to break a sweat. Watching his interviews online always made me cringe and groan from second-hand embarrassment, yet I never missed a single one.

"We already know you're hot," Loren continued. "Is that why you blocked me on Instagram? I just thought I'd return the favor and offer some constructive criticism of *your* performance."

Turning, I faced Loren, but I had to tip my head back to meet his eyes. He was that close. "I'm no more bothered by you than a fly when I swat it. You're a mild inconvenience at best. Besides, there's nothing *constructive* about you knowing the color of my underwear."

"You think so?" Loren pressed in closer until I felt the barest brush of his lips against my forehead. If I still wore my heels, he'd undoubtedly be kissing me right now. "Because I think the ones that you're wearing right now are black like your heart, Braxton Fawn."

He was right. They were.

Against my will, I backed up a step only to trade one wall of fire for another.

Jericho.

I was trapped with nowhere to run.

"What the fuck are you doing?"

My head flew to the right, and I never thought I'd be happy to see Houston. That was until I realized his angry gaze was directed at me, and so was his question. *Unbelievable.*

"Just a little playful hazing," Loren answered when I kept my mouth shut.

"This isn't a frat," I snapped, feeling flustered. Neither Loren nor Rich bothered to move even though Houston had crashed their little party. "And you're not boys. You're grown men."

"You're absolutely right, and I have the dick to prove it." Running his thumb across my lip, Loren's gaze roved my face. "Tell me you're not interested," he challenged. Behind the cocky assurance, I could see the small glimmer of hope that I'd say yes.

"In catching a venereal disease? Not a chance." Feeling a familiar ache between my legs and the taste of cherries stronger than ever before, I pushed past him, and he let me. "Now, if one of you could be professional and point me to a bathroom, please?"

No one said a word or moved a muscle for several tense seconds. Finally, Houston decided. "When you hit the stairs, keep walking. There's one on your right."

I fled the kitchen without saying a word.

By the time I found the bathroom, sweat had poured from my pores as fast as arousal ran from my center. Twisting the faucets on the sink until water rushed from the spouts, I pressed my back against the wall and wrestled my hand down my tight jeans and past my black thong.

The moment my fingers touched my clit, a cry slipped from my lips that I quickly muffled with my free hand. Another brush of my fingers and my eyes rolled back as right there in Bound's powder room, I relieved the ache that had been building since the day I walked into that conference room.

Rich

"SHOULD ONE OF US CHECK ON HER?" I ASKED AFTER TOO MUCH time had passed. It had been twenty minutes since Braxton locked herself in our guest bathroom, and she still hadn't come out.

"No, soft-ass," Loren snapped with a scoff. "She'll come out when she realizes she's screwed like the rest of us."

"Yeah, but why did you have to fuck with her? I thought we agreed to make her one of us."

"We never agreed to like it. Or her."

"I like her."

Fuck me, what wasn't to like? She was hot as hell, a rare gem of intelligence, kind… the icing on the cake was that she talked back when we weren't. I got hard just being in the same room with her—my friends, too, though Houston liked to pretend while Loren had no problem making his attraction known.

Loren made another sound of disgust before waving me off. "You like everyone."

"Yeah, lucky for you, asshole." We've been best friends longer than I can remember, and I still haven't figured out why. Loren slowly looked up from his phone and met my gaze. As much as I wanted to hold my ground, I looked away from the intensity of his stare and what burned inside.

Deciding, I stood from my seat behind my drums. "I'm going to go see if she's okay."

Neither of them bothered to stop me as I made my way out of the living room. I was at war with myself and needed those precious moments it took to reach the bathroom where Braxton was holed up to think about my next step.

She wasn't my enemy, but I was hers. It was just the way the dice rolled, and neither of us was to blame.

I tapped on the bathroom door, using the drumsticks still in my hand before shoving them in the back pocket of my jeans. There wasn't a peep on the other side, making me wonder if she'd slipped out without any of us seeing. I wouldn't blame her if she had.

I didn't realize I was holding my breath until the door slowly opened, and her big brown eyes appeared. How could someone who caused so much trouble look so goddamn innocent? She could fool the entire male population with those eyes. No one would ever see the huntress lurking beneath.

No one but me, apparently.

I shifted my feet. Why the hell was I nervous?

"I guess I overextended my welcome in your bathroom, huh?" she asked me after I just stood there like an imbecile.

"No, it's not weird at all," I lied.

Opening the door, she put her back against the wood, softly biting into that succulent lip. "I was debating."

"If you should leave?"

"And burn this house down with all of you in it," she added. Her steady gaze was unnerving, yet I couldn't look away.

"I'm both terrified and aroused. Look," I rushed to change the subject when I saw her gaze turn wary, "I can't say that we wouldn't deserve it, but can I offer some advice that might be useful?"

She hesitated for only a second before mumbling, "Sure."

"You seem pretty solid."

"For a girl?" She'd called me out on my bullshit with a raise of her brow.

I shrugged when nothing intelligent came to mind. I couldn't deny my sexism, so I ignored it instead. "You're not falling at our feet," I continued as if she hadn't spoken. "It says a lot, but it's not enough. You need to make them respect you, or else they never will. It's now or never."

"And what about you? Do you take your own advice?"

Astute. "I don't know what you mean."

I could see the contemplation in her eyes before she gave an abrupt shake of her head. "Nothing. Why are you being nice to me?"

"That's a risky assumption."

Braxton seemed to see right through me when her eyes formed slits. "You think standing up to them is going to backfire."

It wasn't a question but an accusation. She was right to be paranoid. "Your chances are fifty-fifty."

If my plan worked in her favor, she had a better chance of getting through the tour. If it didn't, Houston, Loren, and I would have someone else to direct our anger toward other than each other. As much as I wanted my friends back, I found myself hoping for the former.

Maybe Loren was right. Perhaps I couldn't commit to being an asshole.

"So, are you toying with them or me, Jericho?"

Braxton's gaze was piercing as she waited for me to respond. I had a hell of a time swallowing past the lump in my throat. Either she was a mind reader, or someone had tipped her off.

Someone else knew that Houston, Loren, and I had become strangers forced to work together rather than best friends who used to build forts to keep everyone else out. The last time we let an outsider in, he almost destroyed us before destroying himself, and whether Braxton knew it or not, she was here to finish what Calvin started.

"It doesn't matter. What matters is making it to the end of the tour...with you."

I swear her red hair looked like a river of flame, matching the fire in her eyes as she stood up straight. I'd insulted her.

"I'm not going to run."

"I'm sure you believe that, but you don't know them. Or me."

"And none of you know *me*. If you don't believe me, consider this. Would anyone else have made it this far?"

Daring to invade her space even more than Houston had at the festival or Loren half an hour ago, I placed my hands on each side of the door frame. I was so close I could feel every one of her quick breaths on my neck. If I placed my hand over her heart right now, I knew I'd feel it racing.

Warmth spread over my lower stomach before shooting to my groin. I dug my fingers into the wood to keep from touching her. Neither Houston nor Loren would have practiced such restraint, but I wasn't them.

"I wouldn't celebrate just yet, Braxton. A year is a long time. Once you get on our tour bus, there'll be nowhere to hide. There will only be the four of us and long, lonely nights with nothing to do but learn what makes you tick."

The twinkle of panic in her eyes was gone as quickly as it appeared, but I knew I hadn't imagined it. Something that raw was too real to fantasize or fabricate.

"Then I suppose it works both ways," she whispered more to herself than to me. I felt her small hand on my stomach, making the muscles spasm and dip before she pushed me out of her way. "Excuse me."

I didn't follow.

Instead, I watched her go, waiting to see if she'd turn toward the noise Houston and Loren were making as they hauled equipment into the living room or keep straight where the front door waited.

I didn't realize how anxious I was anticipating her next move until she pivoted on her bare feet toward our rehearsal space.

My relieved exhale was harsh and swift.

NINE

Braxton

"YOU TOLD LOREN AND EVERY ANUS AT SAVANT RESPONSIBLE FOR you standing here that you knew our material better than he did," Houston began the moment I was plugged into the amplifier.

I sighed, silently cursing my big mouth. It was not only a bold claim but an arrogant one, and now Houston wanted to shut me up.

"If I recall, I said I *probably* knew it better."

"Well then, you *probably* shouldn't have opened your mouth," he shot back. "You'll be responsible for both lead and rhythm, which means I need to trust not only your skills but your instincts. Show me 'Flayed Alive.'"

You mean like you intend to do to me before the day is over? Sweet.

Wisely, I kept those thoughts to myself. Not every battle was worth fighting, and since I was technically there to learn, there was nothing I could argue. It was time to put up or shut up, and I was done letting Houston have his way. Lucky for me, I knew exactly what he was up to.

"Flayed Alive" wasn't a mainstream song. The underground work appeared on their first EP, meaning only a true fan knew of its existence. And the icing on Houston's cherry-topped evil cake is that Calvin wasn't their guitarist at the time.

Nope. That honor belonged to Houston.

Calvin wasn't a founding member of Bound. He didn't join

the band until a deal was already on the table, and rumor had it that none of the three watching and waiting for me to butcher their song had picked him. If not for Calvin and now me, Bound would have been one of the few bands that started and ended with only their original members.

Aw, was that why they hated me?

Boo-fucking-hoo.

Houston folded his long frame onto the couch directly in front of me while Loren and Jericho exchanged wary looks. Neither made a move for their instruments, so I guess I was in this alone. Without bass and drums…

Fuck it.

Taking one last look at the scenery behind Houston, an unobstructed view of downtown Los Angeles, I inhaled the fresh air coming through the open doors of the veranda and cleared away the brine that wasn't there.

I didn't realize how high up we were until now. It was a beautiful home though it didn't seem at all like their style. It was too elegant and modern with clean, white lines—too much like a trophy. I pictured them in a dark castle on a foggy hill much higher than this one, far away from civilization and neighbors, with a haunted graveyard out back.

I let out a short laugh before I could catch myself.

"Something funny?" Houston inquired.

"Yeah." I snorted. "You think you can stump me." His brows dipped, and I cut off his response with a six-bar riff.

With each note, slashes of black and gray whipped the air around me like lightning ripping through the sky, followed by red bursting before pooling down like an open, bleeding wound.

The song was morbid and dark, cutting, and angry.

It hurt.

I wondered which one of them wrote it and decided I didn't care.

The chord progression underneath was a little tricky and not one I practiced often, so I stumbled through the first and second verses with gritted teeth. The greens, yellows, blues, and pinks occasionally lighting up the room made it obvious each time I played the wrong note. I didn't catch on until I reached the chorus, and by the third verse, I'd gained confidence. So much that I tweaked the rhythm of the fourth verse, giving it a smoother transition back into the chorus. It was a minor change, one I doubt they'd notice, and it made me smile at my treachery.

When the song ended, I watched the colors I knew only I could see fade before meeting Houston's black stare.

"What the fuck was that?"

"The beginning was a little rough but—"

"I'm talking about the shit you pulled on the fourth verse. Why did you change it?"

I guess that hadn't gone unnoticed.

Not knowing what else to do, I shrugged. "You said you needed to trust my instincts. I thought what I played sounded better."

"This coming from someone who can't handle more than a three-note chord? Where did you learn to play? Guitar Center?"

"You seemed to approve of my skills, or else why am I here?" When his only response was to stare at me, I glanced at the silent emo, who gave me a subtle nod of his head. Somehow that gave me the courage to dig the hole they would throw me in after a little deeper. "If you want me to do better, insulting me is not the way you're going to get it."

Houston tilted his head to the side, a strand of brown hair falling forward, and his tone deceptively soft when he spoke. "So how will I get it, Fawn?"

"You could show me—"

"We're here to teach you our songs for the tour, not how to play."

Frustrated, I strangled the fretboard of my Strat. "Then neither of us will get what we want."

Chuckling, he stood before making his way over to me. I held my breath until the clove scent of his soap forced me to exhale just so I could get another whiff.

Pathetic.

"Let me let you in on a secret, Bambi. You weren't chosen to succeed. You were chosen to fail. An amateur playing for Bound is a pipe dream. It's time to wake up. You were never meant to get what you want, so I suggest you take that bass out of your voice and do what the fuck I tell you."

Before I could ask what Houston meant because all he'd given me was more questions than answers, he turned away and returned to the couch. This time, he sat forward, bracing his forearms on his thighs and watching me with an intensity that should have frozen me on the spot. And then his lips moved.

"Do it again."

Several hours later, I was shown to the door with the order to return even earlier the next morning. My poor, cramped fingers and abused feet screamed at the atrocity of it all. As I stepped outside, my phone pinged, letting me know that my Uber had arrived. I decided to splurge since there was no way I could make that walk a second time.

Which reminded me…

Turning on my heel and prepared to march back inside, I found Houston, Loren, and Jericho crowding the doorway, stopping me in my tracks. They'd gotten their kicks making me play the same song for ten hours straight until I hit every note the way *Houston* wanted without fail.

"I may not play as well as you, but I'm not stupid. There's a reason you agreed to this, and I may not know what that reason is, but I do know something. I was either your only choice or your best chance. That means you need me."

"Your point?" Loren asked. It didn't escape my notice that he didn't bother to deny it. None of them did.

"My car broke down yesterday."

"Ah, so that's your price. I can't say I'm surprised. Just disappointed." Sliding his hands in his pockets, Loren gave me a jaded look. "What will you have? A Jeep? A mini Coop? A BMW? Let me guess…roof optional, am I right?"

"I don't want you to buy me a new car, jackass. I want a ride."

Loren blinked. "Excuse me?"

"Until I can save enough money to fix my car, I'm on foot. The buses do not come this far uphill. I had to walk a mile this morning to get to you."

Loren shrugged, unimpressed. "So call an Uber."

"Every day, round trip, for the next three months? I don't think so. I bring home minimum wage as a hostess for rich prom queens like you. I can barely afford my bills, let alone catering to your petulant whims. No ride, no Braxton. You can explain to the label why I didn't work out."

"Anything else?" Houston inquired in the most unaccommodating tone ever.

"Yes." Lifting my chin, I didn't let my gaze waver. "I take my coffee black. That shouldn't be too hard for you to remember."

"The fuck?" Loren spat. "Do we look like we give a damn?"

"Do I look like a punching bag? If you want me here before the sun rises, I'll need coffee. Until the three of you see me as your equal, you'll be fetching it until further notice."

My phone pinged again with a warning that my ride would be leaving soon, so I turned and left, leaving my new bandmates without the last word. By the time I made it down the drive, got into the backseat of the Uber, and closed the door on another complicated day, I had three new notifications on my phone. All direct messages on Instagram.

[thebassistLo]: I'm so turned on right now

I frowned at that since I didn't recall unblocking him. I *did* recall leaving my phone unattended when Houston finally let me have a bathroom break. What kind of needy prick unblocks themselves from someone else's social media? Shaking my head, I checked my other messages, not bothering to block Loren again.

[_richnoble]: ;-)

[Houston_Bound]: A car will collect you at six thirty

Ignoring the first two, I responded to Houston's message.

[BraxtheFawn]: How do you know where I live?

Twenty minutes later, the Uber dropped me off. Once inside, I immediately headed for the shower while the bathroom hogs were out. I planned to enjoy the peace—however long it lasted. I knew Griff and Maeko would want every detail, and I wasn't ready to relive my tortuous first day with three jaded rock gods.

They thought *way* too much of themselves.

With a tired sigh, I collapsed on my bed. Unfortunately, it wasn't meant to be. The moment I closed my eyes, my phone chimed. Mustering up the last drop of energy I had, I rolled over and grabbed my phone only to feel my blood boil.

[Houston_Bound]: Don't be late.

He hadn't even bothered to answer my question.

Fucker.

The next morning, a car arrived as promised. The driver introduced himself as Barry before opening my door. He also told me that he sometimes drove Bound to events whenever they were in town. It was all a little surreal. It only got stranger when Barry pulled into the parking lot of a Starbucks and, after going inside, came out carrying a tray filled with four coffee cups.

"For you, ma'am." Barry handed me the one with my name on it, but I was too nervous to drink, so I rode the entire way to the Beverly Hills home, holding the coffee between my shaking hands.

Pull it together, Fawn. They can probably smell fear.

When Barry arrived at the gate, I asked him to stop for a moment before driving through. Rolling down the back window where I sat on the side facing the security booth, I extended my still-hot coffee to the guard from yesterday.

"Truce?" I asked when his gaze moved back and forth between me and the cup.

I bet he thinks I poisoned it.

If I ever decided to risk life in prison, I'd definitely go big.

Perhaps murdering my new bandmates?

Slowly, the guard took the Starbucks before taking a sip, grinning, and waving us through.

Sitting back, I sighed my relief. Maybe today wouldn't be so bad, after all.

TEN

Houston

SHE'S A GODDAMN DISASTER.

Braxton played better than the meatheads we auditioned, but she still needed work. *A lot* of work. Some would argue that my standards were too high, but only pussies with none at all ever said shit like that.

"That was slow and mechanical," I told her the moment she finished butchering one of our bigger hits. "By the time you pieced together the right chords, the song was over. You need to get out of your head. When you're in my session, there's nothing for you in there. Play from here." I tapped my chest where a heart used to be. I felt like a hypocrite. Sighing, I dropped my hand when Braxton stared at me like she wasn't impressed. "Or at least play like you have some fucking guts, Fawn."

Nostrils flaring, she straightened her shoulders. "I want to do it again."

"You say that like you have a choice."

I watched her roll her eyes from my peripheral but didn't comment on it. Three months wasn't enough time to get sidetracked with other shit like her fucking attitude and why it made my dick hard.

Today, she'd pinned her hair up, showing off her long neck and the black choker with a gold, crescent moon hanging from it. She also wore a short, white sundress that made her look virginal and black combat boots that made her look less so. To make matters worse, she'd decided that skipping a bra today had been a smart choice. I didn't get the look she was going for, but it worked for her, nonetheless. It was like she was fighting both sides of the same coin.

Braxton was older than I had guessed initially but still young. She'd only turned twenty-two a few months ago, which meant that as much as she pretended, she was still figuring out who she was.

She tried the song again, which was better, but she still sounded like she was making noise instead of a melody. If I were being fair, she played well enough that it took a trained ear to know the difference. On her third attempt, when she seemed to retreat inside her head again, I shot up from the couch with a growl so loud it roused Loren with a snort from his slumber next to me.

"What the fuck are you playing at?" I demanded as I charged her. She didn't back down to her credit, but I couldn't care less about her mettle. She was wasting my time.

"Excuse me?"

"Where is the girl from the festival? I didn't invite this meek, mild bullshit you brought to my session. Either get out of your head or get out of my sight."

Her thick lips parted in shock before closing only to open once more so she could run her mouth. "Do not talk to me that way." Her fist balled in warning—one I didn't heed. I was willing to risk a broken nose if it meant getting her to play from her marrow.

"Or what?" I pushed up on her, backing her into the wall and trapping her there with my hand next to her head.

Braxton tipped her chin, not willing to break my stare. "Or I'll leave."

"Only if I let you." She was making me contradict my goddamn self.

"What do you want from me, Morrow?"

With my free hand, I fingered the frilly sleeve resting off her shoulder. I wanted to kiss the bare skin there, and had she been a groupie instead of my new guitarist, I would have. "I thought it was obvious."

"Not to me." She searched my gaze before narrowing her own. "It seems like you want me to quit."

"Yesterday, you told me that I needed you. Now you accuse me of trying to get you to quit? I'm confused, Fawn."

"So am I."

I sighed before stepping back and giving her space. "What I want is irrelevant, but you were right. I need you. I need you to play like *you* want to be here. Do you?"

"I'm not sure anymore."

For fuck's sake.

"There's a reason why you turned left instead of right. Whatever that reason is, don't forget it now when there's no turning back. Some good just might come out of this for you, so make the most of it while you can."

She gaped at me in disgust before shrieking, "Is that supposed to be motivating?"

Loren and Rich snorted in response.

"Decide for yourself. Just stop wasting my time." Walking over to one of the cases we'd piled in the living room, I snatched up one of the microphones I'd brought from Portland. Loren and Rich, always in sync with me despite our rocky friendship, were already in place—Rich behind his drums and Loren plugged in and clutching his bass.

"Together this time. Oh, and Fawn?"

"Yes, Houston?" She batted her long lashes sarcastically. When she smiled, I paused, getting lost in it for a moment.

"Don't think for a second that I'm not keeping tabs."

Hours later, the three of us were standing in the kitchen in quiet contemplation as the sun set over Los Angeles. I let Braxton leave early today since she claimed she had to work tonight. I wasn't thrilled about sharing her time, so the moment I was sure she could manage being one of us, she was quitting that job, whether she wanted to or not.

"She played like she wrote it that last time," Loren announced. "So maybe it's time we stop singling her out and get down to business?"

"I'm not singling her out. If one of us sounds bad, we all sound bad. We'll continue like this until I can trust her judgment."

Part of the guitarist's job was to be spontaneous and original, which would allow her to improv when she needed to and keep the rhythm going. Bound's entire sound and direction would be influenced by her abilities and style, which meant this next era of our legacy now belonged to Braxton fucking Fawn. She just hadn't figured that out yet.

"Get the fuck out of here," Loren snapped with a scowl. "Face it, she's good. You're just an asshole. Did you see how fast she caught on to 'Flayed Alive'?" he asked no one in particular.

Jericho was busy scrolling on his phone, and I pretended not to have caught a peek of Braxton's Instagram on his screen moments ago. She had endless thirst traps, making me feel like a kid in a candy store when I went through them last night.

"Calvin still couldn't grasp it, and he'd been playing with us for years." Loren stared at me for a moment before he grinned so wide that I thought his face would split in half. "It must have got you hard as fuck watching her master a Houston Morrow original."

"Not particularly."

"Liar."

"Is there some reason why you think I care if you believe me?"

"Because I'm telling you both now before you get any ideas," Loren began. There was revenge in his eyes when he glanced at Rich, who didn't see it because his gaze was still glued to his phone and a photo of Braxton wearing a green bikini. When Loren met mine, holding my stare for a little too long, a growl rose in my chest at the apparent challenge. "Dibs."

The sound of Rich's phone dropping onto the counter stole our attention from one another. "What do you mean *dibs*? You can't just call it."

"That's literally the entire purpose of *dibs*," Loren shot back dryly.

"How do you know she'd even want you? You're a dick to her."

"It's called flirting, Forrest Gump. Not all of us blush and smile and ask a girl how she's feeling like you do. That's why you don't get laid as much."

"There's more to life than just sex."

Tossing his head back, Loren made this sound that was a cross between a hyena and a donkey. "You sound like a fucking virgin."

"Well, I'm not."

"Oh, I know. I saw your pasty ass going to pound-town one too many times to think that."

Red bloomed on Rich's cheeks before he stood from the stool like he was ready to go to the ground with Loren. "You can't just call dibs, Lo."

"Why not?" Loren asked even though he didn't seem to care too much about the answer or that Rich looked one wrong word from punching him.

"Because she's our guitarist," I answered for him. "No one is touching her. That would be unprofessional."

"Says the asshole who was just dry humping her up the wall two hours ago."

"That didn't happen."

"But you wanted it to. I claimed her, and now suddenly, morals matter? Who do you think you're fooling, Morrow?"

I shot up from my seat and had my hand wrapped around Loren's throat by the time the stool hit the ground. "You don't like it?" I questioned after slamming him against the wall and pinning him there. "Do something about it."

I barely got out the last word before Loren shoved me off him. I immediately braced for him to charge me. It's been a few weeks since we destroyed an entire room, and I was salivating at the chance to see him bleed. The label would no doubt charge us for destroying another rental.

Worth it.

"Can you please fuck each other up later? I'm hungry," Rich announced in a poor attempt to diffuse the situation. My glare was still locked with Loren's when Rich asked, "What's the name of that restaurant where Braxton said she worked?"

That got our attention.

ELEVEN

Loren

FIRST OF ALL, *DIBS*?

Is this what my attraction to Braxton has reduced me to? A fucking twelve-year-old? I knew why I said it—to fuck with my friends. Once it was out, I realized I meant it. I wanted to fuck Braxton, and I was too greedy to share. Fucking the same girls would have never bothered me before but mostly because they were groupies and wouldn't be sticking around.

This was different. *She* was different.

Cue the goddamn violin.

I haven't been this eager for a piece of ass since I learned what it truly meant to free willy.

"You ready?" Rich barged into my room without knocking. "Or do you need another couple of hours to get ready?" he deadpanned.

"I just figured I'd give you time to actually be hungry, chickenshit."

"How does stopping another fight between you two make me a coward?"

"Because you're afraid of the day when Houston is no longer able to protect you." I peered over my shoulder in time to see Rich swallow past the lump in his throat.

"I can protect myself."

"Right." Turning around, I regarded my best friend. "Is that why you can't look me in the eye?"

Rich forced his gaze to meet mine. To fuck with him, I let him see everything I was thinking. Like so many times before, he looked away. I let out a quiet laugh to dull the roaring in my head.

"Get out of my room before you faint, Rich. I wouldn't want you feeling scandalized."

"I need help with my tie." He gestured to the slip of deep purple silk around his neck.

We looked it up, and the restaurant Braxton worked at required the men to wear ties like eating food was ever that serious. Unfortunately, the glitz and glamour of fine dining was nothing new to me. My upbringing had been entirely different from Houston and Rich.

"How are you twenty-seven years old and still can't knot your own tie?" Grabbing his collar after he shrugged, I yanked him into me before getting to work on his tie. "I think you're full of shit, Noble." He didn't say anything, and he wouldn't. Not when we were this close. I could feel his unsteady breath even through my dress shirt. I took my time sprucing him up, and the moment I was finished, I grabbed a handful of his jet-black hair and yanked his head back before he could thank me. "Do not use me again for your little thrills, Rich. I don't like being teased." Before he could lie and deny it, I shoved him out of the door before slamming it in his face.

Twenty minutes later, after I was finally satisfied with my appearance, we found Barry in the driveway waiting. Another forty-five minutes and we were walking through the back door of Succulent and into a private dining room. Our assistant had called ahead and managed to bypass the six-month waiting list once she told them who had inquired.

My ass had barely warmed my seat before we were swarmed by the gushing team the manager selected to wait on us.

"Is Brax working tonight?" Rich's thirsty ass inquired.

The manager frowned in confusion. "Braxton Fawn," I insisted when he simply gaped. "Red hair, banging body, terrible attitude? Ring a bell?"

"Oh, yes! She is working tonight, but unfortunately, she's our hostess. She doesn't wait tables."

"She does tonight. We want her."

"I'm sorry, Mr. James, but—"

"But what?"

His mouth opened and closed like a fish, and I could tell he was torn between pissing me off or just doing what the fuck I asked. "Right away," he eventually decided.

I watched him hurry to the front where Braxton was as I absently sipped water from a glass meant for wine. Our table sat on a raised level. The short stairs were roped off with red velvet, so it was only semi-private, allowing me to see the dining room below. Since it was a Tuesday night, it wasn't as packed, which was a goddamn relief. Still, we'd already been recognized, and I could see the debate in the other patrons' eyes whether to come over and ask for an autograph. I hoped the "fuck off" written on my forehead kept them at bay.

Any other night I would be at the world's beck and call, but tonight, I simply wanted to be a man on the hunt for a woman. Houston and his rules could suck my dick.

It took a few minutes before I spotted them.

As expected, even her boss had a tough time getting Braxton to comply. She was still arguing with him even now as they made their way toward us. Just as I was wondering if he'd told them who had requested her, she climbed the stairs, and her big eyes widened when she saw us sitting there. She was wearing this black number made spectacular only by her subtle curves as the dress hugged her body.

Her brown gaze moved from Houston to Rich before narrowing on me. *Of course*, she assumed this was my idea.

"What the hell are you doing here?" she demanded.

"Miss Fawn!" the managed bellowed his outrage before turning to us and apologizing profusely. "She'll be terminated immediately," he swore.

"Don't you fucking dare," I warned him.

Utterly shocked, he blinked rapidly at me before regaining most of his composure. "I-I don't understand."

"We know her," Rich informed him.

"And we like her," I cheerily added with a wink directed at Braxton.

Houston, of course, said nothing as he looked Braxton over like he was bored. I bet he was already planning to make her quit this gig but wisely kept his mouth shut rather than seize the opportunity that just landed in his lap.

"Nevertheless," the manager began before facing Braxton. If he fired her anyway, I was knocking his toupee-wearing ass down those steps. "Succulent prides itself on providing fine dining and excellent service. These are our special guests who've personally chosen you to wait on them. I expect you to be professional from this point forward and give these gentlemen whatever they desire."

Now you're talking. Maybe he wasn't common-sense deficient, after all.

The manager stormed away, taking the rest of the actual waiters and waitresses with him. They looked disappointed about not being able to wait on us, so I sent a quick text to our assistant before focusing on Braxton.

"You look nice," I complimented after slowly looking her over once more. "Why don't you dress like that when you come to rehearsal?"

"I didn't realize there was a dress code."

"There is now."

Rich kicked me under the table, a nonverbal demand for me to be less verbal, so I knocked his glass over, spilling his water into his lap. He jumped up like he was on fire before snatching up his white napkin cloth and dabbing at the ice-cold water wetting his crotch.

Braxton, catching the entire exchange, shook her head. "You know it's hard to believe that the three of you are grown men."

I had so many dirty responses to that. Wisely, I kept my mouth closed. Jericho, sitting down again, swiped my water for himself since I spilled his and started guzzling it down.

"So," she said with a sigh before lifting the notepad and pen in her hand. "What can I start you off with?" She clicked the pen a little harder than necessary.

"Depends," I spoke before the others could. "What do you recommend?"

"To leave."

Rich choked on his water while Houston frowned down at him. He was so embarrassing.

"Sorry, but I don't think that's on the menu."

Braxton didn't respond. Instead, she leaned over, giving me a full view of her breasts and the freckles there while she flipped open the menu in front of me. I wondered where else she hid her freckles.

"We have an amazing selection of wine—"

"Don't drink the stuff."

She paused, meeting my gaze, which I'd been smart enough to remove from her tits before she caught me. "Well, what about your friends?"

"Birds of a feather."

"We have other drinks—"

"I'll just take a lemonade." She looked surprised, but I wasn't about to elaborate or explain my drinking choices.

Sensing this, she stood up straight before turning to Houston. "And you?"

"Coke."

She wrote it down before turning to Rich. "I'll just take more water," he answered before she could ask. I caught the dirty look he gave me and laughed.

"All right then. I'll be right back."

As soon as she walked away—yes, I watched her walk away—I turned to my friends. "A hundred bucks, she thinks we're alcoholics."

"Does it matter?" Houston asked. Irritation creased his brow.

"If I'm going to bone and possibly marry her, it does."

"You're not, so I guess it doesn't."

I resisted the urge to cause a scene by breaking my best friend's nose. "Afraid I'll beat you to the punch?"

Houston waved me off. "I'm only interested in her guitar skills."

"Which you act like she doesn't have. Care to explain why you're keeping her around then?"

"Because you know as well as I do we don't have a choice. You know what Carl is up to. We all know why he chose her."

"So you think you can get her ready in three goddamn

months? Toot your own horn much?" Houston's frustration was palpable at his point, so I leaned forward, eager to go in for the kill. "Just admit it."

"Admit what?" he snapped.

"That either she's a damn good guitarist, or you want her pussy bad enough to risk everything we've built. Same as me. Same as Rich."

That vein in his forehead looked ready to burst as our staring contest intensified. He couldn't choose, and I, honest to God, had no clue why. It was like someone held him by his heel when he was a child and dipped his complicated ass in a pool of angst, much like Thetis did Achilles in the River Styx.

I figured if anyone could crack that wall, it was Braxton. Maybe that's why he was afraid of her.

"Pussy," I muttered when I caught Braxton making her way over to us while carrying a tray topped with our drinks.

None of us said a word as she set our drinks on the table along with a basket of bread. "Can I start you off with something to sample, or would you like more time to look over the menu?"

Although most of the six menu choices looked foreign even to me, we each rambled off what we wanted. Somehow this world had gotten even more pretentious since I was kicked out of it years ago, and I didn't think that was possible.

"Okay, I'll be back—"

"Wait," Rich interrupted before she could run off again. "Stay."

Braxton shifted from one foot to the other before chewing on her plump lower lip. "I can't. I'm working."

"We obviously know that," I reminded her. "That's why we're here."

"So you purposely came to distract me from my job? You do realize I almost got fired."

"In our defense, no one made you be a bitch," Houston piped in, making me wince. He was definitely the pot in this scenario, but I said nothing since we were on the same side for once.

"Excuse me?" Braxton blinked as she took a step back from the table. It was hard to believe she was that appalled.

"You heard me."

"*You* ambushed *me*. Again. What did you expect?"

"Hi?" Houston suggested with a smirk. He was in rare form today since his weapon of choice was indifference. "Maybe hello?"

Nostrils flaring, Braxton stormed off without another word.

"Could have gone better," I mused out loud. "This next round, I'm going to try to get her in my lap. Think she'll go for it?"

Houston and Rich both looked at me and spoke at the same time. "Shut up, Loren."

Thirty minutes later, Braxton returned with our food, but she didn't give us time to apologize or make things worse before she stormed off again. A starry-eyed waiter refilled our drinks minutes later, and we took turns signing his notepad at his request before he practically skipped away. Braxton still hadn't shown her face by the time we were done eating.

"What I wouldn't give for a cheeseburger right now," I said after I topped off my fish that was smaller than my fist. The food cost so much they didn't even bother to list the prices. Apparently, if you had to ask, you had no business dining here.

"Do you think she left?" Rich asked the moment he swallowed the last of his food. At that moment, Braxton appeared, her face flushed and coated with sweat like she'd just run a mile. I noticed her dress was wrinkled at the hem, making me frown. "Are you okay?" he asked when she couldn't seem to catch her breath.

"Yes. My apologies. Would you like dessert?"

"Are you on the menu?" I flirted.

"You shouldn't ask questions you already know the answer to. Shall I bring the checks?"

"Rich got it," I answered. Since this was his idea, he could pay for the fucking food. Braxton looked at him for confirmation, to which he gave with a nod of his head. She scurried off, and like all the times before, I watched her go. I wondered if she knew that dress was tight enough to tell that she was no longer wearing panties.

Oh, hell yeah.

TWELVE

Braxton

I *KNOW YOUR SECRET.*

I stared at the text message from the unknown number. My heart pounding inside my chest seemed loud to my ears as I walked to the bus stop. My shift was over, and my feet were killing me. The concrete pavement seemed to turn my heels into daggers as I practically limped down the sidewalk. Needing a distraction, I decided to text back.

Who is this?

The response was immediate, like they were just waiting for me to ask.

The reason you're not wearing panties.

I stopped walking as I became painfully aware of the fact that I wasn't. How did they know? I texted back to get an answer.

Tell me who this is, or you're blocked, creep.

A moment later, my phone rang, and my gut painfully twisted when I realized it was the same number. Even worse…it was a video call.

I debated for all of two seconds before quickly tapping the green button. What harm could a phone call do? If it turned out to be a stalker or a creep, I could just block the number.

The call connected, and my jaw dropped when Loren's face appeared. Smiling wide, he moved his gorgeous face closer to the camera.

"Now you know, baby fawn."

"Loren?"

A blond eyebrow arched. "You know anyone else who looks this devilishly handsome?" His nostrils flared as if expecting my answer to piss him off.

"What exactly do you think you know about me?" I asked instead of falling into his trap.

Rolling over in what looked like a bed, he stared at me before responding. "I know that you're incredibly responsive to unusual persuasion."

"What the hell does that even mean?"

Instead of answering, his gaze moved to my background, turning from playful to assessing. "Where are you?"

"Bus stop."

His brows instantly dipped as he shot up from his lazy lounge. "At this time of night?" he spat as if I'd done something out of line.

"Gee, Dad, I didn't realize I had a curfew." After rolling my eyes, I added more amicably, "My car broke down, remember?"

"You could have told us you needed a ride."

"You guys left the restaurant hours ago. You expect me to believe you would have waited around that long?" My coworkers had lost their shit when Bound signed and gave a bunch of free merchandise before finally leaving. They'd also left me a generous tip I hadn't earned before they left—enough to repair my car.

"We would have sent Barry to pick you up."

"I assumed that perk was for rehearsals only."

"Now you know," he responded shortly.

I was thrown for a moment. Utterly bewildered. I couldn't decide if Loren was acting like my father or my boyfriend. What right did he have to be upset about my choices when they affected him in no way? He didn't even know me well enough to care this much as a friend.

"Speaking of late, what do you say we pick this up at a more appropriate hour?" *Or not at all.*

"Don't you dare hang up," he ordered, but it sounded more like a growl.

I hadn't known Loren long, but this side of him had taken

me by surprise. I assumed Houston was the only dominating one. Loren was more of an anarchist, staunchly rejecting authority and proudly boasting his devil-may-care attitude. I envied him.

Right now, though, he looked ready to rip my head off—mine and an imaginary enemy who wished me harm.

"I have pepper spray."

"Do you have a gun?" he countered. "Or even a drop of self-defense skills?"

I wrinkled my nose. "No."

"Then keep your ass on the line."

Something akin to freshly cut grass, morning dew, or what I imagined a meadow would smell like stormed my olfactory senses. When I inhaled, the air felt clean despite the smog covering the city. It was almost familiar and not at all unpleasant. I had no clue what triggered it, but I had a feeling I'd soon find it.

I don't remember what we talked about for the ten minutes it took my bus to arrive, but even after I safely boarded my ride home, Loren refused to let me hang up.

"Okay," I said after I entered my apartment forty minutes later and panned the camera around to show Loren that I was home. Like a smartass, I even showed him that the door was locked, and the windows were closed. Maybe it was me that didn't want to end the call. "Thanks for the talk. Good night."

Ignoring my rush to get him off the phone and my head back on track, he switched topics faster than a race car switched lanes. "You know Houston is going to make you quit that little job of yours, right?"

"What?" For some reason, my vagina reacted to that way before my head, heart, or any other part of me that made sense could catch up.

"Just a heads up." Laughing, he ended the call, leaving me hanging.

I stood there, fuming with the phantom scent of burning wood in my nose to prove it, before storming to the bathroom and a hot shower.

What right did Houston have to think he could make me

quit anything? Maybe Loren was just fucking with me, but in the morning, I would absolutely get to the bottom of it.

"How do you like your eggs?" Loren greeted me hours after our late-night video chat. I couldn't even call it the next morning since it was after midnight when we talked. It was much too intimate for two strangers who didn't even like each other.

I'd just finished storming into Bound's kitchen, where I found Loren and Houston waiting but no Jericho. *Where is he?* I wanted to ask but understood why that wouldn't be wise. Instead, I ignored Loren, who was busy cooking breakfast at the stove and pretending he hadn't planted this seed in the first place.

"You're making me quit Succulent?" I demanded of Houston.

He didn't seem surprised that I'd come in with guns blazing, making my stomach pool with dread when he shot Loren an accusatory glare. Apparently, he already knew who spilled the beans.

"It wasn't high on my list of things to do."

That was all the answer he gave. Not hitting Houston was becoming a full-time job.

Loren turned from the stove, scooping a steaming helping of eggs onto an empty plate and pushing said plate toward me. He didn't seem at all concerned by the storm brewing or the fact that I'd ratted him out. It irritated me how self-assured these guys could be. They were spoiled, entitled, and had more arrogance than the ocean had water. Just once, I'd like to get under their skin as easily as they got under mine.

"I'd ask why Loren would tip you off," Houston drawled, "but I already know why."

Unfortunately, Houston made no move to explain it to *me*. I was more than simply curious. I was obsessed. They hated me, unequivocally, but there was more to it. I'd never experienced hate-sex before, and it was quickly shooting to the top of my fantasies.

"Is there some reason you feel attached to that job to keep it while rehearsing and touring with us?" Houston asked instead.

"That's not the point. I should be allowed to come to that decision myself."

"Why haven't you?"

"Because the tour isn't for three months. I still need to support myself until then. I don't even know when I'll be paid for that." The label had offered me an advance, one I wouldn't receive until the tour began.

Sliding a manila folder that was already waiting on the counter, Houston gave me a pointed look when I simply looked from it to him. After a brief staring contest that I lost, I sighed and flipped it open.

Inside were forms requesting my financial and tax information and what looked like an offer to pay me for rehearsals. It was more than generous and completely unexpected. When I looked up, the question was obviously in my eyes because Houston answered before I could voice it.

"I need you focused and devoted from this point forward." The unspoken "to them" was heavily implied.

"This is a lot of money."

"I agree," Loren chipped in. "Houston seems to think you're worth it."

I guess we were back to square one, where Loren insulted me at every turn. He was a far cry from the concerned friend that he tricked me into thinking he could be last night.

"That remains to be seen," Houston argued. "Nonetheless, do we have an agreement?"

How could I say no to that much money in exchange for quitting a job I hated? It should have been a no-brainer, so why was I hesitating?

Perhaps it was because they'd so very clearly decided this for me without thinking of including me in the discussion. I didn't appreciate the high-handedness, even if it did come wrapped in a pretty bow.

"What if I don't want to quit my job?" I asked them.

"That was never an option," Houston answered, proving me right.

"Hence why we're paying you more than you're worth," Loren added. "So there's no reason for you to say no."

"I can think of one." Holding up the offer, I tore it in half with a smile that would make Miss America look like a sourpuss. "You both can kiss my ass."

"Love to," Loren smoothly and immediately responded.

"I'll quit Succulent and devote myself to this band when the three of you show me some respect."

Loren snorted. Houston stared.

"And not a moment sooner."

Ignoring the plate full of steaming eggs, I pushed away from the island that separated me from them. At the entrance, I peered over my shoulder. Both still stood in the same place, watching me like I was some mystical creature they'd just discovered.

"Shall we?"

THIRTEEN

Rich

I WAS BEGINNING TO THINK MY ADVICE TO BRAXTON HAD DONE MORE harm than good. She'd put her foot down and got our attention.

It turns out it was much more than she'd bargained for.

Since she refused to quit her job, Houston never let up, no matter how much her playing improved. Not once—not for a second, an hour, or a day in the weeks since. If Houston was on her ass anymore, he'd be *in* her ass. No doubt that thought had crossed his mind once or twice.

At least today would offer her some reprieve since we had our first photo shoot and interview with Braxton.

While the magazine that had been promised the exclusive set up, I caught sight of a familiar face entering Clive's. I was holding up one of the cracked concrete walls the owner tried to embellish with celebrity posters, neon signs, and photos of patrons and employees. The molded ceiling looked like it would cave any moment, and the floor appeared as if no one had cleaned it since opening thirty years ago.

This was the most rundown bar the magazine could find in L.A., with Braxton as the centerpiece to commemorate Bound's "discovery."

I snorted.

If we hadn't taken Savant's deal five years ago, this wouldn't be happening right now. This would not be our reality.

"The world must be on fire if you're bothering to show your face," I greeted the suited man approaching me in a blue tailored suit.

As usual he'd forgone a tie, so the top few buttons of his white shirt and suit jacket were left undone, exposing the deep-brown skin of his chest. Xavier Gray, recently forty, stroked his beard trimmed close while his dark brown gaze studied me. His black hair was also cut close and had the appearance of waves so deep they made me seasick whenever I looked at them.

Gray became our manager about a year or so after we signed to Savant. According to him, it was the least he could do after we saved his son, who was now a big-time rapper, from sharing our fate. Raleigh, who'd been nineteen at the time and dead set on fulfilling his dreams, hadn't been willing to listen to his father. The details of how it led to us stepping in were murky, but what mattered now is that it had done some good.

Raleigh signed with a record label that wasn't shady and was now at the top of his game. It was just one reason Carl was determined to take us down, and Braxton was his way to do it.

"Not quite," Xavier answered as he slapped hands with me. "How's it going with your newest addition?"

"You'd know if you brought your ass down sooner to meet her."

He gave me a look as if I were insane. "You mean leave Portland willingly? Pass. I hate L.A. You know that."

I scratched my chin, the lie already on my tongue. "It's not that bad."

"So you're not itching to get back home?"

"I didn't say that."

"You didn't have to." He peered at me then. "You sleeping all right?"

"Like a log," I answered shortly, hoping he didn't push. It's been nearly a year since I gave them cause for concern. I didn't need to be coddled.

Reading the "fuck off" written on my forehead, Xavier nodded before letting it go. I exhaled loudly, making him smirk before asking, "Where are your boys?" He immediately looked around as if he could find the answer for himself.

I shrugged, truly not knowing or caring. Houston and Loren had disappeared, losing interest in the scene as soon as Braxton had been pulled away for hair and makeup. I stuck around to make sure at least one of us was easily found in case…I don't really know. Braxton would chew off her own arm before ever admitting needing us. She put on a brave face, but I was getting good at reading her.

With only a couple of months left until the tour, it was time to introduce Braxton to the world. It was only a week ago that we'd finally assured our fans the tour would go on as scheduled. We hadn't mentioned the fact that we didn't have a choice. It didn't matter. Braxton was good and getting better every day. She'd be ready. Houston's determination not to be bested by Carl would make sure of it.

Because the alternative, extending our contract in exchange for a guitarist with more experience, made me want to put a bullet in my brain.

Carl had not only underestimated us, but he'd clearly underestimated Braxton. If she hadn't impressed us with her performance at that festival weeks ago, he might have gotten what he wanted. We were desperately holding on to the past and too proud to admit that we weren't ready to walk away. It meant giving up on Bound…and each other.

Five years ago, I would have jumped off a cliff, confident that my best friends would magically sprout wings and catch me before I fell. Now I wouldn't so much as cross the street without my own two eyes to guide me. Loren would probably push me in front of a bus just because it's Tuesday.

It was an unholy thing to resent the dead, but if I could bring Calvin back to life, I would without hesitation. All so I could kill him myself. We never let him in, so he ripped us apart instead. By the time we'd caught on to the slow yet agonizing rip, it was already too late. Mistrust and resentment had sunk its claws deep, and though Calvin was dead, we still bore the scars.

The clench in my jaw slackened when Braxton appeared, forcing my thoughts to flee.

Artificial lighting shone on every inch of the dilapidated space. Somehow, she was still the brightest thing in the room.

The ripped jeans and cropped pullover she'd worn to the shoot was gone. In their place, she now wore a tiny number that stopped above her unmarred knees. The A-line dress had long mesh lantern sleeves and an empire waistline. The black pleated material looked like velvet, drawing the light whenever she moved. She was so damn enticing that I couldn't decide if she was wearing a dress or lingerie.

The only thing that mattered was that I couldn't breathe. Not while my eyes were on her. I'd never felt this clench in my gut before. It was hot, twisting, and painful.

Demanding.

Braxton's gaze found mine, and for the first time, she looked unsure. Even when she was afraid, she pretended otherwise. Braxton Fawn was nothing short of a marvel.

And right now, she was waiting for me to say something.

My tongue, unfortunately, had been tied by the vision she made in that damn dress. Her hair had been pinned in a messy knot on top of her head, leaving her neck bare save for the collar around her neck. They'd kept her makeup light, simply enhancing her round eyes, full lips, and long lashes that fooled a sitting duck like me into believing her innocent. Houston and Loren hadn't caught on yet, but they would. When that time came, Braxton would have a different problem on her hands.

I didn't realize I was moving until I was standing in front of her. "You look beautiful."

"You wouldn't happen to think so because I'm practically naked, would you?"

My eyes widened at that. "Are you uncomfortable? I can see if—" Braxton laid her small hand on my arm before I could finish. The simple touch felt like a brand—like I was already hers.

"It's fine," she assured me. "I've worn less in front of a lot more." She smiled, and I had the feeling it was to put me at ease rather than herself. *Fuck.*

I cleared my throat and looked away to keep from being caught in her trance. The door leading to the alley opened, and fucking Houston stepped through. He didn't notice me watching him because he was already locked on to Braxton, whose back was to him. I watched as his attention dropped to her ass, his lips moved to form a swear I couldn't hear, and then he turned and stormed right back out the door.

Loren appeared next, but, of course, he didn't leave like Houston. He sauntered over until he stood in front of her, and Braxton's guard immediately rose. For some reason, it filled me with glee, knowing she was more comfortable with me. I could see why as Loren's dark eyes ran over her, checking her out and offering no apologies for it.

"Looking good, baby fawn."

"Leave her alone," I immediately barked before I could stop myself or Braxton could speak for herself. What the hell was I doing?

Loren didn't even acknowledge me. Reaching out, he fingered the velvet choker around her neck. "Looking damn good."

"Thanks."

She was calm—*too* calm, in my opinion. I wasn't sure I bought it, but it wasn't my problem.

Sighing, I stepped away. Braxton had already proved more than once that she could handle herself. She wouldn't have lasted this long otherwise, and I didn't need more reason to fight with my best friends. Besides, Braxton had no use for a knight with dented armor. We had two months until the tour, and I didn't know how, but I'd find a way to shake Braxton from my thoughts.

Houston returned just as Ingrid, the photographer, was ready to start shooting. She directed Braxton to lie on a red chaise that was out of place in the bar despite having seen better days. With the remaining space left, Houston was placed at the end by Braxton's booted feet. He immediately slouched his frame, resting his arm along the swooped back and getting comfortable against the padded scroll arm. I caught his gaze roving all over Braxton while she was preoccupied adjusting her position to suit Ingrid.

Once her back was arched and her hands braced on the cushion behind her, Loren was directed to stand by Braxton's head. Ingrid wanted the cocky charm he hardly ever needed a reason to display, so with his thumb touching his lip, he gave her that infamous Loren James grin.

Without direction, having done this dance too many times before, I centered myself behind the chaise, crossing my arms, and letting my hair fall forward.

Smiling in satisfaction, Ingrid immediately returned to her camera and proceeded to take what seemed like a million shots. I sighed on the inside, knowing this was only the first pose. After switching positions on and around the chaise countless times, the last one with Braxton lying on her stomach alone with the three of us standing together behind her, we moved to take shots by the bar.

"Doing okay?" I asked Braxton as we waited for Ingrid and her team to adjust the lighting and switch cameras. It was all I could do not to touch her exposed thigh resting near my forearm as she sat on the bar. That fucking dress was so short that I'd caught more than one glimpse of the matching panties she wore underneath. I was surprised the stylist had even bothered.

"I'm not sure," she muttered before smiling down at me. "It's still hard to believe this is really happening."

"Seriously?" Loren remarked with a snort. "A little late to get star-struck, don't you think?" The clinking of glass, followed by the sound of liquid pouring, prompted me to turn my head. I stood up straight when I realized Loren was pouring a shot. The owner stood by the jukebox watching but didn't say a word.

"What the fuck, Lo?"

"Relax," he snapped back before I could say more. "It's not for me." Holding out the shot glass filled to the brim with vodka, he patiently waited, silently daring Braxton to accept it.

Her brow rose as she studied the drink. "Is this appropriate? We're working."

"Don't know, don't care. Drink up."

I watched her chew her lip, utterly unaware of the torture she wrought before finally snatching the drink from Loren and tossing it back.

"You seem to have the most vices," she grumbled when Loren immediately poured her another. This time she didn't hesitate.

"It just means I'm the most fun, baby." Just as he was getting ready to pour Braxton her third shot, Houston appeared, snatching the bottle from Loren and setting it back where it belonged. "Party pooper." Houston didn't respond, walking off with Xavier again while Loren remained unbothered, resting his elbow on the bar by Braxton. "Feel free to thank me for loosening you up."

"I'd rather die first."

Eyes moving around the makeshift studio, Braxton missed the way Loren admired her like she was gold at the end of a very long and bleak rainbow. When her gaze landed on me, I realized she'd caught me staring.

"You don't talk much, do you?" she observed with a rare smile.

"Only when I have something worth saying."

"Think you can teach your friend?" Throwing her thumb over her shoulder, she indicated Loren, who was preoccupied texting on his phone. I knew he had heard every word. He just didn't care.

Laughing, I shook my head, making her pout. "I'm a drummer, not a miracle worker."

Houston only returned when Ingrid was ready to go again. It didn't take a genius to know that he was avoiding Braxton. If she noticed, she didn't let on. It was even less likely that she cared. We were just all lucky we'd chosen to be rock stars and not porn stars.

This time when the camera snapped, she seemed less like a fish out of water. Braxton was a natural if her Instagram was anything to go by. Her problem had been our presence.

The next round of shots was us standing under the spotlight Ingrid's team created with the decrepit bar as our backdrop and Braxton front and center. I admit I was a little eager to see the final shots when I've never cared before. Braxton added an element to Bound that we would never have considered if we hadn't been forced. Whether the change would do some good remained to be seen.

After Braxton changed into black skintight leather pants and a corset, mercifully simple, the magazine took their final round of shots in the alley using a smoke machine to add mystery to an already enigmatic reality.

Whatever.

When I realized it was time for the interview, I knew the hardest part had yet to come. Back on the chaise again, Braxton sitting between Loren and me with Houston perched on the arm next to me, we all pretended we weren't scared shitless as we waited for Holly, the reporter, to begin. It wouldn't be the first time an interview had gone wrong.

Goddamn Loren.

As if he could hear my thoughts, Loren blew a bubble from the gum he was chewing before popping it obnoxiously.

Fuck.

"So," Holly began with a bright and reassuring smile that only made me more eager to get this over with, "on behalf of *Plugged* magazine, we want to thank you for sitting down to talk to us. First, I want to say how terribly sorry I am for your loss. Calvin's life and the legacy he left behind was precious to us all, but for you, it must have been like losing a brother."

Holly paused, waiting for a response or even a proper reaction to the reminder that Calvin was dead. Clearing her throat when we simply waited for her to ask an actual question, she glanced down at her pad before stumbling on.

"W-while Calvin can never truly be replaced in our hearts, we've all been on pins and needles to see who Bound would deem worthy for this next era. Braxton, did you ever think it would be you?"

Braxton inhaled so subtly that if I hadn't been sitting so close or so wrapped up in everything she did down to the flutter of her lashes, I would have missed it.

"I assumed I had a better chance sprouting wings," our fallen angel answered with a nervous laugh. "Sometimes, I think *Punk'd* has been revived, and my life is the pilot episode." I wanted to reach out and hold her hand when I caught her nails digging into her thigh, but that wasn't the message we were here to send. "If someone asked me six weeks ago to list a million impossible things that could happen before I died, playing for Bound would have been one of them."

Tilting her head to the side, Holly's eyes brightened. "Well, you're here," she pointed out with a wave of her hands. "Surely, some part of you must have thought you had a chance."

"Braxton was headhunted," Houston interrupted before Braxton, who was tongue-tied and unsure of how much to reveal, could think of what to say. "She didn't find us. We found her."

"Incredible. So the question must be asked. Why her?" Holly blurted.

I felt Braxton tense next to me.

"Excuse me?" Loren asked, tuning in for what was likely the first time. Even to the most forgiving ears, Holly's question had sounded condescending.

"I-I just mean with all the talent out there, most of whom are either recognized or acclaimed, there must have been a special reason you went with someone unknown."

"I believe you just answered your own question, Hillary."

"Holly."

Loren blinked at her, not bothering to acknowledge his mistake. What he did confess was something that made Braxton stop breathing. "She's special."

I wasn't sure if his statement or the missing sarcasm surprised me the most.

"How so?" Holly inquired.

Squinting, I turned her question over in my mind before deciding for her sake that she was simply curious and not challenging Loren's claim.

"To start, it would be pretty hard to find someone willing to learn after being told a thousand times how perfect they are," Loren answered without missing a beat. "Baby fawn is a sponge. She soaks up everything we give, and the wetter we get her, the more she takes."

I didn't have to see the smirk on Loren's face to know he'd

meant that in more ways than one. Luckily, Holly was too busy scribbling down everything we threw at her to analyze our words.

"She defies," I blurted, causing them all to look my way. I only had eyes for Braxton as she stared up at me, her brown eyes bright with emotion. I noticed her nostrils flaring, not in anger but in response to something teasing her senses. Her brows dipped a moment later as if she didn't recognize whatever it was. "She defies not just us but anyone willing to suppress her. Everything Bound has, we've all contributed—our lyrics, our melodies, every single bit. We chose Braxton because she's willing to look beyond what's been put in front of her." Braxton smiled softly at me, and I found myself grinning back, forgetting where we were. It was that easy to get lost in her.

"Anyone can mimic art that already exists," Houston spoke, stealing her focus from me. I made my fingers ball when I nearly reached out to grip her chin and force her attention back on me. I'd never been this greedy. "That's not a testament of talent. She's unknown, yes, but she's far from unworthy."

A rare blush warmed Braxton's cheeks, and then she quickly looked down so that we wouldn't have a chance to notice.

Too late.

FOURTEEN

Braxton

A MONTH AFTER THE INTERVIEW, AND I WAS ONCE AGAIN QUESTIONING my choices. It all began last weekend when I told Houston I wouldn't be available to rehearse. It had been harder to convince Houston than my *actual* boss to give me the weekend off, and only when I finally confessed the reason I couldn't be at his beck and call.

I'd driven to Faithful and willingly suffered through Mass so that my family wouldn't find out from someone else that I was going on tour with Bound.

I might as well have announced that I'd joined a cult.

As prepared as I thought I was for their disapproval, my parents had topped anything I could have imagined.

There are five stages of grief, and Amelia and David Fawn had only made it to stage two. They'd briefly reached the third when they offered to pay for a lawyer after I brought up the contract I'd already signed. Then they backtracked from bargaining and remained steadfast at anger. The worse part had been the split moment when I was tempted to take them up on their offer.

You can still back out. There's hope. There's a chance.

Except, the hope I felt burning in my gut wasn't for breaking free of Bound.

It was liberating Bound.

I hated Oni for stirring that need in my gut and making it

my burden to bear. I've been inside the lions' den. I've seen the carnage that no one on the outside could see. Something was ripping them apart at the very seam of who they are—Houston, Loren, Jericho—each different in their own way but incomplete when apart.

I thought back to the words I knew would be the last I'd speak to my family for a long time, possibly forever.

"I don't want out. I'm going to see this through."

"See what through?" my father demanded. "This is unacceptable, Braxton."

"Bound," I whispered. "I'm going to see them through."

Fast forward to Monday, and I was left wondering if I'd imagined the interview. Houston, Loren, and Jericho hadn't just convinced that reporter they respected and needed me—they'd convinced me too. Had it been all for show?

"You're playing like you're trying to piss me off today, Fawn, and I'm not in the mood," Houston snapped.

Two hours ago, our interview had appeared online, announcing me as Bound's new guitarist and turning Houston into a bear with a thorn in its paw. Bound had chosen a nobody to replace their beloved Calvin and no one, despite their pretty words, was thrilled about it.

"Do it again," grumpy bear ordered.

Despite my obvious fatigue and despondency, I'd shown up for rehearsal bright and early as expected. I wouldn't have put it past Houston to break into my apartment and drag me out of bed if I hadn't. I would have preferred it—staying in bed, not being pulled out of it.

"Back off, Morrow. I don't need your shit today."

The air became still as soon as I stopped speaking. The world had come to a screeching halt just to witness my punishment for talking back.

"Say that again?"

Behind me, I heard a heavy sigh.

It could have been Loren or Jericho who'd made the sound. Neither were unused to our daily squabbles.

Squaring my shoulders, I looked Houston in the eye. There was no use backing down now. "Allow me to elaborate," I offered. Flipping him off would have been subtler. "I said I had a rough night, so I'd appreciate it if you didn't breathe down my back today."

"You had a rough night?" Houston's tone was gentle, making me instantly wary. I stared at him, not bothering to respond. "And you thought you'd come to my session, play like shit, and then cry on my shoulder about your personal problems?"

"I don't see any tears, do you?"

This time I heard a low, drawn-out groan behind me.

"You know what I see? I see a whiny brat who doesn't want to earn her keep."

I didn't have time to consider the repercussions before I exploded.

"I bust my ass every day, Houston! It's not good enough, though, is it? It never is. We both know I'm good. You were an amateur once too, but I doubt you were half as good as me. So what's your real problem with me, huh? Do I not have the right equipment for you to accept that I deserve to be here? Are you too macho to admit that you're only pretending to be in control? Well, I see you, Houston, and maybe that scares you. If you want me to quit, you're going to have to try harder than being an asshole who thinks too highly of himself. If you're scared, get a nightlight, bitch. I'm not going anywhere."

Exhaling all the air I'd trapped in my lungs, I fooled myself into thinking I'd won. I'd finally shut Houston Morrow up. After my little speech, however, he couldn't even give me the benefit of a reaction. Not unless I counted the fury in his green eyes right before he moved them over my head and spoke to his friends behind me.

"Get out."

I knew he didn't mean me, but I was tempted to flee anyway. The moment the door closed behind Loren and Jericho, Houston moved away from me.

I didn't expect that.

The only problem was that I could no longer see him. It wasn't until I heard the lock turning that I dared look over my shoulder.

Oh, fuck.

This time, when he closed the distance between us, he stood behind me. I could feel every breath he took on my nape, sending chills down my spine. Instead of the coppery scent of fear, I tasted cherries and smelled cinnamon.

"Braxton?"

"Yes, Houston?"

"I want to tell you a secret."

"Oh, good, another one. I'm sure it will be riveting."

Wrapping his hand around my neck from behind, he pulled me even closer before placing his lips at my ear. "Whatever you think you know about me, I promise you I'm much worse. So are they. Loren likes for people to think that what you see is what you get. He saves what's really lurking inside for special occasions. Rich, he's nice, isn't he? He does whatever I tell him to. I can see that desperate need for us to be close again in his eyes. He wants it so much that if I asked him to help me hide a body, he would. Without question."

Houston's arm locked around my waist when I jerked forward from shock. Was he implying what I thought he was implying?

"A horrific thing like that would surely bond us forever, wouldn't it?" I tried to speak, but he gripped my jaw, shutting me up. "It's simple, Bambi. Be a good girl, do what we say, and you'll never have to find out what kind of man I really am." Releasing my neck, he spun me around but kept his hands locked on my waist. "Go home. Take the day. Think about if you really want to have this conversation again."

Houston Morrow just threatened to murder me, and I wasn't quite sure whether I believed him or not.

Knowing that was his intent, I didn't move. My knees were too weak. Sensing this, Houston pulled me close until our hips were pressed together, and I had to tilt my head to look into his eyes.

"Why are you still here, Fawn?"

His warm whisper intensified the ache between my thighs. "I-I don't know," I answered truthfully. I wanted to leave, and I wanted to stay. I wanted to see just how bad and terrible Houston Morrow could get.

Slowly, his hands drifted from my waist to the top of my ass, and something like encouragement ripped from my throat. Just a little lower, and I'd be his.

A moment later, we were forced apart by a knock on the door.

"Is everything okay in there?"

Rich.

"Fine," Houston barked while staring at me. "Braxton was just leaving."

I was? Oh. Right.

Houston threatened to kill me if I didn't fall in line and self-preservation told me to writhe all over him like a bitch in heat.

Unbelievable.

I didn't need any more incentive than that to get the hell out of there. Keeping my gaze off Houston, I left the room, ignoring Rich, who stood there looking confused and concerned. Barry, thankfully, was already waiting outside.

As soon as my ass touched the leather seats inside the SUV, I shifted uncomfortably. The arousal soaking my thong was called The Houston Morrow Effect. It ruined panties and destroyed brain cells.

I had twenty minutes until I was home. Twenty whole minutes until I was alone and could relieve the ache. After that, I'd figure out how I planned to survive a world tour and months of lonely nights spent in close quarters with three men slowly awakening a part of me that I thought was long buried.

FIFTEEN

Braxton

"YOU LOOK *FABULOUS*."

Sherri, who'd been waiting for me when I stepped inside my dressing room, stepped aside after admiring her work. I didn't want to look, but the gasps that came from Griff and Maeko had my eyes flying to the LED mirror in front of me.

I didn't recognize my reflection. She wasn't the girl I'd become these past few months. Sherri had hidden all the sleepless nights and endless days spent worrying over this moment.

When it was discovered I'd be filling Calvin's shoes, *everything* changed. For the past month, I've lived under a microscope. My job, my home—nothing was private anymore.

I'd always feared that I'd do something to trigger this scrutiny—like when Britney flashed her crotch. It turns out I didn't have to be that drastic. Existing was all it took. Rich promised I'd get used to it, Loren swore I'd hate it forever, and Houston told me to suck it up.

Since tonight was the first show of the Bound & Bellicose tour, I'd taken Houston's advice. It turns out three months flew by when you didn't want it to.

The Forum, formerly the Lakers' arena, was our first stop, and all eighteen thousand seats had been sold. My stomach turned as my hands began to shake. At this very moment, those seats were filling, and it was all I could do not to click my heels and wish I were somewhere else. Or *someone* else.

"Thanks, Sherri. You're an artist." I gave her a smile I didn't feel, even though she'd truly done an amazing job, and she excused herself.

"Stop it," Griff ordered once we were alone in my dressing room. "I know that look. You're an amazing guitarist, Brax. They just don't know it yet," she claimed, referring to the stadium full of Bound's adoring fans. "That's why you're going to show them."

I wanted to believe her, but I ended up rolling my eyes instead. "I love you, Griff, but we both know those people didn't spend three hundred bucks on tickets to see me. They're here for *them*."

"Oh, but that's where you're wrong. They might not have good intentions, but that won't matter in a couple of hours. You're going to make those assholes find a heart just so they can eat it."

My head tilted to the side as I turned over her words. "Are we talking about the crowd or Bound?"

Griffin shrugged while staring at me with unflinching confidence and a lack of remorse. She'd make a great lawyer one day. "Both." Nudging Maeko with her elbow, she added, "Back me up here, Ko."

Tapping her clutch, Maeko nodded. "I packed extra panties just for you, Brax."

I couldn't help but laugh. It chased away the butterflies. "If you throw them on stage, the guys might get the wrong idea," I warned her.

"What's your point?" she countered with a straight face. Griff rolled her eyes before fixing her gaze a little too hard on a spot on the other side of the room.

I adored Maeko, but she would not last an hour, much less an entire night, with any of them. Maeko was too soft and sweet, even for Rich, who was an angel compared to his friends. Besides, I was still hoping my absence would give Griff the courage to make her secret feelings known. Maeko might have been oblivious, but I'd caught on a while ago.

At first, I thought maybe they'd connected better than they had with me until I realized it was a different connection entirely. I wasn't sure what was holding Griff back. She was usually straightforward and not the least bit shy, but I hoped she got over it soon. I wanted my friends happy.

"Can we please talk about how hot you look?" Maeko gushed, pulling Griff and me out of our heads. "I'd say you look like a rock star, but that's kind of a moot point. I wonder how much hairspray Yuri used to get your hair to stay like that."

"Judging by how hard it still is to breathe in here, I'd say a lot," Griff deadpanned while fanning the misty air in front of her with a frown.

Rather than shaving the sides of my hair to achieve the faux hawk, Yuri had braided the sides, leaving the larger mass of my hair drifting down my back. Sherri then amplified the edgy look by darkening my eyes with black liner and shadow and painting my naturally red lips with clear gloss.

Tonight's wardrobe consisted of a black halter with criss-crossed strings holding the front together and electric-blue pants, both leather and so tight I wondered if they assumed breathing was optional. The boots adorning my feet were the best thing about the ensemble. I didn't know if I got to keep them, and I didn't care. They were coming home with me.

A knock on the door had my heart falling into my stomach as fear and worry sent my olfactory senses on a joy ride. I knew before the stagehand yelled through the door that it was time.

"I can't believe this is happening," Maeko yelled while jumping up and down excitedly. And then, with tears in her eyes, she added, "My best friend is a rock star."

"Not quite," I denied with a weak smile. I almost choked on the copper and brine I knew only I could smell. "But keep your fingers crossed for me, will ya?"

I left the dressing room with my friends hot on my heels since there was nothing left to say or do. It was so loud I couldn't hear myself think. Perhaps it was best for everyone. Backstage was chaos as the crew hurried to and from to get last-minute things in place. Our opening act would be done any minute and then…

I took a deep breath that shuddered out of me before looking around.

Where the hell were they?

SIXTEEN

Houston

SHE DIDN'T SEE US, BUT WE SAW HER.

We watched as one of our roadies handed Braxton the guitar she'd be using for the first half of our set. She then looked around again as soon as he was gone. It hadn't been my intention to hide, but then I saw her and the last thing on my mind was the goddamn show. Closing my eyes, I leaned my head against the wall and willed my hard-on away.

"Damn," Loren mumbled. I didn't need to see to know that he was referring to Braxton. "Maybe having a chick in our mix isn't such a bad idea after all. She's certainly nicer to look at. Smells good too."

"Not wanting her in our band never had anything to do with her being a girl," Rich claimed.

"Uh-huh," Loren mocked dismissively. There was a beat of silence and then, "If you're picturing your grandmother naked, I wouldn't advise it. She's kind of hot."

My eyes flew open, and I found Loren watching me. "What are you talking about?"

"Braxton. You want to fuck her."

Xavier found us sitting on the staircase even though there were empty couches just a few feet away. We were hiding. "Last I counted, I only had two kids. Why do you three make me feel like I have five?"

"Relax, pops," Loren replied. "We're kind of pros. No big deal."

"Your guitarist isn't," Xavier snapped while pointing at Braxton. She'd given up her search and was now pretending interest in her phone while her friends asked our busy crew a million questions. "She has no idea what she's up against."

Loren shrugged before leaning back to rest on his elbow on the step above him. "Not our problem."

"And when the people who paid to see you perform start demanding their money back? Get your asses over there and make sure she doesn't choke." Shaking his head, Xavier cursed more before storming off to yell at someone else. It was why we paid him the big bucks—to worry so we didn't have to.

Braxton had gravitated toward the stage with her friends huddled around her for support. Sighing, I ran my hand down my face. What the hell did Xavier expect from us? To lie and tell her everything would be okay? We did our part and taught her our music. The rest was up to her, and if she wasn't ready by now, she never would be.

Feeling like I was on autopilot, I pushed to my feet anyway before making my way over. Closer now, I could see her shoulders trembling.

"Hey." Braxton whirled at the sound of my voice, her brown eyes rounder and brighter than ever. She was like a goddamn vortex, pulling me in and swallowing me whole. "Ready?"

I could already read the lie on her lips, but then she surprised me when her shoulders slumped, and the truth came tumbling out.

"Honestly? I'm not sure." Cringing, she looked ready to take it back and assure me that she could do this.

I knew she could, but clearly, she didn't.

"Stop."

I didn't know what I would do if she lied to me. My hands found her shoulders, where I gripped her tightly. It started as an innocent gesture, but now I was just too tempted. Nevertheless, I forced my hands to stay where they were. I didn't get many excuses to touch her.

"No one let you have this moment, Fawn. You took it. You

showed us what you were made of, and we decided we wanted more. So will they," I assured her, referring to the crowd screaming our name. "And so do you."

As if I'd done it a million times, my hands gripped her waist. There was a sliver of bare skin between her top and her pants that burned hot underneath my hands. My thumb absently rubbed the soft skin near her belly button, and even if I wanted to stop, I couldn't.

"You want this, Brax. I know you do." It was questionable whether I meant her newfound career or me. "Forget how you got here. All that matters is why you stayed."

As soon as the words left my lips, I wondered what that reason was. It sure as hell hadn't been anything we did. Braxton wasn't motivated by money or fame. Something else had put that determined look in her eyes.

"The rest is just noise," Loren added as he closed in. I was pulled from my thoughts when Braxton shifted her gaze. "You don't hear it."

Straightening, she nodded at Loren and then returned Rich's smile. When she looked up at me, Braxton no longer looked unsure. I didn't want to admit what that did to me.

"Great! Braxton's motivated," her blonde friend with the big mouth piped in. Sighing, I forced myself to meet her gaze. What was her name again? Gretchen? "But were you giving my best friend a pep talk or copping a feel? I'm confused." To make her point, Braxton's friend fixed her gaze on my hands, still gripping Braxton's waist. My thumb was even still sweeping back and forth.

Fuck.

I took a step back like a kid who'd just been caught stealing from the cookie jar. Loren lifted his chin arrogantly, even while his eyes flashed with jealousy. He was smug because he was right.

I wanted to fuck Braxton.

Loren's anger was because he believed his childish claim would keep me from acting on it. Rich just looked resigned to breaking up a fight between us at any moment now.

"Let's go."

My order broke the tension as everyone shifted gears. The tour had sold out, and right now, they were waiting. We didn't need any more publicity.

The opening act finished, and immediately, the stage crew began to reset for us. Someone handed me a mic, Loren his bass, Rich his drumsticks, and Braxton a headset since she was backup vocals in addition to playing lead and rhythm. It baffled me that anyone could question why I rode her so hard.

When Braxton checked her tuning and headset, even though we trusted our crew to get it right, I caught my smile before it could slip.

She wasn't sloppy. I'd give her that.

Closing my eyes, I inhaled deeply, scattering my thoughts to the wind. It didn't matter how many times I took the stage. Each time felt like the first. With a new member, it was more like I was fresh out of my grandmother's basement.

The apocalyptic backdrop we'd chosen for our stage loomed ahead when the house lights went out, and the screams of eighteen thousand people welcomed Braxton, Loren, and Jericho. I hung back as rehearsed, and while I waited for my cue from Jericho, I watched Braxton closely. No one would ever know she hadn't done this a million times before.

Wisely, I knew nothing with Braxton was ever that simple. The subtle cues she gave were only obvious to someone who watched her too closely and too often. Right now, she avoided looking at the crowd. It was for the best since picturing them in their underwear was a sham.

Jericho didn't wait for the screams to die before he started on the drums. He was my timekeeper, telling me exactly when to start and how to end. All the anger he kept inside, desperate to be the nice guy, he always let loose when he was on stage. Gripping the mic, I closed my eyes and let the foundation he set become my atlas. Loren smoothly followed with the bass and Braxton…she blew my fucking mind. Thirty seconds in, once the rhythm was set, I emerged from the shadows and lifted my mic.

How do I silence these whispers
How do I face what I've become

Castrated by your whims
I drown in my aspiration
Led astray by beautiful lies
You took my blood, sweat, and tears
Trapped in these walls I built
You filled your rivers raging

I'm so tired of feeding my enemies
I'm numb watching them grow
Why do I continue to kneel
No one's keeping me down

Taking all of the good
You left me nothing but hate
You want all I have
Watch me start a revolution

We've waited (So broken)
To find change (Evoked it)
Do you feel it? (Emotion)

After three months of rehearsing, I thought I'd be used to the chemistry between Braxton's voice and mine. I realized now how irrational that was—about as insane as being struck by lightning and expecting it not to hurt twice.

It was no wonder she ran her mouth all the time.

She was impossible to ignore.

Calvin had been good, but Braxton's vocals were infinitely stronger. She had the rare ability to deliver both transparency and power. Our pithy guitarist wasn't afraid to be vulnerable. After seeing her perform at that festival, I knew she was holding back so as not to drown my own.

As soon as we finished the first song, we launched into the

next. The adrenaline had set in, and none of us were willing to lose this rush. No matter how many times my gaze strayed toward Braxton, she never looked out of her element. Eventually, duty was no longer why I couldn't keep my attention where it should have been.

She had me under her spell.

Our gazes met and held as she played, and I sang along to her rhythm. When it was time to deliver one of our harder riffs, she did this thing with her hair, whipping it before dropping into a crouch and letting the crowd have it.

I preferred to think it was all for me.

Hell yeah.

Usually, I didn't approve of the showboating, especially from an amateur since it made room for errors, but at this moment, I could deny Braxton whatever she wanted about as well as I could deny my heart its next beat.

I wondered if she'd feel the same if I dropped my mic and hauled her someplace secluded.

Would she deny me?

I wanted it so much that I convinced myself the look in her eyes was daring me to do just that.

Before I did something stupid, I shifted my focus to the crowd and getting through the set. Nothing else mattered except giving these people the show they came for. Screwing my guitarist was a non-fucking-factor.

We blew through our setlist, and the moment we cleared the stage, Loren swooped Braxton into his arms and twirled her around like a lunatic. For once, I wasn't annoyed by his antics. That show had been one for the record books. Flawless. If anyone had been in danger of screwing it up, it was me.

Her friends stood to the side, impatiently waiting to congratulate her for that perfect performance.

"Braxton whatever-your-middle-name-is Fawn, will you marry me?" Loren shouted after setting her on her feet. To make an even bigger scene, he'd gotten on one knee.

My heart stopped as a frown marred my brow.

I could almost *swear* Loren was serious. I'd caught the look in his eyes before he remembered he was only joking.

Since we were playing here again tomorrow night, the crew mostly had their hands free to stop and watch if this was real.

"Francesca," she answered. Or rather didn't.

"Huh?"

"My middle name," she clarified. "It's Francesca."

That only made Loren's brows dip further. "Your initials are B.F.F.?"

"Yup."

Loren stood, signaling that the proposal wasn't real, which prompted the crew to get back to work. "That's too bad because I have no interest in being your friend," he announced, sounding a little too serious for my liking. He looked a second away from defying my decree that Braxton was off-limits and making his move.

Xavier appeared before I could remind him that it wasn't going to happen. All it did was delay the inevitable since there was always later.

"What the hell are you still doing here?" he shouted. "You only have a short window before that crowd you just finished riling finds you. Get moving unless you want to be followed home."

With that, he was gone again, and so were we.

We made our way through the tunnels that led to a secret exit where two Suburbans were already idling and waiting. I grabbed Braxton's elbow just as she started for one of the cars and held her hostage while her friends climbed inside. I had no doubt they were off to celebrate and envied the days when we were that carefree.

"Something wrong?" she asked me with a deep frown.

"You did great tonight."

Even though I meant it, I could barely form the words. I didn't want her to get comfortable. When she beamed at me, I briefly lost my train of thought. Could she hear my heart beating out of control? Could she feel my palms sweat from the effort not to break my own rules? If she looked down, she'd definitely see a bulge.

"Thanks. That was…surreal."

Her brown eyes brightened even further as she waited for my response. None came to mind that wouldn't jeopardize more than I already had, so I carefully chose my next words. "Same time tomorrow. Don't be late."

I'd already turned away, so I didn't see her glare, but I felt it. I wasn't the least bit sorry, either. If she knew better, she would be thanking me right now instead of thinking of ways to murder me.

This dynamic we set was better for her too.

SEVENTEEN

Braxton

I'D BEEN LOOKING AT THIS WHOLE THING ALL WRONG. I'D ENVISIONED myself alone on the road with Houston, Loren, and Jericho—a recurring plot in all my nightmares. I didn't consider the ninety-seven, ninety-eight, *ninety-nine* people who would be tagging along.

It was the morning after our third show. Ten black sleeper buses were waiting for us in San Jose, where we'd spent the night in a hotel. The crew was busy loading them with our bags and equipment too precious for the one hundred and twenty cargo trucks carrying our stage, screens, lights, and speakers from venue to venue.

Xavier had been kind enough to explain that we were leap-frogging it. We had two identical stages and two teams. While we performed in one city, one of those teams would be setting up in the next.

I shuddered to think of how much this all cost. It was nothing compared to the revenue Bound generated. Their last tour had brought in over three hundred million.

"You look like someone just told you you're a lamb, and we're the wolves come to devour you," Loren greeted me. His hair was perfectly coiffed despite the early hour and his wardrobe impeccable. I had a witty retort in mind, but then he lifted a Starbucks coffee cup with my name scrawled on the side. "For you."

I eagerly accepted it with hearts in my eyes and immediately took a sip, surprised to find that it was not only black—he'd remembered—but that it was piping hot. "I'm surprised," I said instead of a thank-you. Loren seemed like the type to take a mile if I gave him an inch. "I didn't know you made coffee runs."

"That's because I don't. Rich does, apparently. I snagged yours when he wasn't looking. Thought I'd take the credit."

Figures.

I glared at Loren over the top of my cup, and he beamed at me in return. He was an ass, but man, he was gorgeous. It was hard to ignore when he flaunted it so shamelessly. As strong as this coffee was, the phantom taste of cherries easily overpowered it, so I started for the bus that I caught my bags being loaded onto moments ago. Two steps in, I felt someone following, so I peeked over my shoulder.

Loren was hot on my heels.

He was engrossed in his phone as he walked, so sure that water would part for him that he wasn't at all worried about bumping into someone or something.

Climbing the steps onto the bus, I stopped when I came to a barrier separating the living area from the helm. It was a floor-to-ceiling glass door with blackout tint that slid open with the push of a button.

"*Mi casa es su casa*," Loren said after reaching past me to push the button on the wall next to the door.

I wasn't sure what I expected, but I knew this wasn't it. Living on a bus for several months didn't exactly sound like a day spa, but this was close to it. This bus was decked out better than my crappy apartment.

Upon entering, I was standing in a living room with a U-shaped sectional that could easily sleep three grown men comfortably. Hanging above the brown couch was a painting of what I guessed was downtown Portland near the riverfront. Directly across was a sixty-inch flat-screen built into the wall. A black rug even covered the wooden floor spanning most of the living room. It looked so plush that I fought the urge to lie across it. I bet I could sleep there all night and not feel a thing in the morning.

Next to the space was a kitchenette complete with a stove,

microwave, sink, dishwasher, and...*was that a goddamn full-sized fridge?* I gaped at it, forgetting that I wasn't alone.

Yup.

These boys had it made in the shade.

When I ventured deeper, I even found a little nook built into the bus's side, between the sectional and the refrigerator, that could seat four people on the booth-like seats.

This might not be the nightmare I imagined.

The moment the thought entered my mind, the door in front of me slid open, revealing the rest of the bus and an angry-looking Houston. He wore a clean white T-shirt and dark-blue sweats as if he were relaxing at home. I guess, in a way, he was. This was only new to *me.*

"You're late."

His favorite goddamn phrase even when I wasn't.

"I've been standing outside for twenty minutes. If you were so concerned, you would have looked for me yourself."

Houston jerked his head over my shoulder. "Why do you think he found you?"

"Hey, I would have gone," Loren objected. "Eventually."

I rolled my eyes and tried to pass Houston, but the doorway was too narrow, and he filled it too easily. I didn't even know where the hell I was going or what I would do once I got there. I just needed to be away from them.

"Excuse me," I forced myself to say when he refused to move.

"Did Loren give you a tour?"

"He didn't need to. It's not like I could get lost walking a straight line. Excuse me," I repeated when he continued to block my way.

Reaching past me, he wordlessly opened the door next to me, which forced me to back up or be hit. "This is the bathroom we use for guests."

"Which we never have," Loren added. Houston ignored him.

Barely sparing a glance inside, I found a clean half bath and nodded, prompting him to close the door and turn back the way he came.

"This is where you'll be sleeping," Houston said as I followed him.

There were four bunks built into the bus, two on each side, with curtains for privacy. Houston slid back the curtain of the top one perpendicular to my right shoulder. The bed was narrow but long, and the bunk tall enough to sit up fully without bumping my head. It was already covered with bedding even though I'd brought my own, and they looked way more expensive and comfortable than my ten-dollar sheets from Target. Though, what really sold me was the small TV built into the wall at the foot of the bed.

"It has Netflix," Loren announced.

It didn't escape my notice that he'd been quiet until now. Spending the last three months with them with another year to go, I'd already learned that Loren only felt the need to make his presence known when Houston was around. I wondered how much longer it would take me to grasp why. Perhaps it was because Loren didn't like being told what to do, and Houston thrived on giving orders.

My attention shifted back and forth between Houston, who stared at Loren over my shoulder, and Loren silently daring Houston to do what was on his mind. My gut told me their little tiff was because of me, but my head wouldn't allow me to care. I'd already done enough by getting myself trapped between them. The passageway was narrow, and I stood between two alpha males seconds away from ripping into each other. I was probably the only reason they hadn't already come to blows.

Yay me.

"So," I said slowly, interrupting their brooding, "is this it or…?"

Houston's gaze slowly returned to me. I watched his jaw firm before he wordlessly spun on his heel and led me through another doorway. It was a bedroom the size of a standard guest room, and inside was a king-sized bed, a nightstand on each side with trash bins underneath, and another flat-screen spanning the wall it faced. My favorite part of the room was the wall next to the door that had been painted to depict them—Houston, Loren, Jericho, and...Calvin. The aromatic but bitter smell of olive oil suddenly filled my nose.

Calvin should have been the one standing here. Not me. I never thought I'd enjoy filling a dead man's shoes, but I hadn't expected to feel so guilty about it either.

As Houston led me through the bedroom until we reached the bathroom, I realized the walkway between the bed and the wall was narrow. The bathroom was about the size of mine at home, which said more for the bus than it did my apartment. It even had a glass shower big enough to fit two people, a sink with plenty of counter space, and a toilet disappointingly *not* lined with gold.

I felt duped.

Houston and Loren had unconsciously hyped me up for this moment only to show me a normal goddamn toilet. There was no eighteen-karat gold anywhere.

"I wasn't expecting this," I blurted honestly.

"Being rich and famous comes with its advantages," Loren drawled from his perch against the closet by the door. Naturally, he'd mistaken my meaning, and I wisely decided not to share.

"This bedroom is used on an as-needed basis," Houston informed me. At my confused look, he added. "We share it."

"You mean, like, we sleep in here together sometimes?" What the hell would be the reason for that?

"It's interesting that your mind drew that conclusion first, baby fawn."

Since Loren chose to tease me, I decided to pretend he wasn't there as I waited for Houston to explain. Rich was the only one who didn't seem to get off on being cruel, and as usual, he was missing when I needed him. I tried gauging where he went whenever he disappeared, but as expected, neither Houston nor Loren was a welcome fountain of information.

"In the unlikely event that you find yourself needing more privacy than the bunks allow, feel free to use this space."

Houston waited patiently for me to catch his drift. When I did, I nodded rather than protest, which he didn't seem pleased about. He was harder to figure out than a quantum mechanics equation. Why even offer the possibility in the first place? No, scratch that. The better question was why it mattered to him if I slept with anyone.

And that was when I caught on to something he'd said.

"Why unlikely?"

"What?" he snapped a little too aggressively.

"You said *in the unlikely event* I need to fuck someone in here," I paraphrased while returning some of his aggression. "Why is that unlikely?"

"He misspoke," Loren dismissively answered for him. Just as I felt my shoulders began to relax, he added, "What he really meant was there isn't a chance in hell of that happening."

Finally, Loren had my undivided attention, which seemed to be what he wanted anyway. "Yeah?" I crossed my arms as I faced him. "Why is that?"

"Because we don't allow groupies with dicks on board."

"Let me guess. New rule?" Loren stubbornly chose not to answer as he stared me down. "Does this mean you won't be bringing groupies with pussies on board?"

Chuckling, he straightened before flicking imaginary lint off his open shirt. "No can do, baby fawn. It's tradition."

"Ah, but a new member means new traditions, so let's see," I teased as I tapped my chin while pretending to think. "How about…if you're getting laid on tour, so am I."

I had no intention of fucking anyone but being *told* I couldn't by a misogynistic prima donna meant the gloves came off.

"Sounds promising," Loren returned with a smile I didn't trust. He took a step forward, his salacious grin turning feral.

I had the feeling I was one wrong move from being tossed on the bed and fucked. Afraid of how much I wanted that, I started backing up. I only made it two steps before I ran into a hard chest.

Houston.

Why wasn't he stopping Loren? He hadn't said a word all this time. Why?

I was afraid to look over my shoulder. I knew I'd see the same hunger in Houston's eyes that Loren was taunting me with now. What would I do then? I could ignore their desires, but I was powerless against mine.

Another step, and Loren now stood over me with Houston at my back. "You have your pick of dicks already on board, baby fawn. Enough to have a good time. Just say the word, and one of us will service you."

"You're disgusting."

"Oh, I'm filthy, baby. You're fucking right about that."

My mouth filled with the decadent burst of juice, sweet and thick like syrup, just as the refreshing balm of a meadow and its mysterious meaning returned. By then, I was lost in Loren's black gaze. I knew what he was waiting for. My lashes fluttered as I drifted toward him. I was done paying for past sins. I felt more alive when I was damned.

I was standing on the edge of a cliff, waiting to either fall or fly, when I felt strong hands on my hips. It took me a moment longer to realize they were keeping me at bay.

The heat left Loren's gaze, and the rage that took its place seemed endless as he glared at Houston. "Let her go."

Houston's hands tightened even though I hadn't moved an inch. "Nothing's changed, Lo."

"Hasn't it?" Loren challenged. He didn't wait for an answer before moving to grab me.

Houston was quicker since he was already touching me, and I was yanked backward before being blocked by Houston's back. Stumbling, I slammed my hand on the wall to catch my balance. Neither of them noticed as they faced off with one another. I couldn't see Houston's face, so I watched Loren's nostrils flare.

"You don't get a say in where I stick my dick."

"She's one of us now," Houston maintained. "That means she's off-limits."

It was a rather *convenient* time for him to finally admit it, but pride flared in my chest anyway. Unfortunately, it only made me feel guilty for nearly giving in to Loren. Sleeping with my bandmates wasn't just against Houston's rules. It was against mine.

"She's only off-limits if she says so."

The sound of my heart beating was louder and scarier than thunder when the room fell silent. Could they hear it? I struggled with too many emotions at once. I wanted too many things. I'd already made my decision, but my body wanted to renege.

"I say so," I answered, thankfully without any of the reluctance I felt. "I'm not some excuse for the two of you to be at each other's throats. My only desire is to be treated as an equal and to get through this tour in one piece." Meeting Loren's gaze, I let the rest of my decree rip my heart in half. "Everything else is just noise."

Betrayal flitted across Loren's beautiful features. He'd offered those words to me in comfort and encouragement, and I used them as a weapon against him. His lips curled, and I told myself that I deserved the punishment that followed.

"Hard facts, *Fawn*." My soul felt like the imaginary lint he'd flicked off his shirt moments ago. I thought I hated his pet name for me until he cruelly deprived me of it. "You're not our equal. You're barely a step above a groupie, so don't kid yourself." Turning on the heel of his expensive shoes, my heart trapped underneath, Loren started to leave the room. Stopping at the threshold, he looked over his shoulder. "And just so we're all on the same page, Houston doesn't respect you any more than I do. He wants you, too, but he tells himself he can't have you. And if he can't, no one can. Your savior is just a selfish bastard."

Loren was gone before my mind could untwist itself. He couldn't fuck my body, so he'd settled for my head. Houston stood there, watching the space where Loren had just been, his fists balled and muscles bunched tight. I patiently waited for him to turn and deny Loren's claim.

He never did.

EIGHTEEN

Loren

THEY HAD A LOT OF GODDAMN NERVE.

Even though Houston was a hypocrite and Braxton was a tease, I wasn't angry at them. *I* fucked up. I reacted in the heat of the moment only to regret it later—story of my miserable life. A girl didn't want to sleep with me? Big fucking deal. Someone was willing on every corner.

Braxton was different, but she was no less willing, and if Houston hadn't intervened, I'd be rearranging her guts right now. What irritated me most was that I'd lashed out like a prepubescent boy when I didn't get my way.

I wasn't going to apologize. I doubt either was expecting one, and it wouldn't change the fact that I wasn't a nice guy. Unlike Houston and Jericho, I wouldn't pretend to be noble.

We'd been on the road for a couple of hours now with six or seven more to go. Vegas was the third city of the tour and our fourth and fifth shows. I was just eager to get there. If nothing else got me excited, gambling, music, sex, and now Braxton fucking Fawn did the trick.

I was lying in my bunk with the curtain closed, trying to drown out the sound of her voice as she goofed around with Rich. I hated that he knew how to get a smile out of her. It wasn't just because I was jealous.

She was the enemy.

A sexy little insurgent.

If it were up to me, I'd drive her ass to the deepest part of the desert and leave her there. Braxton was trouble, and we caused enough on our own.

My phone began buzzing in my pocket, and I planned to ignore it until I heard Braxton laugh at something Rich said. I'm sure she hadn't meant it to sound sexy…just like Cain hadn't meant to kill Abel.

Shoving my hand in my jeans, I pulled my phone out of my pocket and accepted the call without opening my eyes. I didn't care who was on the other end. I needed to drown her out.

"Son."

Fuck.

I'd been hoping for a telemarketer. Since I couldn't talk to my friends, it wouldn't be the first time I gabbed the ear off a nameless, faceless stranger. So far, I haven't had any complaints. Shit, *they* called *me*.

As for my father, I hadn't heard from him since he kicked me out on my ass and emptied my bank account six years ago. If he hadn't, I'd be married to some white-stocking deb who only spread her legs for me if the lights were out. Standing on my own had been harder than it looked. A few months more and letting my parents decide every facet of my future would have seemed like a small price to pay.

"Loren James speaking." I refused to acknowledge that I was his kid.

I heard his heavy sigh and cracked a smile. "We need to talk."

"Yeah, the phone call clued me in. Besides, we both know you don't give a shit how I am." It was evident in the fact that he hadn't bothered to ask. I've only ever known three types of people: those who cared, those who pretended, and my father.

"You know I'm not one to mince words, boy."

My jaw tightened, and the only thing restraining me was fear of cracking a tooth. I didn't spend years keeping my smile flawless to waste one on him. "It's been six years, *Father*."

"Precisely. It's been six years. It's time you stop goofing around with your friends and come home."

"Hard pass."

"Loren," my father said on a sigh as if he were weary already from our thirty-second talk after six years of silence. "Son—"

"I'm not your son, remember? That's what you said when you threw me out."

"We both did things we regret," he returned, and I recognized it for the bait that it was.

"That's where you're wrong. At least it got one of us far away from you."

"Your mother wants you home."

I let out a bitter laugh. "So? Ornaments are meant to be seen, not heard. She served her purpose twenty-eight years ago."

"Do not talk about your mother that way."

Pulling my lips back, I bared my teeth as if he could see me. "Why not? You do."

"You're a grown man. I'm not going to coddle you. It's no secret your mother and I aren't happy, haven't been for years, but that's none of your concern."

"Is this why you called me? To whine about your marriage? You can afford a licensed therapist, Father. You don't need me."

I was ready to hang up when his next words stopped me. "If you come back home, I'll retire early, and the empire I built will be yours. You have my word."

"What the hell are you talking about?"

"I've underestimated your stubbornness. I don't approve of your method, but the fact still is that you thrived. As a self-made man, I respect that. As my sole heir, your place is here. Come home, take my place as head of the company, and you'll have full control."

Orson James hadn't inherited his fortune as I would have if he hadn't tossed me away. He'd amassed it from nothing using his uncanny ability to exploit the desires of anyone in his way.

My father had just offered mine on a silver platter.

Without me, he had no one to ensure the fruits of his labor wouldn't dissolve like a biodegradable waste after he was gone. In retrospect, I should have seen this coming, but unlike him, I'd overestimated his stubbornness.

"And you think that's good enough? You think I *want* to come back?"

"I know you, son. You think that I don't, and I understand why, but I'm your father. If you were truly happy, you wouldn't have answered the phone. You wouldn't still be talking to me. Come home, and my kingdom is yours. I'll even let you marry whom and when you wish."

Even though my mind was still racing, I answered my father.

"Anything else?" I didn't want him to know that I was considering it, and he wouldn't care that I hated myself for being tempted. I should have been elated. I should have been jumping at his offer. The problem wasn't just that I didn't trust him. It was also because it meant letting go of my friends who I hated. *Figures.*

"Yes. You have three months to decide."

"Three months? Seriously? Cut the crap, *pops*. You know I'm on tour. I literally just left California two hours ago."

"If the decision to abandon your friends is hard for you, ask yourself if you're truly irreplaceable to them. You're my son. I think the answer is quite clear whether or not you are to me."

It took me several stunned seconds to realize he'd hung up. Still shocked, I pulled the phone away from my face and stared at the screen. The background happened to be an old shot of Houston, Jericho, and me laughing at some shit I can't remember because it's been so long since we shared moments like these. Several minutes passed, and I was still trying to decide if I'd dreamt the whole thing.

The faint sound of something hitting the floor, followed by a gasp that was too delicate, caught my attention. I ripped back the privacy curtain that shielded me in my bunk and found Braxton standing there, her already round eyes bugging out of her head. I wasted no time climbing out of my bunk, and then I made a dick move by towering over her in the cramped space.

"What's your problem, Fawn?"

"I—what?"

"Why are you standing here like I'm about to ax you?"

I watched as her attitude returned, and she tried and failed to look like she wasn't intimidated by my closeness. I would have laughed if the conversation with my father wasn't playing in my head on repeat.

"Maybe because you're looking at me like you are?"

"How much did you hear?" I demanded, cutting to the chase.

Of course, she chose to play stupid.

"What?"

"You were eavesdropping on a private conversation." Pushing forward until she was trapped, I rested my forearms on the top bunk she'd claimed. I didn't want to think about the fact that it was directly across from mine. "Someone should teach you some manners."

She snorted, looking genuinely amused. "And you're the man for the job? That's like the pot teaching the kettle how not to be black." She rolled those innocent looking eyes that hid the wickedness beneath.

"You know what else is rude?" I chose to ignore everything she'd just said.

"No." Her eyebrows dipped as a wary look entered her eyes. This one was smart. "What?"

"Offering to let me fuck you and then crashing the party before it even started."

"I didn't offer—"

"You did," I cut her off before she could lie. "I know a woman who wants to be fucked when I see one."

She chewed on her lip before looking away. "Call it a momentary lapse in judgment."

"I had time to think about your momentary lapse and came to a conclusion."

Still refusing to meet my gaze, she shot back, "I'm holding my breath until I hear it."

And she wondered why I was slowly becoming obsessed.

"You said yes to me." Her alarmed gaze flew to me, and I smiled. Rich might have a knack for making her smile, and Houston had mastered making her obey, but I was the only one who lowered her guard. Enough to be vulnerable. "And no one can take that away, baby fawn. Not even you."

"I may not be able to take it back, but I can make sure it never happens again."

Pressing forward until there was no space left between us, I enjoyed the feeling of her soft body against mine as her breathing became short and quick. "You're trying to piss me off."

"Am I? I'd rather not see you throw another tantrum. Can you back up, please?"

Instead of doing as she asked, I studied her. She kept swallowing between pants as if she tasted something, only to sniff the air as if she'd find the answer there. It was subtle and easy to miss if I weren't standing so close. My stomach clenched as a thought occurred to me.

"You're a virgin, aren't you, Braxton?"

She huffed, her face clouded in disbelief. "Why? Because I'm not falling all over you? This conversation is coming dangerously close to sexist, asshole."

I chuckled because I genuinely didn't give a shit. She was naïve to think I would. "If by a snowball's chance in hell you're not a virgin, I'm guessing you haven't been fucked in a while. How long has it been?"

"That's none of your business."

"Maybe it hasn't sunk in yet, but you're not going to get much privacy on this rig. That means we're gonna know each other real well, real soon. Stop clutching those imaginary pearls and tell me."

"If I tell you, will you back off?"

"Sure."

"I mean off *me*. I can feel your dick, dude."

"I'd say I'm sorry, but I'm not. What I am is *waiting*."

She let out a long groan before fidgeting. "It's been a while, okay?"

Interesting.

"What are we talking? Days? Weeks? What?" She refused to look at me, which made my heart rate rise. "Months?" When she didn't respond, I wondered what that meant until she shuffled her feet again and wrinkled her nose. My jaw dropped, making her wince and confirm the conclusion my mind had already drawn. "Are you telling me that you haven't been fucked in *years*?"

"It's not a big deal."

"Oh, but it is. It's a huge deal. Gargantuan. Monstrous. Enormous. How did this happen?" I sounded as if someone had told me the world was going to end in three days. If I wanted inside Braxton before, I was foaming at the mouth to fuck her now. I wanted to howl at the moon over her poor, neglected pussy.

"It was my choice."

"No shit. No one sane would refuse to fuck you, baby fawn. This is one hundred percent your fault. Now tell me why you'd do this to yourself."

"That wasn't part of the deal."

"I want to renegotiate."

"And I don't want to talk about this anymore," she snapped.

I didn't have to look deep to see that the anger brimming her eyes was real. It latched onto my own rage coiling inside of me as my mind turned over the reasons why until it settled on the darkest possible conclusion. I immediately took a step back, giving her the space she coveted and hating myself for not listening sooner.

"Did someone hurt you?"

The words were out of my mouth before I considered whether I had the right to ask them. I was itching to turn this bus around and tear apart California until I found the dead fuck who dared.

Meanwhile, Braxton was blinking up at me in horror. "What? No! Of course not."

I stared back at her, unsure whether to believe her or not. Like I said, I wasn't the most honorable man around, but there were lines even I wouldn't cross. Even if she were lying, wrestling the truth from her would only make me as bad as the man who hurt her.

"Fuck, I need a drink." *Stupid sobriety pact.* I peered down at Braxton. "Ever been to Vegas?" She blinked her confusion at my rapid change of subject, but then her cheeks reddened in embarrassment even as her shoulders deflated in relief.

"I've never been outside of California."

"Well, today's your lucky day. We have two whole days to kill, and I know all the best games in Vegas."

"But I don't gamble."

"You do now. Wear something nice."

NINETEEN

Braxton

When Loren proposed showing me Vegas, I assumed he'd meant we'd be going as a group. Stepping off the bus in my sequin dress and strappy heels, I suddenly felt self-conscious when I discovered the bassist waiting alone. Finally, the question that had been circling my mind had an answer.

This was a date.

Somehow, I'd agreed to a date with Loren James.

Okay, deep breaths.

Maybe it wasn't what I thought. Maybe Houston and Rich were already waiting in the car. They'd disappeared the moment we rolled into town, but they might have come back while I was in the shower.

"I underestimated you," Loren greeted as I approached.

I let his gaze rake over me once I stopped in front of him and returned the favor by doing the same to him. Loren wore all black, making his blond hair appear lighter and his eyes even darker. The double-breasted vest he wore had white pinstripes, and he'd pushed up his shirt sleeves to show off the veins in his forearms and expensive watch. He'd even buttoned the front and tucked his medallion inside.

"How so?"

Pulling me close, Loren gripped my chin before whispering, "I bet you knew exactly how crazy you'd drive me in that dress. A virgin wouldn't have a clue."

"Something tells me you underestimate women in general."

He snorted before letting me go. "No, just you."

I didn't respond as he opened the back door of the silver car that he'd been standing next to. I didn't recognize the brand, but it looked like it cost more than all the pennies I'd ever made.

"After you." He waved me in, and though the gesture was gallant, I knew his motives were less so. I shot him a sharp look before climbing inside.

"Satisfied?" I asked after he settled in next to me. My gold dress only stopped mid-thigh, much shorter than I remembered when I splurged on it a year ago. It wasn't the kind of "flash" I was going for, but it had Vegas written all over it.

"You'd have to be wearing considerably less." I pressed my thighs together, but of course, he clocked my every move. I'd underestimated him too. Loren wasn't the airhead he pretended to be. He was smart, observant, and quick. What I liked most, but would never admit, was that he didn't care about rules. "Just say when."

"Never would be the answer to that, Loren."

"Why? Because Houston said so?" He scoffed at the notion.

"Because I don't want you," I argued as convincingly as I could. The sideways glance he cast me made it clear he wasn't buying my bullshit. *Fuck.*

"Then, why are you here?"

"I recall you offering to show me around."

He laughed at that, an arrogant and husky sound while staring out the window. It was no match for the caustic smile that went with it. I don't think I've ever seen straighter, whiter teeth. His lips that spouted cruelty on a whim was what really dazzled me. They called to my natural need to sin.

The city became brighter, louder, and more chaotic the closer to the center or rather the strip we got. I watched people herd themselves up and down the crowded sidewalk and outdoor escalators. Frantic tourists rushed in and out of casinos, shops, and restaurants, while others were content toting their frozen drinks from Fat Tuesday in the dry heat.

Turning away from watching out the window, I found Loren already studying me. "Are Houston and Rich meeting us?"

He lifted a mocking brow. "You're smarter than that."

My heart began pounding wildly in my chest. If he wouldn't beat around the bush, neither would I. "This is not a date. I didn't agree to that."

"Then call it a pregame to fucking. Feel better?"

My lips parted and closed. Whenever words formed, they became lodged in my throat. Loren didn't seem at all bothered by my stunned silence.

Nope.

He'd already pulled out his phone to play Subway Surf.

I was most disappointed by the fact that if he told me to spread my legs for him right now, I'd do it. It was a slim chance, but still… it was more than he deserved.

When the car slowed to a stop, it wasn't at some glitzy hotel. It was someone's home. A mansion, to be exact. The driveway was lined with more luxury cars as they waited for valet. When it was our turn, Loren took my hand and gently helped me from the car. He then placed that same hand on the small of my back and steered me toward the entrance. I felt his thumb rubbing my spine and took a deep breath. He'd been an asshole far too long for me to be fooled by his charm.

"Where are we?"

"It's called The Palace. It's a low-key spot with high-stakes games."

"How high are we talking?"

Loren and I shared a meaningful look before he focused his attention on the woman in a dress tighter and shorter than mine. Two armed guards surrounded her.

"Mr. James, we're pleased to have you back with us. Is it just you," she asked, completely dismissing the fact that his arm was literally wrapped around me, "or will Mr. Morrow and Mr. Noble be joining you this evening?"

"As you can see, I'm not alone. If you want, though, I can pass Houston your number. I hear the thirty-seventh time is the charm."

The poor girl's cheeks reddened from Loren putting her in her place. Even when he was subtle, he wasn't. She'd snubbed me, and somehow, I still felt bad for her. The fact that she had a crush on Houston and not Loren made her reasons even more confusing. Maybe she wanted them both. It was also possible she was pretending interest in Houston to make Loren jealous and—

Now my head was spinning.

It seemed to be a side effect whenever I strayed too close to Houston, Loren, or Jericho.

"That won't be necessary," she answered. The poor girl looked ready to drop dead.

Loren showed her a matte black card with nothing on it. It wasn't until she scanned it with her phone that it revealed a barcode that spelled out *The Palace*. After that, she waved us in with a tight smile.

"You didn't have to do that."

"I disagree," he casually said as he led me through the dimly lit foyer. "*She* didn't have to be a bitch to you."

"Because only you reserve that right?" How dare he play the hero when he was no different?

Glancing down at me, I wasn't prepared for him to usher me inside a dark alcove and hem me against the wall. When he circled his arms around my waist and pulled me close, I let him. No matter what Loren said or did, when his hands were in play, he had me.

Because his touch felt like finding home, and I was too easily won.

"Haven't you learned that when a boy likes a girl, he treats her like utter shit? It's textbook."

"I've heard that, but I didn't buy it when I was six, and I don't buy it now."

Leaning forward, he skimmed his lips down my neck. "So, what do you suggest I do?"

"About?"

"You. Me." He'd punctuated each word with a soft kiss on my bare shoulder. "I need to fuck you senseless, Braxton Fawn."

"Too bad." Mentally, since he was still holding me, I patted my back in approval. My knees were weak, but my head was still strong.

"Afraid you'll like it?"

"Yes." Surprised, Loren lifted his head from the shoulder he was still kissing. "I'm afraid I'll like it too much, and I won't be able to stop."

He was still grasping for something to say when two men in expensive suits appeared, spotting us as they passed. At once, their steps slowed, their gazes taking the extra time to admire me thoroughly. Loren, not missing a thing, stood up straight. That was all it took for the men to quicken their steps and hurry away.

"Please don't get into a fight," I pleaded with him. The men were gone, but Loren didn't seem the least bit appeased. I could see the contemplation in his eyes to go after them. "Xavier will be pissed if you get arrested."

"Xavier's always pissed," he responded dismissively.

Lacing our fingers together, he pulled me from the alcove, and we walked until we reached a large sitting room with dim lighting, a table in the center with a green felt tabletop, and a bar off to the side.

An older woman sat behind a small desk. She had red hair like mine, hers darker and shorter and reminding me of my mother. She peered over her glasses when we walked inside and smiled. The minute she stood to approach, I noticed that she was tall and busty.

"I'd say I'm surprised to see you, but that would be a lie," she greeted Loren. She didn't wait for Loren's reply before her gaze drifted to me and brightened. "Although I am surprised at your choice of guest this evening. She looks too good for you." She held out her hand for me to shake, and I accepted. "Lorraine."

"Braxton."

"Braxton, would you like a drink?"

"I'm fine, but thank you."

She obviously knew Loren didn't drink since she didn't bother offering him one. He led me over to the table with five other men already seated, and one standing behind the cards and chips before taking the only seat left and… pulling me into his lap. I tensed up even though no one paid us any mind. It wasn't *them* that made me nervous anyway.

I was sitting in Loren James's lap.

"Are you sure this okay? I can—"

"For a quarter-million buy-in, it damn well better be," he grumbled like the spoiled brat he was. I was still reeling over the dollar amount when he wrapped his arm around my waist and nodded at a bearded gentleman wearing a fedora across from us. Based on the look the guy gave Loren in return, they knew each other, but it didn't go further from there.

Once Loren was settled, the cards were dealt, and the game began. I didn't understand any of it, and Loren didn't bother to explain. He promptly withdrew into himself as he concentrated on his hand and the cards on the table.

I was so on edge by the time the first game ended that I didn't object when he placed his hand on my bare thigh and swept this thumb back and forth. He'd won the entire pot.

"Relax," he whispered.

"This is a lot of money," I whispered back. I didn't want to embarrass him by acting like an amateur, but I couldn't seem to keep anything in around him. "Are you sure you should bet so much? What if you lose?"

"After living both sides of the tracks, baby fawn, I've learned that I'm no happier with money than I am without."

I sighed as my shoulders deflated. "Was there a time when you ever gave a fuck?" I sounded utterly drained.

"Once." I turned just enough to catch the faraway look in his eyes. "It was a waste of time, so I wouldn't recommend it."

Still deep in thought, his hand drifted up, and then his fingers slipped just underneath my dress before resting there. I didn't exhale until it was clear he wouldn't try to finger-bang me underneath the table.

"How are you going to play if you're groping me?"

"Easy," he whispered back. "You're going to play this hand for me." As if it weren't insane, he laid the two cards he'd just been dealt facedown on the table.

No way I was touching those cards.

"I'll lose." It was taking all my self-control, which was slipping out the window with him gripping my thigh like he owned me, not to yell. I didn't want to unintentionally alert the others before I could talk him out of his asinine plan.

"So lose." Holding me with his black gaze, his hand resumed its ascent, my leg twitching when his fingers brushed the edge of my thong. "It's worth every penny."

"Are you implying that I'm for sale?"

He snorted. "I know you're not."

"Are we playing poker, or are we watching James sniff after this girl's panties?" snapped the guy Loren had acknowledged earlier. As soon as he was done speaking, he lifted his fedora with an apologetic tilt of his lips and revealed a bald head underneath. Shame didn't come as easily to me these days, but I still caught the faint scent of Father Moore's holy oil.

I started to push Loren's hand away until I realized I wasn't that girl anymore, and I'd miss his touch too much.

"You lose any more money, Vince, and I'll have to take your house as collateral. I'm just giving you time to come to your senses since we both know your wife isn't with you for your charm." The men around the table laughed at Vince's expense, who didn't seem to find it as funny as they did. Without warning, Loren lifted me on my feet before standing. "Give me two minutes."

No one said anything, and he didn't wait for permission.

"Loren, I'm serious," I said the moment we were alone in the hall. "I can't do this. I can't lose your money."

"It's okay. I have more."

"That's not the point."

"Then, how about this? I play this hand." I was already eagerly nodding before he finished. Smiling like he was indulging me, he rested his forearm on the wall next to my head. "But if I win, I make you come. That's the deal."

My heart dropped to the pit of my stomach, but my vagina had a different reaction. If we had still been sitting with his hand on my thigh, I wouldn't have been able to hide my reaction.

"What?"

"You said no one hurt you." It was then I realized he was still obsessing over my confession. "There's only one other thing that makes sense."

"Do tell." I rolled my eyes, but he never lost his serious expression.

"No one ever made it good for you. You can't miss something you never enjoyed."

He patiently waited for me to admit that he was right. And he was…just not about me. Needing something to do with my hands, I placed them on his chest and toyed with the sterling silver clip on his tie. It's where I kept my gaze when I whispered as low as I could, "I do enjoy sex, Loren. I like it very much."

I felt his muscles tense underneath my hand, and when I looked up, I found his brows dipped and his beautiful face twisted in confusion. "Then why—"

The air I'd inhaled shuddered out of me, making him abandon the question he'd been ready to ask. "I told you…if I start, I can't stop, and…"

"And?" he prodded at the same time pressing his hips against mine when I fell silent. He seemed so desperate to get inside my head. Even though he'd done nothing to earn my trust, I still felt the need to let him.

"And no one's ever been able to keep up with me."

Loren's pupils seemed to dilate as his dick grew harder and larger against me. I could feel his heart racing almost as fast as mine. "Oh, baby fawn, it's your lucky day." Before I could respond, his large hand gripped my ass tight enough to bruise. "Because when *I* start, I won't stop until long after you've had enough."

My reaction was visceral.

His promise melted into my skin, burrowing through bones and seizing my heart, gut, and lungs until it set me on fire. I wanted it that much.

Unfortunately, I was wiser now.

"I'm sure you really believe that, Loren, but I played this hand before and lost everything," I said, speaking the language a gambling addict would understand. "You already hate me when I haven't given you a reason. If we sleep together, you'll finally have one."

He stared down at me a long while, turning over my words before tossing them away. "Try me."

A frustrated sound slipped from my lips. "I can't, Loren. Did you forget we work together? It's too messy."

"Sex usually is. With me, it most definitely will be." I didn't respond. When it became clear I wouldn't fall for his bait, he sighed and straightened before taking a step back. "Wait here."

I stayed put as he told me, which was easy since I couldn't trust my legs right now. I needed to find a bathroom to clean up. Removing my thong wasn't possible, thanks to my decision to wear this dress. It didn't matter because Loren returned moments later.

"Let's go."

He barely looked at me before starting down the hall and effectively ending what I still maintained was *not* a date. I also realized this was the second time in a single day that I turned him down. I refused to feel guilt when I knew I was doing the right thing.

The disappointment? That, I allowed myself to feel.

TWENTY

Rich

IF LOREN AND BRAXTON HAD INTENDED TO HIDE WHATEVER HAPPENED between them, they were doing a shit job. To start, it was hard to ignore them disappearing inexplicably only to return hours later. *Together.* I was still obsessing over the vision Braxton made in that sequin dress and whether she'd worn it for Loren.

Houston was still at their throats even though it's been two days. He knew they'd been up to no good too, but what pissed him off was knowing there was nothing he could do about it.

Of course, the only one who seemed guilty was our guitarist. Loren just ignored the problems he caused, as usual, while giving Brax the cold shoulder.

It was Friday night in Vegas, and we were backstage at the T-Mobile Arena. Braxton already looked exhausted even though the night was young. I wasn't sure how much sleep she'd been getting. Our first two nights on the bus together had been tense and wasn't getting any better. Braxton walked on eggshells around us, and we around her.

"You okay?" I asked her when Houston finished berating her for disappearing this morning, this time alone but without security. She was sitting alone on the sofa, heels off, and rubbing her small feet with a grimace.

"Fabulous," she grumbled without looking up.

The link between my brain and my body disconnected long enough for me to take the foot she was rubbing between my hands and kneed the pad of her foot. And I was painfully aware of the fact that this hadn't gone unnoticed.

From the corner of my eye, I saw Loren storm off, bursting through a door marked "No Exit" and setting off the alarm. Thankfully, one of the venue staff ran over a moment later and quickly reset the security system.

"Is this okay?" I asked her once the usual chaos resumed. I was so nervous that you'd think I was fingering her pussy instead of rubbing her feet. Smiling softly, Braxton nodded before closing her eyes and resting her head on the back of the couch. "So I don't know what happened after you and Lo disappeared," I began as I massaged the arch in her foot, "and I don't want to know." Only partly true. "Whatever happened, my unsolicited advice is to put it out of your mind. At least until after the show. Those are not the kind of demons you want out there with you."

Her eyes opened, and I could tell she was considering whether to confide in me.

This is historically the moment when guys too emotionally available end up in the friend zone. We become a shoulder to lean on and nothing more.

You don't care.

And then I told myself to believe it like it was gospel.

"Do you ever get used to it?"

When I simply stared back at her, she gestured toward the stage. I listened for a moment as our opening band wrapped up and then switched to her other foot. I didn't want to know what it meant that she chose to keep what happened between Loren and her a mystery to me. Instead, I concentrated on relieving the ache in her feet and ignoring the one in my chest.

"Fucking up is inevitable. No matter how good you get, you'll always be human. It's not until you screw up the first time and realize the world didn't end that you stop worrying about the times that follow. You're good at what you do, Braxton. You have a gift, and that's something a few bad shows and bloodthirsty critics can never take away from you."

"Wait," she said, making me pause. "I have critics? Already?"

"*That's* what you heard?"

"I'm human, remember?" she tossed back at me sweetly.

"So I'm guessing you haven't been on Twitter lately."

"No." She winced and then grimaced. "Do I want to look?"

"No."

I could see the curiosity burning in her brown eyes and knew the moment my back was turned that she'd find herself in the middle of a shitstorm. We were moments from playing our fourth show, and Braxton had been nothing short of amazing. She hadn't reached Calvin's level, but it was becoming clear that she'd surpass him.

It wasn't enough, though.

She was currently being ripped apart from every corner of the earth, and until I let the cat out of the bag, she'd been oblivious to it. Quiet as it was kept, those critics were why Houston blew his top anytime Braxton was out of his sight.

Because he wanted what was best for those he cared about, even at the expense of himself. Neither of them knew it yet, but that now included Braxton.

The opening band was all smiles when they returned backstage. It was always our cue to get our shit together.

"I guess I'll have to take your word for it," Braxton murmured as she accepted her guitar from a roadie wearing one of our band tees. It was a new design that included one of the shots from the shoot we did weeks ago. The roadies seemed to prefer that one to the choice with just our names on it, and I didn't blame them. Braxton wrapped around me sounded too good to pass up.

Loren reappeared through one of the designated entry / exit doors, and I stiffened when I saw that Houston was right behind him. I didn't trust them alone together, but I'd been too into Braxton to notice anyone else. If they fought without me to break them up, neither would stop until the other was dead, and I'd spend the rest of my life failing to piece the victor back together once the guilt tore them apart.

That's what happens when two competing powerhouses refuse to give up control—Houston had trouble letting go, and Loren hated being told what to do.

I…just wanted my best friends back.

We used to smile whenever one of us walked into a room. Of course, everyone thought it was weird, but we didn't care. And until I fucked that up it never mattered who was in our life at the time. All we had were each other.

"You ready to do this?" Houston grilled.

Braxton nodded, knowing he was speaking to her even though he refused to make eye contact. Meanwhile, she avoided Loren's penetrating gaze at all costs. I knew I wouldn't stop fixating over what happened between them, just like I knew I wouldn't like the answer.

Had they slept together?

Loren might behave like a pig, but he didn't squeal like one, and for once, I wished he was one to kiss and tell.

Houston and Brax started toward the stage. I watched as Houston said something too low for me to hear, and Braxton's spine straightened as her hands made fists.

Yeah, I'd bet Bound's net worth that she'd be taking a swing at him before the tour was over.

Making Houston bleed was sort of our unspoken initiation ritual. Calvin had always been too much of a chump to try. God fuck his soul. We'd never actually sat down and discussed why we couldn't accept him. We never had to. We just lived and bled on the same page and never strayed.

That is until Calvin got his revenge before snorting himself to death.

Good fucking riddance.

Someone handed me drumsticks and handed Loren the bass he called Sharon for no reason at all, and together we made our way to the stage.

"So, are you going to tell me what happened between you and Brax, or are you going to wait until it's awkward for everyone?"

He summoned an arrogant look that only Loren James could. "What makes you think I planned to tell you at all?"

"Because I know you? Because you never seem to keep your mouth shut?"

"When have I ever kissed and told you shit, motherfucker?"

That stopped me dead in my tracks.

Loren was already hysterically laughing, which caused Braxton to peer over her shoulder. Whatever she was thinking, I couldn't pinpoint as her bored gaze moved between Loren and me. Deciding this discussion was better had without Braxton overhearing, I shoved Loren backstage again, even though we were already late.

"You kissed her?"

He peered down his nose at me even though he only had two inches on me. "Maybe she kissed me."

"Bullshit," I spat back. "If something happened, it's all on you."

Yup, I was angry at him.

I wanted to fight my best friend over pussy that wasn't even mine.

"I'm sorry to burst your weird fantasy bubble, but Braxton isn't as innocent as you think."

My heart stopped in my chest.

He fucked her.

He *fucking* fucked her!

How else could he have known? Forcing myself to relax, I started to ask him when he read the look on my face and beat me to the punch. "She told me herself, bro."

"What makes you think she was telling the truth?"

The look he gave me was half bewilderment, half exasperation. "*Why the fuck would she lie*?"

"How many extra fingers would you need to count the virgins who told you their cherries were popped so you'd screw them?"

Slipping a stick of gum in his mouth, he said, "Point taken. I don't think she was lying, though."

"How do you know?"

"Why does it matter?" He smiled sneakily before blowing a bubble and popping it with his teeth. "You got a secret fetish or something?"

"Get fucked, Loren."

"I tried," he mumbled, pushing air from his nostrils. "Believe me, I tried."

Hope shot through me at hearing that. "She turned you down?"

"We wouldn't be *here* if she hadn't." The joy that suddenly overtook my expression was wiped away when he said, "She's got the softest thighs. No way would I leave them this soon."

Loren walked away before I could demand to know where else he had touched her, and I had no choice but to follow. I could hear the crowd outside getting restless. The show had already begun but little did I know, it wasn't one that would be happening on a stage.

TWENTY-ONE

Braxton

THE SHOW WAS INCREDIBLE. THE CROWDS WERE GETTING WILDER. Word had spread about our success in Los Angeles and San Jose, and curiosity made them hungry.

With each song we performed together, it felt less like I was some weird attachment that Bound couldn't shake and more like I *was* Bound.

Mine.

I allowed myself to linger on the fact that I'd claimed them before realizing that it was calmness I felt. They were mine now, but they hadn't earned me yet.

Rich boarded the bus wearing another hoodie despite us being in the desert and gave me another one of those weird looks. I've been getting them ever since the show. He was trying to see past the wall I erected and figure me out, but I didn't like intruders.

On the other hand, it was only fair that I let him since I'd given Loren the cliff notes to my past. At the time, I didn't understand why. After two days of the cold shoulder and long, sullen silences from *all three* of my bandmates, I've had time to ruminate.

I wanted to scare him off.

Instead, I dangled fruit in his face and then forbade him to feast from my garden. Now Loren was pissed, and I understood why, but that didn't mean I would spread my legs to make him feel better.

"You want the shower first?" Rich offered. He was the only

one to do so my first two nights on board. I learned quickly not to shower after Loren, who took longer showers than Houston, Rich, and me combined.

"Sure." I stood and took my dinner plate to the sink. Apparently, Bound traveled with a team of caterers along with a bevy of people eager to do their—our bidding. A girl could get used to this. My dinner usually consisted of cheap wine and string cheese.

After rinsing and sticking my plate in the empty dishwasher, I smiled at Rich, who was busy eyeing one of the three steaming hot plates left on the counter and covertly watching me with the other.

"Thanks, Rich."

"No problem." His lips barely moved—I knew because I was admiring them and his piercing a little too closely—as if it wasn't what he really wanted to say.

I almost stayed to delve into *his* mind before deciding the distance we'd kept was best.

As I headed to the shower, I wondered where Loren and Houston had disappeared. I'm sure they were out turning Vegas on its head. We had one more show in Vegas tomorrow before heading to Glendale, and then it was Denver, Dallas, Houston, and New Orleans after that. The rest of the cities were a blur within my chaotic thoughts.

Figuring Rich would join his friends, I took my time under the hot stream of the shower. I almost felt ready to tackle the world when I finally stepped from the glass enclosure. Steam had completely fogged the mirror and poured from the bathroom when I opened the door to air it out.

I was *not* prepared to find the bedroom occupied.

The steam billowed out, quickly filling the room and clouding the two people rolling around on the bed like they were alone. I didn't recognize the girl with her tiny tits exposed thanks to the dress bunched around her waist, but I did recognize the infuriating asshole on top of her.

He'd just been begging to fuck *me* two days ago, and now he'd already moved on?

As the walls closed in on me, I worked to control my anger before the smell of burning coals could seep into my lungs and strangle me with a phantom hold.

"Was there a sign I missed that I should have hung up, or was the running water not a clue that this room was occupied?"

Loren lifted his head from suckling the girl's brown nipples, letting me see that he was drunk out of his mind.

Oh, that's just great.

"You can join us if you like." Loren's intoxicated gaze dipped to the rest of me, still painted in water droplets and covered only by a towel. "You're almost attired for the occasion. Drop the towel."

The girl beneath him giggled out of control, but I didn't find a damn thing funny.

Neither did Loren.

His head swiveled, and then he was staring down at her like he disapproved. "We were having a conversation."

The girl's lips formed an *O*, and then she lay there pouting while waiting to be used and tossed aside before morning.

Loren's black gaze returned to me.

"So what do you say, baby fawn?"

A quiet chuckle spilled out of me before I threw my head back and stared at the ceiling in defeat. Once I was done feeling sorry for myself, I turned my attention to the clueless, half-naked groupie.

"If you had any brain cells left, you'd get up and go. A spoiled brat, who also happens to be drunk, does not make for an amazing fuck. He's selfish enough when he's sober. You'll regret it in the morning and be too disgusted to tell your friends. It's not worth the bragging rights."

I hid my surprise when the girl looked like she was considering my point.

Seeing this, Loren shot up from the bed.

I didn't know what he planned to do until he was already in front of me with my wrist in his grip. I didn't know why I struggled when he pulled me forward. I already knew he wouldn't force me, and I was right.

He pushed me out of the room and slammed the bedroom door in my face.

As far as I should have been concerned, my problem was solved, so why did I want to throw open the door for round two? The only exception was being left in my towel with no privacy to throw something on. *That* would be the moment Houston or Rich returned. Rich would blush and give me privacy, but Houston would accuse me of trying to seduce them or something.

Sighing, I turned away from the door just as Loren's voice filtered through. "Turn over for me, baby. We don't care about her, do we?"

Rolling my eyes, I listened to her giggle and then Loren giving her more orders as I dug through my suitcase for something to sleep in. Once I found a T-shirt, shorts, and panties, I dropped my towel, deciding I didn't give a shit if someone walked in. As I used my towel to wrap my hair so it would dry quicker, the giggling finally stopped, and I began to hear moans coming through the door.

You don't hear it.

The feminine moans only grew louder and more desperate as I pulled my cheeky underwear up my legs. I forced my teeth to unclench as I shoved on my T-shirt that stopped a few inches below my belly button.

By then, Loren's groupie was coming and announcing it to anyone within hearing distance as if she were going for an Oscar. Staring at my shorts, I loosened my hold and let them fall.

I *hated* sleeping in more than what I had on.

I only wore panties and nothing else most nights, so I repacked the shorts and put my suitcase away in one of the closets built between the bunks and the bedroom. The bed inside was rocking now, and I heard the telltale sound of skin slapping. Listening to Loren and his groupie screw tasted like a glass of sour milk and smelled suspiciously bitter—like jealousy.

Fighting back the urge to gag, I climbed into my bunk and yanked the privacy curtain closed.

My headphones were under my pillow where I'd left them, so

I plugged them into my phone, shoved the buds in my ears, and played the first song my thumb found.

"Love and War" by Fleurie played at full volume, drowning out the sound of Loren fucking someone else after pretending to covet *me*.

Why the hell was I even upset?

I'd known the moment the words left his lips that they were a lie. Loren chose to make her a pawn because I refused to play his fool.

Whatever.

It was his aftermath to deal with.

I didn't realize I'd fallen asleep until I was jerked awake by shouting.

"You're drunk?"

My headphones had fallen out, allowing me to hear the argument taking place at the front of the bus.

Rich was back.

Disoriented, I touched my cheek, feeling the dried tears I must have shed in my sleep. My subconscious must have needed toughening up. There would be no crying over Loren James.

Not wanting them to know I was awake, I carefully settled onto my back before staring at the ceiling of my bunk.

"We agreed to give up this shit, Lo! Look what it did to Calvin."

"Fuck Calvin and fuck you. If I have to look at Braxton's dumb fucking face for the next year, I plan to be shit-faced while doing it. You got a problem? Make her leave."

"Do you hear yourself right now?"

"Yup." I heard something crash as Loren stumbled around. "Shit, man. I must not be drunk enough."

"Just go to bed, Lo. I can't look at you right now."

"Why does everyone think I give a shit?" Loren slurred. "Cuz I don't."

"You felt the need to drown yourself in whiskey. I'd say you're sending mixed signals. I can't believe Houston let you drink."

"He doesn't know," Loren slurred some more. "He's been

with Xavier since we left the show. Dumbass really thinks he can reshape the world just for her. She'll never fit because they know we'll never accept her. She's dooooomed."

Loren started snickering, making Rich sigh. "Please shut the fuck up."

I stilled when they passed through the bunk area and listened as the door to the bedroom opened. A moment later, I heard Rich grunt and then the sound of a body hitting the mattress. Loren was still slurring shit that I couldn't make out. Rich was moving around, and once the snoring started, the door to the bedroom closed. I tracked Rich's sneakered steps as he moved down the narrow passage and held my breath when he stopped in front of my bunk.

"I know you're awake," he whispered, causing my heart to feel like it was falling. "I know you were listening. Loren didn't mean any of it, Braxton. You don't want to believe me right now, but I know him better than you do. He doesn't know how to handle what he feels because he's never felt it before. Just…just give him some time."

I couldn't see him so my imagination conjured Jericho's sad silver eyes and the gold flecks in them pronounced as he pleaded with me to understand his best friend.

I didn't respond or make a peep. Nothing to indicate I'd heard a word of his bullshit. Thankfully, Rich didn't take too long to give up and walk away. Closing my eyes, I began counting the moments I had left.

I would count every second until I never had to see them again.

Morning came, and I decided I needed another shower.

I could still feel Loren's roaming hands and his hard body pressed against mine. Before last night, I'd wanted more, and now I just wanted to forget.

Climbing down from my bunk, it took me a moment to find

my balance, telling me how deeply I'd slept. It's not what I expected after a hard night, but perhaps I'd been more exhausted than troubled.

Houston and Rich were both sleeping soundly in their bottom bunks. I wouldn't allow myself to wonder how late Houston had stayed out or what he'd been doing and with whom.

Opening the bedroom door, I tiptoed inside. As expected, Loren was sprawled face down across the bed in yesterday's clothes and snoring. *Loudly.*

Flipping him off as if he could see me, I hurried for the bathroom. I wanted to be done before he woke—if he even could this early while hungover.

I hated him.

After my shower, I was staring at my reflection in the mirror I'd wiped clear of the fog when the door opened. Loren's black eyes were barely open as he shuffled inside the bathroom. If he noticed me, he ignored me. I watched through the mirror as he stood over the toilet and quickly looked away when he fumbled open his belt and pants.

I lost my train of thought.

How could I have one when his dick was out right now?

From this angle, I'd be able to see it if I dared to look. If he aimed to tempt me, that ship sailed and sank to the bottom of this unforgiving ocean. If he wanted to piss me off by pretending that he missed me standing in a bathroom the size of a shoebox, he was succeeding. He didn't have to know that, though. I didn't have to react.

The sound of Loren's piss hitting the bowl seemed to go on forever. I didn't know how much he drank last night, but it must have been a lot.

Finally, mercifully, it ended.

When he turned, he didn't even blink at finding me standing there. As if nothing was amiss, he stood behind me, trapping me between him and the sink. I could feel his morning wood brushing my ass since I'd stupidly chosen to wear only a T-shirt and panties to bed.

With his arms caging me, he squirted soap into his hand. I just stood there as he lathered for twenty seconds before rinsing the suds away.

"Good morning, baby fawn," he mumbled when he was done.

Good morning? Was he serious?

When I caught him smelling my hair, I lost it. What he did last night was bad enough. Pretending nothing happened was where I drew the goddamn line. As smoke assaulted my olfactory, my first thought was to break his nose and maybe a couple of ribs if I could, but Houston would murder me.

Option two it is.

I spun on my heel and shoved Loren with every ounce of strength I had. Since he was hungover and not expecting it, he was forced back several steps before catching his footing.

The confused look in his eyes only riled me up more because I knew then that he had no recollection of last night. Wasn't that just great?

He hurts me, and I'm the only one left with the memory.

"What the hell is your problem?" he spat when he found his tongue.

"I don't see anyone else two seconds from losing their balls, do you?"

As if I hadn't just threatened him, he closed the distance between us. "Whatever I did, I'm sorry. I'm stupid when I drink."

I had no words as I gaped at him for that lame-ass excuse. Sadly, I'd given him more credit than he'd deserved. "So what's your excuse when you're sober?"

He flinched. "Let me make it up to you."

"It means nothing when you can't remember what you did."

He shook his head, his stare searching the deepest depths of my soul for a chance, even if it was a slim one. "I don't want to. I don't want to think about me hurting you."

"You should have considered that before it was too late."

"Braxton..." He stepped closer to me, and I immediately backed up. All it did was trap me again between him and the sink. Only this time, I was facing him.

"No." I shook my head, warning him off.

He didn't listen, and now he had his arms wrapped tight around me. Loren reeked of whiskey and the girl he screwed while he knew I was listening.

Resting his chin on the top of my head, he sighed. "You're too good for me, Brax. Consider last night me making sure you knew it too."

Slowly, his hand moved over my back, caressing and massaging, until all the tastes and smells assaulting my senses were under control. "You succeeded," I told him while I pushed him away. "You can go now."

His smile was sad as he backed out of the bathroom. When I was finally alone, I tried to make sense of it all. How could it feel as if we'd broken up when we were never together?

Without answers, I had no choice but to face this new day as blind as I was the day before. When I stepped from the bathroom, Loren was sprawled across the bed, out cold again, making me wonder if I'd imagined the whole thing.

I wasn't the only one left awake, though.

Houston, sitting on the side of his bunk, stared at the floor between his planted feet with an expression that gave nothing away. When his head lifted and turned, that changed. He stared at me like I was either a problem to fix or a puzzle to solve. When I lifted my chin in silent defiance, in his eyes, I found I was something more.

An obstacle.

A rock that would force a river to split if he didn't find a way to obliterate it.

TWENTY-TWO

Houston

I wasn't just losing control of Bound. I was losing it altogether. With Braxton around, I didn't know which way was up.

This wasn't going to work.

She was Bound now, and that wasn't changing until the tour ended, but that didn't mean we had to torture ourselves in the meantime. The moment we reached Arizona, I was having her ass sent to another bus. All the easy access made it impossible to think of anything else. Braxton would be safer sticking her head in a lion's mouth.

My chest was still damp from my shower when I yanked my T-shirt over my head, but I didn't care.

I was on a mission.

Leaving the bedroom, I followed Braxton and Rich's voices to the front of our bus. Loren was still sleeping off another binge in his bunk. I wanted to be pissed at him for breaking our pact, but I understood him for the first time in years.

Braxton had that effect.

"The collection is huge," I heard Rich recite. "They have over fifteen thousand from all these different places."

"Sounds amazing," Braxton gushed. "I can't believe I've never heard of it."

"I think you'd like it."

Neither of them said anything more, and it wasn't because

they noticed me standing there. I couldn't see Braxton's face, but Rich practically had hearts in his eyes.

I couldn't catch a goddamn break.

First Loren, and now it looked like Rich would be a problem too. I shouldn't have been surprised.

History was simply repeating itself.

Clearing her throat, Braxton broke the silence before I could trample on their little moment. "Do you think we'd have time to see it? If you don't already have plans, I mean."

"No, I don't have plans," Rich rushed to say.

Instantly, I wracked my brain for some shit to keep him busy until the show. I had a goddamn mutiny on my hands, and Braxton was the cause. She had me wanting to go against myself most days, and she wasn't even my type. I liked something I could bend.

Seeing enough, I made my presence known. Rich had the good sense to look guilty. Braxton watched me with those big round eyes like she saw into my soul and couldn't look away.

"Good morning, Houston." Sensing my mood, her tone was wary. Maybe she'd survive us after all.

Ignoring her good-natured greeting, I got down to business. "The show takes priority over whatever you two have planned today. We're on stage at nine and not a minute later."

"Of course."

I laughed to myself, knowing that I'd pissed her off, but she didn't want me to know.

"You could join us," Rich invited. I was surprised he'd want me tagging along while he followed Brax around like a love-sick poodle. "We're hitting up the museum."

I knew without him elaborating which museum he referred to. The Musical Instrument Museum was by far the most interesting sight Phoenix had to offer, and it was still a snooze fest. They had a zoo and hiking trails with amazing views, but I doubt Braxton would be interested.

"I just hope you're a better tour guide than Loren," Braxton teased Rich. There was still tension between her and Loren. After witnessing that little scene they made in the bathroom three days ago, I expected no less. "He offered to show me Vegas and then took me to some reincarnated version of *Molly's Game*."

Rich and I made eye contact when she described The Palace. Loren was an idiot. I wondered how much money he'd thrown away this time. It's been six years since his father disowned him, and Loren was still flipping him off any chance he could.

"Loren only understands what serves him." Leaning against the small kitchen counter, I crossed my arms as I looked her over. She still wore the clothes she'd worn to bed. Thankfully, I hadn't caught her walking around in her fucking underwear again. "If you're smart, he won't have to show you twice."

Of course, she was quick to catch on.

"What do you mean *if* I'm smart?"

"It remains to be seen."

"Only if you think I give a shit what you think of me."

"You're not special, Bambi. It's understood that you do. Everyone does."

She let out a laugh that was entirely humorless. "It must be exhausting to be so in love with yourself."

"Why am I not surprised that you wouldn't know, little girl? Let me guess…you respond to every little slight so everyone will assume you're strong, and no one will know how insecure you really are."

She regarded me with no emotion, nothing to give her away. "Little girl?" she repeated pointedly.

"Are you even old enough to drink?" I knew she was, but I wasn't missing the opportunity to ignite her fire.

"I'm twenty-two, asshole."

She called me that so much it was starting to sound like an endearment to my ears.

"Wow," I returned, feigning awe. "Old enough to drink for one entire year. Clearly, I had you all wrong."

"I'm only interested in your respect. You can keep your understanding."

"Stop throwing yourself at my bassist, and maybe you'll earn it."

Braxton shot out of her seat, and I thought she'd take a swing at me. She had the intent in her eyes but no real conviction. It would have solved all my problems. I could choke the life from her, claim self-defense, and find a new guitarist—definitely someone who didn't tempt me at every turn.

Rich, who'd been silent, seemed to read my mind. Standing to shield Braxton from me if he had to, he begged me with his eyes.

"I was *not* throwing myself at him."

"Uh-huh."

I didn't want to talk about the two of them anymore. I didn't even want to think of them fucking as a possibility. If one of us claimed her, she'd be off-limits forever. Knowing this made me want to put my fist through a wall. Braxton spoke before I could.

"Why are you so threatened by me?"

"Come again?"

"You behave like a boy who's just been told he has to play nice with girls. You trample, growl, and puff out your chest just to show me who's in charge. It's been three months, Houston. I'm still not convinced, but I finally know the reason why. I've been asking for your respect when I should have told you that you haven't even begun to earn mine. I'll make it super clear and easy for you, caveman. Start with this pretense that you hate me and *drop it.*"

"I see." Stepping toward her, I tossed Rich a warning look when it looked like he'd try to stop me. "And what if I'm not pretending?"

"I haven't done anything to you."

I held her stare for a moment just to gauge if she was serious and snorted. "I'm not buying this babe-in-the-woods bullshit, Bambi."

"I don't know what you're talking about."

"Yes, you do," I returned with finality. I knew it because every time we got too close, her demons called out to mine.

By now, Rich had both hands gripping his black hair, his silver and gold-flecked gaze wild with indecision. He wanted to come to Braxton's rescue but wasn't sure if she was worth the risk. Our friendship was rocky enough without this extra catalyst, which was why she had to go. If I were in his shoes, there's no question what I would do.

I would have never let her attention be stolen in the first place.

"Leave."

Rich had his rare moments of defiance—like now when his gaze shifted to Braxton, silently asking if she wanted him to stay. He wasn't a pussy by any stretch. He just didn't like making waves.

I was always wound tight, Loren forever the rowdy one, which left Rich to be the calm before and after the storm. We balanced each other until Braxton came and tipped the scales.

"It's okay, Rich."

Even after giving him the okay to leave her alone with me, he stood there a moment longer.

"I'll be in the shower if you need me," he finally told her before disappearing behind the door I'd just come through. The moment the sound of his footsteps faded, and the bedroom door closed, I was on Braxton.

"You shouldn't have done that." The ponytail she'd pulled her hair into this morning was now in my grip. It's what I'd been longing to do since the day she wandered into Savant's conference room and turned my world on its head. When her neck was arched, leaving her throat exposed, it was all I could do not to sink my teeth in. "And you shouldn't keep pretending you're not aware of what will happen if you keep giving me lip."

"You'll kill me?" she tossed back, reminding me of my bullshit threat a month ago. I wanted to fuck with her head, and though I succeeded in convincing her, I failed to make her give a shit. I shook my head as a smile crept up on me.

The longer I knew Braxton, the less I understood her.

"Let me go, Houston."

"Convince me that we understand each other."

"I told you what it would take," she returned.

"I don't respect you, Braxton. I never will. You're useful, but that doesn't make you our equal."

For a moment, the little hope she held vanished from her big, round eyes. She looked lost and frustrated until that defiant gleam I hated so much returned tenfold. "Then what are we even talking about?"

"We're discussing the inevitability of you doing as you're told. I'll make sure of that."

"Will you? Good luck with that. The only time I bend is when I'm getting fucked, but we've already established that it's not happening between us."

Unprepared for her response, my hold loosened, so I let my hand fall. I didn't back away from the temptation of her body this close to mine, though. "Last chance, Bambi. Look down or bow down. Just show me who's in charge."

She smiled at me.

What I felt from that simple gesture, that unspoken challenge…I wasn't this excited when Bound scored a record deal or received its first platinum. Braxton made life more than just interesting.

She made it worth living.

Loren and Jericho challenged me, but neither of them ever made my dick hard while doing it.

When I took hold of her again, it was her hips I caught before I yanked her into me. There was no space left between us now. No guarantee I'd let her go this time.

"That's your problem," I whispered to her when she refused to break our stare and submit. "You're always bringing a knife to a gunfight, Fawn. You should have gone for my balls."

One day, I'd figure out how she managed to appear both innocent and insolent at the same time. *This* was the paradox of Braxton Fawn—to look like heaven on earth while wreaking havoc on my peace of mind.

Fear and acceptance of what was about to happen crashed together like a wave returning to the sea. It was the moment I crossed the line I'd drawn with no remorse.

There was only the undeniable truth that I was fucked.

TWENTY-THREE

Braxton

HE KISSED ME.

Houston Morrow was *kissing* me.

Moments are meant to be a seamless transition from one to the next. The cause and the effect. Designed to make sense.

So...how did we go from his arrogant reminder that I was beneath him to...kissing?

And why didn't I pull away?

A good time would have been when I felt his hands slip around my hips until they reached my ass. The shorts I wore to bed didn't leave much for his imagination. I'd put all my cards on the table, and he was calling my bluff.

Groaning his pleasure at the way I filled his hands, he lifted me. My legs ended up wrapped around his trim waist. His lips never left mine.

I was the air he needed to breathe, and he was mine.

Houston moved us to the small table where Rich and I had plotted adventures together just minutes ago. Still, I didn't fight him when he set me down on top of it. I spread my legs to make room for him, and he rewarded me by pressing his cock against the thin layer keeping him from being inside of me.

All he'd done was kiss me.

His tongue slipped between my lips, and I moaned at the taste of him mixing with the cherries that signaled my arousal. It only intensified when his hand slowly wandered underneath my shirt. It was rough and warm against my soft skin.

I wanted him to ruin me.

No question I'd let him tear me apart and piece me back together however he wanted me. I wanted to be the precious thing he took for himself and never let go. I was willing to give him anything if he never stopped touching me in return.

He groaned right then as if he could read my thoughts and shoved his hand underneath my bra. The sensation of his warm palm engulfing my breast and his thumb teasing my nipple made an unintelligible sound slip from my lips. It didn't matter how long it had been. I'd never been touched like this.

"You want to come for me?"

"Yes."

I needed that so much. I'd known no greater thrill than coming apart in front of an avid audience—somehow to watch and appreciate my slow descent from sanity.

It wasn't until Nate Farrow—not my first, second, or last, but the boy who let the guilt eat him alive—that I learned the wildness in my heart, this mania I was a slave to, was truly and irrevocably a sickness.

Dirty whore.

I still believed him as if it had been yesterday.

The pungent scent of olives was heavy in the air as shame gripped me by the throat. Even though I knew it wasn't real, I scrambled away just as Houston was about to kiss me. I didn't stop backing away until I was pressed against the black shade covering the window.

"What just happened?" The confused dip of his brows would have been adorable if I weren't shaking like a leaf in a tornado. "Get your ass back over here, Fawn."

I shook my head, feeling my throat clog when I tried to speak. "You shouldn't have kissed me."

"You shouldn't have asked me to."

I hadn't, but we both know I wanted him to. Denying it when it had been obvious would only make me feel pathetic on top of everything else.

"You don't understand, Houston. When Calvin died,

you didn't get your new start. You just traded one addict for another."

The disgust on his face at my confession was ten times more mortifying than years-old shame.

"You're on drugs?" he spat.

I vehemently shook my head. "Not that kind of addiction."

In my opinion, I had it worse. At least with drugs, I could have been cured. Instead, all I had to cope was to bury a relentless demon.

"Goddamn it," Houston swore through gritted teeth, "tell me and stop beating around the bush!"

"Sex," I told him with a gasp. I couldn't quite catch my breath after that. "I'm addicted to sex, Houston."

I didn't get a response because a noise had stolen Houston's attention. I followed his glower to the door behind him, where Loren and Rich stood looking like a train was barreling toward them.

When I imagined all the ways they might discover my secret, this had been so far from it.

I never made it to the museum.

Houston had stormed from the bus, and the person I'd made plans with had trouble making eye contact with me ever since.

My only ally was Loren.

It was business as usual as far as he was concerned. I didn't allow that small favor to give me hope. There was a chance that he was still drunk or too hungover to process how hard I'd fucked them.

The hours until the show seemed to tick by agonizingly slow. Houston never reappeared during that time, and I didn't see him until the very last moment.

I could feel his gaze as I walked onto the stage, looking amazing but feeling like shit.

Tonight, I wore a black floor-length sheath with slits so high the stylist paired my dress with a bodysuit so that I didn't accidentally flash my vagina. God, who I wasn't sure I believed in, must have decided I'd had enough for today.

That was until the show started.

Yellow and red formed shapes around me as we played, but I didn't listen to the notes through my eyes. Not this time. I was caught up in the words. I dissected each one, and not for the first time, I wondered about the girl in the song. Tonight, it felt like that girl was me even though I knew it was impossible.

She's got claws that scratch me deep
She digs for feelings I never invited
Caught within her cold embrace
I'm falling, stalling, all over again
Just head over heels for her crocodile tears

Why don't you just shut up
Why can't you just get up
Why won't you stop pulling me down (Die)

Bleeding myself dry to give you everything
Then you tell me it's not enough, you want it all
How could I have loved such a heartless bitch
I'm not who I am anymore

Why don't you just shut up
Why can't you just get up
Why won't you stop pulling me down (Die)

Hypnotized by your graceless lies
A fool for what's in cold, dead eyes
You will never be more than a bad memory
So run, run, just keep running away from me

Of course, Houston sang as if it was his pain, but all that proved was how talented he was. It was hard enough to imagine that Houston had a heart. I couldn't fathom him letting it be broken.

I looked to Bound's bassist—the link between the rhythm and the melody, and the most vulnerable of the trio. I'm sure anyone would have assumed that role belonged to Rich, but no. Only someone having trouble burying their pain would feel the need to deceive. Loren's behavior was as much for him as it was for everyone else. He was precisely the type to get his heart broken and then write a diss track.

I admired his perfect smile and the sweat dripping down his exposed abs and wondered who could willingly give him up or hurt him. Tonight, he hadn't bothered with a shirt. All he'd worn were black jeans and matching suspenders hanging down by his hips, boots, and that medallion I hadn't gotten around to asking him about.

His brows that had been dipped with concentration cleared as he turned his head the slightest bit and caught me drooling. I turned away before he could react. It was just in time to switch from rhythm to lead and deliver a solo that brought the house down.

Once the show ended, we were rushed from the stadium. The three of them piled into a separate Suburban, though, and I frowned at that before shrugging it off. It wasn't exactly news that I was the odd man out, but they didn't have to be so blatant about it.

I didn't let it ruin the rush I felt from another successful show, and by the time the short drive was over, I'd successfully cast them from my mind. Texting back and forth with Griff and Maeko helped. They were sending me clips and shots of the show that had already surfaced online as if I hadn't been there. Sweat beaded my brow, and my heart began pounding at the last photo they'd sent.

Someone, somehow, had captured a picture of Loren and me staring at one another.

I wasn't aware before now how much could be said in one look. And it wasn't one of those grainy, faraway shots either.

Nope.

It was a close-up with crystal fucking clarity.

You'd think I'd been caught with my hand down his pants with how quickly I clicked out of the photo. I shoved my phone in my bag just as I reached Bound's tour bus, only to stop dead in my tracks.

Everything I owned was packed and waiting for me on the curb.

Instead of rushing for them, I stared blankly at my bags. My mind and body were unable to react. I didn't know where to begin. Houston had been furious, but I didn't think he'd be *this* upset. Taking a deep breath, I forced myself to think rationally rather than emotionally.

One, they couldn't finish the tour without me.

Two, it was *impossible* that they'd found a replacement in a matter of hours when the reason I was standing here was that they were too damn picky.

I wouldn't figure out what bug was up their ass this time by guessing, so I turned away from the bus to go find them when one of the roadies found me instead.

"Oh, shit. H-hey, Braxton," he said, looking alarmed. "I'm really sorry about this. I was supposed to have this done before you got back, but—"

"It's fine," I reassured before he could finish. "What's going on? Where are you taking my stuff?"

The roadie's blue eyes widened even further at my question. I think his name was either Alan or Alex. Unfortunately, I hadn't been around long enough to be sure. He was cute even with his greasy blond hair that clearly hadn't been washed in a while.

"You didn't know? I was told to move your things to the second bus." Suddenly realizing this was our first conversation, he stuck out his hand. "I'm Alex."

"Braxton," I offered while shaking his hand.

"Yeah, I know," he teased with the beginnings of a blush blooming on his cheeks. "Everyone knows who you are."

"Oh, yeah?" I tried my best to sound excited. Any other time I would have been.

"Yeah, you're pretty awesome."

I could tell he wanted to say more but was trying to play it cool. Perhaps he sensed that I wasn't in the mood to be praised after being discarded like yesterday's trash. Either way, I was grateful. My guard only worked when my back was against the wall. Alex, on the other hand, was nice. I was afraid I'd end up crying on his shoulder if he said too much. I bet he wouldn't find me so awesome then.

"Thanks," I said, giving him a smile that felt real. "Do you know why I'm being moved? Sorry, no one told me."

"Houston thought you'd be more comfortable on another bus." Thankfully, Alex didn't pry. Spilling my guts is what got me in this position, so I wasn't about to do it again. "Should I wait until he's back or...?" Alex let the question hang in the air.

"No. It's fine. I guess he just forgot to tell me," I lied. That pedantic, priggish pile of pig shit hadn't forgotten a damn thing, and neither would I. For now, I breathed in and out through my nose, forcing my anger to wait its turn.

Nodding, Alex lifted my bags from the ground. When I tried to help, he waved me off. "This way."

I followed him to the bus parked behind Bound's bus. When I boarded, I expected to see it occupied and maybe a little crowded. Instead, it was a ghost town.

"Where is everyone?" I questioned while looking around and waiting for someone to appear.

"They were all split up and moved around. This baby's all yours."

This time around, it was hard *not* to react.

Was separating themselves from me really that dire? They'd actually vacated an entire bus so that they wouldn't have to share a space with me anymore.

I had privacy now, but I wasn't grateful for it. I was angry enough to scream and afraid of how alone I'd be by the end of the tour. There would be nothing to distract me from my thoughts and the fear of what was happening hundreds and soon to be thousands of miles away.

No company is better than bad company.

Still, I felt terrible for the crew, who were probably feeling cramped *before* Bound decided to kick me off their island. There was a vast difference between Bound's bus and this one. The most noticeable was the twelve narrow bunks compared to the band's spacious four. This bus also didn't have the slide-out feature that doubled the interior's size when the bus wasn't in motion. Everything here was standard with a straight out of the factory design, not that I cared. I'd be more than comfortable here with no one to share the space. My problem was the real reason I'd been moved, and it wasn't for my comfort.

I'd been exiled.

I could feel the invisible branding of a familiar scarlet letter on my chest even now.

"Is this okay?" Alex asked after I'd been silent for too long. "If not, I can let Houston or Xavier know." His expression didn't match his offer, though. Alex looked like he'd rather swallow rusty nails than play the messenger. The crew was happy and well-treated by the guys, but it didn't change the fact that they were intimidating. It was a natural thing for them.

"This is fine. I'm just worried everyone will think I'm a diva or something." *Thanks for that, Houston.* "If they want to come back, I really don't mind sharing."

"They don't think that. Houston made it clear *he* wanted you to have the privacy."

I bet he did. He managed to cast me aside while looking like the gallant hero. I hated him even more than before.

"I see."

Smiling, Alex made for the exit. "If you need anything, I'll be around!" he shouted before disappearing into the dark. The drivers were set up in hotels for the night, so I was utterly alone until morning.

Sinking onto the worn couch, I tried not to replay the events from this morning, but it was impossible to deny a moment to relive Houston's kiss. If I chose to see it, the silver lining was that I no longer had any secrets.

The problem was that they still had all of theirs.

TWENTY-FOUR

Loren

"I KNEW YOU WERE A DICK. I HAD NO IDEA YOU WERE THIS COLD."

When we returned to the bus, the first thing I noticed was that Braxton was missing. She always came straight home after a show to eat, shower, and ignore us the rest of the night with her headphones in and music on full blast. Sometimes she'd talk to her friends, but never any of her family. Now if I asked her why now, she'd probably tell me to shit a rock or something.

Houston shrugged, making me want to break his collarbone. I had to give him credit, though. He was pulling off pretending he wasn't regretting his latest fuck-up.

No, I wasn't the only one who had them. I was just the only one who got any shit.

"Think what you want, but it was for her sake, too," Houston claimed.

I caught Rich rolling his eyes and smirked. *Interesting.* "Oh, *thank heavens.* I was afraid you only kicked her out for you."

"She was distracting. I did it for everyone since you both seem to forget that she's off-limits."

"You had your tongue down her throat!" Rich spat. His fists were balled when he shot to his feet. One wrong word from Houston, and he was swinging. "We saw you."

"I know," Houston admitted with a solemn nod. I didn't think he felt bad for kissing Braxton, but I believed he wished he regretted it.

"If she hadn't stopped you," Rich continued, "would you have gone further?"

"Of course not," Houston lied through his teeth. I think he'd forgotten that we were there, watching from the moment he asked her if she wanted to come for him.

I snorted.

"Whatever," I cut in before Rich could argue. "This is getting lame. I'm ordering pizza."

No one said shit as I pulled out my phone. I already knew what they liked, so they didn't bother to make requests. After ordering the pies, I remembered that we hadn't stocked up thanks to that stupid, useless pact, so I stepped off the bus, slapped some cash in the hands of a roadie, and sent him off to find booze. Alone, I lingered outside despite the sweltering Arizona heat. Even at night, my balls felt like they were baking.

Thirty seconds must have passed before a thought entered my head. The moment it did, I started for the bus next to ours. I wasn't the type to talk myself out of things. It's the reason I caused the most trouble.

I knew Braxton was awake. She was a night owl like the rest of us. The only morning person was Houston. No matter how late he turned in, he was always up bright and early the next morning. By the time I reached her doorstep, I had my phone out once again.

When in Rome…

Except, this territory that we'd stumbled upon didn't have any rules. This was the first time the three of us had been after the same girl. It would help if one of us had even the smallest claim to her, but she didn't seem to know who she wanted, either. She went on a date with me, kissed Houston, and treated Rich like her white knight.

Braxton wasn't Rome. She was no-man's-land.

Sighing, I sent her a text.

What kind of pizza do you like?

It was a lame attempt to get her to talk to me, but I had nothing else to go on. We weren't friends. Once again, Houston had made that decision for everyone.

Future GF: Not hungry.

It had taken her longer than I liked to respond. My response was short and to the point.

Did I ask?

I imagined her annoyed sigh from my lonely watch under the moon. The buses where our roadies bunked were parked farther away, but I could still hear them enjoying their night.

It must have been nice to live free.

Bound had all of life's luxuries except one.

Future GF: Cheese…with pineapples.

I groaned as I typed back. *You're definitely not marriage material. Men like meat and girls who like meat.*

Future GF: I'll get over it.

I chuckled under my breath when I read her response. She was quicker to text back that time.

Braxton was a challenging book to crack open, but fuck if those pages weren't worth it.

I made a quick call to the same pizza place and ordered a cheese pie—reluctantly with pineapples—and then stood outside for the hour it took both orders to arrive. The time quickly passed since I spent it texting Braxton.

Returning to the bus, I dumped all but two of the pizza boxes on our dining table, grabbed one of the beer cases the roadie had procured and started back out the door.

"Wait. Where are you going?" Rich shouted after me. He was sitting alone on the couch, looking sad as fuck. Houston was gone, and I didn't care where. My guess?

He was brooding in his bunk.

"To the fucking moon."

I stormed off our bus and headed over to Braxton's with the pizza and beer balanced while I sent another text.

I'm outside your door. Open up.

She was back to making me wait longer than fucking necessary for a simple, goddamn response.

Bummer, she sent when she finally texted back. *You should have called first. No one's home.*

I didn't bother to respond. Braxton was anything but coy, so I knew she wasn't opening that door. Setting the case of beer on the ground with the pizzas on top, I headed for the bus where Xavier was bunking. He was busy on a call that had to be personal since it was after midnight.

Lucky me.

Snagging the spare keys to Braxton's rig, I escaped without him asking questions.

Marching back across the lot, I stopped when I noticed the empty ground. Where the hell was the beer and pizza? There wasn't a person in sight.

Unlocking the bus, I stormed up the steps, and to my surprise…Braxton wasn't alone.

She was cozy on the couch with Rich, who had the balls to be eating my pizza and beer on top of ruining my plans.

"So that's how it is? You let him in and not me?"

"He's nice without a motive," she responded with no remorse. "How did you even get in here?"

"Spare key." I teased her by twirling the cheap ring it was attached to around my finger.

"Boundaries, Loren. You need some."

"Not interested," I said as I flopped onto the couch next to Rich and spread my arms along the back, "and it's too late, so don't bother trying."

"It's never too late to grow up, but I digress. Why are you two here? Isn't being alone with me forbidden?"

I sighed and scratched the stubble growing under my chin. "Houston leads when we're in the mood to be led."

"And it was never our decision to kick you off," Rich mumbled.

I agreed with a nod even though I knew Rich's rebellion would pass quicker than a shooting star. He wanted too much for us to be friends again and thought being a doormat was the way to do it.

Braxton perked a brow. "So this is an 'I Hate Houston' party? Are you sure you don't need adult supervision?"

"Yup, you're the guest of honor, and no, unless you're feeling frisky." I winked, but she was too busy staring at the ground with this lost look in her eyes.

"I don't hate Houston."

"We figured when we caught you kissing him." And how could I forget his hand up her shirt? Until this morning, I was the only one who'd copped a feel.

As far as I knew.

I cut my gaze at Rich just as Braxton spoke.

"Jealous?" she shot back.

It turns out I preferred her smug. It sparked my creativity. Sitting three feet from her, I imagined all the ways I'd fuck that look off her face.

"I took you on a date," I answered her. "That should have at least gotten me to third base. Houston blew through first and second, and all he had to do was make you cry."

"The only man around who's made me cry is you." That shut me up, and she noticed too. "Nothing to say?" she challenged.

"No. I'm not proud of that."

Braxton didn't seem impressed by my sincerity. "So what happened, Loren, because nothing's changed. Did you forget to tell your inflated ego?"

I dug my fingers into the couch to keep from reaching for her neck. Braxton had this innate ability to turn the most forward-thinking guy into a prehistoric caveman. I was a sleeping bear, and she was daring me to wake. Houston and Rich were no different. The latter might have been a nice guy, but he was a liar too. She'd learn that sooner or later if Rich ever made a move this century.

"If you're looking for someone to be good to you when he's not inside of you, I'm not your guy. Rich might ask for seconds, but that's about it. Houston will forget you the moment you're gone."

"Why are you telling me this like it matters? First, I'd have to be interested."

"Your head may not be, your heart is still up for debate, but your pussy cries a river whenever one of us walks by, so save your bullshit for the limp dicks and the simps."

Her lips parted at my audacity before she caught herself and narrowed her big, brown eyes.

Yeah, I know.

I'm an asshole who's just leveled up, but it's like I said before. Braxton brought the shit out of me. She was under my skin and getting deeper by the day. I turned to Rich, who had his head back, eyes closed tight as fuck, and face pinched from wincing. I was fucking this up even worse than Houston. "This rig have cable?"

Opening his eyes, Rich looked at Braxton, then me, and sighed. "It should," he mumbled.

I stayed silent as he grabbed the remote from the cushion next to him and turned on the TV. The sound immediately filled the bus. I didn't care what played if it was distracting. Rich channel surfed for a few minutes before settling on a movie that looked like it was just starting. It wasn't until Gal Gadot popped on the screen that I realized what was playing. Snatching the remote from Rich, I cranked up the volume.

A stunningly sexy woman running around in armored lingerie and knocking douchebags on their asses? Count me in.

It wasn't nearly as exciting as Braxton claiming to be a fucking sex addict, though. I didn't buy it, but I couldn't stop thinking about it.

Braxton, the nympho.

Nothing else sounded sweeter.

Or too good to be true.

Rich went to grab three beers from the fridge. They were only slightly chilled, but they would do. Popping the tabs on all three, he handed one to Brax, who surprisingly accepted. He shoved mine into my chest, spilling some on my shirt.

Fuck, I just had this dry cleaned.

We exchanged angry looks, warning each other to back off before focusing on *Wonder Woman.*

Yeah, I got his beef. I kept screwing up. So sue me.

Luckily, the one useful skill my father taught me was how to clean up a mess.

Rich had already eaten most of the three-meat pie meant for me, so I grabbed the one still closed and lifted the top. I watched Braxton pretend to watch the movie for a moment before I spoke. "Cheese and pineapple," I announced like I'd baked it myself.

"I told you I wasn't hungry." Just then, her stomach growled loud enough to be heard over the movie.

Perfect timing. I wasn't surprised since I doubted she had much of an appetite before and after the show.

"Your stomach disagrees. Eat up."

"I don't need you to tell me when to eat, Loren. I'm perfectly capable of reading my body's signals without your help."

On cue, her stomach growled again, only louder this time. Huffing, she leaned forward and snatched one of the slices. After taking a bite, chewing, and swallowing, she tossed me a cheeky smile before rolling her brown eyes.

Grabbing one of the slices from her box instead of mine, I tore off half in one bite as if it would feed me insight into Braxton's mind. It wasn't bad. Of course, I was hungry as fuck. I couldn't recall the last time I ate either. Being on the road could be brutal. There were times when even the most basic human necessities were either optional or forgotten.

We watched the movie mostly in silence. Rich and I made more than a few male appreciation sounds, which disgusted Braxton to no end.

"Do you ever dress up for Halloween?" I asked without preamble, rhyme, or reason.

She cut her gaze toward me. "Where is this going?"

I nodded toward the TV and Gal Godot playing a fierce Amazonian yet clueless demigod. "With the right phone calls, I'm sure we could get you an authentic costume. Then again, I'm thinking of Poison Ivy. Assuming you're a natural redhead."

My eyebrows rose as I waited for an answer. Of course, she didn't take the bait, not that I expected her to, really.

"You're exhausting," she said with a shake of her head.

"I prefer riveting."

"How about pig?"

"You could call me that, but then you'll still want me to fuck you." I shrugged.

Our gazes met and held, but she didn't bother denying it. Falling into bed together was just a matter of when. We were wrong for each other in every facet but one—the chemistry we made could crumble the strongest mountain.

Because I was a gentleman when it suited me, I let her off the hook by focusing on the movie until my eyes started to droop.

The film wasn't even close to ending. How long was this fucking thing?

I'd need a bed soon, preferably with Braxton in it.

Movement from the corner of my eye caught my attention in time to see her yawn for the third time in ten minutes. While she was falling asleep, she must have thought up the perfect punishment for me because she turned on her side, and just before laying her head in Rich's lap, she paused.

"Is this okay?"

Fucker didn't even hesitate before nodding. She rewarded him with a sleepy smile, and then her head was on his fucking thigh.

I saw red.

It bloomed on Rich's cheeks like he was a thirteen-year-old girl.

"Why am I friends with you?" I blurted out of jealousy. I didn't give two shits about hiding it. "You're twenty-seven years old, blushing because a girl asked to touch you *platonically*." I shook my head in envy disguised as disgust. That should have been me Braxton was lying on. "God, you're embarrassing."

"Ignore him," Braxton mumbled as her eyelids drifted closer together. Any moment now, she'd be out cold. "He's jealous because you're sweet, and I like you more."

Feeling evil as fuck, I smiled at them both.

"Too bad he's married," I snitched to Rich's horror.

Lucky for him, Braxton had fallen asleep.

TWENTY-FIVE

Braxton

I WAS RELIEVED THE NEXT MORNING WHEN I WOKE UP ALONE. I JUST wasn't sure I'd slept alone. All I could vaguely recall was being carried into the bedroom and laid gently on the pillow-top mattress. That and a gentle kiss pressed against my forehead. I just wish I could place a face to the lips.

Following the smell of French toast, I entered the kitchen and caught Loren stealing a slice of bacon from a plate meant for me.

"So, you're a thief, too." I shuffled toward the counter and the delicious smell coming from the plate. I could seriously get used to having a chef around. It seemed like a worthwhile investment for a girl who was clueless in the kitchen.

"Morning, baby fawn."

His gruff greeting told me he hadn't been awake long either. I wasn't a morning person, so add what he said to me last night, and I found myself snapping. "Stop calling me that. My name is *Braxton*, but if you insist, can you at least drop 'baby'?"

"I'd rather drop Fawn," he said as cool as a cucumber.

Oh, hell no. I didn't like my stomach's positive reaction to that. "Fine. Whatever. It's a fucking deal." I thrust out my hand for him to shake and pretended I wouldn't like being that intimate with him.

He stared at my hand with amusement before his gaze snapped up to meet mine.

And then he kissed me.

The bastard fucking kissed me.

Loren's kiss wasn't rough like Houston's. He wasn't demanding, but he wasn't generous either. No, he teased and toyed with my lips, heart, and tongue until I was ready to put my soul on the line. He was a playful kisser, leading me in only to pull away. With just one kiss, he taught me how to please him.

"You taste like cheese, beer, and a bad night, *baby*."

In typical Loren fashion, he cruelly shoved me out of the clouds he'd placed me on. I recoiled in horror at the reminder that while Loren looked like a magazine spread, I haven't even brushed my teeth.

I turned to run for the bathroom and my toothbrush when he grabbed me and spun me back around.

"I came to tell you that we're back on the road soon. I didn't mean to kiss you, but I'm not sorry."

"Don't do it again," I forced myself to plead.

"Nah, I'll definitely do it again."

"Loren—"

"It won't be your fault," he interrupted while pulling me close. "You can't help that I don't want to resist you."

I frowned at Loren while pretending my heart wasn't shoving shit aside to make room for him. "You almost sound like you're in love with me," I tried to joke to break the tension.

Loren didn't even blink. "If we're not careful, I will be," he told me seriously.

My lips repeatedly parted and closed until a sane response came to mind. He'd given me no reason to believe him, and yet... the meadow my brain was telling me I smelled right now urged me to. I still hadn't figured out this new emotion. Only that Loren triggered it.

I *so* didn't need this right now.

"What am I supposed to do with that, Loren? We barely know each other."

Our second kiss came sooner than later. It was slow and gentle. The kind that lingered long after the culprit was gone.

"Whatever you want," he whispered against my lips. His head

popped up, and then he was giving me a hard look. Stern on Loren was a foreign look, yet *so* fucking good. "As long as the answer isn't no."

"It has to be." I pulled away, and he let me. "You know my secret."

"Thanks for reminding me," he responded, lips curled. He was definitely pissed now, but I sensed it wasn't at me. "Who the hell told you that you were a nympho? Was it by chance a licensed professional?"

"I'm serious, Loren." I shook my head when my voice failed me. I could feel shame clawing at my skin. It was still too familiar. "You can't joke about this."

"Believe me, no part of me finds this funny. I didn't take it seriously until I realized that someone put this shit in your head. Give me a name. I want to deal with them."

I shook my head while looking down at his Derbies. "You didn't know me then. I crossed too many lines, and I hurt too many people. I was willing to let it destroy me."

"Show me someone who hasn't made mistakes when it comes to sex, Braxton. If I could remember their names, I'd tell you a few I wished I'd met when I was sober," he mumbled.

I didn't want to laugh, but I did. Inside. "If you had an upbringing like mine, you'd understand. They say it takes a village to raise a child. Mine wasn't the most forgiving."

He grabbed me again, holding me by my hips, but it was his eyes that conquered me. Not his hands. "How can I convince you?"

"You can't."

"Have you met me?" he shot back, his voice deep and low. When he kissed me again, he tasted like morning dew. I couldn't get enough. When he finally pulled away, it took us both a moment to catch our breath. "I can run circles around your demons, Braxton. Just let me in, and I'll handle the rest."

The romantic I kept in line with a bat and knuckle dusters sighed in appreciation. He was saying all the right things. Naturally, since it was Loren, I was suspicious. "If this is some ploy to sleep with me, I'll make you sorry."

"Fuck, you're sexy."

It was hard not to fall for his gorgeous smile that lit up my entire life, but I managed. "You won't think so when I slip orange dye in your shampoo or shave your eyebrows while you sleep."

Sliding his hands into the pockets of his jeans, he stared at me for a long, long, *long* time. "Duly noted, baby."

Denver, as it turns out, was a thirteen-hour drive from Phoenix. Add in the frequent stops, including our current one in some town bordering Colorado, and I wondered if we'd ever reach the city. We didn't have another show until Friday, which gave us two days to find trouble.

I didn't know we'd do it in one.

The warning stirred in my gut as I inhaled the air and tried not to fixate on this new turn of events. Houston hated me, Loren had a crush, and...I couldn't figure out Rich's angle. A part of me hoped he didn't have one because I liked being around him a little too much. I didn't have to keep my guard as high.

"Feeling all right?"

The voice was partially obscured by the howling wind, giving me no choice but to face them to solve the mystery. I thought I was the only one hanging around the buses. Everyone else had gone across the street to dine in the only two food options offered. Peeking over my shoulder, I expected to find either Rich or Loren waiting. Maybe even Xavier.

Of course, it had to be Houston. He was best at getting me riled.

Wearing his usual T-shirt and jeans combo, he held a black store bag from the gas station where we filled up the buses.

"For me to answer that, I'd have to believe you cared." Scoffing at the notion, I turned away from him. It hurt too much to look at Houston, knowing he cast me out. I wouldn't dare swim in those gorgeous, green pools and dream.

I listened to the plastic from his store bag rustle, followed by the pop of the tab on a can. "Of course, I care. If you bail, I'm short a guitarist. Again."

I spun on my heel, hoping I'd find remorse or a sign that he was joking. The strong wind whipped through his chocolate hair, but the rest of him remained unmoved. He looked like someone who'd come to conquer me.

"Is the tour really all you care about? You don't give a crap about me. Fine. What about Rich and Loren?"

It was the subtle tells with Houston. The ones like his quick pause before taking a sip that told me I was getting a rise out of him. The last time that happened, he kissed me. "You question me like you have all the facts."

"I've been around a while," I reminded him with a shrug. "I'll be around a lot longer. If I don't have them now, I will soon enough. You're really not that hard to figure out."

"Funny," he said, looking genuinely amused. "I was just thinking the same about you, little girl."

Careful not to hand him my anger on a platter, I let my feet carry me closer and stopped just out of arm's reach. "Now who's bringing a knife to a gunfight? Treating me like I'm inferior, pretending that I don't mean anything... It stopped working when I realized it's your only move."

"Is it?" he whispered before bringing the energy drink to his lips. He eyed me the entire time he drank his fill, and then he closed the last of the distance between us. I already knew his bite was worse than my bark.

I didn't fight him when he pressed me against the bus or rested his forearm on the black surface. The open door a foot away beckoned, and Houston had left the way to it clear. Running was exactly what he wanted me to do.

I stayed put.

The driver was gone, and so was everyone else. We had all the privacy we needed to hash this out. The only distraction was Houston's soap permeating off his warm body. He smelled so good.

"What do you mean to me?" he demanded out of nowhere.

"What?" I could barely catch my breath, much less follow his train of thought. Not with him this close.

"What. Do you. Mean. To me?

"I-I don't know."

"Then how can you be sure you mean anything at all?"

"Because of the way you look at me," I said without thinking. His head jerked back, and he blinked. I'd actually startled Houston Morrow. I lowered my gaze to his chest, expanding with every hard breath he took. "You look at me like I'm someone you never thought you'd see. You want me, but you can't have me, and that pisses you off, so you punish me."

We stood there for maybe thirty seconds, just sharing the silence before he broke it. "Braxton?"

"Yes, Houston?"

"When I look at you, I see something in my way. Nothing more, nothing less."

Pretending that didn't hurt was impossible, so I let him see my pain. "I'm not your enemy, Houston. I don't want to hurt you." When my fingers stretched to reach out to him, I curled them, keeping my hands to myself. "Any of you."

He stared into my eyes, and I watched the internal struggle whether to believe me in his. "Maybe not now," he partially conceded, "but you will. It's what we do to anyone who gets too close. We make them hate us, and then we hurt them before they can hurt us."

Pushing aside the ache in my chest, I let my anger rise.

And then I harnessed it.

"Is that what you did to each other? No wonder Rich and Loren hate you."

He paused, and then his eyes narrowed to slits as he tried to guess how much I knew. By the time his expression cleared, I already knew I'd gone too far.

"I don't cry over spilled milk, Fawn." Lifting his forefinger, wet from the condensation, he traced the edge of my tank's low neckline. On his third pass, the tip of his finger brushed my breasts. The cherries teasing my taste buds told me it wasn't a mistake. "I'd rather clean up the mess."

Tipping his can, he poured his energy drink down my tank until it was empty, and the purple bra I wore underneath was visible.

That. Is. *It.*

When my fist collided with Houston's lip, I didn't care about the consequences. He didn't look surprised, either. He smiled—busted lip and all—like I'd given him exactly what he wanted. I'd proved his point. Eventually, you want to hurt them because that's what they do. They make you crave it.

I went to hit him again.

This time he caught my wrist and squeezed.

"The first one was free. You'll have to work for the rest."

I smiled up at him as he waited for me to beg. "That's the beauty of everyone underestimating you," I told him. "They tend to drop their guard."

Twisting just enough, I brought my sharp heel down on his foot.

"Fuck!" he barked.

He was wearing sneakers today. Lucky me.

Houston's grip loosened enough for me to get away. I made it a single step before he caught me and forced me back under him. I was a little dazed from my back hitting the bus—enough time for him to recover control of the situation.

"Let me go." I tried to wiggle free, but it only drained the energy from me.

"Or what?" he taunted. "It's not like you'll get another shot at me."

Immediately, I stopped fighting and forced my body to relax. "That's what you said last time."

I winked, and Houston responded by crashing his lips against mine. As I tasted the sugar and citrus on his tongue and the cherries on mine, I heard his drink can fall to the ground.

Now both of his hands were free.

They gripped the hem of my skirt before shoving it up until I could feel the wind curling around my inner thighs and failing to cool the heat between them. Eventually, I came to my senses and broke the kiss.

"Houston—"

"No," he cut me off and pressed his forehead against mine. "Don't you say another word." We were so close that with each breath he exhaled, I inhaled. We stayed like that until desire overwhelmed indecision. And then he gripped my panties in his fist. "Goddamn you, Braxton."

One brute tug and they were gone.

My skin smarted from where the fabric had torn, but I was quickly distracted by his fingers. Pushing them between my lower lips, Houston drew my arousal like it only answered to him, and then he pushed inside of me.

"Oh, fuck, I—"

"There's a condom in my back pocket," he informed me. "Get it."

His thumb found my clit, lighting up the nerves like it was the Fourth of July. He didn't stop even when speech was no longer possible. Since I couldn't find the words to argue, I snaked my hips, riding his hand.

And now, we come to the part of my story where I alter not just my ending but three others as well.

"The rubber," he reminded me before pulling his fingers out of me and ripping open his belt. "You're getting fucked with or without it, Braxton. It's your choice."

I shivered at the idea of feeling him hard and raw inside of me, but there was just one problem.

I didn't trust him.

Reaching behind him, I quickly found the condom while he undid his jeans and released his hard dick. He was so long and thick that my breath caught in my throat. Angry veins traveled from the bulbous head down his shaft until reaching the fabric of his black boxers. I was too busy marveling over his cock to notice when he took the condom from me. Once his gorgeous dick was wrapped in latex, he crowded me against the bus.

We'd gone too far to turn back now.

Lifting my right leg into the crook of his arm, he brought the head of his cock to my entrance before meeting my gaze. "I want you to know this isn't personal." Kissing my lips, he whispered against them, "It's just business."

I tossed away his words before I could even consider them. I was too enthralled by the feeling of him slowly pushing inside of me. He took his time, making sure I was aware of every generous inch. We savored it. Our first and last time together.

Even with my arousal, I hadn't been fucked in years. My soft moans turned into a cry of pain when he finally reached the hilt. He filled me so completely I couldn't think of anything but him. And when he started to move…

I didn't feel cherished or loved.

I was something else.

Tainted.

Wild.

Free.

Feeling a grateful sob in my throat, I held onto Houston as if I were hanging from a cliff.

"Jesus, Brax," he croaked in my ear. "Never had…this good." He paused his hammering to push deeper inside, making me choke on my next breath. "*Fuck.*"

Shoving my tank and bra up my chest until my tits were free, his eyes and lips feasted. When he moved his hungry lips to my neck, I tilted my head to make room for him. Houston bit, licked, and sucked until I was sure my skin was bruised.

I didn't care.

There was nothing else I wanted more than to let him have his way.

I could already feel that familiar itch creeping from the shadows. I already wanted more, and we weren't even done.

A smile spread my lips as Houston fucked me harder.

Faster.

My breasts bounced in time with his wild thrusts as his belt buckle slapped my stomach. I welcomed the pain as much as the pleasure. His grunts and groans came more often, his movements more desperate, as his orgasm rose. Never one to do anything half-cocked, Houston's hand pushed between us, seeking out my clit.

"Don't think you're not going to come for me, Fawn."

Holding my gaze, he fucked me hard against the side of the bus. We both accepted that at any moment, someone could turn the corner and see what we were up to. Loren and Rich had gone to get us food and would be back any minute.

What would they do if we were caught? Would they demand a turn? Houston grunted when my pussy contracted excitedly around his dick.

If they did, I'd give it to them.

I'd let Houston, Loren, and Jericho fuck me as if it were their right.

"Right fucking now, Braxton. Come on my dick." Rotating his hips and hitting a spot I didn't know I had, that was precisely what I did. I came all over his fat cock.

Even with all the blood rushing inside me, filling my heart, ears, and pussy, I could hear the approaching footsteps and voices in the distance growing louder. Another minute or two, and we wouldn't be alone.

Hearing them, too, Houston began to pull away.

"No," I moaned, grabbing the back of his shirt and keeping him inside of me. "I don't care if we get caught. Don't stop."

He stared at me as he debated the consequences before giving in like I knew he would. Lifting my left leg over his arm, I was suspended in the air now. Houston then filled both of his hands with my ass and began pounding my pussy to a pulp. Mouth falling open from shock, I clutched his T-shirt tighter as I let him have his way with me.

"Why can't you just do what you're told?" he demanded. I could feel his frustration as he continued to fuck me. He didn't like that I'd made him so powerless.

Knowing that Houston's questions were never rhetorical, I tried to answer, but I couldn't manage anything more than choked cries as I clung to him helplessly. Those desperate sounds mixed with the ones our sweaty skin slapping together made as they filled the air. And when I came a second time, it was a thousand times more intense because Houston joined me with a harsh grunt.

I will never forget the hard yet vulnerable look on his face as he spilled inside the condom. It was so beautiful that for a careless second, I wished it was me he had filled.

Staring into each other's eyes, we shared our vulnerability until the moment ended abruptly when Houston dropped me on my feet. He hadn't been gentle when he was inside of me. I didn't know what I was expecting now that he was done.

We only had moments before we were caught, and keeping what we'd just done a secret was probably the one thing we'd ever agree on. Now that Houston was no longer inside of me, rational thinking had returned.

Houston shoved my skirt back into place before ripping off the condom and tossing it in a nearby bush. I was tempted to scold him for littering but realized how ridiculous that would be under the circumstances. I watched him fix his jeans and wondered how I could find a simple act so damn sexy. He then ran his fingers through his hair, trying to fix what I'd wronged. I couldn't even recall gripping and running my fingers through his thick brown hair as he rode me, but the evidence was there.

"Not a word of this to anyone," he whispered sharply when the roadies along with Loren and Rich were close enough for us to hear their conversations clearly.

I could even make out Loren proselytizing the use of night cream *before* fine lines and wrinkles had a chance to show. I'd never known a guy so meticulous about his appearance. It only made him more unique to me.

"I'm not an idiot, Houston."

What we had done was wrong on so many levels. We played together, and he treated me like shit he'd stepped in and couldn't get off his shoe.

Our biggest offense was Loren.

We both knew he wanted something more with me, and what did I do? I fucked his best friend.

No, no, no, no, no, no, no.

It was happening all over again.

My threads were beginning to unravel, and this was just the start.

Whore.

Harlot.

"Are we done here?" I snapped at Houston. I needed to hide and never show my face again.

"No. One more thing." As he held me arrested with his stern gaze, I knew I wasn't going to like whatever he was about to say. "If you find yourself with an itch you can't control, *I'm* the one who scratches it." He paused to let the words sink in. "The only one, Braxton. We clear on that?"

No. Not even a little bit.

"The only thing you get to tell me is what songs we're playing on Friday night. I'm not interested in anything else." I turned to go when he gripped my nape. My back slammed against his chest a moment later.

"Make this the last time I tell you," he said as he pressed his mouth against my ear. "Stay away from Loren and don't even think about Rich. That pussy's mine now."

He shoved me away.

TWENTY-SIX

Rich

I HAD A KNACK FOR SENSING WHEN SOMETHING HAPPENED BETWEEN BRAXTON and one of my best friends. I found them standing too close and a little disheveled even though they were both fully clothed. It was in the small details, such as the hickey on Braxton's neck that hadn't been there an hour ago and the corner of Houston's shirt sticking through the open fly of his jeans.

A blind man could tell that they'd screwed.

Loren was a few paces behind me, trading fucking beauty tips with the makeup artist we hired for Braxton—who right now looked like she wanted the ground to swallow her whole.

I made a quick decision.

I decided I didn't want to spend the rest of the tour breaking up the fights between Houston and Lo. Yanking Houston's shirt from his fucking jeans, I let him see my disapproval before turning to Braxton. Her hair was pinned up, and for once, I didn't bother asking permission. I undid the messy bun at the top of her head and watched the red waves fall around her shoulder, hiding the hickey taking form.

She stared at me with those wide eyes that I once thought so innocent, and since I wasn't as cruel as Houston or Loren, I didn't let her see my disgust before turning away.

Braxton was every bit the tease Loren accused her of being, but I never took Houston for a hypocrite. Since the day she joined our band, he made it clear Braxton was a no-fucking-go, and then the moment our backs were turned, he fucked her.

The real irony was that I knew him too well. In the space between betraying us, screwing Braxton, and getting caught, I'd bet my life that he'd already claimed her. He couldn't keep us from doing what we wanted, so he switched tactics and decided to take Braxton for himself.

The only silver lining was that Braxton wasn't a doormat.

Clearly, she was going to do whatever the hell she wanted, but Houston was arrogant enough to believe her submission was a sure thing.

Whatever happens next, the two of them deserved each other.

"Rich—"

"Whatever you're about to say, don't. It became meaningless the moment you spread your legs for him." I'd only admit to myself that my disappointment had little to do with Loren. He really liked her, but so had I.

"Back off her."

I couldn't hide my shock at Houston coming to her rescue. Shaking my head, I wondered how we got here. "You're unbelievable," I mumbled.

"Can we please talk about this later?" Braxton begged.

"Why?" I snapped at her. It was her turn to look surprised since I'd never been unkind to her. "Don't want Loren finding out that you're not worth his time?"

I couldn't change that I'd been dealt that blow.

Braxton blinked at me until the tears she tried to hold back slipped from her big, brown eyes. I felt the apology on my lips and swallowed it back. I was sick of being sorry for the way people made me feel. Not this time. She made me believe she was someone I could hold on to. Why not let her suffer the consequences?

Braxton excused herself, disappearing onto the bus. A couple of minutes later, Loren finally stopped being a fucking chatterbox and showed his face.

Immediately sensing something was up, his smile turned into a frown. "What's up?" he questioned as soon as he saw my face. He was clutching the food bags with the takeout he'd brought back for Braxton. He was already doting on her when it had never been his style. "Why do you look like someone shit in your cereal, bro?"

"Ask him." I tilted my head toward Houston. I doubt he regretted fucking Braxton, but at least he didn't look smug. He'd perfected his blank expression so well that when he spoke, his confession was the last thing I expected.

"I fucked Braxton."

"What?" Loren's head swiveled between Houston and me. I could already tell he wouldn't let himself believe it. That's how far gone he was, and she just—I forced my fists to unclench. "What the hell is he talking about?" Loren asked me. Before I could answer, he'd already turned back to Houston. "You fucked Brax?" he echoed. "When?"

"Just now. Right here."

Loren's gaze narrowed to slits. "You're lying."

"Regardless, I'm not interested in convincing you. From this point forward, you two should have no problem concentrating on the tour. If you want to get laid, snag a groupie. They're all around."

If I'd had an inkling of how low Houston would stoop just to keep control, I would have warned Braxton. He'd used her, and the worst part was that she still had no idea.

Loren stepped toward Houston until they were nearly chest to chest. "You think because you fucked her first that makes her untouchable?"

"We both know you're too full of yourself to settle for my sloppy seconds. Get back on the bus."

"Fuck you. Maybe I'm done taking orders from you."

Houston's eyebrow perked before he taunted, "You got a better option?" He already knew that Loren didn't. None of us did. It wasn't about the wealth we'd obtained but the connection to another human life. Without each other, we had no one.

"Maybe I do," Loren returned, making my heart stop. What the hell was he talking about?

"If you want to run back to your daddy's lap, be my guest, but don't kid yourself into thinking the grass will be greener. Oh, and we won't take you back this time."

The air was dipped in so much tension I thought the sky might crack open from the strain. Loren was silent, but his rage rang loudly. Houston was taking a huge gamble. Loren would have appreciated it if it weren't his pride and sanity on the table.

I didn't exhale until he walked away but not before he shoved the bag of takeout that he'd bought for Braxton into Houston's chest. We watched helplessly as Loren stormed away in the opposite direction of the bus.

"Don't," Houston commanded when I started after him. "Loren's not going anywhere. He'll be back."

"I hope you know what you're doing," I said, voicing my hope that this was all part of his plan to bring us back together. I missed my friends.

Scrubbing his hand down his face, Houston gave me a tired look. "I'm doing the best I can, Rich. What more do you want from me?"

"To find a way that doesn't involve you being a major dick. Braxton didn't deserve what you did. Neither did Loren."

He rolled his eyes as if what I said was debatable. "If it helps you sleep better tonight, look at the bright side."

"Which is?"

"No one gets her now."

It took us sixteen hours to find Loren.

"What the hell are you doing here?" he croaked. With one eye open, he peered up at me as I stood over him. We'd found him passed out inside a rundown motel room that I was sure someone had died in. The floor was littered with empty bottles, condom wrappers, and discarded clothes. After bribing the desk clerk for a copy of the room key, Houston had chased off the chicks we found cuddling with drunk-ass Loren.

"What the—" Loren barked. As if he were a vampire, the

drama queen used the floral comforter to shield himself from the sun Houston let in after he ripped open the curtains. "Close the fucking curtains. What the hell is your problem?"

"You," Houston answered coldly. "Now get the hell up."

"Bite me."

It sounded like we'd time-traveled to our teenage years when our hormones made us hate each other for a time as well as ourselves. Now we were men and back to hating each other but with only our egos to blame.

"Braxton's *one* chick. One. You just found three to fuck you in the middle of nowhere," Houston pointed out. "Not to mention we're all better off anyway."

Loren flew from the bed, naked and as shameless as the day he was born. I'd seen his dick so many times that I could probably draw it from memory…

I wasn't quite sure how I felt about that.

"Really? Your solution after screwing me is to insult my fucking intelligence? You didn't screw Braxton for the band. You wanted her for yourself." Shoving Houston, he yelled, "Admit it!" Loren was loud enough, I'm sure, to be heard from the next room.

It was only a matter of time before someone freaked and called the cops. I could read the outlandish headline now.

Bound Spotted: Sources report the purchase of stolen organs at shady Colorado motel.

I shook my head.

"If you understand my motives, why do I need to explain them?" Houston shot back. He really was a dick. "Admitting what you already know is not what you want to hear anyway. You want me to tell you that everything you imagined is true. You want to know that her pussy is fucking crippling. I can't get the feel of her out of my head even while I'm standing here listening to you bitch about it. She let me use her, Lo. She begged me for it. She made me not care if you turned the corner and caught me balls deep. She's fucking insatiable. I may never get enough, but what I do know is that Braxton is mine as of yesterday. It should be easy now for you to keep your hands off and your mind on the music."

Houston's chest expanded as he inhaled deeply and exhaled. "Are we done now? Can we go?"

"That's mighty fucking convenient," Loren replied in the flattest tone ever.

"Come back to the bus."

"Why? Do you need me, Houston?" he taunted. "A monkey could play the bass. That's what you told me once, remember? Find someone else."

Calvin had been a magician at guitar. We never thought replacing him would be possible, but it helped that we hadn't given two shits about that cunt. Loren was different. For Bound, there was no one else. For Houston and me, there was no one else.

Houston had already drawn the same conclusion. The only problem was that he'd never admit it. I watched him silently make a decision and knew what angle he'd play before he even spoke.

"While you might have lost your appetite for money, I know the last thing you want is to hand it all over to Carl fucking Cole when he sues you for breach of contract, so get dressed, and let's go. We've been in this shit-hole too long."

It took another thirty minutes of Houston and Loren bickering like an old married couple before we made it back to the buses. All at once, we stopped in our tracks.

Braxton was leaning against the door of our rig.

She wore a white muscle tee with a black graphic design I couldn't make out from where we stood. What I assumed was supposed to be a dress only extended to the middle of her thighs. If her attempt was to tone down the sexy, she failed miserably. Not when she wore those black, lace stockings that only reached an inch below the hem of her dress. On her feet were distressed brown leather boots that had seen better days. She had the oddest style, but it worked for her. Before yesterday, I would have fucked her just as hard in her weird clothes as I would out of them.

Braxton couldn't seem to decide which of us to focus on since we were all watching her. Glancing at the ground, she pushed away from the bus.

We didn't move to meet her halfway as she approached.

Instead, we stood together like an impenetrable wall, giving no parts of our thoughts away. By the time she stood in front of us, her indecision was gone, and my jealousy was at an all-time high.

She only had eyes for Loren.

"I'm guessing the cat is out of the bag since you can't even look at me," she said to him. Loren wore dark shades to shield his eyes from the sun, but his head was slightly turned, making it obvious he was ignoring her. "I'm sorry."

His head swiveled forward, and then he was pushing up his shades. "You're sorry?" he echoed in a deceptively pleasant tone. Braxton shifted nervously under Loren's piercing gaze. "Whatever for, baby fawn? You're not my bitch." Tilting his head toward Houston, he held her stare. "You're his." Needing to punish her further, he shoved past her as if she weren't there.

Braxton didn't lash out at him, though.

No, she turned her rage on Houston.

"Is this why you fucked me?" she asked as if she didn't already know the answer. Her eyes were red, telling me she'd been crying and on the verge of doing it again. Knowing Braxton, she'd hold it in until she was alone. She hated anyone seeing her weak more than she hated weakness itself.

Houston's gaze held no remorse as he regarded her. "A lot of good it did me. You're the perfect muse, Bambi. If I ever write a song about how shit *can* get worse, I'll be sure to think of you."

Seeing the look in Braxton's eyes, I took a step away from Houston. I watched her debate for a moment, and after several deep breaths through her nose, the anger left her gaze.

"Stay away from me."

"Sure," Houston readily agreed. I knew better, though, and so did Braxton. Hooking his finger under her chin, Houston tilted her head back. "But can you stay away from me?" Too quickly for Braxton to dodge, he placed a kiss on her plump lips and walked away.

I watched her innocent brown eyes turn vengeful and then frantically search the ground. I didn't catch on until she'd already snatched up the largest rock she could find.

"Stop kissing me, asshole!"

Shit.

I barely got my arms around her before she could chuck the rock at the back of Houston's skull. Losing her grip, it fell to the ground with a heavy thud.

She would have knocked him out cold.

God forbid he'd end up with a concussion. It was too early in the tour to have to cancel a show. I could already hear Carl's mouth, and it put me in a foul mood.

"Take it easy," I snapped when she struggled against me.

"I'm going to kill him. Let me go."

"All the more reason not to." Hell, I believed her. Braxton's temper was unmatched. When she kept fighting to get away, I gave up trying to detain her and hauled her over my shoulder.

"Put me down, Jericho!" Gripping my shirt with one hand, she pummeled my back with the other. I'd never let her fall, but I understood why she didn't trust me. Houston and Loren had done a number on her, and it had only been a week. "Where are you taking me?"

Ignoring her, I boarded the bus Houston vacated for her. The driver didn't blink an eye when I passed him. I carried her through the living and bunk area and into the bedroom where she'd slept alone the night before. After putting her to bed myself and forcing Loren back to our bus, I made sure of it. I could still hear that sweet sigh she released after I'd kissed her forehead.

It seemed like it happened a lifetime ago.

Setting her down on the bed, I turned to go.

"Wait."

I paused at the door, but I couldn't face her. I didn't want her to see my anger when I had no right to be.

"Don't go."

"We're leaving soon," I announced as if it explained why I was so eager to go. Every second I spent with her was like barbed wire around my heart. She was bleeding me dry, and she didn't even notice.

"It's still a few hours to Denver." She paused, and I knew she was weighing the chance of me saying yes to the question on her mind. "Keep me company?"

I could no longer hold my thoughts in when I whirled around to face her. I'd have plenty of time to be disappointed in myself later. "Why would I do that?"

Twenty-four hours ago, I would have never told her no.

Braxton paused as if realizing this before drawing her knees to her chest and hugging her legs. "You're mad at me."

What was your first clue?

"No," I lied and shook my head as if that would convince us both. "I have no reason to be."

That part was true, at least. Braxton was free to fuck who she wanted. I just didn't realize how deep it would cut when she didn't choose me.

"Yes, you are," she called me out. "Tell me why."

"It doesn't matter." I turned to go, but my feet felt too heavy to carry me forward.

The mattress was memory foam, making movement impossible to hear. I didn't know she'd stood from the bed until her soft hand was in mine.

"Stay with me, Jericho. You can still hate me. Just stay with me."

"I don't," I said against my will. I swallowed hard, shoving the rest of the idiotic words down. Unfortunately, she pressed her tits against my arm in a move that seemed too calculated for Braxton not to have done it intentionally.

"You don't what?"

"I don't hate you."

"Then why won't you look at me?"

Because I was too busy staring at a spot on the wall as if it held the answers to why I kept fucking up my life. The more I became invested in Braxton, the deeper my hole grew. "Because you're Houston's now. That means I shouldn't want the things I do when I look at you."

She placed her hands on my chest, and I let her push my back against the door.

"I can be yours too."

Rising to the tips of her toes, Braxton pressed her lips against mine. I didn't kiss her back. I held out as long as it took her to flick her tongue against my lip ring and then the seam of my lips. I gave in then with the eagerness of a boy finally reaching first base and the skill of a man who'd been starving.

She tasted too good to be true.

I let her have her way to see what she'd do without anyone leading, and she didn't disappoint. She was as insatiable as Houston claimed. We'd stop in between long enough to take a breath and then be back at it like we couldn't survive being apart for too long. Her lips were softer and fuller than I imagined they'd feel against mine, and the little sounds she made had me thinking of other devious ways to use them.

I always knew Braxton was in my head.

She proved as much when she dropped to her knees in front of me.

I didn't stop her when she unbuckled my belt and pulled the tab on my jeans free. Before she could unzip me, though, I grabbed her wrists. "You don't have to do this," I told her and immediately wished I could take it back. "I'll stay."

"Well, that's a relief." She pulled her hands away.

Fuck.

I wasn't sure how I was going to make it through the night. I'd never been this hard. Instead of standing, however, she held my gaze.

Brown was the most common eye color, but on Braxton, her gaze felt like being caught in a cosmic storm.

No matter how much her eyes gave away, I was always left feeling more befuddled than before.

I was too caught up, wondering what was happening inside her head, to notice her undoing my zipper. I snapped out of it in time to push my jeans and boxers down enough to free my dick.

Braxton wasted no time licking the tip. I felt like I was fourteen again and about to receive my first blow job. Only this time, I was emotionally invested.

After teasing the head until her mouth was nice and wet, she slowly took more of me. I liked that she didn't concentrate too hard on getting me off or think that looking away would somehow make sucking my dick less awkward. Braxton held my gaze, picking up on my cues whenever she gripped me too tight or didn't apply enough pressure. When she found her rhythm, my eyes drifted close, and my head fell back against the door.

Fuck, Braxton.

I kept my eyes closed for maybe two seconds top—long enough to realize I wanted to watch every second. Her cheeks were hollow now as she tried to swallow more of me. She made it halfway before giving up and bobbing her head back and forth. Had she been a groupie, or I'd been Houston or Loren, I would have made her take all of me. Instead, I respected the rhythm she set for as long as I could. The wet sound of me fucking her mouth was curling my goddamn toes.

Eventually, the pleasure she offered trampled all over my good intentions. I was too far gone to think of anything else but dumping my cum down her throat. My fingers slid through her red hair before gripping the lush strands tight. I then did the most challenging part of reaching the orgasm I needed.

I pulled her mouth off my dick.

The lower half of her face was soaked in her effort to please me as she blinked her teary eyes at me in confusion. My dick was angry with me, too, for interrupting. Thick veins ran down my shaft coated in her saliva until reaching the purple head that hung mere inches above her lips.

"I'm going to fuck your mouth now, okay?"

Her brows dipped as I lowered my jeans around my thighs. "Wasn't that what we were doing?" She looked like she wanted the ground to open and swallow her whole. "You didn't like it?"

I smiled down at her before bending, grabbing her hands, and kissing each set of knuckles. "It was perfect."

I didn't know how to explain what I needed without scaring her, so I said nothing. Bringing her hands around to my ass for her to hold, I slipped my fingers through her red hair before getting a good grip.

Her lips were made for sucking cock, and I intended to help

them reach their full potential. The day we met, I thought she'd been wearing a soft shade of red lipstick. And then I realized that everything about Braxton was natural—her red hair, swollen lips, perky tits, curvaceous ass, and her ability to captivate me by just being in the room.

Braxton's lips parted when I teased them with my dick, and I was back in her mouth again with a groan.

This time I didn't hold back.

I wasn't Rich, and she wasn't Braxton.

She was a warm mouth and nothing more.

I used her.

I felt her hands still gripping my ass as I worked her mouth. The sounds that filled the room as I went deeper than she dared were obscene. I pushed her limits and mine. I threw away the nice guy she expected and fucked my way to oblivion. The part of my mind still lucid, worried I might go too far.

And then Braxton opened her mouth as wide as she could and tipped her head back for easier access. Each time my concern for her slipped through the pleasure, she'd dig her fingers in my ass, warning me not to stop. It went like that until the telltale signs of my orgasm approaching washed away all thought.

I didn't even think to stop myself from coming down her throat.

She held me in her gaze, and I held her in mine when I felt my orgasm arrive while my dick was lodged in her throat. Her right hand curved around the back of my thigh, soothing until I gathered enough strength to pull away. I barely got my jeans back up before my knees gave out, and I lowered onto the floor in front of her. It was a narrow space, so I stretched one leg out and bent the other.

Neither of us spoke as we fought to catch our breath. When my vision cleared, I saw the mess I had made of her makeup, the sweat wetting her light freckles, and the drop of cum resting on the corner of her lip.

Reaching out, I thumbed it away. When I never cared before, curiosity had me licking my thumb instead of wiping it on my jeans. I've heard horror stories, and for the first time, I felt insecure. Braxton smirked when I blinked in surprise.

Twenty-seven and I'd never tasted my own cum. It definitely had some zing to it.

"Did I hurt you?"

On the outside, I remained calm. Inside, my heart was punching a hole through my chest. It seemed like a lifetime had passed before she shook her head. It wasn't until she rested her hand on my thigh that I allowed myself to relax.

"It was wonderful, Rich. I loved giving you what you need."

"What about you? I can—"

She waved me off before I could finish. "I can't be alone right now. Just stay with me. I'll have everything I need."

"I've never known a sex addict to turn down sex," I said while eyeing her skeptically.

"Have you ever known a sex addict?"

I chewed my lip as I mulled that one over. None of it made sense. Braxton seemed perfectly in control of whatever desires lurked behind her brown eyes. They weren't the driving force of her actions.

So what could have driven her to think the worse of herself, to see only the ugliest parts? We all had them. Braxton feared hers while Houston wielded, Loren flaunted, and I kept them buried.

"No, I guess not."

Feeling like I could trust my legs again, I stood and helped Braxton to her feet. The bus rumbled to life, and the moment I let go of Braxton's arms, the rig pitched forward, sending her back into my arms. My back connected with the door before I caught my balance while holding Braxton against my chest.

"Let me return the favor," I whispered even though we were alone. Well, mostly, if you didn't count the driver who was separated from the rest of the bus by a door. My dick twitched in my jeans at the thought of going down on Brax. I'd been wondering what her pussy tasted like since I first heard her play.

Too eager to wait for her answer, I walked us the two steps it took to reach the bed before shoving her down on it.

"You don't have to do this," she told me, reversing our roles. If it had been my friends in my shoes earlier, it would never have crossed their minds to turn her down.

Houston was too demanding, and Loren too entitled.

Braxton and I found common ground in our first instinct being to deny ourselves for the sake of others. "I-I'm okay. We can just talk and get to know each other."

You don't want to know me.

It would only shatter the illusion she was already clinging to.

"Sure," I said, pretending I'd play along. "I'll ask the first question." Crouching before her, I removed her boots before standing back up. That damn dress was next to go.

"Um...okay."

I took the time to remove her black bra and thong, both lace like the stockings adorning her legs. I left those on. My gaze raked her naked body, but Braxton didn't cower or move to cover herself. She let me look my fill. When I felt my dick waking up for round two, I pushed Braxton on her back before climbing on top of her, fully clothed. This wasn't about me. If my dick came to play, I'd spend the drive to Denver fucking the memory of every man that came before me from her mind until there was only me.

"Would you rather I eat you from the front or behind? Frankly, I'm partial to you sitting on my face."

TWENTY-SEVEN

Braxton

SURE, ONI ASKED ME TO FIND A WAY TO KEEP THREE STUBBORN ROCK gods from quitting each other. I wasn't so sure my vagina was the tool she had in mind, though. Sridhar was ruthless enough not to care how I got it done, but she would disapprove of me being stupid enough to fall for them. If I took up the charge and somehow pulled it off, I'd be a national hero. Maybe even a savior of the world since the idols' reach was global.

I snorted.

The three of them acted more like prom kings with huge chips on their shoulders—broad as those shoulders might be.

My hand found and desperately gripped Rich's broad shoulder when he asked how I'd like my pussy eaten. It felt like I was falling even though I was lying down.

Rich was the perfect anchor.

Sensing that I needed soothing, he peppered my neck, shoulder, and breasts with kisses while waiting for my answer.

I wanted this night to be about him, so I tried turning him down. He'd seen right through me as I'd seen through him. I didn't know he'd been making room in his heart for me until I allowed his best friend to have me.

Rich had been nothing but friendly and patient and not at all forward. At the risk of sounding arrogant, I'd begun to wonder if he had someone waiting back home. Celebrities hid relationships, sometimes entire families, all the time.

Obviously, I knew now that he wasn't involved.

Even if he did like his blowjobs dirty, he was too much of a sweetie. No way could he be hiding a girlfriend or, worse…a wife. It wouldn't just shatter my trust in him. It would shatter the last piece of myself that I still thought good.

Rich's tongue found my nipple, circling the nub before biting it gently. "Tell me, Braxton. I might go insane if you don't." He punctuated his claim by thrusting his hips and letting me feel his erection. It boded well that he was quick to recover.

"F-from behind," I finally answered. My voice shook since he was still thrusting between my legs. "I want you to taste me from behind."

His jeans and the hard ridge trapped underneath supplied the perfect friction for my clit. It began to throb uncontrollably as my arousal grew. I tossed my head to the side, unwittingly leaving my neck where Houston had already left his mark open for Rich to ravish. I felt his tongue and teeth abusing the skin there and making my toes curl as he humped me with all the vigor of being inside of me. When his hips lost their rhythm, I knew he was close to coming.

And that he was still wearing his jeans.

I wasn't an expert on high-end clothing, but they looked expensive. Eyes closed and close to coming myself, I was fumbling to get them out of the way in time when Rich stopped abruptly and flipped me on my stomach.

I was startled until I remembered his offer to eat my pussy.

Yanked onto my knees so suddenly, I yelped in surprise. A moment later, I was burying my face in the rumpled bedding when his tongue began lashing my clit. The hungry sounds he made, the relentless pressure…he ate me so thoroughly, I came as I fisted the bedspread.

And the only sound I made was a choked scream.

Abandoning my sensitive clit, Rich kissed my lips and then my trembling thighs. The moment my muscles relaxed, and I felt in control of my body, I let myself collapse onto the bed with a satisfied sigh. I wouldn't allow myself to relax too much, though, since I needed a shower and a toothbrush. I felt the bed move and heard Rich settling in next to me before pulling me into his chest. I could feel his erection poking my spine, and even though my body protested moving, the desire to do something about it won.

Turning in his arms, I sat up and reached for his belt. He caught my wrist with a question in his tired eyes. Pulling my hand free, I undid his belt and jeans, and the moment he was in my hand, I swallowed half his dick in one gulp. I was much slower at taking the rest of him. He'd shown me how he liked it, and I was more than eager to give him whatever he needed. I even threw in a few tricks of my own that had him coming down my throat for a second time.

I'd barely finished swallowing his cum before he pulled me to him and began placing gentle kisses on my lips over and over. With his mouth still pressed hard against mine, he whispered, "I think I'm in trouble."

Rich deepened the kiss, which saved me from telling him he had no idea how much.

"It's a fucking wrap, Denver. Good night!" Houston shouted to the roaring crowd. The stage lights at the Broncos Stadium at Mile High were cut—our cue to get the fuck out of Dodge.

We were ushered through the tunnel the players used to enter the field, and as soon as we were behind closed doors of the room we were given to lounge in before the show, Houston rounded on me while ignoring Xavier waiting nearby. I knew he was ready to rip into me for the mistakes I'd made out there tonight. No one except a professional would have noticed, but it didn't matter because Houston Morrow was a persnickety scrooge.

He was also looking for any reason to go to war with me.

"Whatever you're about to say," Xavier cut in before he could start, "it will have to wait. There's been a development."

"Does it require all of us, or can I go?" Loren snapped. When our gazes met, he immediately looked away as if he couldn't stand the sight of me. My tired sigh was drowned out by Xavier, who ignored Loren's bitchiness and began speaking.

"Braxton's popularity has grown to the point that the label felt it wise to sell backstage passes without my knowledge."

"Wait. What?" Loren snapped. He then looked at me and narrowed his gaze as if this were my doing.

"They want to meet Braxton," Xavier answered with a shrug and then an apologetic look thrown my way. For some reason, I hadn't anticipated this part of touring with an international rock band. I'd been too busy trying to keep my wits when they were around. "She's new to Bound and virtually unknown. The public's only knowledge of her is what we tell them."

"We like it that way," Houston pushed through gritted teeth.

"Well, your fans, the reason you're all here and still have a career, *don't*. It won't kill you to mingle for an hour. You've done it before. I don't see the problem."

"The problem is that we should have been told."

"I'm telling you now," Xavier returned unperturbed. "Besides, they didn't pay extra to meet you three anyway. They want her."

"Yeah," Loren returned with a scoff, "right. I'll believe that when my dick falls off." He stormed off, making it clear he wasn't looking for someone to argue.

"This is nuts," Rich said, surprising me with his objection. "This is Brax's first tour. We've only done a few shows. How do they know it won't be too much for her?"

I raised my eyebrows at that. I'm sure I could handle a polite conversation with complete strangers. I did it almost every day working at Succulent. "Well, if you guys could manage it with your sparkling personalities, I'm sure I'll be just fine."

Rich's gaze swung to me, his silver eyes panicking when he realized he'd offended me. I already knew that wasn't what he intended. He wanted to protect me, but I could handle myself. I was getting good at dealing with their shit. "No, that's not—I didn't mean—"

I took his much larger hand in mine and squeezed. "It's fine. I know."

My palm tingled from touching him so soon after last night. I knew from the twinkle in his eye that he was reliving it too. Since I couldn't entirely blame my reaction on lust, I let him go and calmly waited for the sweet scent of berries to dissipate.

First Loren and now Jericho.

What did these new emotions mean?

As if nothing was amiss, I turned, intending to address Xavier only to have my attention stolen by something else. Houston was beautiful even when he was foreboding. Right now, his eyes and the set of his lips told me I'd have a long night ahead of me. I squared my shoulders, pretending I didn't care that he knew something happened between Rich and me.

"When do the meet-and-greets begin?" I questioned Xavier.

He looked at his watch and then at the door behind me, which had just opened. "Now."

I was glad that I wasn't still holding Rich's hand. I didn't want the first impression Bound's fans had of me to be that I screwed my way to the top. Everyone knew that assumptions spread rumors, and facts were optional.

I *happened* to have fucked, sucked, and made out with each member of Bound.

It wasn't how I'd borrowed a place in their world. I had no intention of sticking around. All that mattered was that I'd have the strength to walk away when it was time.

I tried to follow Xavier when he started for the small group teeming with excitement, but a hand wrapping around my wrist stopped me.

I knew by the cruel grip that it was Houston.

Rich was too gentle when he wasn't getting blown, and Loren was still off somewhere sulking. Besides, Loren would have grabbed my ass and wouldn't care who saw.

"This isn't happening," he announced once I spun on my heel to face him. I was still debating whether to break his nose or not. "Go back to the bus. I'll tell Xavier you were feeling sick. The label will refund them their money."

I pulled my wrist free, and to keep from making a scene, Houston let me.

"You might be okay with that, but I'm not. Look at them." Of course, he ignored my order and kept his gaze on me instead. "I'll bet you at least one of those people over there sacrificed more than just a couple hundred bucks. You can refund their money, but you can't give that back. I won't disappoint them."

"That's exactly what you'll do if you go over there. They want something that we can't give them, Braxton. Not now, maybe never. We're expected to act like friends, like we can stand to breathe the same air. We can't."

I considered his point. I knew surliness couldn't be the reason Houston, Loren, and Rich would be willing to turn their fans away. Bound was the glass bottle they used to trap their emotions.

On stage, they were free to let them run wild.

Once the lights died, they shoved it all back inside, keeping it corked until the next show.

The problem with glass was that it shattered under pressure.

Rage, defiance, and sorrow were all they had to give, so they channeled it into their music and harnessed it on stage. They showed their ugly truth through a beautiful lens. The world believed that it was all a performance, and they let them because rejection was almost certain.

Obscurity protected them.

Until now, I assumed they were immune. I thought their devil-may-care attitude was the truth behind the façade. It wasn't. It was the mask itself.

And what of my own need to dissimulate?

Tonight, I'd stumbled my way through the setlist because I couldn't get past the sex occupying every corner of my mind. If it weren't for the meet-and-greet, I'd have gone after Loren, maybe cornered Rich, or convinced Houston to let go once more.

Spoiler alert: It would have been a lie.

I was incapable of not wanting more. I warned them as much at the festival.

Running back to the bus and hiding sounded like a no-brainer—until I remembered that I was on this tour to do the opposite.

"So what?" I said, pissing Houston off enough to fry an egg on his head. "You think they're looking for perfection? Your pain is what called to them, Houston. They won't turn away. Not as long as you keep giving them something real."

"Flaws over frauds," Rich mumbled behind me.

I flashed him a grateful smile over my shoulder.

Yeah.

Flaws over frauds.

TWENTY-EIGHT

Houston

Braxton and Rich took off for the group before I could stop them. If she wanted to learn the hard way, who was I to object? I'd never be bored, that was for goddamn sure. She was perfect smiles and bright eyes as she greeted the group eager to meet her, while Rich hovered like her goddamn lady-in-waiting.

Resigned to whatever this night turned into, I headed for the opposite side of the room. There, from my perch on the sofa, I clocked every move Braxton made.

Five minutes passed, ten, and then fifteen.

I'd just managed to relax when Loren showed his face.

Leaning forward, the knot in my belly returned as I watched the public relations nightmare make a beeline for her. I wouldn't put it past him to purposely say or do something that would piss Braxton off and make everyone uncomfortable.

If I were forced to make another public apology because of him, I was breaking every bone in his body.

He was barely in the room before Braxton noticed him. She tensed with each step he took toward them. I could tell even from here that she was holding her breath. He'd completely stolen her attention. When he reached the group, Loren waited until the last second before it was awkward to hold out his hand. The guy closest to him shook it vigorously, and Braxton visibly relaxed.

Knowing the group would eventually make their way over to me, I waved over one of the roadies waiting nearby and had him lay out some free merchandise on the table in front of me. They might have been here to meet Braxton, but there was no way that I'd get away with brooding alone in the corner. Not as Bound's front man.

I loved meeting the people who connected with our music. Just not so much when I wanted to choke Braxton while fucking the shit out of her. It was all I could think about. We were playing with fire, but they pretended it didn't burn.

Ten minutes later, I was shaking hands and signing T-shirts. Another half-hour and I was waving them out the door. I turned to Braxton the moment we were alone.

Well, mostly.

"Good job," I told her once I had her attention. I wanted to say more, perhaps something less condescending, but my lips wouldn't move.

The blank look she gave me told me she wasn't flattered. "I didn't do it to impress you."

My smirk I failed to catch made her eyes light up like a Christmas tree—if that tree were on fire. "Nonetheless."

Sighing, she turned to walk off. "Get fucked, Houston. I'm busy."

I studied the curve of her ass as she stormed for the door.

She was heading back to the buses, and I swallowed the urge to follow her. I wondered if she could read my thoughts or simply felt me watching her, and that was why she peeked over her shoulder at the last minute.

The cold look she gave me before disappearing through the door had the opposite effect she intended.

I had two choices at this point.

Get a grip or get a groupie.

I followed Braxton to the open door, leaning my shoulder on the jamb as she spoke to one of the roadies. He pointed her in the direction of the buses, and she took off, unaware of the chaos around her as the crew tore down and prepared to load our equipment in the cargo trucks.

Meanwhile, there was another crew with a replica setting up

in Dallas for Monday night's show. The label had greedily packed our schedule to squeeze every penny they could, knowing it would be the last they would make out of us. Negotiations were already in the works to buy back every one of our masters, even if it bankrupted us.

The moment I was sure Braxton was gone, I found Rich, who was talking shop with one of our stage techs. The roadie, seeing the look on my face, scrammed mid-sentence. Rich looked confused until he noticed me.

"You really need to work on your people skills," he preached for the thousandth time.

As usual, I ignored him.

People rarely saw a good person when you were too nice. All they saw was a mark.

"Did something happen between you and Braxton?" I got right to the point.

Rich's silence said it all, but I still wanted to hear him say it. "Do you really want to do this right now? Right here?"

"Yes or no, Rich?" He shrugged before looking off and keeping his mouth closed. The last time Rich was this stubborn he'd lit a match to his life and was still trying to clean up the mess. Braxton's defiance was spreading through my camp like an incurable disease. She needed to be stopped. "Have it your way."

I started for the tunnel that Braxton had just disappeared through.

"Wait. Where are you going?" Rich called out. When I didn't stop or turn back, he rushed after me until he reached my side.

"If you won't tell me, I'll make Braxton."

"Are you serious right now?"

"As a fucking heart attack."

"Fine! All right!" he yelled, making me stop in my tracks halfway through the tunnel. "We fooled around, but we didn't have sex, so just leave her alone. You've done enough."

Had I?

I thought I'd made myself clear, but every move I made, the three of them found a way to outmaneuver me.

I moved Braxton to another bus, and they followed her.

I fucked her, knowing Loren was too proud and Rich too cautious, and Braxton somehow convinced them to act outside of their nature. I know because she'd done the same to me.

Fucking her hadn't been planned.

Wanting more was the most shocking surprise of all.

When I reached the end of the tunnel and burst through the security door, I found an even bigger problem on my hands. Braxton's bus was being towed away as she stood on the side with everything she owned at her feet.

Again.

"What the hell happened?" Rich wondered out loud. I didn't respond, knowing it was rhetorical since I'd been with him. He repeated his question to Braxton the moment we reached her side.

"Bus broke down. Something about the radiator. They're towing it to the nearest shop to see if they can get it running again by morning."

Xavier spotted us and quickly made his way over. I already knew what he'd say before he even spoke. "So here's the deal, Braxton's bunking with you again until we get the rig fixed," he announced in a way that brooked no argument. "And before you ask, I've already checked. There are no extra bunks anywhere else. The crew is doubled up as it is."

Xavier, Braxton, and Rich all paused, waiting for my reaction. I silently weighed the pros and cons before deciding the damage had already been done. I needed time to rethink my strategy.

"Let me know when the bus is back in commission."

Taking Braxton's elbow, I pulled her toward our bus. The silver lining was that now I might get a good night of sleep. The moment Braxton occupied a room, the air changed, making the people inside feel lighter on their feet. Sometimes she had me thinking I could fly. It was hard to forget that, even when she was gone.

Even after you pushed her away.

I didn't worry about her bags, knowing one of the roadies would grab and store them on our bus, but Rich didn't seem to want to take any chances. He was just as eager as me to get Braxton settled back in with us.

"You do know both of my feet work, right? I'm capable of putting one foot in front of the other," she sassed.

She never. Fucking. Let up.

Neither did I.

I smiled down at her right before I let her go, only to haul her over my shoulder. Her surprised yelp and cry of outrage had every head in the vicinity turning our way. They watched her being carried back to our cave where she belonged. I even caught some of the house staff recording on the sly. Our roadies already knew not to pull that shit. Xavier was already on it, though, handing out threats of injunctions like it was Christmas.

Once we boarded our bus, I set Braxton on her feet, and she looked around like she was seeing it all for the first time.

"Welcome home," Rich said sappily.

I rolled my eyes while Braxton's back was still turned.

Looking over her shoulder, she smiled at him in a way that implied they shared a secret between them.

Jealousy was an ugly thing, and mine was about to rear its head. I didn't like them having a thing.

"Thanks." She looked around again. "Where's Loren?"

He'd disappeared again after the meet-and-greet. I knew he couldn't have gone far since we weren't sticking around. The drive from Denver to Dallas was too long, and after his latest stunt, I wasn't taking any chances.

"He's around."

Whenever Loren wasn't getting his way, the social butterfly tucked his wings and cocooned himself in hate. His absence was his way of punishing the world for not appreciating him enough.

The crestfallen look on Braxton's face told me it was working flawlessly. For once, she didn't try to hide it, meeting both of our gazes before disappearing inside the bedroom. The sound of the lock sliding into place echoed through me.

I turned to Rich.

He was watching the closed door at the end of the hall like he was debating whether to go after her or not. Feeling my stare, he turned to me.

"Find him."

TWENTY-NINE

Loren

"ARE YOU SURE YOU DON'T MISS IT?" I ASKED OUR ASSISTANT. SHE'D just finished slipping me the weed I sent her to find.

"For the last time, Loren. *No*."

Danielle, formerly known as Daniel, stormed off, swaying her hips paid for by me—so to speak. Her insurance company had refused to cover her surgery because it hadn't been "medically" necessary.

And there lies the problem with our inherited human nature.

We only bothered to take care of one another when it was too goddamn late.

I was trying to talk myself into going back to the bus when Rich found me. The look on his face told me that I was pissing him off, but I couldn't find it in me to care. I knew he was just as fucked up about Braxton and Houston screwing, but he and I had different ways of handling our problems. He dealt with them. I didn't.

Simple.

"Are you really going to do this now?" he asked me as he came to stand in front of me.

"Do what?"

"Sulk and pout and make everyone around you as miserable as you are."

I nodded once just to piss him off more. "Sounds like a plan to me."

"What Houston did was fucked up, but you're no better than he is. You weren't playing fair either."

"What are you talking about?"

"Arizona. You told Braxton about Emily."

I'd forgotten all about that.

To make him feel better, I chose to pretend I hadn't. "Good fucking thing for you that she was asleep. Close one, huh? Are you planning to tell Braxton that you're already married, or are you waiting to knock her up first and put a ring on her finger? Bigamy is illegal, you know."

"I wasn't going to tell her anything because it wouldn't have mattered."

I heard the "but" at the end of his statement and waited for the other shoe to drop. The longer he took to spit it out, the more guilt I read all over his stupid face. "So, what changed?" I finally pried, keeping my voice casual.

At least I have weed.

"Let me guess," I drawled when he said nothing. "You fucked her too?" I felt my heart beating out of control as I waited for him to admit it.

"She kissed me."

I balled my fists and put all my focus on not using them on my best friend. "And?"

No way that was all they'd done. Rich had stayed with her for the rest of the drive up to Denver. I just assumed they'd been playing Scrabble or something since they were both Houston's doormats.

"We didn't have sex."

"So what did you do?"

"Not all of us kiss and tell. Now come the fuck on. Time to go."

I smiled even though he'd already turned away, and it wasn't entirely forced. "I didn't think you had it in you." That made him stop in his tracks. "I didn't think you'd cheat on your wife, fuck behind your best friend, and screw over your other best friend. Good job growing some balls, man."

"Fuck you, Loren."

"You did, remember? You're just mad that I didn't want seconds."

Rich stormed off, and I smirked as I watched him go. Maybe now he'd finally give up this dream of us being friends again. The next time I was in L.A., I'd be sure to spit on Calvin's grave. He hadn't been from Portland like us, hadn't grown up with us either. We didn't owe him shit.

Sometime around one in the morning, I moseyed back over to where the buses were parked. Even high as fuck, I still noticed one missing.

Best couple of grand I'd ever spent.

THIRTY

Braxton

I woke up much earlier than I liked for a Saturday morning. I wasn't sure I'd ever get used to the rocking of the bus that told me when we were back on the road. I didn't leave the stateroom last night even after Loren made his presence loud and clear. I didn't want to allow him to take his anger out on me—even if it wasn't entirely misplaced. Guilt didn't mean I had to be his punching bag.

By now, he and Houston probably knew what I'd done with Rich. I didn't think that Rich would kiss and tell, but something had tipped them off. It was hard not to remember the thrill of Rich fucking my mouth and the power I felt when pleasing him.

Some have a natural instinct for sex. Some need to be taught to let go. The rest spend their entire lives fucking and never quite get it.

Anyone who knew what to look for would see right through me.

I'd been taught that sex outside of the marriage bed was a sin for which there could be no forgiveness. It contradicted the teachings of a merciful God, but my parents had been adamant. I'd burn in hell for all of eternity.

Whore.

Sinner.

Doomed.

How else could I rationalize dropping to my knees for Rich less than a day after spreading my legs for Houston?

I loved every moment.

Being with Houston and Rich had bared more than just my body. I hadn't felt free until I let them touch me, hold me…use me. I had an agenda when I agreed to do this tour, and now there was something in it for *me*.

If I truly had a sickness, I hoped I never found a cure.

This time I wouldn't be left alone. The three rock stars sleeping on the other side of the door wouldn't use my body and then blame me for enticing them. They wouldn't run into the light and beg for salvation. Houston, Loren, and Jericho had no interest in being saved. It was in the darkness that they thrived.

My thoughts were too chaotic to lull me back to sleep, so I dragged myself from the bed and relieved my bladder. With only one eye barely open, I shuffled out of the bedroom as quietly as I could. The last thing I wanted was to wake the prom queens. The windowless bunk area was still dark despite it being morning and filled with the loud snores of a slumbering bear.

Rich.

Now that I was back on the island, I planned to invest in a pair of noise-canceling headphones. Otherwise, I had a year of sleepless nights ahead of me.

I made it three more steps before I was stopped by a muscled arm lined with thick veins that shot out and blocked my path. The passage was narrow and the arm long enough for the strong, talented fingers to connect with my empty bunk. Staring back at me were eyes so dark that in the shadows of his bunk, I could only *feel* Loren watching me.

He was the last person I expected to find awake before dawn.

Houston was usually the early riser. My theory was that he used the quiet time alone to plot how to make the rest of our lives hell.

Leaning forward, the faint glow of the LED lights activated by the dark allowed me to see Loren's tired eyes. I wondered if he'd been up all night and if it was for the same reasons that plagued me?

I'm so sorry.

I couldn't tell him that, though, because Loren was too used to getting his way. I owed him nothing.

"Are you going to let me through? It's too early in the morning for your shit, Lo."

Loren stared at me for several heart-pounding moments before moving his arm. I thought I'd gotten off scot-free when that same arm hooked around my waist and proved me wrong.

I was lifted off my feet before I could tell him to let me go. I was then dragged inside the bunk and the darkness surrounding him.

I didn't fight him when he placed me on the mattress next to him. Even with all the custom modifications they'd done, the bunks were narrow, and Loren took up a lot of space.

There was nowhere for me to go.

Spooning me from behind, Loren trapped me between his naked body and the wall. Who the hell slept in the nude with other people sleeping less than five feet away? All he wore was his medallion.

"Sorry, were you going somewhere?" the sarcastic ass finally spoke.

With sleep adding an extra dose of gruffness to his voice, my reaction was the same as drinking fine liquor. My belly warmed, and I was drunk instantly. If I were standing right now, I'd be swaying on my feet and then lying about the cause to keep my dignity.

"Yup." Before I could push his hand away, his arm tightened around me, and I knew it wasn't a reflex. By now, he knew my natural instinct was to fight even when I didn't want to. "Do you mind?" I snapped. It was obvious he wouldn't let go.

"Actually, I do. I've been staring at this fucking ceiling and listening to that whore snore all night," he griped, referring to Rich. "I was finally drifting off when your rude ass stomped through here like you wanted to be noticed."

"I was not stomping."

"But you wanted to be noticed?"

I didn't respond. Whatever I said, he'd find a way to twist it.

Unfortunately, my silence spoke louder. I couldn't see Loren's face, but I knew he was smug.

"Jericho is not a whore," I whispered and immediately felt lame. It was the only thing I could think to say with his footlong spreading my ass like a bun. I wanted to see for myself if he was truly as long and thick as he felt.

Please, God, no. It wouldn't be fair for Loren to be this cocky *and* back it up.

Houston was big.

Rich was bigger.

Statistically, *one* of them had to have a little dick, right?

"Defending your boyfriend while you're spooning his best friend's dick? Real classy, baby fawn." I rolled my eyes at his insistence on using a nickname that didn't make any sense. I'd asked him a dozen times to stop, but he was determined to claim me any way he could.

Was Loren that desperate to have me or using me to provoke his friends? Houston wanted them to keep their hands off, but he never banked on me being the problem. Men never do. It's why women made better spies and were ten times as lethal.

Rather than waste time explaining that Rich and I weren't together when he already knew, I decided to kick him while he was already down. Loren's mind might be sharp, but my claws were sharper.

"Jealous?"

I waited and waited for a response that never came. Had he finally fallen asleep? I tried to peer over my shoulder, but he held me too tight.

"Loren?"

"I don't answer stupid questions."

Don't head butt him, Braxton. "No. You only ask them and then throw a tantrum when you don't like the answer."

Loren tucked his face inside my neck with a tired exhale that I felt in my bones. I hated myself even more for being the cause.

As if he could hear my mind turning, he said, "Go back to sleep, baby fawn."

This time I found myself smiling at the nickname. I hadn't broken him, after all. "I thought we had an agreement?"

"Yeah. So did I."

I didn't say anything after that. Shutting me up had been his plan, and it worked. There was no way I was going back to sleep, so I decided to recite the musical alphabet in my head. I needed something to distract me from wanting to ride his morning wood. By the time I reached F-sharp, the slow sound of his breathing, which told me he was asleep, pulled me under.

I woke up for the second time that morning, and the notable difference was that I wasn't alone. The bus was still rocking, but I barely noticed it.

I noticed the hand underneath my shirt.

I noticed how it palmed my tit as if it belonged there.

If only I wore bras to bed. Honestly, I didn't get those chicks. I hardly wore them when I was awake.

Loren's audacity didn't surprise me. Nor did the thrill I felt by it either. I'd been asking for trouble when I allowed Loren to snuggle me in the first place.

There was too much between us to pretend nothing was there at all. We'd already ruined each other, and when the pain began to dull, we stupidly ask for more.

"I know you're awake," he mumbled before kissing my neck and squeezing me until my hard nipple stabbed his palm. Realizing the bunk had grown darker despite the sun rising while we slept, I glanced over my shoulder.

The privacy curtain had been drawn.

Whatever was about to happen, Loren had planned it. Probably from the moment he put me in his bed. I guess he had to get his beauty rest first. With the two of us being the only ones awake, there was no one to stop us from causing more trouble.

"I'm awake."

I didn't object when he licked his thumb before finding my nipple and teasing it. "Want to play?"

"You were an ass to me, Loren. Why would I?"

Why indeed. Secretly, I wanted him to pull down my shorts and slip inside me in the dark. No one had to know.

"You fucked Houston," he reminded me, but there was no anger in his voice. "And I'm not sure what you did with Rich, but, baby, I'm *pissed*."

"We weren't exclusive."

"And now we'll never be." I felt him skim his lips over my shoulder. "We can still have some fun, though."

Like icy shards cutting me deep and leaving me bleeding, I shut down. "Get off me."

When he pretended not to hear me, I took his hand and flung it away. I felt the loss, but I ignored it. I tried to climb over him and leave, but he pushed me back and climbed between my legs. There wasn't enough space for me to fight him and win.

"Shh, stop," he whispered when I squirmed anyway. I was a second from damaging his pride and calling out to Houston when he said, "I'm sorry."

"Fuck you." I turned my head away to stare at the drawn curtain.

"Just say when as long as the answer is now." From my peripheral, I could see him smiling down at me. He knew the effect his smile had on me. He knew how often it got me wet.

"I'm so sick of your toxic, narcissistic shit. Either treat me right or leave me alone." Still refusing to look at Loren, I shook my head. I'd done nothing but dole ultimatums since meeting these assholes.

"That's an easy one." Leaning down, he brushed the tips of our noses together and then our lips. I hated how sweet his kisses were. They were the dangerous kind. The ones that convinced you to put up with more than you should. "I really am sorry, baby."

"Are you?" I turned my head, letting our eyes meet. His gaze reminded me of the way light deceived when it broke the surface of the water. You never realize how deep the water reached until you were already drowning. "Prove it."

"How?"

He sounded eager, and I was almost sorry for intending to make him regret it. "I want to sightsee today, and I want you to take me."

"Done."

"I'm not finished." He looked wary now, and my sweet smile of false reassurance didn't wipe the look away. "I want Houston and Jericho to come, I want you to be nice to them, and I want you to be nice to me. At least for today."

I'll just have to figure a way to convince him when tomorrow comes.

"You want me to do what?"

I didn't repeat myself. He'd heard me the first time.

Blowing frustrated air through his nose, he considered my proposal.

"This isn't a good idea," he warned with a shake of his head. He had the cutest bed hair. The blond strands were ruffled from sleep, and I liked the look on him.

As he stared down at me, I felt sixteen again—only he'd be the cute boy next door. I wished I'd known him then. I wished it had been Loren I'd given my virginity and let use my body. I knew he would have stood by me.

"I don't care. I'm done living my life afraid of what tomorrow brings."

"Cool, so when we kill each other?"

I dug my nails into his naked back. "You're going to be nice, remember?"

Loren rolled his eyes, and then slowly, his demeanor changed. I wasn't sure I'd ever seen him look so defeated as he stared at the bedspread beneath me. "Tell that to them," he mumbled.

When his gaze shifted to me, and I saw the uncertainty in it, I finally asked the question that had been nagging me since Oni brought it up. "What happened between you? Why aren't you close anymore?"

Once again, I watched his mood shift. There was distrust in his eyes now since I shouldn't know that they secretly hated each other. "Who says we aren't close anymore?"

"You still call them your best friends, but you fight them like you're not. Am I not supposed to notice how you're always eager to get away from each other?"

"Friends fight," he argued with a shrug. The careless demeanor he tried to give off didn't match the angry curl of his lip. He was defensive, and that gave me hope when I shouldn't care.

"They do," I agreed. "But not like you. Not as often as you."

I tried not to look so disappointed when Loren moved from between my legs to lay on his back next to me. When he was settled, he folded one arm beneath his head. "It's this life," he mumbled while staring at the ceiling. "We didn't know how much we'd be giving up. We started to blame each other for our choices, even though we'd made them together."

"You resent being famous?"

He shook his head. "I resent how much I needed it. I traded one fucked-up existence for another. We all did. The only one who really had a choice was Houston."

I frowned at that. "So why did he do it?"

Turning his head, Loren stared at me for a long time, probably deciding whether it was safe to confide in me. I wish I knew the answer. I told Houston that I didn't want to hurt them, but pain was often caused unintentionally.

"Rich…and me."

Just as I was getting close, Loren decided he was done sharing. Ripping back the privacy curtain, he left me in his bunk alone.

Throwing my arm over my eyes, I wondered if, like them, I'd agreed to more than I had bargained. They were complicated at best and completely hopeless at their worst. Guarded, they were a labyrinth of emotions, questions, and riddles. I was traveling up this winding creek without a paddle, a map, or a clue. The hurdles they forced me to jump to reach them were high. I was already bearing the scrapes and bruises.

I summoned the energy to pull myself out of bed with a groan for the second time today. The moment I lifted my arm, I found Houston awake, sitting up and staring at me as if I'd kicked his kitten. Sensing I needed it to face the day, my mind conjured the image of Houston with a dozen kittens crawling all over him. I made sure he noticed the smile it brought as I hopped from the top bunk and landed on my feet.

"Coffee?"

I didn't wait for his answer before prancing through the door leading to the kitchen.

He followed me, of course.

Houston was silent as he sat down at the small table no one ever used. I knew he was trying to figure out what I was up to and how far I'd gone with Loren in his bed. I hummed to myself just to piss him off as I tinkered with their fancy coffee machine. I was slowly getting the hang of all the bells and whistles.

"What are you up to, Fawn?"

Ah, so it speaks. I kept my back to him while the first cup filled. "What do you mean?"

"Why are you asking questions that are none of your business?"

"That's your perspective. It's not mine."

"Cut it out, Brax. I fucking mean it. No more questions and no more pretending you care. None of us are going to fall in love with you."

Jesus.

Every day, Houston gave me a new motive to murder him. I wondered if there was a time when he wasn't so arrogant. I doubted it.

Grabbing the full cup when the machine stopped spurting, I set it down in front of him, knowing he liked it strong like me. Our black hearts beat the same hard rhythm.

"You're right. I don't care. I'm just curious." I chose to ignore his claim that I was looking for love. I wouldn't dignify his assumptions by answering them.

"Why?" he questioned after eyeing his coffee before pushing

the cup away. I smirked. Surprisingly, it never crossed my mind to poison him.

"Why what?"

"Why are you curious?"

"That's the thing about curiosity, Morrow. It's random and often pointless. A passing fancy. Oh, look, I'm already bored."

He stared at me a beat before his gaze narrowed.

Why yes, Houston, I do mean you.

"You're bored?" he echoed so low I almost didn't catch it.

I gripped the counter behind me in an attempt to appear casual. All it did was push out my chest. His gaze dipped briefly to my nipples poking through the thin tank before returning to me.

"Completely."

"So you're saying if I tried to kiss you right now, you wouldn't let me?"

"Are you asking permission? You never cared about it before," I tossed back.

"Irrelevant. Yes or no, Fawn?"

I kept my mouth shut.

When he slowly stood from his chair, I forced myself not to move. We both had a point to prove, and neither of us considered the consequences.

After all these months, he still hadn't learned that I would never make it easy for him.

I could already feel Houston's kiss intensifying the ache Loren had started between my legs. We both still had morning breath, for fuck's sake, but it didn't matter when he was this close. I was trapped against the counter with his hands on my hips. The tiny shorts I wore did nothing to protect me from his warmth.

Houston was a blazing inferno, and I was the match that lit him.

"Last chance, Braxton."

"Go to hell, Houston."

Smiling, he took his time, letting our lips meet. He was giving me the chance to make a choice, and I was still pretending

I didn't have one. It was irresponsible. Neither of us wanted to take the blame for what happened next.

He kissed me slowly and gently. The way he stroked my tongue with his reminded me of lazy Sunday mornings spent in bed with the sheets twisted around our tangled legs.

It was not at all what I expected.

With one kiss, Houston proved that he was the storm and the calm, and I, the destruction he left behind. As our lips continued to dance, my hands found his bare chest, moaning at the hard muscles there. I wanted him wrapped around me.

Feeling him pull away, I whimpered. If I weren't too far gone, I would have been embarrassed. So much need in such a broken sound. I didn't want to leave this dream world.

When I opened my eyes, he was staring down at me, mistrust and desire swirling in his green gaze.

"Play your stunts, Fawn. I do enjoy making you sorry."

Undoubtedly, if there were a girl out there more daring than me, of the three, Houston would be the hardest to conquer. He considered himself responsible for his friends and what remained of everything they shared. Letting someone in meant lowering his guard and taking a chance that the person didn't mean them harm.

I ached at the thought even as I spoke.

"Then piss me off, Morrow. That shouldn't be too hard for you."

THIRTY-ONE

Rich

THIS WAS GETTING WEIRD.

But not in the way that made me think shit was totally fucked. The hope stirring in my gut was real, and it wouldn't go away. Each day it grew stronger. Before, it never lasted past noon because my friends were jerks.

Whether she knew it or not, Braxton had taken up our cause.

Houston was suspicious and fearing the worst. Loren was still convinced he only wanted to get his dick wet. He claimed he was allergic to commitment, but I think he craved it more than he knew. At some point, we start to believe a certain perspective of ourselves, and no evidence otherwise can change our minds. The strongest illusion was delusion.

Loren looked at Braxton like she fed his soul, and he was eagerly waiting for just a little more. It wouldn't go over well when he finally realized it. He'd rather be told he had terminal cancer than to hear that he was falling for our insatiable rebel.

Right now, he was too occupied with Braxton's lips to worry about his heart. It was all I could do to keep my gaze forward while Houston navigated Dallas. Security trailed us in separate cars while we did this little outing. Braxton had invited us to go sightseeing, and none of us had the willpower to say no. Even if it was weird as fuck.

"Headstrong" by Trapt started to play, and Houston turned up the volume. I was pretty sure he was trying to drown out the sound of Loren and Braxton making out in the back seat. It didn't matter how high he cranked the volume, though. We were too tuned in to every move they made.

Even now, I could hear clothes rustling, followed by Braxton's soft sighs.

"It's a shame," Loren muttered when they finally stopped sucking face long enough. "I could be knuckles deep in your pussy right now, but you insisted on bringing food to a buffet."

Yeah, he was definitely taking a dig at Houston and me.

"How will I ever survive?" Braxton returned.

Loren chuckled, but I knew him. He didn't find it all that funny. Out of the corner of my eye, I saw him glowering at his phone.

I was just relieved it was over.

Braxton was no longer hiding that she was attracted to all of us. Before we left, she'd kissed me good morning while Houston and Loren looked on. I saw their jealousy when she pulled away, but they hadn't said a word. I didn't know what it meant that we weren't acting on it. We've never so much as double-dipped inside of a groupie, and now we were sharing our guitarist?

One of our songs started playing through the speakers, and listening to Calvin's insane riff was the first drop of grief I've felt since he died. As much as I hated him even after death, I couldn't deny his gift.

"Can we change the song?" Braxton grumbled from the back seat. "No offense, but I get enough of you guys when we're playing."

"You mean us," Houston corrected, darkness edging his tone. He even risked taking his attention off the road to pin Braxton with his gaze. "You're Bound now, or should I find a more effective way to remind you?"

I think everyone held their breath as they waited for her response. When it came, she didn't disappoint. She never did. Sarcasm and defiance were her weapons of choice. It didn't take us long to learn, but we were still figuring out how to know better.

"I don't know," Braxton mocked. She sounded deceptively

pliable. "I think the hundred and fifteenth time is the charm. Why don't you remind me again?"

Sinking lower in my seat, I turned my head toward the window to hide the smile playing on my lips.

I just knew she was batting those big, brown eyes at Houston and daring him to do something about it. I was itching to turn in my seat and see for myself, but I didn't want her to think that I was helping Houston back her against another wall.

Not this time.

Not when she made my knees this weak.

"Maybe Braxton should deejay," Lo suggested, breaking the tension. Houston had already refocused on the road. Since he was strangling the steering wheel, I knew the conversation wasn't over. At least for them. He'd resume it the moment he got her alone. "We all know Morrow only likes the sound of his own voice."

I couldn't help myself this time, so I peered into the back seat and found Braxton cutting her gaze at Loren. I also spotted the hickey he'd left on her neck right next to Houston's and mine.

"Why me?" she asked him when no one objected.

I couldn't tell if she was nervous about sharing her music choices or too smart to think that Loren was up to any good.

Maybe it was a little of both.

She didn't want us figuring her out because of what we might do with that information. Someone should have told her that she couldn't peer into our minds without baring a little of herself in return.

I see you.

Loren paused his brooding to focus on Brax. He licked his lips as he watched her as if he could already taste her tears. Or maybe he had something else in mind. If he only knew how good she tasted.

"Why not? Afraid we'll find out that you secretly love the Backstreet Boys? I suppose you think "I Want it That Way" was the greatest love song ever written."

"No," she returned, sounding confident even when Loren was forcing her to play defense. "But I do think "Goodbye Earl" is pretty killer."

"'Goodbye Earl,'" I echoed from shotgun. "Isn't that a song about a woman who killed her husband?"

Braxton shrugged, still staring at Loren.

I need you to notice me.

My head had my heart all twisted up. The feeling only intensified when Braxton finally looked my way. Her attention was like phantom fingers tiptoeing down my spine. Goose bumps appeared on my skin just as those full, red lips of hers moved. "I said it was killer."

She smiled at me like I deserved the privilege.

My heart skipped a beat while warmth filled my belly. Braxton must have read it on my face because her smile disappeared, and then she was pulling out her phone. I watched her tap the screen a few times, and after helping her connect her phone to the car using Bluetooth, Tool's "Sober" spilled through the speakers.

Unable to forget her confession four days ago, the lyrics took hold with an icy grip. They did their job and left only a warning.

I'm no good for you.

Braxton stared at me until she was satisfied that I'd gotten the message. Her red hair became a veil shielding her expression as she stared out her window. I could reach out my hand and touch her easily, yet she'd never felt so far away. Shifting my body forward, I rested my head against the back of the seat before closing my eyes.

I wouldn't listen.

I never did.

Emily hadn't warned me away like Braxton just tried to, but my friends did.

No one spoke again for the rest of the drive. We were too distracted, dissecting the lyrics of each song she played. We hit up the zoo first after Braxton admitted she'd never been. I didn't even want to know how someone reached adulthood without ever visiting a zoo. Even a petting one would have counted.

Xavier had made some calls and was able to get the place shut down for a couple of hours. Braxton's excitement level, which had been stuck on neutral, revved once we got inside, and she saw the first exhibit.

She actually thought those creepy-ass fucking lemurs were cute. I swear one of them stared at me as if he knew me or something.

Loren griped the entire time about the smell.

Houston remained impassive even when a male lion charged the fence and roared. It baffled even the keepers who admitted he was a pretty vocal lion…just never toward guests.

Braxton explained that Houston had that effect. Apparently, it wasn't limited to humans. Houston got some curious looks from the staff after that as they not-so-covertly whispered to each other. We moved on, and when we reached the giraffes, Braxton lost her shit. She talked endlessly with our tour guide about some chick named April, who'd given birth last year. I was confused along with Houston and Loren until she saw the looks we exchanged and filled us in.

April wasn't a friend of hers.

She was a giraffe we'd never heard of before. At the time, we were too busy fighting in vain to keep Calvin alive to realize a fucking giraffe had set the internet ablaze.

Braxton claimed the wave had only lasted a couple of months but that it helped the world lose themselves in something meaningful. At least for a while. As she talked, we nodded, pretending to give a damn until she turned back to our tour guide.

At some point, as we made our way through the park and for no reason at all, Braxton slipped her hand in mine. I wasn't sure if she planned it or was just caught up in the moment, but I didn't let go. If she noticed my tension, she didn't comment on it. She was thoroughly enthralled by the guide's boring facts about fucking flamingos.

I glanced at Houston, who was currently hiding behind his black shades. I could tell by the set of his lips that he'd noticed, and he wasn't thrilled. Braxton wasn't only defying orders. She was risking it getting out that we were making more than just music behind closed doors. Liking the fact that she'd chosen me to make her stand, I tightened my grip.

Houston could kill me and then pry her from my dead body if he wanted me to let go.

Braxton's hand was soft and small in mine, and I suddenly had this urge to go all alpha-dick and stake my claim. That was usually Houston's speed. I'd never felt this way with Emily. With Braxton, the possibilities of who I wanted to be for her were endless. I wanted to protect her from everyone.

Including me.

Knowing that when Braxton found out about my wife, she would never forgive me, I loosened my grip. When I started to pull away, Braxton's head turned, and then she was staring up at me, a question in that deceptively innocent gaze. My heart began to pound out of control.

Fuck.

She had me.

She so fucking had me.

I tangled our fingers once more, but she kept staring at me like she could read my guilty thoughts. She wanted to know why I tried to pull away. She wouldn't let it go unless I made her.

Desperate to avoid the inevitable, I did the first thing I could think of.

I kissed her right there in front of the tour guide and the other keepers trailing us while pretending to work. With a moan, she melted into me, not bothering to think twice as we spiraled deeper within each other's souls. I haven't been able to stop thinking about her lips since she wrapped them around my cock. I will never forget how it felt to have her on her knees for me.

I was vaguely aware of the guide trailing off mid-sentence, Loren storming off like I'd stolen his favorite toy, and Houston plotting to make us both pay. Xavier had faxed over NDAs for the employees to sign in exchange for our patronage, so word wasn't getting out, but that was never Houston's problem.

He wanted Braxton for himself.

He'd rather scheme and plot and make arbitrary rules than simply admit it so that we could deal with the fact that we wanted her too.

Braxton broke the kiss, and when our gazes met, we were the only two people in the world.

"Take me somewhere, Jericho. Just you and me."

It only took me half a second to pick up what she was putting down. Grabbing her hand, I pulled her back the way we came. We hurried over a bridge and underneath a covered walkway before crossing over to the tunnel that separated the park's east and west side. Or maybe it was north and south.

There wasn't enough blood left in my brain for critical thinking, let alone navigation skills.

The moment we were under cover of darkness and the prying eyes of the security cameras, I kissed Braxton again. With my hands on her waist, I kept kissing her as I backed her against the wall of the tunnel. I could hardly see shit, but I felt how crazy she was making me.

My hands drifted up, teasing her hard nipples through her thin T-shirt. She hardly ever wore a bra, and before now, I had no clue how much easy access turned me on. I groaned, thanking God for small favors as I shoved her shirt up, baring her breasts and wrapping my lips around her nipple.

She let me have my fun for a while, gripping my hair like she was hanging from a cliff, and I was her only lifeline but then…

"Rich."

I felt her trying to pull me away. My heart skipped a beat before plummeting to my stomach. Had she already changed her mind?

"I know this is our first time, and as much as I appreciate the foreplay, I assure you I'm good to go," she told me through her panting. "We don't have much time."

She smiled so sweetly that even though I'd been thinking about going down on her again, I didn't have it in me to deny her. She wanted to be fucked now, and I was more than willing to make that happen.

Today, she wore black denim shorts, which told me getting fucked in a zoo hadn't been her plan. She needed me bad enough not to care if we were caught. I quickly unbuttoned her shorts and helped her shimmy out of them since they were tight as fuck. She wore fishnet tights, but instead of patiently pulling them down her legs, I tore them at her crotch. After she gasped, I watched her surprise morph into desire. She was looking at me like all my past lovers had when it dawned on them that my lovemaking didn't match my personality. They expected sweet and gentle. This was the first time I wished I could oblige.

"I wish we had a bed right now."

She made this purring sound that reverberated deep in my gut and down to my dick. "Me too, but there's always later."

I kissed her again before turning her to face the wall. Her hair was pulled up, and her nape beckoned, so I kissed that too before bending her over. She stayed like that, her hands braced on the wall while I quickly undid my jeans and pulled my dick free. I silently prayed I had protection while I fished out my wallet and plucked out the single condom inside. *Thank fuck.*

"Hurry," she urged me.

I wrapped my dick up as fast as I could without breaking the rubber and fucking up my chances. We were all so hot and cold. There was no guarantee there'd be another.

With that reminder, I quickly found her soaked entrance. I needed inside her now. Slowly filling her pussy, I realized she was even tighter than I imagined. If not for Houston, I'd think she was a virgin.

"Rich..."

I couldn't respond.

She was too hot, too wet, and I needed her too desperately.

Gripping her hip with one hand and planting the other on the wall above her, I begin fucking her hard, showing her just how much.

I pulled her body into me even as I shoved into her from behind.

The sound of our skin slapping and my dick moving in and out of her pussy echoed around the tunnel, mixing with her moans and my grunts.

Sweat dotted my temple and collected on her back.

I lost awareness of my surroundings and didn't care if someone watched. All that mattered was that I chased this feeling.

This—fuck, I didn't know.

Whatever it was, it wasn't supposed to happen. She wasn't supposed to mean anything to me. Now it felt like I couldn't live without her.

Pulling her upright, I forced her front against the wall, and then I gripped her chin before turning her head. "What are you doing to me, Brax?"

"I don't know," she whimpered.

"You don't know?" I echoed as I pumped inside her. She shook her head as much as my grip allowed. "Bullshit."

I should have only cared about getting my friends back, but instead, my only concern was which of us got to keep her. If she chose Houston or Loren…I wouldn't be able to stay. I wouldn't be able to watch her be happy with them. I was a selfish prick, but I wanted to be *her* selfish prick.

Much too soon, I felt the familiar stirring in my gut as my heart rate increased. My body took over, pushing me toward the point of no return.

My hips began to thrust of their own accord.

Faster. Harder. Fucking with single-minded intent.

I fucked her so hard I feared Braxton would bruise from the force of my body using hers. Trapped against the wall, she had nowhere to go, no other choice than to accept my savage lovemaking.

Anyone nearby would immediately know what we were doing. The gallant hero I wanted to be had thought about stopping, but then my muscles tensed, and I held onto Braxton as my seed flooded the condom.

Feeling boneless and drowsy, I slumped forward while making sure to keep most of my weight off Braxton. I crushed her hopes of getting off. I didn't want to destroy her bones too.

Under the guise of catching my breath and making sure my legs could hold me up, I stood up straight. Only when I found the courage to meet her gaze did I turn Braxton around to face me.

"You know you do amazing things to a girl's self-esteem."

I huffed out a laugh even as I felt my cheeks warm. By my count, she'd given me three orgasms, and I'd given her…one.

Shit.

"Sorry," I whispered as I pulled her close. "It's been a while." I'd been too busy hunting my demons to worry about getting laid.

Do it, my conscience urged me. Now was the perfect time to tell her about Emily.

Then again, maybe not.

My dick had been inside her less than a minute ago. Learning that you screwed a married man is not something a girl wants to hear right after sex. It was too late for there to ever be a right time, but there couldn't have been a worse moment than now.

I kept my mouth shut by kissing her.

Placing my booted foot between her legs, I kicked her feet apart. I then dropped to my haunches, where I gripped her hips and attacked her clit with my tongue.

As soon as I added my fingers to the mix, she came apart in my arms.

It didn't come close to the sordid things I wanted to do to her, but until we had a shower, a bed, and some privacy, it would have to suffice.

THIRTY-TWO

Braxton

IN CASE ANYONE WAS WONDERING...NO.

I have no idea what I'm doing.

Being around them, I seemed to have developed this habit where I say one thing and do another. I was more than fine with the sex, but I was starting to think that it wouldn't be enough. Why did I insist on spending the day with them? Why had I taken Rich's hand? Why was I already plotting how to get Loren alone and Houston on board?

I didn't understand any of it.

My body was winning this internal war while my heart was staging a coup and my brain was screaming that I was a fool.

We hit up Ripley's Believe It or Not and then the Reunion Tower, an observation deck almost six hundred feet in the air. Unfortunately, Houston and Loren's bad mood had cast a permanent cloud over our outing. Loren had broken his promise and was back to pretending I didn't exist while Houston ramped up the dark looks that promised I'd regret crossing him. He intimidated me more than I let on, but as long as I didn't turn into a doormat for Houston to wipe his feet on, I was fine pretending.

After the tower, Rich suggested that we find somewhere to eat, to which Loren claimed to have lost his appetite. By then, my guilt had dissipated entirely, and I was done with his bratty behavior. Letting go of Rich's hand for the first time since we emerged from that tunnel hours ago, I used both of them now to press against Loren's chest. It was hard and warm beneath my hands, but that was no longer relevant. I shoved Bound's bassist backward right there on the crowded sidewalk.

He blinked those onyx eyes at me in surprise before steeling his gaze and pushing up on me. I was eight inches shorter and maybe a hundred pounds lighter, but that wouldn't keep me from standing up to him. I was the first to speak since I started this in the first place. This was my show.

"Stop pouting."

Loren never looked so offended in his life. "Come again?"

"None of you are entitled to me. *I* decide who gets me when I want to be had. You want something from me? Convince me you're worth the time. Otherwise, suck it up. You might be used to getting your way, but I'm your new reality."

He bared his teeth in a smile that was condescending and more condescending. "That's big talk for someone who won't be able to back it up. Make no mistake, Braxton, I'll get you. You just better hope I don't toss you back after I'm bored."

I felt the words parting my lips. Loren wiped them away by yanking me into him and kissing me with everything he felt but was too much of a coward to say.

It was hard, passionate, raw, and messy—the culmination of everything Loren and I would be together if we ever gave in.

"Let's get something straight," he whispered darkly against my lips. "I'm the only one who had the balls to admit wanting you. Houston still denies you because you'll always come second to Bound, and Rich…you might want to open your eyes, baby. He'll never belong to you."

I refused to let him see that he was getting to me. Everything he'd just said was everything I feared. "You might be right, but you're also the only one who forced me to listen to him as he fucked someone else."

In his eyes, I saw his guilt and the acceptance that he'd screwed our chance before we ever knew we wanted it before he pushed me away.

I stumbled, but then gentle hands helped me find my balance.

I knew they belonged to Rich. I wanted to pull away and hated myself for letting the seeds Loren planted grow. What if he wasn't just screwing with my head?

Feeling my stomach roil like a storm at sea, I pulled away from Rich's touch just as Loren turned back in the direction of the car. We had no choice but to follow.

I'd lost my appetite too.

None of us spoke during the drive back to the bus. There was no handholding, kisses, or secret touches. Houston didn't look at me, not even to make me squirm. Rich, on the other hand, couldn't stop watching me as if he expected me to shatter at any moment.

Maybe I would.

Loren's anger and accusations filled me with bitterness and insecurity until I slowly came to my senses.

I could never have all three of them. I didn't factor in Loren's volatility, Houston's mistrust, and the secrets Rich was apparently keeping. Feeling the wonderful ache between my legs, I conceded that the day hadn't been all bad. It had been great until Loren ruined it by being a brat.

I was even willing to shoulder some of the blame.

Seducing them was the easy part. What happens in the unlikely event that sex is no longer enough? What if I fell for one of them or worse…all of them? What. Happens. Then?

The only thing messier than sex was feelings.

Do I ask three men used to playing dirty to share me? How would I convince them? How would I convince myself? I'm not sure many women would jump at the chance.

In theory, my body reacted in favor of it.

Reality, however, was a judgmental bitch.

I tried putting myself in Rich's shoes after hearing that I wasn't complete with only him. He'd try just to please me until it shattered him completely. Loren gave me the strong suspicion that he'd been an only child. He's never had to share before. Why should he start now?

And then there was Houston.

Morrow suffered a complex that told him he must control

what he could possess and eclipse anything he couldn't. Hoping he'd claim me while allowing his friends to stake their piece was a fool's dream.

Making the sensible choice wasn't something I was used to.

I gave up my innocence, knowing what it meant for my soul. I left home accepting that I may never fit in. I joined Bound, knowing that my bandmates hated me. I've filled my existence with challenges. They gave me purpose, a reason to keep fighting until the bloody end, and a distraction from the knowledge that nothing was waiting on the other side. I could live now and forget it all later.

Once again, defiance was staring me in the eye, waiting for me to pick up the gauntlet. I learned Bound's music. I earned their respect and monopolized their desires.

But I couldn't do this.

I couldn't do what Oni had hoped when she chose me. All I'd end up doing was piling my broken pieces on top of theirs. Pain was all I had to offer Bound. That and my guitar.

THIRTY-THREE

Houston

"You won," Braxton said to me the moment we were back on the bus.

Loren, Rich, and I crowded the door because she hadn't allowed us a step further. She stood there with her head high and shoulders back, but it was the coldness in her eyes that bothered me. Braxton looked at us as if I'd never been inside her, as if she'd never felt Loren's touch, and her clothes weren't torn from fucking Rich mere hours ago.

She even bore all of our marks.

Staring at the spot where mine was starting to fade, I forced myself to stay put. No question she wouldn't welcome my mouth on her right now.

"What are you talking about?" Loren demanded. He shoved past me to get closer to Brax as if he could stop her from saying or doing whatever came next.

"From this point forward, I'd like to keep it about the music."

Loren stilled while Rich shifted next to me. My reaction was also nonverbal. I let my suspicion show as I regarded Braxton. I never took her for a schemer. It had to be a ploy to get us under heel because the only alternative was that she was completely fucking serious.

"When has it not been about the music?" Loren pushed through gritted teeth. Brows dipped and nostrils flaring, his breathing turned heavy from the exertion not to grab Brax and shake her until she was pliant. He'd calmed down on the drive home and even looked like he wanted to take it all back. He didn't count on Braxton deciding for everyone that it was too late.

I toyed with the possibility that she meant every word. What I didn't expect was for it to piss me off more.

"Since I let myself cross too many lines with you," Braxton said with too much passion to be faked. Her gaze slowly met each of ours. "All of you."

Fuck.

She was serious.

"You don't want to accept me," she continued. "It was wrong to think I could make you. I'm temporary. It should never have mattered."

Braxton turned to me, and I read the confusion in her expression when I didn't immediately agree. Victory had always tasted sweet. At the moment, I had a hard time swallowing my nausea.

"Houston?"

I held her stare, but I didn't respond. I was afraid of what might come out. I'd wanted this, and now that I had it, I—

Doesn't matter.

Her mind was made up. Braxton wasn't looking for me to change her mind. She wanted an ally, at least in this. Rich and Loren wouldn't accept a strictly business relationship—not when it was three against one. And if I gave even an ounce of fight, my best friends would immediately pounce. Braxton could hold her own against one of us, maybe even two. She stood no chance if all three of us decided we wanted everything she had to give. Every. Single. Thing.

"Appreciate ya," I finally spoke. I heard the words, but I didn't feel them.

Braxton, however, did.

In the split second it took for her true feelings to show, she recovered, saving me from taking it back. Something inside of me shifted though at seeing her so crestfallen. The wheels in my mind were beginning to turn, and there was no stopping them. Braxton nodded, but before she could speak the gratitude I read on her lips, Rich exploded.

"Wait, so that's it? The two of you get to decide for us?"

"I'm in charge," I reminded him, "and it's what she wants, so…yeah."

Rich and Loren stared at each other, then Brax, and finally me. I'd never been one to wear my thoughts, and right now, it served me well. Betrayal, confusion, disappointment, anger—it was all there in their eyes. There was a time when I'd walk through fire just to bring them an ice cream cone. Back then, I never said no. I never left them behind, and I never left them wanting. It wasn't until we signed with Savant that I failed them and have ever since.

I couldn't dwell on the past anymore, though. It meant wasting the chance I had in the present to right my many wrongs.

Starting with Braxton.

Sometimes pissing off the people you love is how you do them the most good in the end.

THIRTY-FOUR

Loren

All right, I'll confess.

That bullshit Braxton was spitting had gone in one ear and out of the other.

It wasn't until a week of getting the cold shoulder passed that she made a believer out of me. Tomorrow night was our show in New Orleans, and then we were finally getting some time off.

It's been exactly three weeks since the tour started, and I was already beginning to feel the effects. The first leg of our tour wouldn't even be over for another three months. It would have been less demanding had we used a private plane, but we always insisted on the open road because it kept us close to our roots.

A lot of good it did. Braxton claimed we had no humility.

New Orleans had the weirdest fucking food, but damn if wasn't good as fuck. Doggy bag in tow, I rushed up the steps of our bus, hoping to catch a certain redhead before she could disappear.

After Dallas, she still went exploring when we touched down in Houston, but we hadn't been invited. Braxton stayed gone most of the forty-eight hours we were there, and she always took security, leaving us no reason to object.

Even if I was a patient man, she'd be trying mine.

The sliding door separating our living quarters from the driver slid open, revealing Braxton dressed for the day and brushing her long hair. She was wearing shorts, a Bound & Bellicose tee cut to expose her navel, a plaid flannel three sizes too big, and combat boots.

"Good morning," she said when she caught me staring. It was the most we could get out of her this past week if it weren't about a show.

"Morning," I returned, wanting to ask where the hell she was going. Obviously, I didn't. Not only would she not tell me, but I'd ruin my plan to get her to talk to me. "I brought you something."

Holding up the paper bag from Café Du Monde, I let her see the beignets I'd brought back. I remember her excitement over trying one when she learned a few months ago that New Orleans was one of our stops.

Looking at the bag and then at me, she smiled brightly. Just as I was about to celebrate, she turned away. "No, thanks."

I didn't even have time to ask her why not before she grabbed her bag and was gone.

The moment I was alone, Rich and Houston appeared, and I knew they'd been eavesdropping. They didn't say anything, though, as they settled on the couch since absolutely nothing happened. Braxton was sticking to her guns.

Rich and Houston ended up eating the beignets while I spent the day becoming more and more pissed off.

"Whatever you're thinking of doing, don't," Houston said to me as the sun started to set.

Braxton still wasn't back yet. New Orleans was three feet long and our show tomorrow night was the only thing happening. What the hell could she be doing? Even though she had security, I didn't like that she was alone. Someone was bound to recognize her.

"Don't tell me how to deal with a decision that didn't include me," I snapped at my best friend. "This is your fucking fault."

"When she wanted in, we didn't give her that," he shot back. "The least we could do now that she wants distance is to respect her wishes, Lo."

"Nah." I was slumped on the couch with my arms folded, head back, and staring at the bus ceiling.

"So what do you suggest we do?" Houston inquired. I was

about to tell him *he* could go eat a dick when I realized that was curiosity in his tone and not him trying to make a point.

"We change her mind."

"How?"

I don't. Fucking. Know.

"We wear her down," Rich piped in.

"Thank you, Captain Obvious. What do you think the beignets were for?" Without lifting my head, I cut my gaze toward Rich, who had his face screwed up in disgust.

"So you think her pride and self-worth can be bought with a three-dollar pastry?"

No.

God, I hated when he was right. It would be convenient as fuck for me if it could, but then, would I want her so desperately?

Nope.

Fuck no.

"If you have a plan, I'm waiting to hear it," was all I said in return.

"We wear her down by giving her what she wants. That means leaving her alone, Lo."

Feigning excitement, I quickly sat up. "Oh, I think I'm picking up what you're putting down. Your genius plan is to act fifteen and ignore a girl in the hope that she notices us."

"It will piss her off," Rich said like that explained anything.

"Exactly why it's dumb as fuck."

"Loren," Rich said while pinching the bridge of his nose. "When have you known Braxton *not* to react when she's pissed the hell off?"

I paused to consider his words.

"So reverse psychology…that's your play?" Houston asked skeptically. He shook his head. "It's not like you."

"Braxton has been forcing us to play by different rules since the day she walked into that conference room. I've never wanted anything this bad before, so the gloves never had to come off."

"Not even your wife?" I taunted him. "That's cold."

"Shut the fuck up, Lo. You know she's as much my wife as she is yours."

"That would be incorrect. I didn't give her my last name. You did."

"No, you're just the reason she's gone."

Staring at Jericho, I silently prayed that he wasn't still pining for that bitch. "I'd do it again," I told him.

Just so we're all clear.

Shaking his head, Rich refused to look at me when he changed the subject back to Braxton. I didn't give a fuck about Emily. "Are we doing this or not?" he questioned angrily.

I hated myself for looking to Houston first. We all knew this wasn't happening without him on board. He sat on the arm of the sectional, forearms braced on his thighs, and staring at the floor for too goddamn long. "I'm in," he finally said with a slow nod.

"Sweet. Me too." I snatched up my phone when Instagram notified me that someone I followed had posted. There was only one person I cared enough to use the setting. Tapping on the notification, it took me to Braxton's profile and the new photo she'd posted ten minutes ago.

It was a goddamn selfie of her eating a beignet.

Unable to help myself, I left a comment.

[thebassistLo]: petty

There were already hundreds flooding her comment section since her follower count had reached over three million. Before coming out as our new guitarist, she'd garnered thirty thousand on her own. Not bad for someone who hadn't wanted to be found.

Oni made sure to let us know how hard she worked to sell Braxton so that we didn't fuck it up.

I snorted.

It's like she didn't know us.

After scrolling through some of the comments, I refreshed Braxton's page to see if she'd replied.

She didn't.

Instagram told me her account was not found, which meant I was blocked again.

Tapping my handle at the top of the page, I switched to the ghost profile I'd made the last time she blocked me, found her page, and typed another comment.

Yeah, I was supposed to leave her alone, but I couldn't help it.

Braxton was addicting.

[brax_n_lo_4eva]: You look like your pussy tastes better

Done trolling since I knew she wouldn't respond, I pocketed my phone and turned to my friends. "I just have one question."

Rich still wasn't talking to me, so Houston stepped to the plate with a sigh. "What, Lo?"

"Assuming we win her over, how do we decide who gets her?"

"*We* don't," Houston informed me. "It has to be her choice."

I liked the sound of that since I had more charm and charisma than both of them put together. I also had a leg up. Braxton would never speak to Rich again once she found out he was married, and Houston would have to grovel more since he'd been the biggest dick to her.

Lacing my fingers behind my head, I grinned at my evil master plan.

"Sounds good to me," I said excitedly.

"I have a better plan," Rich said slowly. He looked to Houston and then to me, and I knew I wasn't going to like whatever the fuck came out of his mouth. "We share her."

It was late as fuck when Braxton finally returned to the bus. I was lying in my bunk, smoking, and forcing my eyes to stay on the movie playing as she got her shit together for a shower.

She was going to be mad as fuck when she realized I didn't leave her any hot water again.

It was the first time I'd done the shit on purpose, hoping she yelled at me again. I was willing to take any scraps she gave me at this point. If I felt like this after only a week, I couldn't imagine what I'd do when the year was up. She said she was just temporary, but maybe she didn't have to be.

Drawing as much weed as I could into my lungs, I slowly exhaled.

One step at a time.

As soon as Braxton disappeared inside the bedroom, I rolled out of my bunk and snatched her bag from her bed.

"Lo!" Rich hissed so that Braxton wouldn't hear. He'd been sulking in his bunk for the last hour too. "What are you doing?"

"Staying out of your business," I tossed over my shoulder. "Return the favor?"

A joint in one hand and Braxton's phone in the other, I typed in her passcode and then tapped the Instagram icon only to realize she'd logged out.

Fuck.

Not willing to give up, I tried a few combinations.

When I struck out on her full name, birthday, and all that simple shit, I switched tactics.

bambi
babyfawn
richisawimp
houstonisabadlay

I snorted when I struck gold on my final attempt before Instagram locked me out.

lorenisadick

I started to put her phone back once I unblocked myself until I realized there was no rush, unlike last time. Getting comfortable on the edge of Houston's bunk since he was still out discussing shit with Xavier, I went to her photos. I thought her Instagram feed was good until I saw all the shit she *didn't* post.

Damn.

I was praying for a nude as I scrolled through all her photos, and just when I thought I wasn't that lucky…

There was an aerial shot of her without a stitch of clothing, lying in her bunk alone, thick lips pursed, and staring at the camera as if she knew someone would find these photos. Her hair was spread out like wings on her pillow and around her shoulders while the light from the TV illuminated her pale skin.

She looked like an angel cast from heaven, but she didn't fall.

She dove.

I felt my mouth watering as I stared at her dusky nipples and the gentle swell of her breasts. Her stomach was taut, the skin there smooth, and I even felt the urge to dip my tongue inside her belly button.

Just as I was admiring what I knew were soft thighs and thinking about what I really wanted hidden between them, her phone was snatched from my hands.

I'd been so caught up in her photo that I failed to hear Rich climb out of his bunk. He stood over me, holding Braxton's phone in his fist and staring down at me in disapproval.

Toking on my joint, I watched as Rich glanced at the screen and then as he sucked in a breath at what he saw. It took him a second longer to realize he shouldn't be looking either before exiting the photo and stuffing the phone back in her bag.

"Enjoyed that, did you?" I teased.

"Seriously, Lo. Grow up." Shaking his head, he slid back into his bunk, and I chuckled under my breath when he stared at the top like he couldn't get Braxton's nude out of his head.

Welcome to the party.

Hearing the shower cut off, I climbed back in my bunk to resume my nightly ritual of smoking. Before I gave it up, I could never seem to sleep without getting high as fuck first, but I managed. Now it seemed to be having the opposite effect. I was too wired.

Braxton was keeping me on edge.

Rubbing my eyes with the heel of my hands, I sighed. *Fuck it.* I climbed out of my bunk just as Braxton entered wearing a camisole and… Where the hell were her shorts? She usually wore them, or maybe it was the other way around. Perhaps she was tired of accommodating us by being decent, which was more than fine with me.

Panties covered her perky bottom—if you could even call them that. They went up her ass like a thong, but they had a little more material. I had no idea what chicks called those shits. It was sexy as fuck, and that's all I needed to know.

Since I was just standing there in my boxers like a dope, Braxton eyed me warily as she finished towel drying her hair. More than once, her gaze strayed to my chest before catching herself and meeting my eyes. I could feel Rich silently warning me from his bunk to stick to the plan.

Fuck the plan.

"Enjoy your beignet?"

There was amusement in Braxton's eyes as she regarded me. "Does the answer have anything to do with tomorrow night's show?"

Cheeky bitch.

"It would if you got food poisoning." I wasn't quite sure if she could from eating fried dough and powdered sugar but...anything to keep her talking.

Tossing her towel at the foot of her bunk, she turned away from me. "I think I'll be fine, Loren. Good night." As Braxton climbed in her bunk, Houston showed up and got an eyeful of her nice, round ass.

He looked like he wanted to say something to her, but one glance at Rich, and he swallowed it. It was good to know he followed someone else's rules better than he did his own.

Tucked inside her bunk and nestled under the covers now, Braxton met Houston's gaze, and a moment later, she turned, giving him—us—her back.

"Ouch."

Rich promptly threw his pillow at my head, a final warning before he lost his shit. Rolling my eyes, I decided to brush my teeth before Houston could finish getting ready for his shower. Once I was done, I borrowed a couple of things and was back in my bunk after hiding them under my pillow.

Eyes shut, left arm tucked underneath my head, I listened to Braxton's nails click against her phone screen as she texted her friends. I knew it could be no one else. She didn't seem to have a lot of people in her corner, and we were planning to change that the moment she let us in.

Houston returned from his shower, and by then, it was two in the morning. I wasn't even a little bit sleepy, though, and apparently, neither was Braxton. Rich was already snoring loud as fuck, and Houston's breathing had turned deep.

Perfect.

Keeping my eyes closed, I drew the items I'd hidden from under my pillow. The lube I'd taken from the bedroom. After squirting some into my palm, I pushed my boxers down enough to free my cock.

I didn't bother drawing the curtains.

I wanted her to see.

Her back was still turned as she faced the wall, but I knew she wouldn't be like that for long. My mind then conjured her photo as my muse, the memory as vivid as if I still held it in my hand. I kept my rhythm nice and easy, squeezing the head on every upstroke until I began to fantasize, drawing her nipples between my lips.

"Shit," I let slip when I imagined their taste.

I heard the rustling of sheets and knew that it was her turning over to see. I stroked my dick faster, my hips rising off the bed now and then as I chased my orgasm. I imagined her legs wrapped around me as I slowly slipped inside of her. She'd coat my dick with her arousal, making it easy for me to have my way inside her tight, warm walls. I'd bury myself so deep I'd never be able to find my way out.

"Fuck, Braxton."

I didn't even care that she knew it was her I was imagining. It could never be anyone else ever again. No use pretending.

When my movements turned jerky, and I couldn't control my grunts, I knew there was no turning back. Grabbing the second item I borrowed, I groaned long and hard as I used it to catch my cum.

I heard the growl Braxton tried to conceal when she recognized the purple panties she'd been wearing earlier.

I smiled to myself.

After cleaning my dick off with them and figuring she might want 'em back, I tossed them on the floor before rolling onto my stomach.

Now I could sleep.

You might lose love
It might fade in the wind as if it had never been
You might mourn the good years left behind
You might curse the lonely ones that follow
And when you wake up, you realize
It's only the beginning

Listening to Houston sing the words I'd written, I thought about my father's offer for the first time since he made it. I didn't count Colorado because I'd been bluffing as usual whenever Houston pissed me off.

The bitter truth is that my feet were firmly planted.

I couldn't walk away from my friends as easily as I'd done my parents. It's why I hated them so much. I loved them just as deeply.

No matter how much Houston and Rich hurt me, I'd keep coming back for more. The three of us were toxic as fuck, together and apart, but we were all we had. It hadn't always been like this, and I think remembering all the good is why we stayed through the bad.

Seventy-thousand people were on their feet by the time we walked off the stage at the Mercedes-Benz Superdome. It was a rush I never got tired off. We had maybe twenty minutes to collect ourselves before the first round of meet-and-greets began. I was actually looking forward to it since it was the only time we got to see Braxton smile these days.

When she wasn't cursing one of us in her head, that is.

She hadn't remarked on the stunt I pulled last night, but I expected no less. I think she figured out that I thrived on attention, so she punished me by depriving me of it. *Figures.* It was like she'd flipped a switch and became the center of my universe. Everything I am revolved around her. I never even considered trying to undo what she'd done.

Two hours later, the meet-and-greets were over, and Braxton immediately headed back for the bus.

Houston, Rich, and I stayed behind to give her "space."

We used that time to have a powwow with a few roadies as if they didn't have an entire stage to tear down.

"Has it been enough time?" I snapped once we were done distracting our crew. They had enough shit on their plate without us adding in our melodrama. "Can we go back to the bus now?"

"Relax," Houston responded dryly. "It's only been ten minutes."

"This is dumb as fuck if you ask me." I cut my gaze at Rich, who noticed.

"There's a reason no one asks you."

Fuck this.

I walked off, and they shouted my name once they realized the direction I was headed. It didn't take them long before they were hot on my heels. They didn't try to stop me either—not that they could—when I climbed inside the back of the SUV.

The drive back to the bus was only fifteen minutes, but it felt like fifteen hours. I couldn't understand why my palms were sweating, and my heart was racing. I only knew the stirring in my gut that told me Braxton was up to no good.

I screwed with her, and she'd been compliant.

I should have known better than to trust it.

She was a devious little thing.

Before the SUV fully rolled to a stop, I was out and taking off for our bus. I could hear a baffled Houston and Rich talking shit behind me, but I paid them no mind. They were unaware of what I'd done last night. If they knew, they'd be going crazy too.

Bounding up the bus's stairs, I slammed my palm on the button to activate the sliding door. Stepping inside, I peered through the dark interior. It wasn't until a low whimper drew my attention that I spotted Braxton on the couch, naked as the day she was born, red hair cascading down her back, and straddling my goddam pillow.

I knew it was mine because of the dark-green pillowcase.

"Holy shit," I heard Rich whisper like a virgin. I don't know why he bothered to conceal his presence.

Braxton knew we were here.

She planned this.

I watched her ass and tits jiggle every time she moved her hips. My pillow was providing the friction her clit needed as she rode it like a professional jockey. She was at the perfect angle for me to see everything while she performed like we weren't even here. *Hell yes.*

"What the hell is she doing?" Houston asked no one in particular.

Without taking my eyes off Braxton, I answered my best friend. "She's upping the ante."

I was willing to give whatever at this point to make her mine.

Ours.

Whatever.

I wanted to move in closer, maybe touch her or join in. I knew the second I did that it would be over, so I stayed put.

Meanwhile, Braxton sped up her pace, her cries becoming more desperate as she humped my pillow with reckless abandon. Her small hands clutched the casing, her nails digging in as she held on for dear life.

The only thing that could make this moment more perfect was if she were sitting on my face and not my pillow. Swallowing when my mouth-watered, I admired the moonlight washing over her and the sweat glistening on her skin.

If this was her way of punishing me, she could count on more trouble.

The closer she drew to her orgasm, the more captivated I became. And when she finally reached her peak, I was hard enough to break a brick.

The three of us looked on as she slumped on the couch, her

chest rising and falling rapidly as she fought to catch her breath. She wasn't at all shy or bothered by her nakedness even though we stood fully clothed.

A minute or two must have passed, and no one said a goddamn word. I think Houston and Rich were as speechless as I was. Maybe even more so since they didn't know the reason behind her stunt.

When she could trust her legs again, Braxton stood, grabbed my pillow, and tossed it at my feet. While she disappeared inside the bunks, I stared at my pillow, admiring the wet spot she'd left behind.

Touché.

THIRTY-FIVE

Rich

I wasn't sure how much longer I could keep this up.

Loren was too loose a cannon and a terrible influence. He made me want to throw caution to the wind and beg Braxton to give us a second chance.

We hadn't come to that part of the plan yet.

Right now, we were trying to make her see that she didn't want to be without us. I knew whatever the reason for Braxton's behavior tonight, Loren was behind it. And with him off his leash, for every step forward, we were bound to take two steps back.

I heard the shower running when I pushed inside the bunk area and knew Braxton was washing away the remnants of her private show. Spotting a scrap of purple lace on the floor, I swooped them up just as Loren pushed through the door. Feeling my fingers brush something white and sticky, I immediately tossed the material away.

"What the—is that jizz?" I yelped.

Staring at the lace hanging from the toe of Loren's boot now, I realized they were Braxton's panties. Why was there cum on Braxton's panties? I was pissed off, wondering who it had come from since it sure as fuck hadn't been me. It couldn't have been Houston or Loren either since we were all in the doghouse together. I don't recall ever being this angry as I considered the possibility that Braxton had fucked someone else.

I didn't realize I was storming toward the bathroom, ready to interrupt Braxton's shower, until Loren caught me.

"Relax, man. It's mine."

Whirling on him, I shoved him back. "How did your cum get on Braxton's panties?"

"As much as I wish it was what you think, it's not, so chill. I used them last night."

"You used them," I echoed. I waited for him to explain.

Loren's face balled up in irritation. "I beat my dick and nutted in them, bro. You want a fucking play-by-play?"

"So you left them for her to find, and that's why she put on that show?"

"Not quite." Loren scratched his fucked-up head while I waited for the other shoe to drop. "She kind of saw me, and that's the reason for her show." I didn't realize my desire to hit him until I'd already bloodied his nose. "What the hell was that for?" he had the nerve to shout.

Gripping his collar with both hands, I shoved him against the door hard enough to make the wood splinter. He tried to push me off, but with his head tilted back and one hand busy trying to stop the bleeding, he couldn't.

"Make this the last time I tell you to leave her the hell alone or you're out."

Forgetting about his busted nose, Loren dropped his hand to stare at me through the slits his eyes made. "You think I need you to win over Brax?"

"I think you know she won't just choose one of us. She won't risk what it will do to our friendship." Or what's left of it. "It's all or nothing with Brax."

"Does she know that?" he quipped.

Probably not. "She will."

"So you're willing to screw yourself just to make sure I don't get her?"

"Doing this means we're a unit. Every move you make, you make for all of us, so if you don't deserve her, neither do we."

I could see Loren mulling over my point before he gave in

with a sigh. "Still seems a little dramatic. I practically admitted I'm in love with her."

Letting him go, I took a step back with my brow raised. "I can always put you in a wheelchair. You won't need your legs to give her your heart."

Flipping me off, he yanked open the door and rushed for the half bath we never used instead of the one Braxton still occupied.

While Loren took care of his face, I washed my hands in the kitchen sink. I then sat on the couch where Houston was watching a clip from our show tonight.

"You guys all right?" Houston muttered without taking his eyes off the TV. I knew he'd heard every word.

"I'm not sure this is going to work," I admitted in defeat.

I could feel Houston's gaze as I stared at the ground. "It's only been a day, Jericho. We can't know for sure."

Loren was shirtless when he came out of the bathroom and wisely kept Houston between us as he sat on the couch.

The conceited ass kept checking his nose, and I knew it was to make sure it wasn't crooked. I heard the shower cut off in the bedroom and forced myself to follow my own plan by staying put. Loren began to roll up as we watched TV, and after a few tokes, he passed it to Houston, who surprisingly accepted. I was next, and just like that, a rotation began.

So much for sobriety.

Back then, we indulged here and there to keep moving when life was just too much to handle sober. It wasn't until Calvin was beyond saving that we realized we couldn't bear losing each other that way. It wouldn't be quick. It wouldn't be sudden. It would be slow and agonizing. It meant being helpless while one or all of us withered away. I hated Everill's guts, and it had still ripped me apart to see him destroy himself.

So we gave it all up—the weed, the pills, the alcohol, and the coke.

My stomach had been in knots ever since Loren started back drinking. Now that he was smoking as well, I wondered if it was too late. Our lives aren't nearly as hectic now as it had been when we were building our name, and we'd never developed a dependency like Calvin, but the fear and the possibility were still very real.

"Should we be doing this?" I blurted when I felt my lids begin to lower.

"We've been smoking since we were pups. If it were going to ruin our lives, it would have done so by now," Loren reasoned. "Besides, Calvin's not around to talk us into the harder shit."

"We can't put all the blame on a dead man. He didn't force us to say yes, Lo."

"No," he returned while meeting my eyes. "He just made sure it was always around."

I didn't bother trying to argue him down. Loren was determined to be the victim, and it was nearly impossible to change his mind once it was set.

It wasn't until I was into my high that I realized that it'd been years since we tolerated each other enough to be in the same room for longer than five minutes.

Had to be the weed.

I would have smiled had Braxton not made an appearance.

She didn't seem bothered by our smoking, but perhaps it was because she was determined to ignore us. I watched from the corner of my eye as she warmed up her portion of the food the chefs had left for us. Sticking to the plan, Houston pulled out a deck of cards and started dealing while Loren whooped and rubbed his hands together.

"What's the bet tonight, boys?"

A pang of nostalgia hit me like a lightning strike.

Frustrated, I shook it away. I didn't want to hope. I snatched up my cards when Houston was done dealing, only to tense when Braxton sat next to me with her dinner. There was a table, but she'd chosen the couch. I didn't want to think about what that meant. As she settled in, Loren immediately ashed the joint and waved the smoke away. Braxton was careful not to sit too close, but I could smell her soap, or maybe her shampoo, and that was enough. For now.

There was no forgetting how it felt to be inside her.

"Does anyone mind if I change the channel?" she asked us while reaching for the remote.

Houston, without giving her his full attention, nodded his consent.

"Thanks." She channel surfed for a while before settling on a movie.

When we saw she'd chosen *The Legend of Tarzan* with Alexander Skarsgård, Loren snorted. I sent him a warning look, and he piped the fuck down.

Pretending not to hear him, Braxton closed her eyes, and I watched as her lips moved in silent prayer. My eyes bucked as I looked on because I'd never taken her for religious.

The moment her eyes opened, I looked away, and she immediately dug into her shrimp scampi. It looked good as hell, and I felt my stomach tighten. The only problem was that I only had a taste for her.

Near the end of the movie, when the villain was leading Tarzan into a trap using his girl, my phone chimed once, signaling I had a text. Houston's phone had also gone off at the same time.

Frowning, I checked the screen and saw that it was a message from Loren in our group chat.

Lo: I bet if one of us yells like Tarzan, Brax will be so turned on she talks to us.

Our phones chimed again with another text from him.

Lo: Not it.

Houston and I looked up from our phones to stare at Loren. I already knew he was serious. Grinning, he sent two more texts.

Lo: Houston's got the pipes.

Lo: Can't hurt to try.

Just as he started to send another, Houston slapped Loren's phone out of his hand. It skipped and scattered across the floor, making Braxton jump and drawing her attention to us. I could see the question in her brown eyes, but it was gone in one blink, and then she turned back to the movie.

Loren ignored his phone lying on the floor across the room

while we played another hand, which I won. Possibly the hardest thing I'd ever done was sit here and ignore Braxton's presence. Every time she shifted on the couch, laughed under her breath, or let it catch from something happening in the movie, I was aware, yet I had to pretend otherwise.

Once the movie finally ended, Braxton stood and began washing her plate. Since her back was turned, I felt free to watch her.

She was fully clothed tonight even though she'd been completely naked and riding Loren's pillow three hours ago.

When she was done, I felt like all the air had been kicked from my lungs when she bent to pick up Loren's phone near her bare feet. The three of us went still as she straightened while staring at the lit screen.

Loren didn't keep a lock on his phone so all she had to do was tap and swipe up to see his last open window. She didn't even bother to conceal her curiosity from us either.

Helplessly, we watched as Braxton read Loren's texts.

When she was done, without a word, she calmly placed his phone on the counter before leaving the room.

"Shit," Loren swore.

Feeling our glares, he hung his head.

Pissed was an understatement when I shot to my feet, but I didn't bother pummeling him. Braxton had already made him feel worse than I ever could. "Find somewhere else to sleep tonight."

Loren's head shot up. When he saw I was dead serious, he looked to Houston, who shrugged. This was my show and my shot to call, but we were both still caught off guard by Houston's refusal to interfere. Control was not something he relinquished without a bloody fight.

Braxton was changing everything.

"This is bullshit," Loren spat like I gave a damn.

"Wheelchair."

It was all the reminder he needed before he stormed off the bus.

Sighing, I headed for the shower while Houston cleaned up. With Loren gone, at least there'd be hot water.

THIRTY-SIX

Braxton

ONE CITY BLURRED INTO THE NEXT AS WE MADE OUR WAY EAST. Exhaustion from performing nonstop, with only two real breaks to recharge in between, had drained my excitement for new places. I didn't feel the spark I'd left behind in New Orleans until we reached the Big Apple two months later.

Now all I could smell since we arrived this morning was cinnamon.

Visiting had always been a dream of mine, and not even the pall Dallas put on the tour could ruin it.

My bus had been repaired and met us in New Orleans, but Houston had given it back to the crew rather than exile me again. Even though I was relieved for the crew, I wondered if Houston's motive was to punish me since it meant staying on the bus with them. We didn't speak unless it was absolutely necessary, and the three of them avoided me like I carried a flesh-eating virus.

I know I said I wanted space but going so far as to avoid even a shoulder brush was a bit much. All three seemed to jump out of their skin whenever I got too close and would hurriedly leave the room.

They still argued almost every night, but something had changed. They didn't lash out anymore, and I was no longer a bystander. Blossom, Bubbles, and Buttercup made sure to hash their beef out of earshot, though it was always close enough for me to watch them through the window.

Sometimes I had to remind myself that I'd asked for this. We were Pandora's box, better left untouched than explored. I just didn't count on it hurting this bad.

Against my will, I missed them.

I'd gone from feeling nothing to feeling sad, and now something else. I wasn't sure at what point during the two months prior that anger had set in, but the chip on my shoulder was *huge*.

New York was as loud, smelly, and crowded as portrayed on television, but the magic was real too. Los Angeles had gotten me used to large cities, but there was an edge to New York that the City of Angels just didn't have. No other place in the world could match the grit, speed, and glitz of the metropolis.

The best part was that we'd be here for a week before moving further north. After Boston, we'd storm through Canada, and then it was back to the west coast for our last two shows of the first leg—Seattle and Portland. I'm sure the guys were excited about returning home—at least until the European leg of our tour began.

The number of shows packed into one tour seemed…excessive, even for a band as notable as Bound.

I also wondered why we weren't flying to each show instead of being crammed onto a bus. It was public knowledge how much money Bound's tours made. I'm sure the label could afford to charter a plane. None of it made any sense.

I told myself I didn't care, but the thought only went so far as the corner of my mind where it waited to spring out again at the most inopportune time.

At least Savant had sprung for us to stay in a hotel while we were here. It was a five-star hotel, and nothing I could have afforded on my own. Even with my large advance, I wouldn't squander it on a few nights' stay. Meanwhile, the crew was put up in a less expensive hotel nearby, which didn't seem fair. I would have been fine without the glamour—even Stevens.

When I texted my friends to complain, Griff called me a self-sacrificing headache and ordered me to shut up and enjoy the all-expense-paid vacay.

I'd been talking to them practically nonstop since I no longer had the guys to distract me. Before, I'd been too caught up in life on the road and my whirlwind emotions to realize how much I missed home.

I hadn't talked to my parents since they wouldn't pick up the phone and wouldn't allow Rosalie to, either. She *did* manage to sneak me DMs here and there since my parents didn't understand social media. I wasn't sure they even knew Instagram existed.

During our last talk, I tried to get a sense of where her head was, but Rosalie had been reluctant to let me inside. That was more than two months ago, so I knew she was avoiding me. She'd even abandoned her mission to convince me to fly her out despite our parents forbidding her any contact with me.

Rosalie believed I could move mountains while sometimes I wished she would beg me to come home. At least then, I'd have an excuse to leave Bound without wounding my pride.

Annoyed with myself, I sat up into a sitting position where'd I'd been lying in the middle of my hotel bed. I'd already wasted two months of new adventures. I wasn't going to let Bound take away another.

Digging my brown crossbody from my suitcase, I filled it with things I thought I'd need for the day before shoving on my most comfortable pair of boots and heading out of my room. The white summer dress with long sleeves that hung off my shoulders would do just fine.

The four of us had been given the twenty-six hundred square foot duplex for our stay. It had four beds, four baths, and a view of Central Park and the city. There were only three bedrooms, so Loren and Rich had doubled up while Houston took the second bedroom, and I was left with the master.

I'd forgotten what it was like to sleep on a full-sized bed. The bedroom on our bus had been left empty since I refused to run and hide. And despite its purpose that Houston had made known, the guys never used it for any groupies—not since Loren that one time.

Nope. I've been content with my bunk, putting up with Rich's loud snoring, Houston's quiet contempt, and Loren jerking off every morning and night.

At least he used his curtain for privacy now.

I wouldn't think about what I'd done with his pillow.

I was seeing red at the time, but I didn't regret it. Sometimes you have to stoop to beat your opponent at their own game.

Emerging from my room for the first time since arriving, I descended the five or six stairs separating the master bedroom on the suite's second floor from the other rooms.

Loren was sitting alone on the couch closest to the stairs, with his arms spread along the back, and his body sprawled as if the couch were his throne, and he was king.

Houston stood in front of the floor-to-ceiling windows gazing out at the city with his brows dipped even though the view was breathtaking.

Rich stood in the kitchen, sucking on an orange, and I tried not to remember how good he was with his tongue.

I pretended they weren't there as I headed for the door.

"Stop."

When my feet actually obeyed, I cursed him and me under my breath. None of them had spoken to me in nearly twenty-four hours. What made Houston think I'd want to listen now?

"Where do you think you're going?" he asked when I peered over my shoulder.

"Does the answer affect our show four days from now?"

Houston's expression morphed into something that warned me to back down now. Loren watched me like he wanted in on the action, and for the first time, Rich wasn't jumping to my defense.

Looks like I'd bonded them, after all.

"It does if you don't plan on coming back," Houston returned.

Spinning around to face them, I crossed my arms. "No need to flatter yourself, Morrow. I'm not going anywhere."

"That's right, Braxton. You're not. Get back in your room."

The room suddenly smelled as if we were standing inside an inferno. I was so angry it almost slipped my notice that he'd called me Braxton and not Fawn. "Excuse me?"

"We dismissed our security team. They needed some time off. That means we're staying put for a couple of days."

How convenient.

"I don't need buff men with guns to tell me not to wander down dark alleys."

"It wasn't an offer, and I'm definitely not asking. This isn't a negotiation or a goddamn democracy. Sit. The fuck. Down."

Houston's voice had gotten rougher with each word he spoke, but he never reached the point of shouting. I was one thousand percent sure I'd walk out on them and this tour if that ever happened.

Savant could sue me.

This time, I didn't bother to stop or offer another caustic remark. It would only give them the chance to corner me, so...

I bolted for the door.

Rich was closest, so I knew it was his arm around my waist, lifting me in the air while his free hand slammed closed the door I'd barely gotten open.

"It's been two months," he whispered in my ear as he held me. I could have sworn I felt his lips skim my cheek. "You've made your point."

"I doubt it," I returned dryly.

The only thing I felt was confusion as Jericho carried me to the empty sofa across from the one Loren occupied. How had I gone from being ignored to locked inside our hotel suite?

My angry gaze traveled from Rich, who'd taken a couple of steps away, to Loren and finally Houston.

"What is this really about?" I was certain my new status in life hadn't reached me being unable to walk the streets in an overcrowded city without being recognized. Most people only knew who I was if one of Bound was standing next to me. I wasn't buying Houston's reason for keeping me here. Besides, he had no say in what I did off stage.

"What makes you think that we have an agenda?" Loren asked.

When I responded, I kept my gaze on Houston, knowing it would piss Loren off. "Tell me a time when you didn't have one."

"Touché."

Unable to resist him any longer, I looked into Loren's eyes. I missed staring within those endless depths. "Screw you."

They all reacted one after another to my aggression.

"Someone's cranky."

"Could it be that she's hard up?"

"Whatever shall we do about that?"

I so wasn't interested in this game.

Rich didn't move to sit me back down when I stood, but I was ready for him if he tried. "Nothing," I said, answering Houston's question. "It's being covered."

"What the hell do you mean by that?" Loren snapped.

"Figure it out."

I didn't consider that I'd have to walk by him to get to my room and through Rich to get to the front door. The moment I tried to pass him, Loren pulled me down onto his lap, and he wasted no time locking his arms at my waist to keep me there. I could feel my limbs wanting to relax. My body missed being close to his. Knowing better, I kept my spine ramrod straight.

"Tell us who he is so you can watch us beat the shit out him."

"Why would you do that?"

As Loren spoke, his hand caressed my lower belly, drawing heat there and filling my mouth with sweet syrup. I was beginning to despise the taste of cherries. "Because we're spoiled, possessive, jealous…and we only like to share with each other."

Loren caught me off guard. The only part of me that moved was my heart pounding inside my chest. "What are you saying?"

"We'd like to propose an experiment."

"An experiment?" I echoed when I couldn't think of what else to say.

"We've been kind of losing our shit without you," Rich admitted.

"I've been right here." And from my viewpoint, it looked like they'd been just fine.

"It felt like you were on another planet."

I didn't expect the admission to come from Houston. When my gaze shot to him, he wore an uncomfortable look as if the lead singer of a fucking rock band wasn't used to baring his soul. I guess it was easier in front of a stadium of faceless strangers.

I was floored.

But I wouldn't fall for it.

No one else had ever made me feel so alone. Not even my parents after they'd thrown me to the wolves.

There was a chance they'd gotten bored ignoring me and were just toying with me for their amusement. It wouldn't be the first time.

Chuckling, I pried Loren's arms from around me, and he reluctantly let me go. "I'm not doing this," I said after I was standing on my feet. "I'm not playing this game."

"You haven't even heard what we have to say," Rich accused me. He sounded disappointed and angry, but I didn't care. I'd given into them too many times.

I recalled how I'd found them when I finally left my room. I realized now that they had been waiting for me. For this. Whatever *this* was.

Swallowing past the lump in my throat, I nodded even as my stomach twisted, and the air began to fill with the scent of roses. It's been a long time since I felt sorrow this deep.

"I'm okay with that."

"Braxton," Loren called after me when I started for the stairs.

I'd stay put for now, but I had no interest in hearing what they had to say. They don't get to ignore me and discard me until they're ready to play again.

Yes, I asked for it, but they had no problem giving in.

It was all too easy for them to shut me out. They hadn't even tried. They just taunted me as usual until even that grew boring.

The thick tension in the suite weighed my feet down, but eventually, I made it to my room.

The last thing I saw before I shut myself inside was Rich's bowed head, Loren's tense shoulders, and Houston staring out the windows once more.

THIRTY-SEVEN

Houston

"THAT WENT WELL," LOREN DRAWLED SARCASTICALLY THE MOMENT Braxton shut her door. I already knew she was smart, but when I heard the snick of her bedroom lock turning, I realized she had great instincts too. "Great idea, Rich. I'm so glad you talked us into this."

"I didn't talk you into anything. You were already thinking it. We all were."

Loren sighed rather than argue. "Back to the drawing board, I guess. Fuck this three-musketeer shit. I'd rather be all for me and none for you anyway."

"She never said no."

"She never gave us the middle finger either, but the *fuck you* was implied."

"We iced her out for two months, Lo. Just give her a couple of days. We can try again."

Loren's sneer that he directed at Rich told me we'd already lost him. It seemed there was no hope for a plan that didn't fail when it came to Braxton Fawn. She was too complex to strategize, and we still weren't worthy opponents.

Rich's suggestion of not making her choose had so many holes in it, I couldn't blame Loren for jumping a sinking ship. There was only one option left, but I couldn't help wondering if the cost was too great. Not one of us would stick around and watch her be happy with whoever she chose. It would mean the end of our friendship that was barely hanging on. It would mean the end of Bound.

"Why the hell are you pushing this so hard anyway?" Lo grilled Rich. "It was a crap idea, to begin with. *Share her*? Do you know how much that makes my balls itch? Fuck you."

"I don't see you coming up with ideas."

"Sure, I have." Loren grinned, kicking his legs up on the suite's coffee table and lacing his fingers behind his head. "My plan is to make her fall in love with me. Whichever one of you cries the least about it can be my best man at our wedding."

Rich, who had more patience than was wise, looked ready to swing on Lo. "What makes you so sure she'll choose you over one of us?"

"Have you seen my rock-hard abs and gorgeous hair? What am I saying? Of course, you have." The look Loren gave him was mocking and knowing, which Rich avoided by turning his head. Naturally, Loren wasn't ready to let it go. He'd push every button necessary to get the reaction he needed. "Oh, no, don't be ashamed, Jericho. I'm honored, you being so straight and all, took it up the ass so that I'd stick around."

Rich shot to his feet, his angry gaze like liquid silver as he fixed it on Lo. "I'm not ashamed," he snapped. "I'm just wondering why I bothered."

Something in Rich's gaze made Loren hesitate before he said, "Me too."

Rich stormed off and closed himself up in the room they were supposed to share before Loren got himself thrown into the doghouse. Again. Now he'd be sleeping on the couch instead of the spare bed, and I doubted the opulent piece of furniture had been designed for comfort.

Feeling Loren's gaze, I found him silently attempting to pry open my mind so he could piss me off and push me away too. He probably thought it would make it easier when he tried to take Braxton for himself. It hadn't worked out for him the first time but being pigheaded was at the top of his vices. I had yet to figure out how he'd gotten so smart learning shit the hard way. Maybe it was because he insisted on having to be told everything twice.

I sighed. "Unless you want the room's security deposit taken out of our cut for this tour, I suggest you swallow whatever you're about to say to me, Lo."

"I'm just wondering how you sleep at night." Unlacing his fingers from behind his head and lowering his arms, he spread them once again along the back of the couch. "First, you convince us Savant's shitty deal was a dream, and then you let Rich believe that sharing a woman was actually possible."

"Why are you so sure it's not?"

"Because that's not how love works."

"How do you know when you've never been in love, Lo? Our only knowledge of it is what we've been told. It's second-hand information."

"But have you thought about what happens when this gets out? Don't kid yourself into thinking it won't, and I'm not keeping Braxton a secret."

"Neither will I, but whose opinion are you so concerned about? Strangers we pass on the street? People we'll never meet? Our families who don't give a shit if we're sad, much less if we're happy? We get to define what true love is for ourselves. No one is entitled to do it for you. Once she's mine, I'd never hurt her, neglect her, or let her forget that she's the axis on which I spin. I can do the same with my best friends hanging around. We were already family, Lo. We built a career together. We share a house... *We don't even have separate bank accounts.* What's mine has always been yours. This world is a wolf in sheep's clothing, and the people in it would rather you be miserable as long as they're comfortable. Why not carve out our own piece and be free to love how we choose?"

Loren was quiet for a moment, staring at the wall ahead of him before muttering, "Maybe."

Afraid I might be forcing him into something his soul couldn't take, I continued. "I'm not telling you that it's wrong to want Braxton for yourself. It doesn't make you anything other than *who you are.* But if your only objection is what other people will think—"

"It's not me I'm worried about," he said, cutting me off.

It was probably for the best since I could feel my heart racing inside my chest. This was the closest I'd come to keeping us all together. It wasn't just about Bound. Besides my grandmother, Rich and Loren were the only family I ever truly cared about. I had to seize the opportunity Brax had unwittingly given us. I never thought sharing my woman was something I'd ever do. It contradicted everything I thought I knew about myself as a man, and I had the feeling no other woman could have convinced me to take such a leap of faith. No one.

"The girl always gets the most shit during a scandal," he pointed out. "Men will pat us on our backs while Braxton is belittled by the same women vying to take her spot. Guys will assume she's easy game. It—" A frustrated look twisted Loren's features. "I already want to commit murder, and nothing's even happened. She won't even hear us out."

"She will."

"How?" Loren returned skeptically. "We buy her diamonds and flowers? You know Braxton better than that. She'll just find the highest window and throw them out."

I scratched my chin because he had a point. Braxton could hold a grudge and had the temper to keep it going. It definitely made me think twice about crossing her in the future.

"We'll figure something out." I tipped my chin toward the closed door of the spare bedroom. "Go make up with Rich. He's always been Braxton's favorite, and three heads are better than two."

THIRTY-EIGHT

Braxton

EAVESDROPPING IS ONLY WRONG WHEN YOU'RE NOT THE TOPIC OF conversation, right? It hadn't been my intention to listen.

Okay, so maybe it had.

Their muffled voices had drawn me to the door, and when I heard Loren vowing not to keep me a secret, I couldn't walk away. Once again, my heart and mind were at war.

All night, I replayed their conversation.

When the clock read a quarter to five in the morning, and I still couldn't sleep, I found myself slipping into another dress and tiptoeing from our hotel suite. Not even Houston was awake, and he was the early riser. I'm sure it crossed their minds that I'd sneak out, but they'd never count on it being this early.

The sun was still a couple of hours from rising, and since the streets would be mostly empty this early, I wasn't worried about being recognized.

Just to be sure, I borrowed the ball cap Houston had left on the kitchen counter. I might have even sniffed it a little for a hint of his shampoo before throwing it on and keeping the bill low.

I emerged from the hotel without being accosted as Houston would have claimed and spotted a French café just across the street. Even though they weren't open yet, I could still smell the coffee and pastries.

My stomach growled, reminding me that I'd been too stubborn to come out last night to eat. Rich, Houston, and Loren had even knocked on my door twice each to ask if I was hungry.

So nice of them to be concerned when they thought it was too late.

As I wandered down East Seventy-Sixth and cut across Fifth Ave toward Central Park, I set my mind on deciding what I'd do once the tour was over. My advance had been generous, with more to come once the tour's profits were divvied and distributed. I knew I wouldn't get nearly as much as the guys, but I hoped I'd at least bank enough to buy a crappy house in a questionable neighborhood.

What more could an average girl with no real ambition ask for?

I only needed to decide if Los Angeles was the endgame. Wherever I chose to go, I had to make sure it was somewhere my parents would never step foot in.

I hated that Portland was the only city that came to mind. My parents *did* say it was much too liberal, but they weren't why I thought of it.

I had no clue if Portland is where Bound still lived or if that house in Beverley Hills belonged to them. I only knew that it was home. Calvin, who they never mentioned, was the only one who hadn't grown up there.

I knew there was no correct way to grieve, but my gut told me they didn't mourn him—only his guitar skills.

Under Bound's tutelage, mine have certainly grown. Houston hadn't corrected my methods or complained about my mistakes since our show in Denver. I just assumed he'd been too angry to deign even ripping me apart like usual.

I should have been accustomed to complicated, but the Powerpuff Girls were tossing out everything I thought I knew of the meaning.

It was still too early for joggers and dog-walkers, so I walked for five minutes, passing a small playground and seeing no one until I came across an amazing bronze statue of a little girl perched on top of a giant mushroom surrounded by woodland creatures. It was Alice in Wonderland with the Mad Hatter looking on, the White Rabbit checking his pocket watch, and a dormouse eating something at her feet.

Digging out my phone, I snapped a selfie with the Mad Hatter and then the White Rabbit. I wasn't sure I wanted to risk slipping and falling if I climbed the mushroom for Alice.

Sorry, Alice.

I walked for another ten minutes passing a boathouse before I stumbled upon a miniature castle next to a pond that wouldn't open for a few hours. If I hadn't been too early, I would have dipped inside, but it wouldn't have been for the panoramic views.

I had less chance of being found if I were undercover.

Even though I'd left Houston, Loren, and Jericho sound asleep in their beds, I felt like a kid skipping school and avoiding all the places my parents or someone who knows them might show up. A few more hours and the park would fill up since it was summer, and parents were looking to keep their kids entertained until they wore themselves out.

Smiling as an idea formed, I took a selfie and smiled into the camera while biting the tip of my finger. I made sure not to show too much of the stone and brick castle in the background. It was dark, so my flash still came in handy. Once I was satisfied nothing else gave my location away, I opened the texting app. After unblocking Loren, I started a new thread, and typed a message. I already knew they liked group chats.

I decided to take a walk. Find me before sunrise, and I'll grant five minutes of my undivided attention.

Attaching the photos I'd taken, including my selfies with the Mad Hatter and White Rabbit, I hit send and pocketed my phone. I figured I had about a twenty-minute head start.

THIRTY-NINE

Loren

"Stop playing, girl. You know I like it when you do that."

Smiling, I was just getting to the good part of my dream when my eyes drifted open for some reason.

I jumped and screamed like a bitch at the sight of Houston standing over me with no expression whatsoever.

"What the hell are you doing?" I shouted at him. I'd even startled Rich awake. Weirded the hell out, I clutched the covers to my chest. I couldn't tell if Houston had been about to stab me or rape me. Rich creeped us both out plenty whenever he had trouble sleeping. Thankfully, it's been a while since he had an episode.

I'd been a sphincter's hair from having a wet dream, and strangely, I was okay with that—as long as Braxton was playing a starring role.

"You were talking in your sleep," Houston announced.

"So you decided to stand over me like you're Michael fucking Myers?"

"Fuck you. I was coming to wake you up." Looking like he could barely restrain himself, he took a deep breath and exhaled. "Braxton's gone."

Glancing out the window with the curtains drawn since we were so high up, I saw that the sun wasn't even up yet.

Sucking my teeth, I rolled onto my stomach. Braxton was like a frat boy, keeping late hours and sleeping until noon. No way she was awake yet. I don't care how mad she was.

It's too early for this shit.

"She's sleeping. *I'm* sleeping. Now leave us both the hell alone," I mumbled with a face full of pillow.

"Check your phone." It was all he said before he left the room.

Ignoring him, I concentrated on picking up where my dream had left off. A moment later, I rolled my eyes when I heard Rich grabbing his phone from the nightstand. I was starting to drift off again when I heard his sheets rustling as he got out of bed.

If she's really gone, I'm going to wring her neck.

"Get up," Jericho ordered, confirming my worst fears. "Houston wasn't fucking kidding. Check your texts."

Heart pounding, I frantically searched the sheets. The last time I recalled having it was before I fell asleep texting her. Not a single message had been delivered since she'd blocked my number. It only gave me the courage to pour my heart out and let loose my anger since I knew she'd never see them.

By the time I found my goddamn phone, Rich had already thrown on a white T-shirt and sneakers since he'd worn basketball shorts to bed. When I finally saw the texts, my reaction was different than Houston and Rich's.

I smiled.

I loved the balls on this kid.

She wasn't predictable or needy like Houston and Rich preferred in that order. She made us play the games we liked her way.

Sitting on the edge of my bed, I shook my head at the responses Houston and Rich had sent, telling her to bring her ass back. Underneath my excitement, I admit I was pissed too. It wasn't even five in the morning yet, and she was out there in a strange city alone and in the dark. Not to mention she no longer had the luxury of obscurity. If someone recognized her, who knows what they would do.

The upside to overthinking everything is that you're smarter than the people who don't think at all. I knew nothing I said would make her obey. The only way to ensure no one got to her first was to find her as quickly as possible, so I'd play.

We could get our pound of flesh after we found her.

I'd never gotten dressed so quickly in my life. I'd also never stepped foot in public looking quite so disheveled. It was a first for me and yet another reason to return the favor to Brax when I got my hands on hers. I'd take my time unraveling her.

I had my shoes on and met my friends at the door just as they were storming through it.

Ten minutes later, we'd reached the park.

"What the hell is that supposed to be?" Rich griped as he stared at the last photo Braxton had sent. She'd been giving us "clues" for which direction to head once I assured her that we were up for the hunt.

I shook my head as I smiled to myself.

She'd really lured us into the city to chase her unruly ass at five in the goddamn morning.

"It's clearly an arch," I snapped back. "What else could it be?"

I *really* wasn't a morning person.

"But where is it?" Rich questioned, unbothered by my crankiness. He only had his mind on finding Brax.

"How would I know?" I tossed my head toward Houston. "He's the map."

Currently, we were standing in front of the Alice in Wonderland statue as the smell of horse shit clung to the air.

I wasn't an outdoors person either.

And we only had ten minutes tops left to find her.

"There's something called a Ramble Arch half a mile from here, but she won't be there. She's already gone."

"She hasn't sent us another clue," Rich pointed out.

Houston shook his head. "The clues are only meant to point us in her direction. She's not going to wait around for us to catch up."

"She had maybe a twenty-minute head start," I surmised out loud. "How far could she walk in that amount of time?"

The three of us huddled around Houston's phone as we stared at the map of Central Park. After only a few seconds of trying to guess, I felt more of my patience slipping. "This is pointless. We won't know for sure which direction she's gone until she sends another clue."

Just then, Houston's phone chimed with another text from Braxton. I hurriedly tapped the banner before it could disappear from the top of his phone.

It was a picture of her standing against the railing of what must have been a bridge. It was still dark, but I could just make out the still water in the lake behind her and the leaves from the trees reflecting on the surface.

"That has to be here," Houston said, pointing at something called the Bow Bridge.

"There are two directions she could go once she crosses it. I say we haul ass and cut her off here," I suggested, pointing at Bethesda Terrace.

She was probably expecting us to be off our game and actually retrace her steps. By the time we caught up, even though we were faster, it would be well after sunrise.

Who knows if or when Braxton would give us another shot. I shuddered to think of what other trial she'd feel the unneccssary need to put us through.

"And if she heads in the other direction?" Rich questioned.

"One, it's why I said we should haul ass. Two, she won't. She wants us to find her."

Neither of them wasted time trying to argue. Pocketing his phone, Houston took off for Bethesda Terrace with Rich and I hot on his heels.

FORTY

Braxton

I didn't realize I'd been cut off and cornered until I stepped off the paved path and onto the red brick at Bethesda Terrace. Purple had begun to give way to orange in the sky while just ahead, three brooding figures waited for my arrival. I'd been too busy admiring the fountain to notice them closing in from the other side.

Looking around as if nothing was amiss, I took in my surroundings, secretly plotting my escape. To my right loomed grand staircases leading to the upper terrace and an arcade offering access to the shadowed lower half. Both provided passage to the rest of the park.

To my left was the lake.

I never realized before how tall they were until now. Standing shoulder to shoulder in front of the fountain now, they were a reckoning force united in anger and blocking my only other escape.

It was Houston who broke the silence first. "You really should be careful who you toy with, Braxton Fawn."

I knew better than to get too close, so I stayed where I was a few paces away. Centered in the fountain behind them was a bronze, eight-foot statue of a winged angel blessing the water cascading into the upper basin before spilling into the pool that surrounded it. Looking on underneath the angel's feet were four cherubs—Temperance, Purity, Health, and Peace.

I had the feeling all of mine were about to be tested.

"How did you know I'd be here?" I asked to keep them talking and distracted. The last clue I sent them had been the bridge, so it really wouldn't have been all that hard to figure out. It wasn't their intelligence I'd underestimated, though. I hadn't counted on their eagerness to get to me. Sunrise was only a few moments away. I thought I'd be long gone before they ever made it here.

Keeping my face unreadable, I quickly ran through my options. Obviously, the path behind me was the only viable one. Maybe they wouldn't notice if I started inching away? I could run, but then what? They'd definitely catch me.

"You made it too easy," Loren quipped as he pulled a stick of gum from his pocket and unwrapped it. "Lucky for you." He slipped the gum between his lips.

"I—"

"Come here," Rich commanded before I could utter another syllable. His gaze and his tone were so flat I didn't know if it was caution or surprise that made me step back. He was supposed to be the sweetheart of the group—the even-tempered one. Right now, he had my heart racing more than the others.

"I believe we were promised five minutes of your *undivided attention*," Loren reminded me.

"Yes," I agreed, gulping as I folded my arms. If I couldn't beat 'em, I'd bluff like hell. "It started two minutes ago."

"Well, then," he returned with a smile that didn't reach his eyes. "I guess we better not waste any more time." Tossing down his gum wrapper, Loren shot forward with a gleam in his eyes that said I'd bitten off more than I could chew.

Despite me knowing how useless it would be, I turned and ran anyway. I could hear Loren's feet pounding the red and white brick as I rushed back the way I had come and under cover of trees. It wouldn't make a difference. At least not for me.

The thick brush kept the rising sun from lighting the path, so I was led by instinct alone as Loren chased me. I was too afraid I'd trip over a rock if I looked behind me to see if he was alone, so I kept going. Loren toyed with my mind by letting me think I'd get away, and just when I was about to round the first bend, he deftly swooped me off my feet.

Laughing as I struggled, he carried me two steps before throwing me down into the grass that lined the path.

He was on me before I could think of what to do next, and then his soft lips crashed into mine. I could taste the mint on his tongue mingling with the cherries on mine and the scent of morning dew that I couldn't tell was real or fake.

Yes, he had my emotions in a whirlwind, but he also had me pressed into the grass while he lay between my legs as if he belonged there.

"This is not how I imagined our first time would be," he complained with a groan against my lips.

I was still panting from the run, and Loren kissing me so deeply. "Who said this would be our first time?"

Ignoring me, Loren rose to his knees before searching the pockets of the jeans he wore. When he came up empty for whatever he was looking for, he closed his eyes, tilted his head back, and swore.

He opened them a moment later, and I didn't like the contemplation in his eyes—like he was considering something he shouldn't. His angry, black gaze was darker than usual under cover of trees just before sunlight. I shivered in desire laced with fear just as the sound of something hitting the ground drew our attention.

Lying in the grass next to my hip was a square packet of gold foil with *Magnum Extra Large* written in black.

My gaze shot to the path behind Loren to see that Houston and Rich had caught up. Houston was still slipping his wallet back into the pockets of his sweats when our gazes met. It figures he'd be the one that came prepared.

"Make it count," he said to Loren when the bassist looked over his shoulder.

I guess it was the only protection they'd brought, which told me getting fucked in a public park that would be filling up with people soon hadn't been their plan for me.

"Oh, I will," Loren promised while gazing down at me.

Snatching up the rubber, he kissed me again before I could remember that I should be saying no.

"Your five minutes are up," I whined when he started ripping open his jeans. It was a weak attempt to resist him at best.

"Not quite," he said with a cocky twist of his lips before shoving his jeans down his thighs and revealing his thick and veiny cock. He was already leaking pre-cum at the tip. I let my gaze travel the length of him and knew I'd feel him long after he was done with me. I watched him tear open the condom with his teeth before skillfully slipping it on.

Still, I didn't object.

As I lay there trembling and growing wetter by the second, he yanked my panties down my thighs and pushed my legs apart to make room for him.

"I want to see her tits," Rich whispered from his perch against a tree.

Loren smiled as he obliged him. Once my dress was shoved around my waist, leaving me bare above and below, Loren ran a long finger down my sopping wet opening.

"Is all this for me, Miss Fawn?" Chuckling when I refused to answer him, he slipped his finger inside. "Maybe I won't give you my dick," he mused as he gently fingered me. "You've been a bad girl this morning."

Refusing to let him have all the power, I forced a smile to my lips. "If you won't, they will. Either way, I'll have some fun."

Never losing his infuriating smirk, Loren took his finger away.

My legs immediately cradled him as he settled between my thighs, and then I felt this dick prodding my entrance when he whispered in my ear.

"That won't work anymore, baby fawn. We've decided you're ours." Slowly, he began to fill me, making my lips part as he stared into my eyes. He didn't speak again until he reached the hilt, and we both released a low, satisfied sound. "*All* of ours."

Instantly, I was coming around his dick.

"Aw, fuck," Loren moaned under his breath. My pussy had locked him in a vice grip.

"She's coming, isn't she?" Houston remarked. They'd been so silent until now I'd almost forgotten they were there.

"I think she likes the idea of belonging to all of us," Rich teased as he looked on.

I was still releasing soft whimpers, my chest heaving from each hard breath when Loren began to move. "She's as tight as you described her," he remarked in a strained voice. His thrusts were slow and gentle, allowing me to get used to his size and invasion. "Holy fuck, I'm not going to last."

"I blew my load in three when I had her," Rich admitted.

"Hurry the fuck up," Houston groused as he kept watch. "Sun's coming up, and we need to get back."

I can't explain why the three of them talking around me, like I was something to use turned me on, but as Loren sped up his thrusts, I found myself coming for a second time.

"Do I still have your motherfucking attention?" he questioned as he pounded me with short brutal thrusts.

The medallion around his neck swung like a pendulum, beating against his chest already dripping with sweat, and making a clinking sound that was mostly drowned by the sound of his hips meeting mine.

I could feel my breasts swaying from his rough movements and knew Rich watched them with a hunger there'd be no time to sate.

Lost in the feeling of being thoroughly fucked, my head fell to the side. I couldn't stifle the sounds I made, either. If someone wandered over, there'd be no question what we were up to.

Loren increased his tempo, and my fingers began ripping the grass from the ground in an attempt to hold on.

"Answer me."

I tried.

Every time my voice was cut short with a choked cry when he'd shove deeper inside of me.

Loren was a remorseless fuck.

He drew out my pleasure even when it caused me pain. I felt like I was being driven wild, trapped in the den they made for me.

"Yes," I managed to moan only when he finally let up. He was back to fucking me slow, but there was nothing gentle about it.

"Show me." I didn't understand how until he flipped onto his back, leaving me on top and gazing down at him. "Ride my dick like you rode my pillow, you insolent little thing."

Rich released a groan that sounded like he was being tortured, and then I heard clothes rustling, prompting me to look over my shoulder. Rich had his dick out now and was stroking it furiously as he watched me ride his friend. I licked my lips, remembering his taste, and deciding I wanted more. Seeing the invitation in my eyes, he ambled over.

A moment later, I had my left hand wrapped around Rich and my right planted on Loren's chest.

"Eyes on me," Loren growled. He'd drawn my attention back to him. "He's had his turn."

Bouncing on his rod, I dug my long nails into Loren's chest, making him grunt in pain as I continued to stroke Rich. Not done making him sorry, I began to carve my name over and over.

"Fuck, she's ambidextrous," Loren breathed before tossing his head back and groaning. "She's fucking ambidextrous."

Feeling another orgasm rising, I rocked my hips at a furious pace, using Loren for the friction I needed to come.

This time I wasn't alone.

Unable to hold back any longer, Loren seized my hips to keep me still and began pounding me hard from below. My mouth fell open from the sensation of Loren completely wrecking my middle. His movements became jerky soon after, and then he froze as he flooded the condom. The grunt he released was cut off when my pussy began contracting around him. The look in his eyes said I owned him as I held his dick in yet another vice grip.

Turning to Rich, no words were spoken between us before I swallowed his dick in three gulps. It took maybe thirty seconds of rough deep throating before he was coming with a groan that I felt in my bones. Breathing hard, his knees shook a little when he took a step back and pulled up his shorts.

I winked at Rich, and once he smiled, I turned my attention back to Loren.

Still nestled inside of me, he lay there with his eyes closed, body relaxed, and his breathing slow and deep. It took me five seconds of calling his name to realize he'd fallen asleep.

"We need to talk," Houston informed me the moment we were through the door. We were back inside our hotel suite, and we'd almost gotten here unscathed.

At the edge of the park, we were spotted by early joggers who'd paid no mind to our rumpled clothing or the grass in our hair as they excitedly requested our autographs. By that time, we'd drawn more attention. Once the crowd had gotten too big for us to handle safely, Loren took my hand, and the four of us made a run for it.

Sighing, I stopped at the bottom of the stairs leading to my room before turning and gripping the railing. "Is the topic in any way related to our next show?"

I watched the three of them gape at me with matching, confused frowns. If I weren't so exhausted and knew better by now, I'd think that they were adorable.

"I didn't think so," I said when none of them responded.

I bet they thought me spreading my legs meant all would be forgiven. I'd given them time to plead their case and be heard, and they hadn't used it wisely, so…no. All was not forgiven.

"Thanks for the orgasms." Turning, I gingerly climbed the sweeping stairs. Loren and his friends had done a number on me in more ways than one.

FORTY-ONE

Rich

WHAT...THE HELL?

How is it that we kept making the same mistakes? Or maybe we were making all new ones. I didn't know anymore. I couldn't tell which way was up.

Houston hadn't said a word after Braxton left us with our dicks in our hands...so to speak. He'd disappeared inside his room, and not long after, I heard the shower running.

Me, I was sitting at the kitchen island, rubbing my temples and contemplating our next move.

Not all of us had taken her rejection so calmly, though.

"Braxton Francesca Fawn, you open this goddamn door, right now!" Loren shouted as he pummeled her bedroom door.

"Damn it, Lo!" I snapped when my head began to throb out of control. "You know that's not going to work, so sit the hell down."

Loren looked at me, back to the door, and then me again before giving her door one last look and kicking it hard as hell.

Returning to the lower level, he dashed into the spare we shared and returned with his stash before rolling up. If nothing else, weed definitely mellowed him whenever he was off his fucking rocker.

"How the fuck is it that she still won't talk to us?" he said after passing me the joint.

I shrugged as I brought it to my lips and inhaled. "Maybe it's because she gave us the chance, and you chose to have sex with her instead?"

"Easy for you to judge when you already had her. Sue me. I was feeling left out."

I shook my head as I regarded my best friend. He was the smartest idiot I knew. "You were better off not knowing how good she feels—at least until she's done icing us out."

"I really thought we were coming back for round two," he admitted before chuckling bitterly. *Me too.* "I would have even been happy just getting to hold her."

Laughing at Loren's expense as he slumped in his stool, I eyed him. "I never took you for a sap."

He shrugged while staring somberly at the granite countertop. "And I never thought you'd grow some balls, yet here we are."

Since I was still holding his joint and knew it was the last of his stash, I tossed his shit in the sink and flipped the garbage disposal switch near my leg.

"What did you do that for?" he yelled. His mouth was open as he stared inside the sink in horror.

"Cuz you're a bitch," I said while standing up. I flipped the switch when I was sure there was nothing left. "And we agreed a long time ago to quit this shit. Nothing's changed."

"Everything's changed," he bit back.

I was already walking away from him, so I didn't respond. I needed a shower, and even though cleaning up was the last thing on my mind, I was hoping it would distract me for a while. As soon as I was done, Loren hopped in, and I knew he'd be occupied for a while.

Motherfucker stayed in there for hours, it seemed.

As soon as I had finished dressing, I called Danielle, our assistant. After telling her what I wanted, I hung up.

It only took her an hour to get the things I needed, and after checking to make sure it was all there, I climbed the short stairs to Braxton's room. It was quiet as hell on the other side, making me paranoid that she'd snuck out again. Knocking, I waited, and still, there was no sound. Had she fallen asleep?

I knocked again, and finally, thankfully, I heard her footsteps.

"Go away, Loren," she whispered when she came and stood by the door.

"It's Rich." I didn't like that she still hesitated instead of immediately opening her door. Two months ago, she would have welcomed me in with a smile I took for granted. When the door cracked, and I was staring into her big, brown eyes, I exhaled.

My relief was short-winded by her cold tone. "What do you want?"

"I want to apologize. I've been a jerk."

"It's fine," she said in a tone that assured me it wasn't.

"If that were true, you wouldn't feel the need to keep this door between us. That's my fault, and I want to make it up to you."

When her brows dipped, I knew I had her curiosity, if not her forgiveness. Not yet anyway. "How?"

Unable to help my smile, I wordlessly held up the bag from the wig and costume store.

"You weren't kidding!" Braxton exclaimed as she stood in front of the wax replicas.

I chuckled as she gaped at Houston's likeness. He was the only one in our exhibit who *wasn't* smiling. That was pretty goddamn accurate if you asked me.

When she was finally satisfied that it really wasn't him, she moved to the one of me. I was standing next to Houston, wearing one of my hoodies, and holding a set of drumsticks—lip piercing, silver eyes with gold flecks, and all.

"It looks just like you," she whispered so no one would overhear.

I was wearing a disguise too.

Braxton had laughed for ten minutes straight when I donned the brown Annie wig, sideburns, mustache, and black-rimmed glasses. I looked like the nerdy version of Jacques Grande from *The Love Guru*.

I have no idea what made Dani choose the short, purple wig for Braxton—or why it worked.

I just knew with those expressive brown eyes and adorable freckles that she looked like a goddamn manga character.

And now, all I could think about when I looked at her was the anime porn I used to watch as a kid. She'd changed into a black, sleeveless ribbed dress so form-fitting I wondered if she was wearing panties. And she'd paired it with black thigh-high socks and her combat boots.

"Loren's going to be pissed when he finds out they made his nose too big," she remarked with a snort.

She was now standing in front of Loren's that was placed on the other side of mine, leaving me sandwiched between Houston and Loren. The museum had captured his abs since his shirt was depicted open, the medallion he never took off, and even his signature smirk.

With an evil gleam in her eye, she posed next to the statue and quickly snapped a selfie. I was pretty sure she was planning to show it to him later.

I know it seemed shady not to have invited Houston and Loren, but I'd barely talked her into letting *me* come. I was hoping to at least soften her up enough for them to win her over on their own.

"I can't believe this is your first time seeing it," she said absently after she'd moved on. Calvin's wax replica was right next to Loren's.

"It's only been six months since they added it, and this is our first time back in the city since our last tour."

"Do you miss him?" she blurted.

I was a little startled at her rapid change of subject.

"Who?" I don't know why I asked when I already knew.

"Calvin," she said while still admiring his statue. "You guys don't seem like you mourn him."

Because we don't. I forced myself not to shrug or sound too defensive when I spoke. "It's been months."

Her head turned, and then she stared at me.

I knew she was disappointed by my cold answer. She left me under the scrutiny of her gaze for what seemed like forever before nodding as if she accepted my answer. I could already see her shutting down and cursed Calvin from the grave. I was not going to let him take anything else of mine away.

"We weren't friends," I heard myself say. My tone was hesitant as I chose my words carefully. I didn't want to give her another reason to run. "Far from it."

Spinning around, she faced me. When her arms crossed, I tried not to focus too much on the extra sliver of thigh exposed by her dress lifting slightly. *She better have on panties.* "Why?"

"The label chose him for Bound when they decided they wanted Houston to focus on vocals. It was a rocky start that we never recovered from." I'd given her the beginning and the end, but I purposely left out the middle. Now was not the time to tell Braxton about Emily.

"Like me."

"*Nothing* like you," I denied vehemently. "We *want* you, Braxton, and we've been trying to make you see that."

"Have you?"

"*Yes.*"

"I see," she snapped. I knew at that moment that I wasn't getting to her. Not even close. "So if Calvin had convenient pussy for you to fuck whenever you liked, things would have been different with him?"

"We were dicks to him, Braxton. Just like we were dicks to you, but Calvin was no angel."

"Neither am I."

"Yeah, but he never had me convinced that I was falling for him, Braxton. *You do.*"

I didn't realize my voice had risen until I noticed the attention we'd garnered.

I didn't want to risk anyone looking too closely and recognizing us, so I grabbed Braxton's elbow and led her through the rest of the exhibit so we could get the hell out of there. It seemed to take forever, and not once had she commented on what I'd said to her.

It was like it never happened.

"Let me go," she quietly requested once we were on the street.

In an instant, I was in her face and trapping her against the wall of the museum.

I didn't care about the fact that we were standing in the middle of a potential mob. My heart was racing for other reasons. "I tell you I'm falling in love with you, and your answer is to let you go?"

"My arm, Jericho. Let my *arm* go."

"Oh."

I released her elbow only to take her hand, earning an irritated look from her when she tried not to blush. As I threaded our fingers together, the black Suburban we had drive us here pulled up to the curb, so we climbed inside.

"Where to next?" I asked her once the back door closed behind me. At that exact moment, her stomach growled loud enough to scare a bear. I laughed to myself at her sheepish look as she attempted to avoid my eyes. "Dinner it is."

While our driver was distracted, pulling us safely into traffic, I decided to settle a certain burning curiosity. Otherwise, I'd never get through dinner in one piece.

Placing my hand on her thigh, I watched her face as I slowly slipped it higher and higher. I wanted to give her time to stop me, but she never blinked, and she never spoke a word.

By the time my fingers reached the apex of her thigh, I knew what I would find, but I kept going anyway.

"Braxton..." Using my knuckle, I teased her wet pussy that she'd left bare, knowing I'd be curious. Her breathing started to quicken when I didn't let up even after I'd gotten my answer.

"Yes?"

"Where are your panties, baby?"

As if she wasn't on the verge of coming, she smiled at me like the cat that ate the canary. "I knew I was forgetting something."

FORTY-TWO

Houston

WE'RE ON OUR WAY UP, RICH TEXTED OUR GROUP CHAT.

He and Braxton had disappeared without saying shit, and each hour they were gone, I grew more and more pissed. Our security team wouldn't be back on duty until tomorrow. Rich should have known better than to risk Braxton and himself. Before I could respond from my perch on the couch, he sent another text.

Rich: I think I figured out Braxton's beef.

Loren: Which one?

I didn't have to hear Loren's voice to know it was dry as fuck. Right now, he was shut up in the spare bedroom where he'd been since realizing Braxton had left with Rich.

Rich: Shut up, Lo. For once. Just shut up.

Rich: When we fight, she feels responsible

So she shuts us out, I texted before he could finish his train of thought.

Rich: Yup.

Rich: We're almost there. Don't say shit unless you're playing nice.

Loren: So you want us to pretend to like each other long enough to trick her into a relationship?

Loren's objection to Rich's plan genuinely surprised me. I thought he'd be all out for playing dirty. Instead, he was willing to jump through whatever hoops to get her fair and square.

Rich: We won't be pretending.

It was the last text he was able to send before they walked through the door. I had my eyes on her from the moment she stepped through wearing a purple wig that caught me off guard. Rich had claimed they'd worn a disguise, but I hadn't been convinced that it was enough. He looked like that character Justin Timberlake played in a movie I couldn't remember.

Unable to look away from Braxton, I knew the moment her apprehension sunk in for what awaited her now that playtime was over.

It's true.

I wanted to ask where the hell she'd been and who told her she could leave, but I didn't. I couldn't bring myself to be the reason for that depleted look in her eyes. Instead of Braxton sucking the happiness out of the room, the room had sucked the happiness out of Braxton. It was a bruising blow to my ego, to be sure.

Loren appeared on the spare's threshold, and the moment Braxton spotted him, she made a break for her room. "Have fun?" he asked before she could get too far.

She spun on her heel to regard him with a curious squint as if she were trying to figure out whether he was being genuine or not.

Deciding to make a stand, she lifted her chin. "I did."

"Oh." Loren scratched his chin. His eyes darted around the room as he searched for something else to say in an to attempt to make small talk. He was never without words when he was being an asshole, though. "So what did you see?"

"You."

Smooth as fuck, as if he'd actually understood her cryptic reply, he didn't miss a beat. "Doubt it, baby. I was here all day."

Setting down the bag of souvenirs she'd bought, she dug out her phone from…somewhere. Her dress, which had no pockets, was tight and short as fuck. I watched her through narrowed eyes as she crossed the room and made her way toward Loren.

No way she was wearing panties.

My gaze shot to Rich, wondering what else they'd been up to. He caught me staring and smirked. He had another one of his idiotic plans to thank for the reason I didn't pummel him.

"What the hell," Loren barked out of nowhere, drawing my attention away from Rich. Braxton was showing Loren something on her phone, and whatever it was made his face turn purple. He looked like an angry eggplant emoji.

"What is it?" I asked when no one bothered to explain. Rich had his lips tucked, and his body shook as he fought to keep himself from losing it.

Braxton took her phone from Loren, who looked like he wanted to snatch it back before he stormed over to the mirror by the door and started inspecting his nose for some reason. When Braxton reached me with her phone in tow, I accepted it from her before pulling her down onto my lap and before she could realize my intent.

She didn't fight me.

I pretended my heart wasn't skipping inside my chest when she sat in my lap like she'd accepted that she belonged there. After getting my fill of staring at the goofy face Braxton was making in the photo, I finally glanced at the wax replica of Loren that she was posing with and burst out laughing.

The sound made Rich lose his composure, followed by Brax before we were all laughing at Loren's expense.

Truth be told, it wasn't that bad. The difference was minuscule, and the statue was pretty accurate.

To Loren, it looked like his nose should have its own zip code.

Without thinking to ask for permission, I went through the rest of the photos she'd taken, wanting to see her day through her eyes.

I wasn't surprised to see she'd even taken some with Rich since she was being so agreeable with me. I felt her gaze on me as I scrolled through them.

He'd taken her everywhere.

Times Square, the Statue of Liberty, the MET, the Empire State Building—everywhere I'd been too stubborn and stupid not to take her myself.

When I reached the last entry and realized it was actually a video, she tried to snatch her phone back, but I held it out of reach.

Our gazes met, mine steady, hers nervous.

"Houston—"

I held her tighter before pressing play. The video was dark, but I could still make out the wig Rich wore, and his head buried between Braxton's legs as she recorded. He was eating her pussy in what looked like the back seat of a car, but I couldn't tell anything else about their surroundings.

"Rich," Braxton moaned in the video as he attacked her clit.

My mouth began to water as I wondered what she tasted like. It was a problem I'd have to rectify soon.

Her soft moans filled the room, and even Loren paused his bitching to listen in. In the video, she wound her hips, fucking Rich's face as he slurped and sucked her nectar as if she were cool spring water on a hot summer day.

"I'm coming, Jericho."

She wasn't lying.

I was hard and getting harder at the sounds she made. I didn't have to question whether she could feel me when she squirmed in my lap. The footage became shaky before her grip must have slipped, and she dropped the phone, ending the video.

I took my eyes off the phone for the first time since the video started to look at Braxton, who was refusing to let us see how embarrassed she was. It made me wonder why she'd taken the video in the first place.

"Did you enjoy that?" I asked her even though I'd seen the proof.

"Yes." Her tone was flat. "Can I please have my phone back now?"

This time I gave it up since I'd seen all I needed to. Standing, she walked to where she'd left her bags before climbing the steps to her room and closing the door behind her. I didn't hear the lock turn this time, which had me feeling like a kid in the candy store.

First things first.

"Tell me you didn't do that in front of the driver," I demanded as soon as we were alone.

"Of course not," Rich bit back. "I told him to take a walk.

You're welcome, by the way. I made her record that so you two wouldn't feel left out."

Loren was beaming as he regarded Jericho. "Good looking out, best friend." Just as quickly, a frown took over his face as he looked Rich over like he was seeing him for the first time. "Bro, what the hell are you wearing?"

"It's a disguise."

"Clearly. You look like someone I should be telling to stay away from schools and playgrounds." Rich immediately snatched off the wig and shoved it against Loren's chest. The mustache, sideburns, and glasses quickly followed. "That's better," Loren said with a sigh. "I'm honestly questioning how Braxton let you go down on her looking like a pervert." When Rich looked ready to hit him, Loren smiled. "We're supposed to be getting along, remember?"

Braxton stayed in her room for the rest of the night, and I wasn't sure how we managed it, but none of us bothered her. Loren and Rich had grown bored waiting and were currently sound asleep in the spare. Meanwhile, I was wide awake and feeling anxious. I couldn't stop replaying in my head every fucked-up thing I'd ever said to her. I couldn't stop wanting to undo my brutal treatment of her. My desperate desire for the impossible, to travel in time to change the past, is what kept me up. I wouldn't be surprised if I never slept again from the fear that Braxton may never forgive me.

Sometime around one in the morning, she finally showed her face. I caught her sneaking into the kitchen and cornered her against the fridge.

"Enjoy your day?" I whispered to her with my hands on her hips. I didn't want to risk waking Loren and Rich. I was willing to share her with them any other time and for the rest of our lives, but I needed to do this alone.

"Yes. There was so much to see." Her nose wrinkled as she frowned. "I'm not sure I'll get to see everything before we go."

"No one ever sees the whole city in one visit," I reassured her. "It just gives you an excuse to come back."

She beamed up at me as she clutched her glass of warm milk to her chest. I guess I wasn't the only one having trouble sleeping.

"That's true. Besides, next time, I'll be regular Braxton Fawn again and won't need to wear a disguise."

I didn't like hearing her making plans to leave us, so I ignored the inevitable for another truth. "You were never ordinary. You lit up the universe, and that's how we found you."

"Pretty words, Morrow, but you didn't find me. Oni did."

My lips twisted in amusement as my hands slipped around from her hips to her panty-clad ass. "Semantics."

She smiled softly. "Good night, Houston."

As soon as she tried to escape, my lips found hers. I took the glass from her hands and set it on top of the fridge before deepening the kiss. Like every time we kissed, Braxton followed my lead, giving in and letting me take as much as I wanted. She was pliant when she wanted to be and only when it mattered.

"Let me stay with you tonight," I said when I finally pulled away.

She stared up at me, contemplating whether or not to trust me. "I don't know what's happening," she whispered so low I could barely make her words out despite how close we stood, "but whatever it is, I'd like to take it slow." She suddenly looked wary as she waited for my response.

Nodding, I took a step back. "All right."

Grabbing her glass from the top of the fridge, I handed it to her before turning away to leave. When she grabbed my hand to keep me from going, I paused.

"No sex," she said.

I didn't understand until she led me to her room and into her bed to sleep in my arms until morning came.

FORTY-THREE

Braxton

I couldn't remember the last time I'd slept this soundly. It definitely hadn't been in the last two months. As I reluctantly came to, the warm body underneath me was the first clue that I wasn't alone. The second was the morning wood poking my belly.

A king-size bed, complete with pillow-top mattress, and I'd chosen to sleep on top of a chest as hard as brick.

When my eyes finally chose to open, the last person I expected to see was Houston underneath me. I knew it was him because I recognized his nipple of all things.

It all came flooding back.

The wild goose chase I'd sent them on yesterday, and Houston worming his way into my bed. I was just grateful I kept my word and didn't have sex with him. My motives hadn't been entirely pure, though. Like me, he'd been having trouble sleeping, and I figured we'd have a better chance together than apart. I hated that I was right because it complicated feelings that were already complex.

I was staring at the fantastic view of New York that twenty-nine floors high offered when I felt Houston's hand curve around my nape. I hadn't realized he was awake the entire time I was brooding. Still, I let him pull my attention away from the panoramic windows and kiss me until I was fully awake.

I never thought Houston Morrow could ever make me feel like I was floating, but alas, here I was. I just wondered how soon before I came crashing down.

"Good morning," he whispered against my lips. On stage, Houston had the kind of voice that altered the construct of your soul. It changed you. In bed and heavy with sleep, however, he had a different kind of effect. The kind that made you do things you knew you shouldn't.

"Hey."

He stared into my eyes for one long, breathless moment, and I could tell something was heavy on his mind. He didn't leave me in suspense for long, and when he finally spoke the words that I never thought I'd hear, I was glad I was lying down for them.

"I'm sorry, Braxton."

"For?" I didn't care how weak he made my knees. I'd return the favor by not making whatever he hoped to achieve easy for him.

"For not realizing what I had before it was too late."

I didn't react mostly out of confusion. I became his guitarist, so he made me his enemy. He'd never given me the chance to be anything else.

"I'd like to start over," he proposed when I chose to say nothing.

Frowning, I felt my heart race as I sat up a little. I couldn't take this suspense any longer. I had to know what they were plotting, and I wanted it in plain terms. They'd alluded, they'd made hints, but never in a setting or in a way that I could take with a grain of salt.

"What's going on, Houston?"

His gaze was stern as he held my eyes. "You know exactly what's going on, Braxton Francesca."

I should have never told them my middle name.

The coldness in my voice wasn't forged when I spoke. I could be stern too. "Actually, I don't. Why don't you spell it out for me?"

I yelped when I was suddenly thrown on my back. Houston was on top of me now, holding me down with his weight. He made sure I couldn't walk away from this conversation until he was ready to let me.

"I want you," he said as easily as if we hadn't spent the last six months warring.

"You had me." I may not have gotten enough, but I was sure

he'd gotten his fill. That goes for Loren and Rich too. Even with my past, I couldn't believe I'd fucked all three of them.

Suddenly, I heard angry voices urging me to repent.

Houston squinted as he stared down at me. "Why do I think you're purposefully misunderstanding everything that I'm saying?" I heard the warning in his tone not to push him. Naturally, that meant none of his buttons were safe.

"Because you're still beating around the bush, and before you, my patience was never this thin."

Houston blinked at me before groaning and burying his face in my neck. "I deserved that," he mumbled as if it'd been up for debate. We lay there, listening to one another breathe for a while before he spoke again. "I've never done this before."

"Done what?"

"Ask a girl to be with me."

I stared at the ceiling, pretending my heart didn't skip a beat. Houston was too used to having his desires handed to him. I wouldn't be just another thing on a platter. "Boo-hoo."

His head lifted from my neck, and when our gazes met, I was immersed in the warm and inviting scent of vanilla. For a third time, I was hit with an emotion I couldn't define. Loren was first, then Rich, and finally Houston. He'd never looked so vulnerable. At least not while I'd known him. Lowering his head again, I met him halfway. This time when we kissed, it was a meeting of broken souls, each hoping our pieces fit to make something whole.

Between kisses, he finally whispered, "Be my girlfriend, Braxton Fawn."

My head knew what to say. My heart was in my throat. I knew it was coming, and somehow, I was still unprepared. I wanted to say yes. I felt it on my tongue, overwhelmed by green apples. All I had to do was shut my mind away, and I'd be his. There was only one problem.

He was asking too much.

I couldn't pretend Loren and Rich weren't chasing me too.

I wanted them all equally, but I craved them for different

reasons. Houston challenged me, Loren worshiped me, and Rich made me feel like I was worthy of redemption.

I didn't want to give that up.

This tour would end, but the wreckage they will have left of my heart would be permanent. There was only one way I could survive. One way no one got hurt, and…it was impossible. Almost as hopeless as choosing.

I sighed.

I had three birds and only one stone to conquer them.

And Houston, the mercurial rock god whose opinion of me swayed with the wind, was asking me to risk it all. Suddenly, the room became awash in the paralyzing scent of copper.

Breaking his kiss, I looked into his eyes and swallowed desire that wasn't sexual but still tasted the same.

"Give me a reason."

FORTY-FOUR

Loren

BRAXTON WAS POUTING.

We were back on our bus with New York in the rearview, and we'd all been more than reluctant to leave. It wasn't the confined space I minded.

It was the fear in Braxton's eyes that the fairytale was over.

All the good memories we'd made were left behind in the city, and back on the bus, we were only left with the bad. With the help of the disguises Danielle had obtained for us, we'd been able to show Braxton around as much as we could before leaving this morning.

"I don't know if I can go back to my bunk after sleeping on a real bed again."

She was sitting on our sectional with her feet in Rich's lap, nibbling on the hero she'd been eating for the last hour. I don't think she'd even made it halfway through yet, but I enjoyed watching her try. Braxton's lips were insane. She always looked like she'd been sucking face for hours. I was jealous of the fact that Rich had gotten to feel them around his dick and didn't know when I'd ever have that privilege. At the moment, I had more important matters regarding Braxton Fawn.

"Take the bedroom," Rich immediately offered.

Smiling softly, she shook her head. "It wouldn't be fair."

Rich's gaze shifted to me at the same time mine fell on him. "We don't mind," we said at the same time. I'm pretty sure it wasn't the only thought we shared.

Houston appeared after taking a phone call in his bunk, but she didn't see him because her back was to him. He approached on silent feet with his eyes on her and purpose in each step.

I didn't realize his intent until it was too late.

Bending over her shoulder, Houston bit off half her sandwich in one bite.

"I was eating that!" she yelled after he rounded the couch to sit next to her. She stared at him angrily the entire time he chewed.

After gulping down the last of it, he smiled at her. "Didn't look like it."

I snorted at the look on his face when Braxton made him wear what was left of her sandwich. Houston said nothing as he gripped his T-shirt from behind before pulling it off and using it to clean his face. I knew he wasn't upset, but he was good with mind games. He kept his expression neutral, making Braxton watch him warily until he leaned over to tongue her down. I rolled my eyes as I watched them go at it, but I knew to keep my jealousy to myself.

Three hours later, we were at the Mohegan Sun, a resort and casino with an arena we were playing tomorrow night.

Our security was back on duty, so we didn't bother with disguises. It didn't take long for the paparazzi and a few wild cards to get wind of our presence either. The only part that bugged me about having so many eyes around was remembering to keep my hands to myself. Houston and Rich struggled with the same whenever they ventured too close or lingered too long.

One of us involved with our new guitarist was bad enough. All three of us publicly claiming a piece would be inviting trouble that we weren't prepared for. Not yet. Eventually, we'd break the news to Xavier and warn our publicist.

At the moment, there wasn't much to tell.

Houston and Rich had gotten back on her good side, but they hadn't been allowed more than a foot each. While they treaded carefully, I was still figuring out how to get her to talk to me and what I would say once I succeeded. I told her how I felt long before either of them dared.

Yet you still fucked up.

I knew it was the reason she was so cold with me, never sparing me more than a glance while allowing my best friends to kiss and touch their fill. Claiming one thing only to do another, I'd hurt her more, so she trusted me less.

Braxton had wandered off with two of our guards trailing her, and eventually, after fifteen minutes of searching, I found her standing at one of the slot machines.

The floor was mostly empty on a Monday afternoon, so there was no one around to see when I wrapped myself around her from behind. I didn't count our guards because, as far as their jobs were concerned, they were Three Blind Mice.

"Are you running from me?" I whispered when my hands found her hips. Braxton was almost the perfect height. She wasn't so short that my dick was in her shoulder blades, but I wouldn't have minded her with a few more inches either. Right now, Loren Jr. was busy giving her a tramp stamp when it was her ass that had woken him up to party. She was also stiff in my arms, and I didn't like that. I wanted the days back when she melted against me.

Right now, she refused to even look at me.

"You found me, didn't you?"

I chuckled to myself.

Her smartass mouth was at the top of the list of things I'd missed. I'd rather she give me her anger than nothing at all. I found myself kissing her nape since her hair was hanging over her shoulder and inhaling the brown sugar body wash that I knew she used. When she still didn't react, I sighed and closed my eyes.

"Tell me what to do, Braxton."

"Now, why would I do that?"

"Because you want me to fix it as bad as I do."

Hearing someone approach, I forced myself to let her go. Luckily, the group passed without us being recognized, and the moment the coast was clear, I was back in Braxton's space. This was the closest I'd gotten to her since we fucked in Central Park. I wasn't about to let the possibility of being seen stop me from taking whatever scraps she threw me. I hated having to keep my feelings a secret, and it was solely for Braxton's sake that I did. Anyone else could swallow thumbtacks.

I watched Braxton play that stupid slot machine for thirty minutes before running out of cash and winning only ten of it back.

Taking her hand, I led her away, and after losing all her cash, she didn't object. Houston and Rich were busy putting money on the races, and I had the feeling the clingy fucks had backed off Braxton to make room for me to get my shit together.

After asking Braxton if she was hungry and getting her to agree to have dinner with me, I managed to get us a table in a private room without reservations. Arranging it was chaotic as fuck, but getting some time alone with Braxton was worth it. Once we were seated, closed off from prying eyes, and left alone with our drinks, I got up from my side of the tall booth to sit next to her.

Sticking to the pact I'd already broken once, I'd ordered lemonade instead of something hard like I needed, and she did the same. Right now, her eyes were glued to her drink as she tried to avoid mine.

"Look at me." I couldn't take it anymore.

After taking a deep breath, she did, and I finally learned the reason why she wouldn't before. A drop of liquid slipped from her eye, and I knew she hated me even more for that tear.

It was the second time I'd made her cry.

"Don't say you're sorry," she snapped when she read the words on my lips. Shaking her head, she angrily wiped the ugly truth away. "I'm sick of hearing it."

"I don't deserve your forgiveness, but I'm asking for it anyway."

"Tell me why you think you need it."

She already knew why.

She wanted to hear me admit everything I'd done out loud. She wanted my shame and regret and my anger. She wanted me to see her pain.

"I tried to push you out of my life the moment you walked into it. I let Houston belittle you because it took the heat off me.

I knew Rich was using you to pull us back together again. I made a fake account just to troll you on Instagram. I told you I had feelings for you when I knew I wasn't ready. I acted like a spoiled prick because you were smart enough not to return them. I made you feel guilty for being attracted to my friends. I was an idiot to believe that pushing us away was what you needed. I broke into your phone and found all your nudes. And then I stole your panties and jerked off in front of you. I didn't fight for you even though I knew you were waiting." Inhaling and exhaling, I closed my eyes and winced. "And I treated you like a groupie instead of my future wife by fucking you on the ground without asking you to dinner first."

Braxton was staring at me when I opened my eyes while giving away nothing of what was happening inside her head.

"Aren't you forgetting something?" she prompted when I was quiet for too long. I started sweating bullets as I ran through the list in my head. When I drew a blank and just stared at her, she pursed her lips before lifting her glass. "You left the toilet seat up this morning." Eyeing me, she took a sip of her lemonade and then set the glass down. "I fell in."

So that's what her squealing was all about.

I was surprised she hadn't ripped into me, but then again, I wasn't. I would have seized any opening for this moment, but until now, she hadn't been ready to listen. Another time and I would have laughed or made a joke, but at the moment, I was feeling a little dead inside.

"Tell me you forgive me." It sounded like a demand, but we both knew it wasn't. I was begging at this point, and I wasn't the least bit ashamed.

Braxton was back to not looking at me again when she shrugged and offered me a nonchalant answer. "I'm working on it."

My phone notifying me of a text kept me from begging her to work faster, damn it. Sighing, I checked my screen.

Houston: Where are you?

I texted back using one hand because the other was busy toying with the ends of Braxton's hair.

Fuck off. I'm almost there.

My phone buzzed again since I'd put it on silent. This time it was a text from Rich since Houston had used our group chat.

Rich: Lol. I doubt it. Let us come help you.

Houston: Before you fuck it up for all of us.

Our gushing waitress returned to take our orders, and while Braxton told her what she wanted, I texted Houston and Rich the name of the restaurant. Maybe I *could* use some help since Braxton held onto her grudges so tightly, you'd need the jaws of life to pry them apart.

Feeling Braxton nudge me, I looked up from my phone to see the beaming waitress waiting for my order.

"Hey, sweetheart. I'll take three Porterhouses and a side of fries. I want two of those steaks cooked medium and one medium-rare. I'll also take some of those mini crab cakes you charge a left nut a piece for, the creamed spinach, and some bread for the table. Oh, and a coke and water." I winked at our waitress as Braxton gaped at me.

"Are you really going to eat all of that?" she asked me.

"Not for me."

Just as the waitress pranced off with our orders, Houston and Jericho entered the room, which saved me from having to explain further. She didn't say anything when they slid into the booth across from us.

"I hope your luck was better than mine," I said to kill the awkward silence. Braxton cut her gaze at me, so I guess I wasn't as cryptic as I thought.

"I lost ten grand," Houston announced as I put my hand on Braxton's thigh. She'd worn a skirt today.

"How? It was a cheap bet."

"He wasn't betting on the horses," Rich answered with a smirk.

My hand paused from inching up Braxton's leg when I caught his drift. Each time I forgot why I hated my friends, they reminded me. "Night's not over."

"You know I can leave, and then you three won't need to talk about me like I'm not here…because I won't be." She pushed my hand off her leg, and it felt like I'd taken three steps back from the half a step I'd gained.

So much for help.

Our food came, so I shut the fuck up and ate as I thought of my next move. I'd been honest. I'd been sincere. I didn't know what else I could do to get through to her.

"What does your medallion mean?" she asked me out of the blue halfway through our meal. Houston and Rich both paused mid-chew as their gazes darted between Braxton and me.

Swallowing my food, I sat back as I looked at her. My appetite was gone. "What makes you think it means something?"

"You never take it off."

I could tell by her tone that she wouldn't just shrug it off if I chose not to give her the full and honest truth. *Fuck.* "Instead of a car for my sixteenth birthday, my father gave me this."

Lifting the heavy chain off my neck, I slipped it up and over my head for the first time in six years. Before Braxton could react, I placed the medallion depicting a man with the head of a lion forging a sword around her neck. The rest of the crest included the family name and "solum initium est" engraved in the platinum. I don't remember the exact value, but it was somewhere around a hundred and fifty thousand.

"Just before he kicked me out and left me with nothing, he told me to pawn it because it was the last cent I'd ever get out of him."

"But you didn't."

It wasn't a question since she wore it around her lovely neck, but I answered her anyway. "Nope."

"And that's why you've never taken it off and always wore your shirt open," she pieced together out loud. I could see the wheels in her mind turning as she looked at me. "You knew he'd be keeping tabs and wanted him to know that you didn't need his money."

"Yup."

I let myself be an open book as she studied me, but I didn't mention my father's offer to give me everything I once thought I wanted if I quit Bound and came home.

Nodding once, Braxton signaled that her curiosity was settled, and I released a quiet breath for small favors. My old man was the last thing I wanted to discuss while trying to win over my girl. I never thought I'd be capable of wanting more after watching my parents crap all over their marriage. I couldn't risk anything giving me second thoughts. Spending another moment without Braxton was crippling enough. No way was I willing to go the rest of my life.

We headed back to the bus after eating, but by then, the night was no longer young. I still had no idea where I stood with her.

Instead of asking, I watched her disappear inside the bedroom that was now hers after we assured her it was fine. It's not like we were planning to bring groupies on board.

"So what happened?" Rich asked the moment we heard the shower turn on.

I shrugged as I flopped onto the couch. "We talked, I told her everything I'd done wrong, and that was it."

"She didn't say anything else?" Houston questioned with a frown.

"Nope."

"Did you apologize?" Rich asked me like he really believed it wouldn't have occurred to me on my own to do so.

"In a way."

"In a way?" they both echoed like some jackasses.

"She wouldn't let me, and...I don't blame her." I had no idea why I was coming to her defense like she could hear me and would forgive me on the spot. *If only.* "Look, there's no rush," I lied as I put my feet up on the table. "The tour doesn't end for another nine months. One way or another, she's all ours whether she wants to be or not."

"Do me a favor and don't say that to her," Rich advised.

I waved him off. "I'm done listening to you. All you've done is dig us into deeper shit."

"He's also the only one of us who's ever gotten a woman to marry him," Houston pointed out.

Barking a bitter laugh, I leaned my head back against the sectional and closed my eyes. "He was the only one dumb enough to ask."

FORTY-FIVE

Braxton

I KNEW THE THREE OF THEM WERE WAITING FOR SOME KIND OF SIGN OR answer from me. My heart knew what it wanted, but my head still wouldn't agree. I knew the only solution to my dilemma was to sit them all down at once. I just didn't know what I'd say or what I'd do once I did.

Would I say yes and take a chance, or would I turn them away out of pride? I wasn't all that convinced they'd suffered enough.

I certainly had.

Sighing, I finished pulling my wet hair up. I didn't realize until I looked in the mirror that I was still wearing Loren's medallion. I wasn't sure if he meant for me to keep it, but I liked wearing something that belonged to him, even if it was temporary.

Smiling, I left the bathroom only to find the bedroom occupied. The room seemed ten times smaller with three rock gods invading it.

Houston sat at the edge closest to me, Loren at the foot of the bed, and Jericho taking up the opposite edge. I stupidly thought I had until morning before I was forced to face them again. I could see the restraint dwindling in their eyes and knew my time was up.

"Come sit down," Houston told me.

I garnered by his tone that it wasn't up for debate. "What are you guys doing in here?"

"Waiting for you, obviously," Loren answered. The glare he bestowed on me was full of accusations.

"Sit down, Braxton," Houston ordered once again.

Huffing, I stormed over to the bed. I felt their eyes on me as I climbed the mattress, braced my back against the headboard, and held my legs up to my chest with my arms wrapped around them. It was all the distance I could put between them and me. All the protection I could hope for.

Jericho chuckled as he read my mind, and a teasing light entered his eyes. "That won't help you, baby."

My lips parted slightly as I felt my legs tremble. I didn't know what to say. I didn't know how to fight these feelings they evoked. They obviously knew how to wield them against me.

"Now that we've had *your* undivided attention," Loren stated, "you have ours."

"Tell us what you're thinking." The request had come from Houston.

"I don't know. I'm not done yet," I snapped.

"Maybe that's the problem," Loren said to his friends instead of me. They were talking around me again. "She's overthinking."

"It must be all the space we've been giving her."

Jericho.

I never thought he'd be the one to betray me.

All at once, they closed in around me. The room began to smell like I was on a boat in the middle of the ocean, and there was no one else around. Only the four of us.

We were lost and drifting, resigned to our fate with only each other, and the last of our hope left to sustain us.

Houston reached me first, and I was plucked from the bed and set in his lap once he took the spot he'd forced me to vacate. Loren lay on his stomach now between Houston's legs and propped his chin in his hand while Jericho lounged on his side, using his arm to keep him up.

"That's better," Loren said before kissing my naked thigh. All I'd managed to put on were panties and a muscle tank that stopped just below my belly button.

"You're not playing fair," I accused no one in particular. They were all at the top of my shit list.

"Fair doesn't get us what we want," Houston lashed harshly in my ear. I could feel the scrape of his teeth against my neck as his lips moved. "So no. We won't be playing fair. It's going to get real dirty from here on fucking out."

I gulped. "You think that will make me say yes?"

"Oh, I know it will." I knew he was looking at Loren now because that onyx gaze shifted over my shoulder to Houston. "Her panties. Remove them."

"With pleasure," Loren agreed with a devious grin.

It was then I knew.

Before the night was over, I'd give each one of them everything. All of me. Irrevocably.

My panties were no match for Loren's eagerness to be rid of them, and so he accidentally tore them while wrangling them down my legs.

"That's two pair you've ruined," I reminded him. Why wasn't I fighting?

"I'll buy you more," he stated absently. He looked between my legs once Houston spread them and released a long, agonizing groan. "Fuck, that pussy is pretty."

"I want you to eat it," Houston commanded, making a whine spill from my lips. "And I want you to keep eating it until she gives us what we came for."

If there was ever a time for Loren to rebel, this moment unfolding would have been it. Of course, he chose *now* to follow Houston's orders blindly.

Gripping me underneath my thighs, Loren pushed my legs up and out until I was open and bared for him completely. Houston took over, holding me hostage by hooking my legs in the crook of his arms from behind.

There was nowhere for me to go.

Nothing I could do but let Loren sate that hungry look in his eyes. They slowly shifted over to Rich, and my breath caught in my throat because I knew what he would say before he ever spoke.

"Two heads are better than one."

Oh, God.

I squirmed in Houston's lap to get away, but he only held me tighter. I could feel his chest heaving as his breathing increased, and his hard dick under me growing even harder.

"Wait!" I yelped as Rich slowly stood up. My heart began racing as he joined Loren between my legs. "I..." I swallowed. I could barely speak around the taste of cherries coating my tongue.

"You what?" Loren challenged. My silence was heavy as the three of them waited for me to agree to a relationship. "Didn't think so." The soft chuckle he released was nothing compared to his smile. It was taunting and promising more than I could handle.

"Bon appétit," Houston inserted from behind me.

It was an order for his friends to enjoy their meal and also for them to hurry the hell up.

Neither Rich nor Loren wasted another second before their heads lowered at the same time. I knew whose mouth found me first when I felt the cold metal from Jericho's lip ring. His tongue lapped me in an open-mouth kiss, and then he pulled back for Loren to have his turn.

They continued like that.

They took turns attacking my clit and dipping their tongues inside of me.

Each time I tried to move away from the horde of sensations they stirred, Houston held me tighter. They weren't playful or teasing, either. They were aggressive, leaving no part of me untouched. The greedy sounds Loren and Rich made as they ate me filled the room until they were drowned only by my cries. Resting my head on Houston's shoulder and burying my face inside his neck, I closed my eyes, thinking it would bring me relief, but it only heightened the intensity of their touch.

Turning his head, Houston kissed me deeply as his best friends went down on me.

"Open your eyes," he whispered against my lips. "It would be a shame if you missed anything." Houston spread my legs even wider, and I could feel both of their lips on me now. I felt my bottom clench at the ramification, and giving a weak shake of my head, I kept them closed.

I knew the image that would be waiting for me once I did.

Loren and Rich weren't taking turns anymore.

Against my will, my eyes drifted open.

What I saw…my pussy began throbbing uncontrollably.

"Oh—" My words were cut off as I came hard watching them. I couldn't tell where Loren's mouth began, and Jericho's ended. They were enjoying each other as much as they were enjoying me. And when the remnants of my orgasm trickled out of me, Loren eagerly lapped it up before turning his head and sharing with Jericho. I watched them kiss as if it was nothing they hadn't done before, and just like that…another orgasm ripped through me.

I couldn't say if multiple orgasms were something I was capable of before the three of them. All that mattered now was that I couldn't seem to stop.

"Jericho," I moaned when he kissed my pussy one last time.

It was the only warning I got before he took me from Houston. I was yanked off his lap and brought to the center of the bed. Once my muscle shirt was gone, he pushed me down onto the bed until I was flat and naked on my back.

The impassive look in his eyes both frightened and excited me, the emotions blending when he reached for his belt.

"Something to say?" Loren teased me. His finger lazily brushed my nipple as he waited for my response.

"Yeah," I breathed out as I struggled to catch my breath. Even Rich paused from undoing his jeans, and we locked gazes as the three of them waited. "Do your worst."

"Aw shit," Loren instigated as he fell onto his back. He locked his hands behind his head as he cheesed at the ceiling. I wasn't as confused by his response as I was by Rich's.

He wasn't cocky or angry as he nodded. He simply held out his hand to Houston without breaking our stare, and I didn't understand until Houston passed Jericho a condom from the nightstand.

I could say no to whatever was about to happen, but everyone in this room, including me, knew I wouldn't.

I wanted them to convince me.

I wanted them to force my mind to finally let go.

My heart and body were already on board.

Rich tore the condom open with his teeth before shoving his jeans and boxers around his thighs and quickly sheathing himself. He talked the least shit, so it made sense that he had the biggest dick. I could already feel him inside me, forcing my body to accept him and carving his name on my walls.

He took the time to partially remove his shirt, lifting the neck over his head but leaving the material bunched around his shoulders. I watched his abs flex as he moved between my legs and brought the fat head of his dick to my entrance.

I wasn't expecting for him to go slow. I could feel Houston and Loren watching every inch that disappeared inside of me until Jericho was buried to the hilt. My breath caught in my throat at how deeply he reached and how completely he filled me.

"Braxton." My eyes had begun to drift close when I heard Jericho's whisper. I opened them, and he smiled down at me gently. "Tell us what we want to know." He was still fucking me slowly when he lifted my hips off the bed and gripped my ass hard enough to bruise. "Say yes."

"Make me."

As if he had expected me to defy him, Jericho's lids lowered as he bit into his bottom lip. There was no warning before he changed his pace. My bottom half was still completely at his mercy when he began slamming into me with thrusts that could be heard fifty feet away.

"Oh, my God," I yelped.

But Jericho had no mercy to give.

He pounded me as I gripped the mattress above me with both hands. I even started twisting my body to try to get away, but that only made him growl and fuck me harder.

I smelled the bergamot and orange in Loren's cologne as he moved closer, and then he was kissing me and swallowing my cries.

"I know," Loren cooed when the sounds I made turned broken. "Give us what we want, and it stops." He kissed me again, and it was gentle. A complete mockery of everything Jericho was doing to me below. "I promise, baby."

I felt my head being turned, and then Houston was kissing me. His kiss was rough and demanding, a warning that there was only more to come. "Otherwise, you'll keep coming, but he'll go all night," he said when he was done.

"Why do you think Rich is the nicest?" Loren taunted. "He's always had the most restraint. The most discipline. The most self-control. He won't let himself come until he's gotten what he wants, and even if he does lose control..." Loren smiled. "There are two more cocks waiting to service you."

As if the three of them commanded it, I flooded Rich's dick.

It was only the beginning.

Jericho came down on me as my pussy convulsed on his cock, and with a groan, he began fucking me into the mattress. I had no choice but to hold onto him as my sharp nails scoured his back, and my heels dug into his ass. The sound of his dick tunneling into me was all that could be heard for a while as I came again on a silent scream.

I wasn't sure how much more I could take. I could already feel my mind splintering apart.

One word, and he'd let himself come.

He'd offer a reprieve—if only until his friends were ready for a turn.

"Jericho, please," I found myself sobbing when I came for the third time in mere minutes. I wanted mercy, and he wanted me.

Only one of us was getting what we wanted.

"You want me to stop?" he whispered in my ear.

I shook my head.

"You want me to come?"

I nodded.

Logically, it made no sense, but I knew what he was asking when he offered to stop. I wasn't denying him my body. I denied him my heart. The only way to end this was for him to give in by releasing or for me to give in by saying yes to being theirs.

Tangled was an understatement to describe the web we'd weaved.

"Then you know what to do," he responded without mercy.

As if he knew I was standing on a precipice, his strokes slowed, becoming deeper, longer.

And then he lifted his head to stare into my eyes.

The genuine need for me in his own is what captured me in the end. I was lost in his silver gaze and the scent of berries when I heard myself say it. I leapt off the cliff, but I didn't fall.

I flew.

"Yes." My voice was lower than a whisper, but it rang loud in my heart.

"What was that?" Jericho's eyes had lit up as if he were watching me fly, so I knew he'd heard me. He just wouldn't make this easy.

"Yes." I was louder now, but still not enough.

"They can't hear you, Braxton. Let them hear you," he urged. His pace was picking up again, his breathing deepening, telling me he was close to coming. On either side of us, Houston and Loren looked on, both silent and still and waiting.

"Yes."

"Louder!" Jericho barked while shoving himself inside of me.

"Yes!" I repeated on a short, high cry. He'd never gone that deep before. "Yes, I'm yours. I'm yours."

"Aw, fuck," he moaned lowly before smashing his lips against mine. His thrusts shortened, becoming more erratic and frenzied as he chased his orgasm. "Fuck, baby," he growled with his lips still attached to mine. "I—"

Suddenly, Jericho stiffened with a grunt, and I knew he'd let himself come.

I wondered what he'd been about to say.

He started kissing me again, and all thought fled as I melted under his tenderness now that I was his.

"All right, you stingy motherfucker," Loren griped. "Quit hogging her. We want to celebrate too."

Jericho kissed me a few seconds more before carefully sliding himself out of me as he lifted up.

I felt the soreness right away.

"What?" he asked with a confused frown when he noticed his friends watching him. Turning my head to Houston and then Loren, I realized that they were as shocked by Rich's dominance as I had been despite the show they put on.

"Nothing," Loren answered, keeping his amusement from his gaze. "I'm just glad to be a top and not a bottom, is all."

As Loren took over kissing me while Rich fixed his clothes, Houston stood from the bed. I didn't know where he'd gone until I heard the water in the bathroom running. Loren was still kissing me and promising to be the best boyfriend ever when the bed dipped with Houston's weight again. A moment later, I felt the warmth from a wet cloth between my legs as he gently began to clean me.

We didn't have sex again.

As the events of the night came rushing back, I knew it was because I'd fallen asleep before Houston was even done cleaning me. The next morning I woke up and found myself lying on Jericho's chest and still wearing Loren's medallion. I didn't understand why I was on top of Rich until I turned my head left and then right and found that Houston and Loren were in bed with us too.

They'd kept Jericho and me in the middle while they slept on opposite edges. The sun must have barely risen because not even Houston was awake yet.

As I admired his mussed hair, pursed lips, and naked chest slowly rising and falling, I wondered why I'd woken so early.

I knew the answer before the question could fully form. My mind was too restless to sleep through the morning. Houston, Loren, and Jericho had gotten me out of my head, but it had only lasted a short while.

The questions and doubt were back now and with a vengeance.

As carefully and quietly as I could, I left the bed and my bandmates sleeping in it.

I guess…technically…they were my boyfriends now.

I'm sure that's what I had agreed to last night. I just wasn't sure if I was up to deliver.

Shuffling out of the bedroom and through the bunk area, I intended to use the half bath in the front because I didn't want to risk waking the guys. I needed the quiet time alone to think without one of them *literally* trying to fuck me out of my mind.

The moment I stepped through the sliding door, I stopped in my tracks at the sight of a dark-haired woman sitting with her back to me at the kitchen table like she belonged there.

"Hello?"

FORTY-SIX

Rich

"Dude, why the fuck is your dick in my hip?" Loren shoved me off him before I could respond.

Slowly, my eyes opened, and I looked around.

Where the hell was I?

It wasn't until my vision cleared that I recognized the bedroom and noticed the fact that my best friends and I were in it alone. I immediately climbed off, my motion startling Houston awake and annoying Loren, who sucked his teeth. Houston slowly rose to sit on the edge of the bed while Loren rolled over onto his stomach and fell back asleep.

After checking the bathroom for Braxton, I hurried to the front of the bus where I could have sworn I heard two voices speaking. I couldn't think of any reason someone would bother us this early, but nevertheless, I smelled trouble.

When I made it to the front, that's exactly what I found, but it was the last person I expected to see.

Braxton was sitting at the table with Oni fucking Sridhar.

"What the hell are you doing?" I immediately barked. She was a long way from Los Angeles, and her presence didn't make any sense. Nor was it welcome. Braxton gave me a look that said she disapproved of my rudeness, and I found myself dialing it back.

Day one, and she already owned me.

Oni, however, castrated me with her gaze as she looked me over. Ever the professional, she wore a tailored, navy blue suit, nude heels on her feet, and dark hair falling in waves down her back. She was beautiful, but a viper, nonetheless. "Carl sent me to check on things."

"I don't remember that being a part of your job description."

"It's not."

At the moment, I was regretting making Loren stick to our pact. I could really use a drink, and it was only seven in the morning.

"Now it's my turn to ask the questions. I checked the bunks when I arrived and didn't see anyone." Her manicured finger waved back and forth between Braxton and me. "What's going on here?"

"None of your business."

I sat down at the table next to my girl, and because I felt like being a dick, I pulled her into my lap. Braxton didn't fight me or pull away, but I could tell she was uncomfortable. There was nothing I was willing to do about that, though, since I refused to hide her in private. There was nothing we could do to prevent the backlash, but as soon as we found a suitable way to announce our relationship, I wouldn't be denying her in public either.

Loren and Houston felt the same.

"I see," Oni said in response to my claim. I noticed how her gaze immediately shifted to meet Braxton's.

I didn't get the chance to decipher that look because the bunk door had slid open, and Houston walked through. He noticed Oni immediately but didn't react. As if she weren't even there, he walked over to the table and took his time kissing Braxton good morning.

"Sridhar," he finally acknowledged before moving over to the couch.

"Morrow," she returned as the wheels in her mind turned.

I didn't want to care what Oni was thinking, but I would if it in any way altered the decision Braxton had made last night. I knew not everyone would accept or understand the unconventional aspect of our relationship, but my ability to care only extended as far as how it would affect Braxton. The rest of the world could eat itself.

Sitting down, Houston grabbed the pad and pen he used to jot down lyrics from the ottoman we used as a table. He'd been writing last night while Braxton was in the shower and didn't get to finish before we decided to corner her.

Thank God it worked. Braxton saying yes was the only reason I was in the mood to deal with Oni's shit right now.

"So will you be joining us for the rest of the tour?" Braxton inquired with a deep frown on her face. I don't think she was opposed to the possibility like I was—just confused.

I prayed Oni said no.

"Thankfully, no," she said, answering my prayers. "I'm only here to see the show tonight, and then I'm on a red-eye back to Los Angeles."

The troubled look didn't leave Braxton's eyes, and I cursed Calvin and Oni both for putting this shit on her shoulders when she was already dealing with enough. Mainly us. "Why would Carl choose me to replace Calvin if he didn't think I could handle it?"

"He didn't choose you," Oni reminded her. "I did."

For some reason, she gave me a pointed look at that last part. Was I supposed to be thanking her or something?

Yeah, without Oni, we would never have found Braxton, but it's not like she knew what would happen. She didn't know we'd fall for our rebel, and I doubt she'd have chosen Braxton if she had known. Oni had a lot of reasons to feel guilty, but she never showed it. Not even once. Why would she care to right her wrongs now?

I glanced over my shoulder at Houston, who was pretending he wasn't listening to every word as he continued to scribble new lyrics. He'd tweak it again later once he was ready to establish a melody. I wondered if he'd let Braxton help since I knew he had her to thank for the inspiration. Yes, I'd sneaked a peek at some of the lyrics.

Braxton nodded, acknowledging Oni's claim, but didn't say more about it. She probably sensed, like I had, that it wasn't actually meant for her. "Would you like some coffee?" she offered Sridhar.

Immediately, I tightened my hold on her hips. I didn't want her getting up just yet.

"I'll take tea if you have it."

The bunk door slid open again just as Braxton was standing. I noticed how she moved a little gingerly and smirked. I'd never fucked anyone as hard as I had her last night and was already eager to do it again. I knew she'd let me despite the fight she put up.

Loren was awake, hair sticking up, and wearing a frown that cleared the moment he noticed Oni. Without a word or making a sound, he turned on his heel and disappeared again. It was probably for the best since Loren was cranky enough in the mornings without throwing someone he hated into the mix.

Braxton fixed Oni's tea, and as she handed it to her along with the milk and sugar Oni had requested, a knock sounded on the door. Without looking up from his pad, Houston shouted for the person to enter, and the door slid open, revealing Xavier.

"You got to be fucking kidding me," he snapped the moment he saw Oni.

"That's funny," she said without missing a beat. "I was going to say the same about your tie."

"I'm not wearing one."

She gave him that same deprecating look she gave me, except much slower—like she was taking her time. Xavier always wore his suits without a tie. He preferred to keep the top buttons of his shirt undone, showing off his chest and the dark skin underneath.

"My point exactly."

I stood from the table and joined Houston on the couch. He had to be the one who'd called Xavier over here though I didn't know why. Those two hated each other even more than we did. "You know they're just going to argue all day and pretend we're the reason for it, right?"

Houston looked up from the line he was writing down and over at me.

"Exactly." After glancing at Braxton, whose brown eyes were

darting between Xavier and Oni as they traded insults, he met my gaze again. "They can keep each other occupied. I'd much rather we handle that."

Houston tipped his head toward Braxton, and I knew he was referring to the doubt in her eyes and the fact that she was back inside her head.

Content with his plan, I nodded as I sat back. All the while, I kept Braxton in my line of sight. Making sure she didn't change her mind was at the top of my priorities. Not even our show tonight would keep me from her if she tried to run away from us again.

FORTY-SEVEN

Houston

Braxton finally showed her face, and I must admit, the wait had been worth it. I loved her in leather pants because they always showed off the shape of her ass. We were backstage at the Mohegan Sun's arena, waiting to go on stage. I'd never been this anxious to get through a show before.

Here, with the combined eyes of the house staff and our road crew, I was forced to keep my hands to myself, and I didn't like it one bit.

Braxton had been taking advantage of the berth we were forced to give her and hiding out in the private space they'd given her to double as a dressing room. In addition to the black leather pants driving my head and dick crazy, she wore a loose, white tank that was shorter around her midriff and longer on the sides. Her jewelry included a silver cuff on her wrist, Loren's medallion around her neck, and rings that covered each finger from knuckle to knuckle on her left hand, and heels I wanted to feel in my back when this was over.

Feeling my gaze, she caught me staring, but I didn't look away. She was my girl, right?

After a moment of indecision that I hoped she broke free of soon, she slowly made her way over to me. I smelled the sweetness of her brown sugar body wash long before she reached me. When she was close enough, I pushed away from the wall I'd been leaning against and nodded for her to follow me.

She did.

All the way to the secluded spot I'd scoped out almost immediately upon our arrival at the arena. Because I knew I wouldn't be able to get through the concert without touching her.

I fucking knew.

There was shit everywhere as house crew and road crew rushed back and forth. They were too focused on getting the job done to pay attention to me luring Braxton into the dark corner underneath the stairs. We were perfectly hidden in plain sight.

Leaning down, I began to kiss her because I couldn't focus on anything else right now. She eagerly kissed me back, and I silently thanked God for small favors. Her lips always tasted like succulent fruit, and I'd developed a dependency. She began to whimper when I deepened the tangle of our lips, so I pulled away. I couldn't risk anyone discovering us…or me fucking her up this wall.

Sighing, I rested my forehead against hers and closed my eyes. "Why does it feel like I'm still chasing you, Bambi?"

She sighed too before shaking her head. "I don't know." I was starting to fear that she didn't want to be with me after all when she cupped my face with both hands. "Just don't stop. Please."

Feeling this spark in my chest that I couldn't put a name on, I gripped her ass in both hands and yanked her closer to me. "I wasn't planning to."

I'd run her ass down, however long it took, to get her to see things my way. There was no curing my obsession with Braxton Francesca Fawn.

We ended up kissing again, but this time she was the one to pull away with her hands pressing against my chest. "Where did Rich and Loren go?"

I shrugged only to answer absently, "I don't know." I didn't care either, but I kept that bit of honesty to myself.

I was strangely okay with sharing Braxton with them, and I didn't quite understand why, but that didn't mean there wouldn't be times I needed her all to myself. Rich and Loren would just have to deal.

"Something you need?" I forced myself to ask. Obviously,

I was at her beck and call. I just didn't want that something she needed to be Rich or Loren.

Braxton's hands reached for my belt, and while holding my gaze, she began to undo it slowly. "You."

I didn't object when she pulled my hard dick out or when she dropped to her haunches to wrap her lips around it. Forgetting where we were, I gasped against my will at the feel of her warm tongue stroking me.

Rich had warned me that her mouth was like no other, but I hadn't been prepared for the crippling truth of it. I held her hair in my fist that had been loosely curled for tonight as she slowly bobbed her head while gripping the back of my thighs for balance. The sight of her red lips stretched around me had my hips moving, and my toes curling in my sneakers as she stared up at me through those innocent brown eyes.

Wanting to enjoy this as long as I possibly could, I started to count the freckles under her eyes and around her nose, but each time, I lost count by the time I got to three. Picking up the pace, drool began to wet her chin as she grew more enthusiastic. The ardent sounds she couldn't seem to control as she worked for my cum made me realize that we'd be caught if she didn't get it soon.

Luckily, I was right there on the edge.

"I'm going to come in your mouth, and you're going to swallow every drop. Understand?"

Braxton barely finished nodding before I was pressing forward with a groan and spilling down her throat. I had to quickly grab the wall behind her for support before my legs could buckle from under me. Once I was sure not a single drop was wasted, I pulled free of her mouth and helped her to her feet.

After fixing my jeans, I walked her back to her now empty dressing room. Her little glam team, as they liked to call themselves, had packed up and gone, so I waited on the leather sofa while Braxton brushed her teeth and cleaned her face.

Loren and Rich found us by the time she was done and quickly closed the door behind them before locking it for some privacy. We only had about ten minutes before we were due on stage, so I knew they weren't planning to act on that itch I could see in their eyes.

Braxton must have known it too because she sat between them on the couch instead of keeping her distance like she'd been doing all day. It had been harder than I thought keeping Oni distracted, but at least now, she'd found somewhere else to be. I didn't know where that was, and I didn't care as long as she stayed out of our way.

"Having seconds thoughts?" Loren asked her when he couldn't take the suspense any longer. It was the question on all of our minds, and I didn't know what I'd do if she said yes. She told me to keep chasing, but what if she woke up one day and realized she didn't want to be caught? At least not by three jaded and broken men.

"Not really," she answered hesitantly. "Just…questions."

"We're as new to this as you, but we'll do our best to ease your mind," Rich promised. "Just tell us where to start. That's all we want."

"How does this work…me with all of you?" She looked from Rich, then to me, and finally, Loren, who answered.

"To start, it helps that you're ambidextrous."

I turned my head just in case so Braxton wouldn't see me laugh. I wasn't all that certain she'd appreciate it when she was trying to be serious.

"Thanks," she said dryly. "That really helps. I'm so glad we had this discussion."

Loren slumped in his seat before looking at her and taking her hand in his. I watched his thumb caress the back of her hand as he silently wooed his way back into her good graces. "It works however we want it to work. Tell us what you're comfortable with, and we'll go from there."

"No other women," she blurted immediately.

I don't know if it had been heavy on her mind all this time or if it was just the first thing that popped into her head, but her quick response had caught us all off guard. Mostly because we'd never even considered other women since deciding to make her ours. Until now, it had only been an unspoken agreement, so I could understand why Braxton insisted on having it spelled out.

"I know it's selfish of me and unfair," she said in a low tone before wincing and shaking free of her guilt. "I get the three of you, and all you get is me, but it's what I want."

Rich gently gripped her chin and turned her face toward him. I could tell he didn't like what she said. Not one fucking bit.

"*All* we get is you?" he echoed.

I could see the hurt in her eyes when she misunderstood him, but she kept her gaze steady as she looked into his eyes. "Yes."

Loren's hand fell to her thigh, drawing Braxton's attention back to him. "Do you see us turning into stage four clingers for anyone else, baby fawn?"

I could hear the smile in her voice when she spoke. "Only stage four?"

The bassist smirked as he held her gaze. "I haven't asked you to marry me yet."

I knew her smile had fallen long before she turned to look at Rich and then me. "If this becomes serious—"

"It's serious," the three of us stated at the same time. The only one still fighting this was her.

"Then I can't marry any of you," she said, keeping her serious expression. "It wouldn't be right for me to marry one of you and not all of you. I'm sorry."

Laying my head back, I closed my eyes as I let reality and the first hitch in our relationship sink in. I would never be able to give Braxton my last name. She would never fully belong to me. The only solution would be to make her choose and lose her altogether just to sate my ego.

"Stop it, Morrow," I heard Loren bark.

My eyes flew open to find him staring me down. His black gaze was intense enough without anger doubling the effect.

"I know exactly what's going on in your head," he continued, "and it's bullshit. Marriage is as binding as shoelaces tied by a five-year-old. They're hastily thrown together and easily unraveled." I didn't miss the pointed look he gave Rich, but Braxton did. "We don't need an old fart in a robe to tell us that what we have with Braxton will last for-fucking-ever." Glancing down at our girl, he pressed a kiss to her lips before pulling back a smidge so she could see the threat in his eyes. "That's what duct tape and rope are for."

"Are you implying you'll tie me up if I try to leave?" Braxton asked for clarity. I always liked the push she gave no matter how hard we pulled.

"No implication necessary, baby. I'm sure I made myself pretty fucking clear."

Braxton simply rolled her eyes at Loren as he began to kiss on her neck. He was still sucking and biting on her skin like they were seventeen when a knock came at the door.

It was time to hit the stage, and as much as I wanted to stay here and continue to get shit understood, I accepted that the sooner we got out there, the sooner we could get her back home to finish what we started last night.

Sighing, I stood from the sofa and left the dressing room, followed by Rich, Braxton, and Loren.

"If you do change your mind and you insist on marriage," Loren rambled as he trailed us to the stage, "you could just get divorced and remarried every four months. You might raise some brows, but at least you'll hold the world record."

FORTY-EIGHT

Loren

BRAXTON WALKED LIKE SHE WAS FUCKING FLOATING, AND CALL ME arrogant, but I knew we were the reason. There was only pride and the ambition to do better whenever I looked at her and was reminded that she was mine.

She was actually mine.

We were back on the bus after another successful show, and even though I was exhausted, I knew I'd catch my second wind. It arrived right at the moment Braxton started stripping off her clothes. She was taking her time, too, like she wanted us to watch.

I was tuned the fuck in.

"Does anyone mind if I use the shower first?" she asked once she was down to her thong. I was caught between being jealous of that little piece of string between her ass and wishing the broom closet we called a shower was spacious enough to do what was on my mind.

The three of us mumbled our agreement, and she smiled before disappearing inside the bedroom. Once she was done, Rich was next to shower, and then Houston took his turn. We had an unspoken agreement that I shower last since I liked to take my time and didn't feel like hearing anyone bitch about it. No one gets to look this hot cutting corners.

An hour later, as I was wrapping a towel around my waist, I heard the sound of something crashing and rushed from the bedroom to investigate.

My steps slowed when I reached the front of the bus and found Braxton on her back, legs spread, and getting her pussy pummeled by Houston. Head thrown back, her arms were stretched above her head while her hands gripped the edge of the table like she was holding on for dear life.

It looked like they'd been getting ready to eat the dinner our chefs had prepared since the porcelain plates and food that used to be on them lay broken and splattered all over the goddamn floor.

I searched the room for Jericho only to see that he'd disappeared. One look through the window, however, showed him outside taking a call. I knew what it had to be about if he'd felt the need to take it out of earshot while Houston worked to keep Braxton distracted.

Chicken Alfredo was his favorite meal.

He wouldn't waste the chance to enjoy it without a damn good reason.

Then again, fucking Braxton was reason enough.

Ignoring my best friend and our girl still going at it like I wasn't even standing here, I returned to the bedroom. It was hard keeping my focus just from the noise they made as I found a pair of sweats, socks, and shoes.

Dressed, I joined Rich outside just as he ended the call.

"Any luck?" I hadn't bothered giving him time to notice my presence before making it known.

"No," he mumbled.

At least he hadn't run off this time with divorce papers in hand just to hit another dead end. In the beginning, Braxton had been curious about his sudden disappearances, but we'd always blown her off whenever she allowed herself to ask. I knew we wouldn't be able to pull that shit now. At least not without serious repercussions.

"So maybe you should just tell Braxton about Emily now instead of waiting until you're both old and gray." He'd have one foot in the grave, but Braxton would still send him to it early if he waited that long to tell her about his wife.

"She's not my wife," Rich claimed like he was still in denial after all this time.

"Technically, she is. How you feel about it doesn't matter. Only the facts do, and the *fact is* you married her, you're still married to her, and your girlfriend doesn't know about it."

"Why do you care so much?" he snapped after rounding on me. He knew there was nothing else he could say. I was right, per-fucking-usual. It was always my delivery that people hated.

"I care because Houston's in there fucking the shit out of Braxton, and while I'm sure he's having a jolly good time, I'm also positive that it's for *your* benefit. That makes him an accomplice. I am too since I knew about Emily and chose not to say shit...*for you*. That means when this blows up in your face, it blows up in all our faces, and I'm not letting you fuck this up for me."

Braxton was my first and only girlfriend. If she broke up with me, mark my words, I would never have another.

I could still see the stubbornness and reluctance in his silver eyes and sighed. "You said it yourself, man. If one of us doesn't deserve her, none of us do. Houston and I risk losing her too because we don't want to do this without you." Eyeing Rich suspiciously, I added, "It's starting to feel awfully one-sided."

My gaze began to narrow when he stayed silent for too damn long. I knew he was considering my point, but I needed him to see the light *this* century.

"A few more weeks," he eventually begged me. "I'll find Emily, get her to sign the papers, and then I'll tell Braxton."

"Why wait?" I snapped. "It's not like you need her consent. Just get the damn divorce." I wanted to grab him by his collar, march his secretive ass inside that bus, and force him to come clean. I only cared about him doing the right thing for Braxton. Emily could go jump off a cliff.

The only thing that stopped me was the utter misery on Rich's face as he took a silent trip down memory lane. He was staring into the distance as if the past was replaying itself right before him. "You know why."

Rolling my eyes, I exhaled through my nose because, unfortunately, I did know why. And it was all my fucking fault. The least I could do, I suppose, was buy him the time to finally right the wrongs we made.

"Fine."

My gut twisted painfully the moment I heard myself agree. I knew without this shit going left that I was making a huge mistake. I just hoped Braxton would be able to forgive us a second time. Unquestionably, it would be more than we deserved.

"On one condition," I added the moment he relaxed.

He was eyeing me warily now. "What's that?"

"You back off. Unless she initiates, you don't touch her. Not until you tell her about Emily."

"No."

It was funny how he wasted no time thinking about his answer when doing the right thing still made him hesitate. "Cool. Then I will."

I turned to do exactly that when he shoved me into the side of the bus. My reflexes were quicker than his, though, so I elbowed him in the nose, making him back off a step as he gripped it and swore. I was planning to blow off some steam between Braxton's legs, but this worked too, at least for the moment.

Turning to face my best friend fully, I waited patiently in case he wanted more. I could see the temptation in his eyes, but he didn't act on it.

Because Rich was in the wrong, and he knew it.

Scoffing at the irony of how well his last name fit, I shook my head. Jericho's need to be noble, if not all that candid, was the reason we were in this mess.

"Braxton isn't stupid," he warned me. "She'll notice."

"Not my problem."

Baby fawn noticing his distance if he backed off could be avoided if he just told her the truth. Rich, still as blind as a bat in a cave, stared at me as he waited for me to relent. When I didn't, he wordlessly turned away from the bus, and I watched him go until he disappeared into the dark.

He didn't realize it now, and considering how stupid he was being, maybe he never would, but I was doing this for him too. When Braxton inevitably finds out, she'd know he'd at least felt guilty about lying to her. He'd have a minuscule chance at earning her forgiveness rather than none at all.

After boarding the bus, I noticed the mess Braxton and Houston had made was cleaned up, and they were nowhere to be found. They weren't in their bunks either, so I pushed inside the bedroom and found them in the middle of round two.

Undressing until there wasn't a stitch left and not caring one goddamn bit, I tapped Houston on his shoulder, interrupting him mid-stroke. When he looked over his shoulder and scowled, I stared back at him impassively.

"Move."

He stared at me long enough to make me consider knocking him out cold. I only refrained because I knew Braxton wouldn't find us fighting over her cunt endearing. Apparently drawing the same conclusion, Houston lifted off Braxton after pressing a kiss to her lips. She looked a little dazed and out of it, but by the time I slipped on a condom and took Houston's place between her legs, her gaze had cleared enough to notice me.

"Loren?"

Pussy warm and sopping wet, I slid right in with a groan. "Yeah, baby, it's me." My hips began to move, stroking her slowly as we kissed. "I missed you."

Widening her legs to make room for me, she whispered, "I missed you too."

FORTY-NINE

Braxton

MY GRANDMOTHER HAD ALWAYS WARNED ME TO APPRECIATE THE tortoise because I'd be up against the hare one day.

The days were flying by faster than I liked, and the last thing I expected when we ditched the bus for good was that I'd miss it. The cities as we made our way through Canada became a blur. Montréal had been fun. Toronto, where we'd ditched the bus and said goodbye to the crew, was even better. After only one night in Edmonton, however, we were boarding a flight to Vancouver.

The SUV we rode from the hotel to the private hanger pulled to a stop, and we all climbed out. People were waiting to load our bags onto the plane, so Houston, Loren, Jericho and I immediately climbed the steps leading up to the plane.

Xavier and Dani had already arrived and boarded and were the only ones still traveling with us since they were Bound's manager and assistant, respectively. The road crew had been booked on commercial flights and would be meeting us at the venues now.

I was nervous about the flight since this was only my second time flying, and I still hadn't decided whether I liked it or not. Loren had to hold my hand the entire four-hour flight from Toronto, so I was determined to get through this one on my own. In another month, we'd be making our way to Europe, and I couldn't expect him to coddle me the whole way there, now could I?

As if he'd heard my thoughts and wanted to prove me wrong, Loren grabbed my hand the moment we boarded the small, private plane.

As I looked around the cabin with its plush leather recliners and wood-grain interior, I couldn't believe how much my life had changed. I suddenly wished Griffin and Maeko were along for the ride since they were the ones who'd known I'd be here. I'd been too afraid to chase my dreams, so my dreams found me instead. There was only a one-in-a-million chance of that happening, really dumb-blind luck, and it only made me regret not finding the courage sooner.

But I hadn't been afraid that I'd fail.

The problem had always been that I'd succeed.

Even my baby sister had known, and she'd called me out on it.

My eyes squeezed tightly together as I unwillingly recalled the moment I decided to give into Oni and sealed my fate with Bound.

Rosalie's face had been coated in tears, her sobs cutting me deep as her fragile body shook with rage and frustration from being tugged in two directions as she glared at me. *"Why should I listen to you, Braxton? I looked up to you! I thought you were strong, but you're not!" No longer yelling, she whispered, "You're still afraid of them too."*

"Hey, you all right?"

Hearing Loren's voice, I hadn't realized he'd been watching me as he stood in front of me now with his hands on my hips. I didn't want to explain, so I offered him a smile that he saw right through. After taking a seat in the recliner across from Rich, Loren immediately pulled me into his lap. Xavier and Danielle were sitting together on the bench a few feet behind us as they discussed the arrangement for tonight's show.

"You know I can't stay in your lap, Loren. You might as well let me go."

Burying his face in my neck, he growled, "Not yet."

I stayed put until it was time for takeoff, and he reluctantly let me go so I could take my seat next to him, which also faced Houston. Jericho was seated diagonally from me, and my gaze couldn't help but linger as he stared out the window and brooded.

It's been seventeen days.

Two weeks and three days of climbing the mountain he'd put between us. And every day, it became more apparent that Rich had grown bored with me.

I'd expected that possibility from Houston, maybe even Loren, but not Jericho. I couldn't ignore that he only seemed interested in me whenever I practically threw myself at him. I was beginning to wonder if he only gave me even that small mercy out of pity. He'd been enthusiastic each time, if not a little troubled, but he was a guy, so that didn't mean shit.

The reason nagged at me because his interest hadn't slowly waned.

It'd been abrupt.

The morning after our show in Connecticut, he'd been distant, and the only logical explanation was that he'd considered my terms and decided I wasn't enough. I knew I'd been unfair, so I didn't want to blame him, and yet...I absolutely did. Houston, Loren, and Jericho had all driven me to the edge, but it was his hand that shoved me over.

I almost felt like I didn't deserve Oni's praise, not that I ever wanted it. *"Not quite the apple on your head, but effective nonetheless."* Before returning to Los Angeles, it had been all she'd said about the task she'd given me when she chose me to replace Calvin. Knowing this, I wasn't as convinced as the guys that Carl had been the one to send her in the first place.

The short flight to Vancouver was over quickly.

The moment we were shown to our suite at one of the waterfront hotels, Loren proposed we hit the jet skis. Two hours later, after sending Dani out to get a bathing suit for me, three swim trunks, and four wetsuits since germophobic Loren was too prissy to use a loaner, we were back in the disguises we'd used in New York and standing on a dock in Granville Island.

After checking the straps on my lifejacket for the third time, I regarded the guys who were already mounted on the jet skis while I still stood on the dock. "So which of my doting boyfriends am I doubling up with?"

No way in hell was I riding one of those things alone. I barely trusted myself not to drown in the shallow end of a pool even though I knew how to swim.

I'd posed the question to all three of them, but my attention was steadfast on Rich as I waited for him to offer. I needed to know if I was reading too much into the distance he kept.

Noticing my gaze, he immediately looked away, and I sucked in a quiet breath as my heart cracked in two.

"You're riding with me," Houston said as if it had already been established.

He might be my boyfriend now, but he was still bossy and controlling as hell, and the perverted demoness squatting inside of me liked it.

I couldn't even count on the pompadour wig and cheap, gold shades to detract from his appeal.

Even though I was disappointed in Rich, I didn't hesitate to go to Houston. I slipped my hand in his when he held it out for me, and with his assistance, I climbed on behind him.

I didn't allow myself to look too long at Rich and the muscle in his cheek, jumping as if he was restraining himself. Instead, I held onto Houston's waist and pressed my cheek to his strong back. Despite the summer sun and the wetsuits we wore, my face was still at the mercy of the ocean's breeze. It was cool, almost chilling, but no match for the heat Houston's body generated. I was in awe, considering how cold he'd been when we met. Nevertheless, he was a furnace, and he warmed me right up.

Whooping, Loren was the first to take off, shooting forward on his red and blue jet ski. Rich, straddling a black and gray watercraft, was right behind him. As soon as Houston's green and white Sea-Doo lurched forward, I tightened my grip so hard I was surprised he hadn't complained. The brine attacking my senses was stronger than ever with the water's natural scent mixing with my uneasiness.

Gradually, Houston accelerated, giving me time to get used to the motion each time we crested a wave. The moment we hit English Bay, the three of them opened up, and we were soon flying up the coastline.

I had no idea where we were going and no idea if they did either.

None of that mattered once I was brave enough to lift my head. The creamy sweetness of chocolate melted on my tongue as I watched the three of them enjoy the journey without a destination in mind. My heart swelled, and it was the first time I'd tasted true happiness in a while. The last time I'd been too young to realize that it would always be temporary.

Birds flew by closer than I would have given them credit, but as we raced past swimmers, groups on guided tours, and other rogues like us, I surmised they had no reason to be afraid.

Loren and Rich raced each other past Horseshoe Bay and Bowen Island and all the way up the Howe Sound while Houston and I followed closely behind but much slower. It wasn't until they were done with their pissing contest that they slowed down, allowing us to catch up.

It didn't occur to me they'd have a motive until they began to circle.

"So what do you say?" Loren shouted since they had to keep enough of their speed to turn their vessels. Houston and I were idle in the water now as they continued to circle and taunt. "Did you bring your big girl panties?"

"I'm not wearing any!" I reminded him—not unless I counted my bikini.

It seemed to have the desired effect on Loren either way because he was staring at me now like he wanted me to read his mind and every filthy thought inside it.

And I didn't even care how utterly ridiculous he looked wearing that black, eighties mullet on his head, which had drawn more attention than it diverted. Luckily, he'd kept his disguise authentic with a pair of dark shades and a beard he'd glued onto the lower half of his face.

"How about a race then?"

"I don't know," I shouted at the top of my voice. "What do Houston and I get when we win?"

Loren pretended to mull it over even though we both knew he'd had his prize in mind long before he posed the challenge. "First one back chooses a dare for the loser to do. No exceptions. No excuses."

I nodded as I thought it over.

"What will it be, baby fawn?"

"It's not really up to me since I won't be driving, is it?" I pretended to lean forward as if I was gauging Houston's interest and whispered, "When I pinch you, punch it."

The only indication I got that he'd heard and was on board was the subtle quirk of his lips as he waited for my signal.

"Hey, Loren?"

He was grinning already as he anticipated my answer. "Yeah?"

"We're in!" Before I was even fully done speaking, I pinched the hell out of Houston, who immediately pushed on the throttle, shooting us forward and narrowly clipping Rich as we raced through the closing gap.

I heard Loren shouting obscenities, and one look behind me confirmed that they were hot on our tail. I smiled as Houston pushed the Sea-Doo to the max and laughed as Rich and Loren desperately fought to catch up. Since we'd had the element of surprise, we'd gained enough of a head start that it would take an act of God for us to lose.

It came just as Houston made a sharp turn around a bend I didn't know to brace for because I'd twisted in my seat to watch our opponents.

Slipping off the side of the Sea-Doo, my scream was cut short when I fell into the cold water and plunged beneath the surface. Fear of drowning had me grappling to reach the top again, even as my life jacket brought me back up. I broke the water with a gasp, and then I looked around for my rescue.

Rich was the first to reach me since he'd been in last place. He twisted around in his seat as I boarded from behind and offered me a hand that I didn't need but was all too eager to accept.

I missed him touching me because he wanted it too.

I might have preferred not taking an unintentional dip in the ocean and losing my wig to learn that he still cared, but I wouldn't turn my nose up at the knowledge either.

Once I got him alone, I'd make him explain.

I got plenty of their hot and cold mood swings when they were just my bandmates. I wouldn't accept them now that they were my boyfriends.

Houston and Loren had caught up when I was settled on the Sea-Doo with my arms around Jericho's waist as if nothing had occurred.

"What the hell happened?" Loren shouted at Houston.

Instantly irritated, I pursed my lips. I was a grown woman—their woman—yet when it came to their expectations of each other, they treated me like a child. It was me who wasn't being careful. Houston wasn't to blame.

However, I could tell by the rigid look on his face that he disagreed.

Since Houston was staring at me, asking without words if I was okay while ignoring Loren, I refrained from rolling my eyes and nodded. Jericho must have felt my nod because he took off without another word spoken. Houston and Loren followed, but this time, we didn't race back.

Unfortunately for them, I was still feeling devious.

Standing on the dock now with Rich hovering next to me, I faced Houston and Loren, who were still straddling their jet skis. "I guess this means Jericho and I win."

"What? How?" Loren challenged with a frown. "We didn't finish the race."

"You said the first one back chooses the dare. You didn't say anything about finishing the race." Houston and Loren's response to my loophole was to stare at me with their lips parted. I smiled. "No exceptions, no excuses, right?"

They grumbled what sounded like an agreement, and after returning our Sea-Doos to the rental company, we headed back to the hotel. I wasn't so sure the jet skis were a good idea since tonight's show started in a few hours, and I was already bone tired. The guys removed their disguises while I moved onto the private terrace overlooking the North Shore mountains' jagged edges and rough slopes.

I stood there a few moments, just enjoying the view, when I felt a warm exhale on my nape. The zipper on my wet suit was slowly dragged down, and then strong hands peeled it from my body. The suit pooled around my ankles on the wooden planks of the deck where we stood. I stepped out of them before turning around to face Houston, who had already removed his own wetsuit and now wore cotton shorts that hung off his hips. He wasted no time kissing me deeply once I looked up at him.

"Come with me," he whispered when he finally let me catch my breath.

Left only in my blue bikini, I followed him through the suite and into the bathroom with an L-shaped view overlooking the harbor.

There I found Jericho dressed only in jeans and sitting on the lip of the bathtub centered in the room as he checked the temperature of the water pouring from the spout. Loren had shed only the top half of his wet suit and stood at the end of the tub, pouring a generous stream of bubble bath into the tub. I knew it had to be the source of the lavender aroma filling the room and not another new emotion I couldn't name. Watching the tub fill, I felt my muscles ache at the promise of soaking them.

Houston made short work of my two-piece, pulling the string at my neck and the ones at my hips until they both fell from my body and decorated the marble floor.

"Bath's ready," Jericho announced when he was satisfied with the temperature of the water.

Houston immediately lifted me off my feet bridal style before carrying me over to the tub. After placing me in the water, I realized just how deep the tub was. I was covered almost to my chin in warm, lavender-scented water.

Houston accepted a bottle from Loren while Rich worked to wet my hair. I didn't realize their intention until I felt Houston's fingers in my hair, massaging my scalp with shampoo and making me moan as I tilted my head back.

I hadn't expected this when I said yes to them.

Any of it.

But I couldn't say I wasn't pleased.

Loofah in hand, Loren lifted my left leg and gently began washing me. Rich disappeared from the bathroom for a minute or two, and when he returned, it was with a platter filled with fruit that he began to feed to me from his lounge beside the tub.

It was never far from my lips to ask what brought this on, but for some reason, I never did. I shut up and let them dote on me as if it was always meant to be this way—as if we hadn't hated each other once upon a time.

Loren moved onto my other leg just as Houston began rinsing the shampoo from my hair and adding conditioner. Together, the trio worked in perfect harmony and comfortable silence. I blushed when I saw how dedicated they were to their tasks.

Or maybe they were hoping I'd forget about the dare or have mercy on them.

Not a chance.

I was yawning uncontrollably by the time my skin was pruned and rubbed raw because the three of them were having too much fun to leave me be.

Houston stood me up, Jericho wrapped me in a towel, and Loren carried me into the bedroom with the biggest bed. Once I was under the covers, I tried to pull him down with me for a quick nap, but he mumbled something about needing to shower. I pouted, causing him to smile and kiss my lips before placing my phone on the nightstand and walking away.

I didn't even know he had it.

The door made a soft click when it closed behind him, but my eyes were already closed, so I didn't watch him go. Everything felt good and hurt at the same time as I shuffled my feet and burrowed deeper under the cool, expensive covers with a satisfied sigh.

I'd almost made it too.

It would have been the nap of the century.

But no.

My phone played the specially assigned ringtone, "Dear God" by XTC, and the last person I expected was calling.

FIFTY

Houston

CANCELING A SHOW MERE HOURS BEFORE THE START WITHOUT demanding a reason why was a pretty accurate measure of how far I'd fallen.

We were currently back on the private jet and headed to some town I'd never heard of called Faithful. I watched Braxton's knee bounce rapidly before giving Loren and Rich the same quizzical look we'd been sharing since she told us she had to return to California.

We tried to get answers, but she hadn't been willing to give them. Our only option had been to watch her grab her shit, leaving us no choice but to grab ours the moment she darted out the door without an explanation.

We could have made her stay and talk, but that anxious look in her eyes only turned mine up a few thousand notches. I've never been very empathetic, but how else could I explain leaving Xavier behind to manage the chaos and barking orders at Dani to arrange a last-minute flight?

I didn't bother to think about the phone call we'd be getting when it got back to the label that we'd missed a show. I didn't care. The refunded tickets would come out of our meager cut, though it wouldn't be enough for slimy, fucking Carl Cole.

I sat back as we continued to make our way south and wondered how I got here. Seven, hell, *three months* ago, I would have never let Braxton pull the shit she did today.

I was addicted to controlling everything around me.

More so than her claim to be a sex addict.

Braxton hadn't torn apart her own life and her friends as well just to feed it.

At this very moment, she wasn't contemplating ruining a relationship still in its honeymoon stage, one that could eclipse all others, by ordering the plane around and heading back to Vancouver.

I was.

Feeling someone's gaze, I looked away from the window I was staring through and found Loren watching me. The look in his raven eyes as he sat across from me was intense yet worried. Elbows braced on his strong thighs and hands clasped together at the set line of his mouth, he subtly shook his head.

He'd read my mind and was telling me it wasn't worth it.

There would be other shows, but our chances with Braxton were limited. She was more important. Making sure she continued standing whenever life knocked her around was more important. Our mutual agreement to put her first always and never look back had been instinctual, so I knew my decision to keep moving forward well before I leaned my head back and closed my eyes.

A few hours later, we were climbing inside the rental we had Dani arrange to be waiting for us when we landed. It was a thirty-minute drive from the airport to the town where Braxton grew up, and the moment I looked around, I felt a crawling sensation on my skin.

Braxton hadn't grown up with much.

The sign welcoming us to Faithful informed us of the nine hundred people residing here. It made me think of our first meeting and how innocent she'd looked. Eventually, I'd kicked myself for judging a book by its cover only for it to have been a clue all along. It's not who she was now or even seven months ago, but once upon a time, it had been.

Is that why she'd fled to Los Angeles? Had she needed something more than the minuscule town could offer her? Braxton was larger than life, at least to my infatuated eyes, so I could see that being a real possibility.

The three of us stayed silent as Braxton directed Rich, who was driving, on where to go.

I almost snorted.

It's not like he could get lost since the town couldn't have had more than three streets. I bet the jail only had one cell, no one ever bothered to use a turn signal, teachers called students by their older sibling's name, and all the high school parties were held at "the lake" or in a cornfield.

We rode for a couple of more minutes before I shook my head when we passed some teenagers racing down the street on a lawnmower.

It was just after one in the morning when we arrived at a small hospital. Rich parked, and after sending a quick text, Braxton climbed out, and we followed.

I expected her to rush inside, considering her urgency to get here, but she just stood on the sidewalk, staring at the entrance while she breathed in and out deeply through her nose.

Turning her toward me, I noticed how her lips trembled and tucked her against my chest while Loren and Rich hovered behind her.

"This was a mistake," she whispered. "We should just go back."

Loren chose that moment to yawn as wide as he could with a look that said he wasn't going anywhere but to a bed anytime soon. As he looked around, I could hear him talking shit in his head about being dragged to the middle of nowhere for nothing but wisely kept his mouth shut. He was always his bitchiest when he was exhausted, but we all were, so he'd just have to deal.

"Talk to me," I urged Braxton.

She didn't immediately jump at the chance, and I swallowed my wounded pride when I wondered why.

"It's my sister," she eventually mumbled against my chest. "She's inside."

Blinking at nothing, I was floored as I replayed her confession. Until now, it had never occurred to me how little we knew about her. She'd managed to get away with uncovering pieces of our past while giving away nothing of hers in return. Unfortunately, it wasn't the time to ask her why or berate myself for not demanding to know more.

Later.

Asking if her sister was okay would have been redundant since no one goes to hospitals for fun, so I asked instead, "What happened?"

Before she could answer me, though, someone with a deep voice called her name.

I felt Braxton stiffen in my arms while her face stayed planted in my chest. She was taking careful, controlled breaths now as if she were psyching herself up to face an opponent in the ring. I was seconds from telling the older man dressed in brown corduroy and a plaid flannel who had her eyes to get lost when she lifted her head and turned her attention toward him.

"Hi, Dad," she said brightly despite her trembling in my arms. "It's nice to see you."

He was lucky to be her father when he didn't return her greeting or her sentiments. "Your mother sent me down here to see what's keeping you."

The look he gave me said he didn't approve of me touching his daughter and the look I returned dared him and his mustache to do something about it. Braxton's father was tall like me and well-built, so it would be an evenly matched fight if it came to that, but hopefully, it wouldn't. I'd hate to fuck up my future father-in-law.

Braxton, noticing our silent pissing contest, pulled away before walking inside without another word spoken. I didn't like how she seemed to make herself small as her father followed closely behind, so I added that to the growing list of problems to tackle later.

Since visiting hours were over and we weren't entitled to the same perks Braxton got being a local, the three of us waited in the lobby while Braxton visited with her sister.

"Please tell me I'm not the only one who didn't know she had a sister," Loren blurted the moment we were alone. His frown was deep, telling me this bothered him as much as it disturbed me. "Did I miss something?"

"We all did," I told him.

It didn't make any of us feel better, though, since there were three of us, and we still sucked at this boyfriend thing.

Rich scrubbed a hand down his face as he stared off in the direction she'd gone. "What else don't we know about her?" he mused out loud.

"If she's secretly married, I'm kicking your ass," Loren informed him. "That bit of karma's all on you, bro."

"More importantly, what's been up with you lately?" I finally asked Rich. It pissed me off to see him pulling away from Braxton and not being able to do anything about it. We were supposed to be in this together, not to mention sharing her had been his goddamn idea.

For some reason, Rich tipped his head toward Loren as if that answered anything. "Ask him."

"I'm asking you."

Loren taunted Jericho with a Cheshire smile in my peripheral, telling me he had something to do with it, after all.

Nevertheless.

I kept my gaze steady on Rich, who sighed.

"Loren threatened to tell Braxton about Emily if I didn't back off until I told her myself."

My gaze immediately swung to Loren, who looked unapologetic as fuck. "Why would you do that? No, scratch that," I said before he could answer me. "Why would you do that without talking to me first?"

"Because last I checked, my balls were attached to my body and not in your pocket."

Closing my eyes, I blew air through my nose as I reminded myself that we were in a strange town in the middle of nowhere. Getting arrested because I put Loren in a hospital while *in* a hospital was not the way I wanted the rest of my weekend to go.

I decided to let it go for now and focus on something I could change. "When are you planning to tell her?" I asked Rich.

"He wants to wait until he's actually divorced as if that will make any goddamn difference." Loren rolled his eyes. "Actually, it will," he quickly backtracked. "Because the longer he waits, the deeper her feelings get. Dip shit can't see that, though."

"How hard can it be to find one damn woman? And how much are you paying those detectives?"

"Finding her is the easy part," Loren butted in again. The motherfucker couldn't keep his mouth closed if someone paid him. "Getting to her before she's tipped off and takes off is where he's failing. If he would just do what I told him, we'd be square."

"I'm not having her kidnapped," Rich snapped, drawing the attention of the pretty receptionist a few feet away.

When she continued to stare, waiting to hear more, Loren immediately scowled. "Can we help you?"

She quickly looked away, and we made sure to lower our voices before resuming our conversation.

"Maybe it's time you consider it," I heard myself say. Normally, I would have agreed with Rich, but that was before Braxton. I didn't give a fuck about that she-demon we warned him not to marry.

"No," he said with a finality that left me no choice but to respect.

Loren, however, narrowed his eyes at Rich. "I'm starting to think you still have feelings for her."

Rich never answered because his attention had been stolen by Braxton coming down the hall. She was alone as she walked with her head down like she was deep in thought as she stared at the freshly waxed floors.

Pick your head up. Give me your eyes.

As if she heard me, that's precisely what she did. I just wasn't prepared for the utter look of failure in them. Braxton looked defeated, something I once thought impossible even when I relentlessly pursued it for my own satisfaction. I didn't know what to do as she came toward us. How could I when I didn't know what put that look in her eyes?

Loren and Rich were frozen like me when she finally stood before us.

"We can go now," she announced before turning toward the

exit. She walked through it without looking back, expecting, or perhaps not caring whether we followed or not. Braxton moved like she was on autopilot—like she was drifting in the desert without a direction to go in.

We were supposed to be her compass.

There were no words spoken between us before we stood and followed after her.

When Braxton told us we were leaving, none of us expected her to mean California altogether. It was obvious she wanted to put as much distance between her and whatever happened as fast as she could. It took us putting our foot down when reasoning with our girlfriend hadn't worked. She'd been reacting off pure emotion while Loren, Rich, and I were still scrambling to catch up.

Braxton was no help as we searched for accommodations. The brat sat and brooded in the backseat with Rich while Loren rode up front as I drove around aimlessly for half an hour.

I'd fix her, though.

Eventually, we found a motel near the airport ran by someone who hadn't recognized us. The innkeeper smiled like he was in on the joke when I asked for one room, and he noticed there were three of us and only one of her.

I wrote his name on my mental checklist and accepted the key to our room.

We were given one on the first floor that smelled like mothballs and smoke even though I'd asked for non-smoking. The small room had wood paneling for walls and shag carpeting in a deep shade of red. There was a box TV on top of an old dresser that I doubt turned on much less worked, a table with two chairs in front of the one window draped by white curtains that had a green, geometric pattern. All I cared about was the king bed centered in the room as exhaustion washed over me for the third time since arriving.

"So," Loren said after we were all inside, and he'd taken a seat at the foot of the bed. Rich was sitting in one of the chairs staring at his phone as he checked for updates on how well canceling our show had gone while I hovered by the door. I didn't trust Braxton not to run through it the moment our guard was down. "You have a sister."

Braxton looked up from the suitcase she was now rifling through to look at each of us. The anger and disappointment in her eyes were momentarily replaced by guilt when she realized we were still in the dark where she'd left us nine, almost ten hours ago.

"I guess I haven't been very forthcoming."

Understatement.

"We should have asked," Rich told her, hefting some of the blame onto our shoulders, which I accepted.

How could I feel this deeply without knowing everything about her?

I knew she preferred her left hand even though she was dominant in both. I knew that she held onto her grudges because she hated the truth that she was hopelessly forgiving. I knew she took her coffee black, gorged on action movies, and preferred sleeping in the nude until well after noon. I knew she didn't wholly believe in the God she prayed to when she thought no one was looking. I knew that her voice's pitch had been perfected by the synesthesia she'd only hinted at when she told Loren the lyrics he was working on sounded blue.

I knew all of that, yet there were large and notable gaps that needed to be filled. I was also sure there was nothing else I could learn that would alter my course and that scared the shit out of me.

"I have a younger sister," she supplied with a nod. "Her name is Rosalie." Standing with the items she needed for her shower, she stared at the floor as her mind turned over the thoughts and fears plaguing her. "She wanted to be a doctor someday."

I wasn't sure how many dots she expected us to connect with that, but Braxton made it obvious she was done sharing when she disappeared inside the bathroom before closing and locking the door.

FIFTY-ONE

Braxton

MY EYES HAD BARELY OPENED THE NEXT MORNING WHEN I WAS thrown on my back by Houston, who I'd apparently draped half my body on top of while I slept. He quickly settled between my legs, keeping me trapped with his weight as he peered down into my eyes.

He was angry, and I understood why.

Last night, I refused to talk when I knew they were eager to listen. I'd made demands with no explanation of why I needed them. They hadn't complained. They simply gave. The only exception had been letting me run away from my problems.

The sweet and woodsy scent of his clove soap wafted off his warm skin, so I knew he must have taken a shower last night. Combined with the intensity of his green gaze, I felt like I was standing in the middle of an evergreen forest. If that forest also smelled like vanilla.

"I know you're mad," I blurted when he shoved his sweats off his hips. He then reached over Loren, still sleeping deeply next to us, to flip open the wallet he'd left on the nightstand. I knew already what Houston would grab from inside.

"Mad? No." Plucking a condom free from Loren's wallet, Houston tore it open with his teeth before I watched him roll it down his long, thick dick. "I'm livid, baby."

I tasted cherries on my tongue while my head was scrambling to figure my way out of the trouble I'd landed myself in.

"Okay, I hear you, and I'm ready to talk now."

"I'm sure you are," he returned dismissively.

I felt him tug my panties to the side, the only thing I'd worn last night, before testing my readiness with the head of his dick. I was wet for him, but he already knew that.

He slowly pushed inside once he was done teasing me, and he didn't stop until I'd taken every inch. Still unused to him, he stole my breath even as my legs fell open to make room for him. I felt his mouth skim my neck as he took his time fucking me, and lost in the sensation, I turned my head to kiss him.

As if the war he waged on my body wasn't enough, he chose to play with my heart as well when he dodged my lips.

"Houston," I heard myself whine.

I tried to kiss him again, but he continued to elude me. Turning my head away in frustration, I saw the hint of his smile from the corner of my eye and hated him even as I loved what he did to my body.

Houston inevitably picked up the pace, making the bed rock and the headboard slam into the wall as he fucked me harder and deeper under the covers while Loren and Rich slept next to us. I knew I must have worn them out yesterday since they didn't stir once the entire time Houston fucked me.

We didn't even try to keep quiet.

If Loren and Rich woke up, I'd let them have a turn too until they were sated, and I was drained of every drop.

I was the whore of Faithful, after all.

The scarlet who'd corrupted good Catholic sons.

The incarnate Hester Prynne who didn't just stop at one or even two.

I moaned as Houston rose onto his forearm. His other hand then gripped my hip as he wildly slammed his hips against mine with short, brutal thrusts that told me he was close to coming.

Panic and desperation rose inside me even as I cried out from the pleasure.

I wasn't there yet.

I was close but not as close as him.

It didn't occur to me the punishment Houston intended to enact until he shoved inside me one last time with a groan as he flooded the condom.

Still breathing hard and seeing the confusion on my face, he quickly leaned down and finally kissed me. I was already wrapping my legs around his waist, eager for round two, when he abruptly ended the kiss. Houston didn't offer a word of explanation before throwing my legs off him and rising from the bed.

I quickly sat up, holding the covers to my chest as I watched him saunter toward the bathroom while removing the condom from his dick.

He couldn't be serious.

When he closed the bathroom door behind him, and I heard the lock turn, I realized he had no intention of finishing what he had started. After peeking at Loren and Rich, who were both still sound asleep, I slammed my back onto the bed with a frustrated growl.

I could wake them up, but I couldn't handle being rejected three times in one morning. I may have deserved it. I may have even loved whenever they used me for their needs, but being here was having the opposite effect.

Suddenly, I was sixteen again and standing on a scaffold.

Instead of the boys whose faces and names I couldn't remember, it was Houston, Loren, and Rich staring back at me. It was their fingers pointed my way as they forced me to bear all the blame.

My heart rejected the possibility even as the bitter aroma of olive oil assaulted me. Shame was the reason I always stopped myself from talking to them about Rosalie—my reason for joining Bound. It meant revealing everything I'd done and why I was given no choice but to leave home.

Even with five years and hundreds of miles between us, Faithful hadn't forgotten me.

I didn't realize Houston and I were no longer the only ones awake until the bed shifted, and the covers were snatched from my body.

There was no time to react before my panties were discarded, my legs pushed open, and a head with hair as dark as black ink fell between them. His warm tongue swiped my wet opening, soothing the soreness there and making me forget my woes. Soon, he began to attack my throbbing clit, bringing back the orgasm Houston had stolen from me as the sweet smell of berries pushed away the shame.

Winding my hips as I pushed my fingers through the gorgeous stands, I tossed my head back and sighed his name.

"Rich."

We sat alone at the back of the quiet church.

Communion had just been given, and after receiving it, the congregation belonging to the Angels of Purity & Faith fell into reflective silence. Houston, Loren, Rich, and I went ignored but not forgotten.

There was only one sweet exception.

My sister turned in her seat once more since learning I was here and smiled brightly as if she was seeing me for the first time today.

I smiled back.

We had the same brown eyes from our father and red hair from our mother, although Rosalie's tresses were paler and cropped at her shoulder. Our mother maintained that long hair was the mark of a wanton woman. I made sure when I left home to trim mine less often, and now my hair stretched toward the end of my spine.

Rosalie's excited gaze shifted to the rock gods fidgeting in the wooden pew we shared as if they'd burst into flames any moment now.

I shared their anxiety.

I never thought I'd be here again.

After my mother made it clear last night that I wasn't welcome in their home, I knew this would be my only chance to see Rosalie before leaving. We had a show in Seattle tomorrow night, and I didn't want to force my boyfriends to cancel another performance just to stay where we weren't wanted.

Amelia Fawn, catching her youngest daughter distracted, voiced her disapproval in a quiet tone, making Rosalie pout as she turned and faced the front. I swallowed the bitterness as my gaze shifted to the boy sitting next to her and his parents sitting on his other side while our parents flanked Rosalie's right, keeping them together.

I would never forgive my parents for forcing a life on my sister that she didn't want, and my parents would never forgive me for derailing the one she did.

"Go in peace," Father Moore dismissed moments later, "glorifying the Lord by your life."

I nudged Loren next to me, who'd fallen asleep, and he awoke with a loud snort that drew unwanted attention our way. I pushed air through my nose when I was recognized immediately. Now that Mass was over and they were done pretending to be God's innocent children, the whispering and the stares began.

"What the hell is everyone staring at?" Loren griped.

It never took any of them long to notice much, which never seemed to work in my favor. I was still hoping to get out of this without having to come clean about my past. They knew I wasn't innocent when they met me, but they had no idea just how much I had sinned.

"You're not supposed to curse in a church, Lo," Rich scolded.

Loren paid him no mind as he continued to look around. I stood up, smoothing down the brown, long-sleeved midi dress I carefully chose for the occasion, so he did too. Once the four of us were standing in the aisle, I waited near the narthex.

No way was I going near Father Moore or the chancel.

Standing here, I could almost feel the smear of anointing oil on my forehead while the pungent smell of olives never left me. Father Moore had used it to cure my "sickness" as I stood before distraught parents and the sons they'd brought with them for absolution.

My only regret had been not having the wisdom to give my body to a boy who deserved me, someone who would have stood by me as a friend or even just a hand to hold.

None of the nine who'd been there that night did.

As I waited for my parents and sister to reach us, I fought to push away the memories before my knees could collapse. I almost gave up and let the shame take hold when a large hand slipped into mine, tangling our fingers together.

I looked up and into the green gaze of Houston Morrow and knew he'd noticed the stares too.

Shrugging at the question in his eyes, I offered him a wry smile that wasn't entirely a façade. I was used to being the outcast. I'd lived that way for two years until I was able to escape when I turned eighteen.

And I never would have looked back if it hadn't been for my baby sister.

She'd been too young at the time to understand what was happening to me, but it didn't change that she never abandoned me.

The last of Father Moore's flock who weren't intending to stay now that Mass was over and continue their prayers finally passed us.

I knew the moment Houston spotted my family because his hand tightened around mine ever so slightly.

Jericho was next to recognize my sister, and I could hear his soft swear even after just moments ago berating Loren for doing the same.

The bassist was last to notice them. His gaze skirted over my mother and father dismissively before landing on my sister as she approached with a very swollen belly and a diamond ring adorning her left hand.

She was only thirteen.

FIFTY-TWO

Loren

BRAXTON'S SISTER LOOKED BARELY OLD ENOUGH TO KNOW LONG division. How the hell could this kid be pregnant and married already? My gaze moved around the church, stuck playing duck, duck, goose, because I didn't know where else to put it.

This was so fucking fucked.

Braxton should have warned us. I'd get in her ass later, but right now…

Rosalie's cheery voice, despite the palpable tension around her, brought my attention right back to her. "Hi, I'm Braxton's sister, Rosalie," she introduced. She never lost that sweet smile on her face despite my feeling and probably looking like I needed a drink.

"Loren." I forced a smile as I held out my hand, which she eagerly shook as she jumped up and down. She didn't appear to be someone who'd spent the night in the hospital, though I still didn't know the reason why.

"I can't believe it's really you! Braxton talks about you all the time, except she mostly calls you names I can't repeat, or I'll be grounded until I'm thirty."

Jesus.

I didn't know how much more I could take of this shit. I couldn't believe I'd ever mistaken Braxton for innocent when her sister really took the cake. Thankfully, she moved on to Houston, who was better at hiding his chaotic thoughts.

Rosalie talked his ear off about her going into labor early—the reason for her short hospital stay and our visit—and was too excited to notice his short responses. Meanwhile, I studied Braxton's parents, who had pulled her aside. Braxton was the spitting image of her mother, a stone-cold fox even with her mouth's rigid set and the added years. I knew I had the coldness right, at least as I witnessed the way Mrs. Fawn regarded her own daughter.

I recognized that look a mile away.

It was the same disdain my father had shown me many times, and my mother was too weak to tell him any different.

When it looked like they started to argue, I made up my mind to come to Braxton's rescue when she caught my gaze at that exact moment and subtly shook her head.

Blowing out air, I forced myself to stay put as I shifted my attention to the trio hovering near Rosalie. I dismissed the older couple, and I narrowed my eyes on the pimple-faced shit standing next to them. I knew he was the one responsible for knocking up baby sis. His blond hair covered his eyes as he stood there slouched in black slacks and a tie like he was bored out of his mind and uninterested in anything—including his new wife.

When he noticed me staring, he hesitated for only a moment or two before inching away from his parents.

"I'm Pete," he said excitedly as if I gave a shit. "I'm a huge fan, man."

As I pulled a stick of gum from my pocket, unwrapped it, and slipped the stick between my lips, I did some soul searching and reminded myself that he was just a kid too. I seriously doubted the marriage and baby carriage were his doing any more than Rosalie's.

I knew what had been his bright idea, though.

"Not of wrapping up, apparently."

Stupid shit frowned before realizing what I meant. He looked a little older than Rosalie, maybe a year or two, so I knew who was the predator and who had been the prey.

It was always the same shit, just a different generation.

"Oh. Yeah," he said, his gaze turning shifty as he chuckled

nervously. "It's cool though because Rosalie and I…um…oh, we're in love. Hey, do you think I could get an autograph?"

I kept my expression blank as I stared at him. I couldn't believe Braxton's parents allowed a precious thing like Rosalie to marry someone who sounded like he ate paint chips for an afterschool snack.

I turned to Rich, who'd been watching and listening the entire time. Rosalie was still talking Houston's ear off, so she hadn't gotten to him yet. Now that she wasn't fangirling anymore, it sounded like she was ripping him a new one for being mean to her big sister. I laughed to myself at the fire in her already before getting pissed all over again.

What a waste.

"I'll be outside," I told Jericho, ignoring Peter the Skeeter's request for an autograph. One of the others could hook him up.

I was outside for maybe ten minutes before Braxton found me. Houston and Rich were right behind her, and the three of us watched her stare off in the distance at nothing in particular before turning to us. "Can we go now?"

I was nodding before I could even form words. "Hell yeah."

We started for the rental before the sound of Rosalie's voice stopped Braxton in her tracks. I almost groaned out loud when she turned around. I needed to get her the hell out of here and sooner rather than later. If I could get away with it, I'd take baby sis with me too.

Rosalie was timid now as she slowly approached with a blush staining her cheeks when she noticed she had more than just her sister's attention. Brushing her hair behind her ear, she stared at the ground while she spoke, and I almost snapped at her to pick her damn head up. Braxton would have castrated me, even if she did agree because it wasn't my place and never would be.

Leaning back against the rental, I kept my mouth shut by blowing bubbles with my gum as Houston and Rich stood next to me.

"I know you're mad at me, Brax, but I really wish you wouldn't be," Rosalie pleaded. "I'm okay. I promise."

"And that's the problem, Rosalie. You shouldn't be okay. This is not what you told me you wanted."

Rosalie finally looked up from the ground only to burst into hysterical tears when her gaze met her sister's. They poured down her face relentlessly as she sobbed and attempted to talk through them. My heart ached for her, knowing she was being pulled in two directions and much too fragile to endure the strain.

"I know, but I was scared," she wailed. "They were going to hate me forever, but I knew you never would, so I just did what they wanted, but I was wrong because now you do hate me, and I wish I could take it back, but I can't."

It took me several seconds longer than Braxton to decode and decipher Rosalie's ramble. By the time I did, Braxton had her arms around her sister's body as she held and attempted to soothe her.

"You were absolutely right," Braxton told her sister. "I could never and will never hate you. I'm disappointed, and I feel responsible, but that's *my* burden to bear, not yours. Take it off your shoulders because it doesn't belong there. I told you to make the decision that was best for you, and that's what you did. You didn't make the one you wanted, but you made the one you thought you could live with. I get it." Braxton took Rosalie's drenched face in her hands and lifted her head from her chest to make their eyes meet. "And know this…no matter what, no matter when, every time you look in your corner, I'll be right there, babe. Gloves up."

Rosalie giggled, her eyes even bigger than Braxton's, as her big sister attacked her sweet face with kisses. Our girl seemed reluctant to let go of her sister when she finally did pull away. Each step backward seemed weighed down as their hands held until the very last.

Their parents stood several feet away, watching their daughters closely but not intervening. I really didn't know what to make of them. Obviously, they were devout, but that didn't necessarily make them cruel. I guess I had no choice but to wait to hear the full story before forming an opinion, and I wouldn't need both sides since I only gave a fuck about Braxton's. There were still pieces of her missing, and I was eager to complete the puzzle.

"Braxton!" Rosalie called out again once the four of us were in our rental.

Rich was in the driver's seat, ready to take us to the airport since our bags were already in the car. It was a good thing, too, since Houston decided to break the clerk's nose before we left this morning. No one bothered asking him why, and he didn't enlighten us.

"Yeah?"

"Don't you want to know if you're having a niece or nephew?"

Braxton simply smiled when words failed her. There was a strain to it that she fought like hell to hide from her sister. She didn't want to cause her any more anguish, and it only made me love her even more.

Fuck.

I never even heard the gender baby sis shouted out.

I was too busy freaking the fuck out.

I was silent the entire drive to the airport, but everyone was trapped in their own thoughts as well, so no one noticed. I was completely still as I watched the scenery pass through the window and let my mind turn on itself.

Did I love Braxton?

I felt my heart lurch in answer.

We were back at the airport and boarding the plane to Seattle before I knew it. We had a show tomorrow, but our gig was the last thing on my mind. I was tripping all over my feelings and Braxton's.

Whatever hers may be.

I wanted to sit her the fuck down, take her hands in mine, and ask if she loved me too. Even with my zero experience, though, I was smart enough to know I'd only look like a lunatic, so I refrained.

Thankfully, Houston was around to distract me by being a dick per usual. When he spoke, I sat back in my seat as we waited for the plane to take off and pretended I didn't want to make demands of my own.

"Start talking, Fawn."

FIFTY-THREE

Rich

BRAXTON ROLLED HER EYES WHEN HOUSTON ORDERED HER TO TALK, but then her gaze landed on me when I leaned forward to listen, and somehow, I made her soften. It could have been the orgasms I'd given her this morning when Morrow left her hanging, or it could have been my desperate need to know that I didn't bother to hide. Either way, she gave us what we wanted.

"Did I ever tell you how I learned to play?"

"No," we each said at the same time.

Deep in thought, she nodded absently as she fidgeted with the ends of her red hair.

"Faithful isn't the kind of place that grows, you know? It closes in until you feel like you're trapped in a box with no escape and no air to breathe. The only people who stay long enough to be buried are the ones who were born and raised, unless they get out and don't look back."

"Like you," Loren filled in.

Braxton nodded. "Seven years ago, I met a stranger named Jacob Fried. He was on the road with his band, and they were passing through our town when their drummer fell asleep behind the wheel. The van was totaled and everyone died except Jacob. His injuries were so bad that he slipped into a coma while the doctors were fighting to save him. When he woke up six months later, Father Moore claimed God had delivered him to Faithful, and the reason for it was why he was spared. Jacob believed him."

Braxton fell quiet, but I could tell her mind was still sifting through her memories.

"In hindsight, I realize now that he was a broken, grieving man desperate to understand why he'd lost all his friends in one night and was left to bear it alone. He needed to believe there was a higher purpose to keep going. He stayed in Faithful, but it wasn't to find his calling like he thought. He couldn't bring himself to leave the last place he'd seen his friends alive."

Braxton studied each of us, and I knew she was wondering if we would have done the same.

Yes.

"Did he ever find his calling?" Houston asked. His eyes narrowed as he tried to piece together Braxton's memories for himself. He was anxious to understand her. We all were.

"Eventually," she said with a shrug. "Despite being the pious Christians they claim to be, Faithful isn't welcoming to strangers or strange people—even if we're all His children." She rolled her eyes. "Jacob was left utterly alone in a strange town for weeks until a sixteen-year-old girl decided to befriend him."

I stopped breathing.

I tried to fill my lungs, but it was like I'd forgotten how.

There was only the hope that this story wouldn't take the turn I knew it would.

"I was on my way home from school when I heard him play. He'd gotten a place, and when I walked by…I don't know why I turned in…or why he never sent me away. We didn't speak. I listened until he had nothing left, and then I went home. It was the same the next day, and we continued like that for a week before he finally spoke to me. He asked me if I played. I told him maybe one day."

She stopped speaking for a while when the plane began to take off, and she didn't speak again until we were in the air. "It started with him just showing me a few things. Once he realized how quickly I was catching on, he started to challenge me. I adapted, and Jacob found his calling. He never talked about himself during those times, and neither did I. We never stopped being strangers.

I was his student, and he was my teacher. That was all we were to each other…at least for a while."

"What happened?" I heard myself ask.

"He fucked her," Loren blurted bitterly. His eyes were angry when his gaze met mine briefly, and then he slowly turned it on Braxton. "Am I right?"

"It was my idea," she argued as if it made a goddamn difference. Her eyes were wild and determined as she met each of our gazes. She didn't want to be a victim. "I came on to him."

"Oh, was he just a kid who mistook gratitude and adoration for love and attraction too?"

Loren and Braxton stared at each other, neither willing to concede. For once, I sided with Loren, and I couldn't recall the last time that happened. Braxton might have been the aggressor, but it didn't change the gut-turning truth that she'd been taken advantage of by someone she not only trusted but idolized.

And what about you?

I tried to shove the thought away, but it kept coming back.

I wasn't ready to face the truth that I'd waited too long to tell her about Emily. I wasn't prepared to accept that Braxton may never forgive me. My betrayal would hurt her more than Houston or Loren's ever could because she never expected it from me. I could see the unshakable trust in Braxton's eyes each time she looked at me.

Fuck.

"How old was he?" Houston asked, and I knew he wasn't merely curious. The dick wanted her to admit out loud, even indirectly, that she wasn't to blame.

Braxton fidgeted in her seat, her eyes and voice low when she mumbled, "Thirty-six."

There was nothing but the sound of the plane's engine and the air circulating through the cabin.

I watched as Braxton forced herself to meet Houston's gaze, who never wavered. Her shoulders were back now, but her breathing seemed erratic. She was swallowing and flaring her nostrils at whatever teased her senses. It was a reaction, easily missed, that I've seen from her before. The cause was something else we needed to unveil and soon.

"Come here."

Braxton hesitated for only a moment before unbuckling her seatbelt and crossing the small space between them. Houston made sure she faced us too when he pulled her into his lap. Her legs were thrown over the arm of his seat as she stared down at him.

"What if it had been Rosalie?" he questioned softly, going straight for the motherfucking kill. There was a reason Houston was our unspoken leader. "Would you have blamed her?"

Braxton's brown eyes were hard when she stiffened in Houston's lap. "Never."

"So how could you think we would ever accept that what happened to you was your fault?"

Seeing for myself what Braxton's parents made Rosalie do before she'd even learned to drive, nausea slammed into me like a relentless tidal wave.

It could have been Braxton.

If they'd known, if Jacob had knocked her up…the Fawns would have made their daughter marry a man old enough to be her father. They would have done it to hold their heads high in a middle-of-nowhere town.

Justice wouldn't have been an option.

Braxton wouldn't have been an option.

Their beliefs and their pride would have mattered more.

Braxton's gaze snapped to me as if she'd read my thoughts, and it was at that moment, the first crack in her armor appeared. I could see it in her eyes even as she tried to reason with us. "It was a long time ago."

Houston closed his eyes, and Loren responded.

I couldn't do anything. My goddamn stomach was in my throat.

"And the fact that you've been carrying it ever since is what pisses us off, baby fawn. You're never going to convince us any differently."

She looked at Loren, who was strangling his seat as if it were Jacob fucking Fried. I was tempted to call my private eyes and pull them off Emily's trail. I had a new mission.

"Is he still in Faithful?" I whispered.

Catching my drift, Houston didn't react, but Loren was grinning like a Cheshire cat. Neither would stop me if I put the play in motion.

Braxton was none the wiser when she shook her head. "I promised him I'd never tell anyone, but it didn't matter. He skipped town, and I never saw him again."

"Is Fried the reason you believe you're a sex addict?"

"No." Laying her head on Houston's shoulder, Braxton closed her eyes. "It was the ones who came after. It was their parents. It was my parents. It was everything I was taught. I was stuck inside a town too rigid to understand what was happening inside of me. I had all this energy and no conduit. All I wanted was to *breathe.* Jacob gave me that when he taught me to play. I had an outlet. I could express myself. I could follow my soul through the dark and find the light that called to me. The world my parents chose was no longer my sole reality. I understood who I was meant to be, and what I was meant to be—free."

Her eyes slowly opened, trapping Loren within their depths.

"You were right. Jacob used me, but I used him too. Music wasn't enough anymore, and he was the only one I trusted to understand. I preyed on his grief, and he preyed on my desperation. We were both too alone in this world to say no. After he left, I fought it. I was afraid of my parents finding out what I'd done. I didn't just sin, I enjoyed it, and I wanted to do it again. Sex consumed me. I didn't sleep. I didn't eat. Eventually, I didn't fear my parents as much as slipping back into my shell."

Braxton rose from Houston's lap before returning to her own seat and curling into herself. I didn't know why until she spoke again.

"It was three months before it got back to my parents." She looked at the three of us before inhaling deeply and exhaling slowly. "By then, I'd seduced twelve boys from our parish."

"How did your parents find out?"

Braxton blinked at me as if she'd expected a different reaction. I admit I was stunned by her confession. Most of my shock, however, was due to my first impression of her. I'd never been so wrong.

I didn't care, though. It changed nothing.

She'd been around the block, but her body count was only shocking to her. It didn't alter my feelings or diminish our determination to possess the only thing that truly mattered.

From the start, our existence has been so thoroughly entangled. We've only ever been one entity.

Houston, Loren, and I were bound.

Braxton would only ever give her heart once.

"One of them feared for his soul enough to come forward. What I didn't know until my parents dragged me to the church and before all of Faithful was that he wasn't alone. Eight more had confessed to sleeping with me, and their parents wanted justice."

I didn't miss her hesitation and the indecision in her eyes whether to tell us the rest.

"I was allowed to atone for my wanton behavior by standing before the altar for three days without food or water or sleep so that the *good* people of Faithful could be restored and comforted by my sacrifice."

Braxton's gaze traveled between the three of us, attempting to gauge the reactions we were careful to hide. Whatever we decided to do regarding her past, our first step was making sure she retained her innocence.

"The others never said a word," she slowly proceeded when we said and gave nothing, "but they avoided me after that."

Because they'd gotten what they wanted from her and had been fine letting her walk through hell alone.

I blew air through my nose.

"Names."

I didn't miss Houston and Loren's heads snapping toward me and their silent demand for me to keep it together.

They could blow me.

I was too far gone to regain my composure.

Braxton pursed her lips at me in disapproval, and it took the last of my control not to grab and shake this need to punish herself out of her.

"I disregarded their beliefs and who they were to get what I wanted. The only guilty party here is me, Jericho."

I couldn't accept that.

Neither Jacob Fried nor any of those assholes were forced into anything.

And if it had been someone else, anyone else, Braxton would never let them feel this shame she was so determined to hold on to.

"What about the three who didn't feel guilty?" The temperature in the cabin dropped sharply at the quiet fury in my tone. "Tell me where to find the ones who fucked you and then abandoned you. I have questions."

I'd simply beat the nine names out of the three when I got my hands on them instead.

No question they knew since men gossip as much as women do.

We were just too macho to admit it.

"What will that solve?" she challenged with a raise of her brow. "What will it change? By now, they've forgotten me." She looked away, staring out the window as she whispered, "I've forgotten them too."

I could tell she had another pointless argument to make when her head swiveled toward us, and her big, brown eyes narrowed to slits.

"I'll make a deal with you," she offered to all of us. "I'll consider that you might be right when you explain how you're any different. How many women have you tossed aside? Do you even remember their names?"

The cabin was silent as the three of us watched her, and I wondered if they were considering pulling Braxton over their knee as well.

Loren, as usual, chose to bat first.

"For one, I've never blamed and shamed a girl for a decision *I* made using the wrong head," he deadpanned. "Only pricks with small dicks do that."

I swallowed my laugh, and I could tell Braxton was fighting back a smile.

She was a scrapper, which meant changing her mind wouldn't be easy. She'd lived with her shame for too long. Since we had plans to stick around, there would be plenty of time to open her eyes.

Shaking her head while still fighting her smile, she mumbled, "Whatever," before returning to staring out her window.

"I still haven't heard the reason you think you're a nympho," Houston said.

He'd drawn her attention back to us, and she frowned her confusion. "I just told you."

"Sounds to me like it was never about fucking," Loren told her. "It was always about your need to rebel. Music was your battle cry. Sex was your weapon."

"Your only mistake," Houston added, "is that you waged war only to run and hide when the other side fought back."

"You weren't ready then," I told her while holding her gaze. "Are you ready now?"

Houston, Loren, and I wouldn't have the luxury of hiding our relationship with Braxton. The four of us would be ripped apart from every corner of the world by people who couldn't and wouldn't understand it. Braxton would bear the brunt of it, and we'd shield her as best as we could. We just had to be sure she wouldn't fold under pressure.

The three of us waited for her answer.

We waited to see that fire in her eyes that consumed us from the start.

When it came, I felt it burn inside my chest while my goddamn dick saluted her.

"I'm ready."

FIFTY-FOUR

Braxton

Immediately after the show in Seattle, we decided to leave for Portland. Our performance in the City of Roses wasn't scheduled until tomorrow, but there was a reason we couldn't wait.

Just before tonight's show, my boyfriends had cornered me, literally, and asked me to stay with them instead of returning to Los Angeles. We had a month before the second leg in Europe began, so I agreed, of course.

I've been tasting chocolate and smelling cinnamon ever since.

Loren held my hand tight in his grip—enough to make it numb. I'm guessing he didn't want me to get away in case I changed my mind. However, I was a thousand percent sure the three of them would kidnap me if I tried.

After returning to the hotel to pack and grab our shit, we were rushing down the hall from the suite we'd abandoned while Houston and Rich trailed us much slower while carrying our luggage.

I didn't think to slow down until Loren burst through the heavy door leading to the stairs.

"Wait, why aren't we taking the elevator?" I asked him as soon as we started to climb. "And why are we going up instead of down?"

My question was answered, not by Loren, when we pushed through another door, this one opening to the roof.

The same matte black helicopter they rode in when they

crashed my festival was waiting for us. The blades spinning made my hair whip my face and neck as Loren pulled me toward it without stopping.

He then wordlessly helped me inside while Houston and Rich caught up. After our bags were loaded, they climbed in, and the pilot wasted no time lifting us in the air. As I hurriedly buckled myself in, Loren pointlessly placed a headset with a microphone on my head while Houston and Rich did the same.

We didn't talk.

The four of us were silent the short hour or so it took to reach Portland. I was immobile the entire time. Flying in a helicopter, especially at night, was twice as nerve-wracking as a plane.

Despite the brine and copper enflaming my senses, the moment I felt the bird began to land, I leaned toward the window nearest me. I could feel the three of them watching me as a smile slowly split my face.

It wasn't on a hill.

I couldn't really see much.

But I knew in my heart that I got the dark colors and sharp edges right.

Their home was definitely secluded.

Trees literally swallowed it whole.

The only clue I was given that something was even there was the orange glow shining through. In complete darkness, someone passing over wouldn't be able to tell anyone lived there.

Not unless they knew where to look.

We flew over the house until we reached an open field not far away where a helipad and even a small hanger had been built.

The crisp and sour taste of green apples burst on my tongue since it hadn't occurred to me until now that the bird belonged to them. I assumed they chartered it like the planes, though it was obvious they owned their tour bus.

Once the blades stopped spinning, Houston slid the door open. Loren hopped out first before lifting me down. He didn't wait for his friends before walking me over to the row of golf carts lined up and waiting nearby.

I climbed inside, and he got behind the wheel.

As Houston and Rich approached with our bags, however, they both gave Loren a look I couldn't decipher. Before I could ask, Rich dropped the bags he was carrying, lifted me back out of the golf cart, and sat me inside the one next to it while Houston filled Loren's cart with our bags.

Whatever the reason, it amused Loren to no end as he laughed uncontrollably before flipping off his friends. He then winked at me before taking off down the path leading to their home.

I was still frowning when Rich sat in the driver's seat next to me, and Houston climbed on the back.

Too exhausted to care about the reason, I didn't bother to ask questions.

I admired the quiet scenery as Rich drove us much slower down the tree-lined path. It was maybe a three-minute ride to their house.

Once it came into view, my heart began thundering in my chest. I couldn't make sense of the taste and smells lighting up my senses. My emotions blended too finely together as I stared up at their home.

Gothic.

Victorian.

Dark.

Towering.

I fell in love instantly.

The light I'd glimpsed from above filtered through the elegant tracery, keeping the forest from completely shrouding the home in darkness and allowing me to see the thin vines draping the black stone, the pointed arches that made up the windows and doors, and the tower I was all too eager to explore. The circular driveway was paved, interrupted only by the grass island in the middle, and extending into the forbidding darkness the forest created as it obscured the only way out.

Loren waited, hands in his pockets and ankles crossed as he leaned against one of the thick columns of the carriage porch. The golf cart stopped in front of him, and I didn't wait for one or all of them to show me inside.

I felt like I was floating as I drifted over to their front door.

Loren caught me just as I was passing him and lifted me bridal style. I grinned up at him, allowing the nameless emotion he stirred, the one that smelled like I was rolling down a grassy hill, to imbue as he gazed down at me. I could feel his excitement to show me their private, hidden kingdom rolling off him in waves as he carried me over the threshold.

I kept smiling even when I heard Houston and Rich suck their teeth for not thinking of it first. Sometimes I found their jealousy adorable because they forgot they weren't teenage boys anymore.

Loren carried me inside, and I gaped as I admired the high ceiling, carved moldings, dark walls, and arched doorways. There were even three black chandeliers whose candles illuminated the lush, blue rug decorating the long path to the stairs. It continued up the steps that split on the second level and continued in opposite directions.

"Welcome to our treehouse," he flirted as he carried me across the foyer. "No girls allowed, but for you, we'll make an exception."

"I'm honored," I returned dryly. "So will you be giving me the tour then?"

Loren's footsteps echoed with each step he took, warning me just how large and how easily I could get lost in their home.

"Sure. Let's start with my bedroom."

He flashed me a sexy grin that was way too tempting, so I made him put me down. By the time Houston and Rich made it inside with our bags, no thanks to Loren, I'd already kicked off the booted heels I'd worn before finding and exploring their kitchen, dining room, and the small sitting room I could tell they never used.

Obviously, the house wasn't new construction, but I could tell it had been well restored, which couldn't have been easy.

I didn't have to guess why that made me smile.

The three of them could have purchased or built something separate and more befitting to their individual styles. Instead, they'd chosen to revive a long, lost castle that had been cast aside and forgotten. They'd thrown themselves into the project and then used their labor and sacrifice as an excuse to share it and stay together.

I wouldn't bother to ask if my theory was correct.

I knew them too well by now.

Just as I was wandering into another room, since Loren had rudely chosen to disappear, Rich appeared out of nowhere, cutting off my path and making me yelp in surprise. As the taste of green apples and the scent of copper dissipated, he grabbed my waist when I tried to move around him.

"I promise we'll give you the tour in the morning, okay?"

Feeling shy and embarrassed for some reason, I nodded as I smiled, and then I let him pick me up and wrap my legs around his trim waist before he carried me off.

I'd forgotten it was almost three in the morning.

Just like I'd forgotten the show tonight after our long weekend thanks to me dragging them to Faithful to deal with my family and then around Seattle to sightsee.

We climbed the stairs and traveled down a long hallway and then another, and I didn't realize I should have been paying attention to where we were going just in case until we were already entering a bedroom.

I peeked over my shoulder since my back was to the room as Rich carried me.

The walls were decorated with periwinkle wallpaper that had a dark-gold filigree print. Each of the six arched windows taking up three of the bedroom's walls were draped by long, heavy panels of dark purple while another chandelier, this one a mix of crystal and candle, hung from the black lacquered ceiling that matched the wooden floors.

Braced against the furthest wall was a large four-poster bed made of black iron and an elegantly carved headboard.

Jericho immediately started for it.

I looked around as he crossed the large room. His sneakered feet were silent, but without carpeting, and thanks to the high ceiling, there was still a soft echo as he walked. When he reached the bed, instead of laying me on it, he swung around until I was facing the bed instead of the door. He then dropped down, draping his legs over the foot of the bed as he lay on his back.

His breathing began to deepen immediately as I felt his grip on my ass loosening.

"Is this your bedroom?" I asked before he could fall asleep. It didn't seem like his style.

Eyes closed, he confirmed my suspicions when he sleepily shook his head no. I tried to climb off him so he could sleep in peace, but his arms tightened around me, a silent order to stay put.

Five maybe ten minutes passed with me lying on his rising chest and grinning at him as he fought to stay awake. I didn't understand why he bothered considering how late it was, but he's never looked more adorable to me.

Me, on the other hand, I was too excited to sleep.

I toyed with the black hair falling over his bunched brows as I began to sing softly to him. Rosalie was the only one I'd ever done it for whenever she used to have trouble sleeping. It didn't seem to be working on Jericho, though, as the troubled dip between his brows grew deeper. I knew each time he clenched his teeth as if he were restraining or frustrated with himself as the muscle in his pale cheek ticked.

Whatever had been keeping him awake most nights and moody during the day these past three weeks had not gone away.

In the morning, I vowed to get to the bottom of it, and I wouldn't take no for an answer. They couldn't expect me to bear my demons while they kept their own hidden under lock and key.

As I silently brooded, Jericho's eyes started to drift shut again when Houston walked into the room.

Eyeing him over my shoulder with the side of my face in my palm, I watched as he pulled his shirt over his head and admired his abs flex as he did it. I liked that none of them were overly muscular. What they did possess made it more than clear that they were strong and able men.

After tossing his shirt on the floor, he made his way over to the bed, his amused gaze shifting from me to Jericho and back again.

"You're not going to let the man sleep?" he teased.

"It's not me. It's him," I told Houston as he towered over me while I stared down at Jericho. "I tried singing, but he's stubborn."

I felt the bed dip under Houston's weight as he braced his knee on the mattress next to me, and then he was pulling my head back using my hair as his personal reins and kissing my lips.

"So wake him up."

As if his tone hadn't made it clear it wasn't a suggestion, Houston lifted me off Jericho and the bed until I was standing in front of him with my back to his chest. His hands then gripped the hem of the distressed, black cotton dress I'd worn to our show tonight over my head.

I immediately shivered as the cool air brushed my skin, and I stood there in only my panties, garter, and stockings.

I hadn't bothered with a bra tonight.

Houston made quick work of my garter and panties but left my black thigh-high stockings on my legs. The three of them seemed to like whenever I wore them because they always took off everything except them, so I made a mental note to buy and wear them more often.

I tilted my head back, resting on Houston's shoulder when his hands cupped my breasts from behind, and he began kissing my neck. His chest was hard and warm against my back, and the comforting aroma of vanilla gave me no choice but to lean against him.

I always felt like I could rule the world when I was in Houston Morrow's arms.

His fingers slowly drifted down my stomach, making the muscles quiver in anticipation, and he didn't stop until he was possessively palming the smooth, bare skin of my pussy in a show of ownership.

"Yours," I gasped around the cherries drenching my tongue. I knew what he wanted to hear.

Moving my hair over my shoulder, Houston kissed my nape in response.

He didn't make me beg before he moved to my clit, teasing and circling until my back arched and then tunneling two of his fingers inside of me. He groaned the moment he was knuckle-deep and discovered how wet he'd gotten me.

Suddenly, I felt like I'd been caught red-handed.

I knew just by the sound that poured deep from his chest that I had a long night ahead of me.

"Houston—"

"Sit on his face."

My lips parted, but I couldn't respond.

Houston was still fucking me with his fingers when my gaze shot to Jericho, who watched us through half-lidded eyes.

He was no longer fighting sleep.

By the second, Rich was becoming more and more alert.

A shiver shook my body, but I was quickly distracted from my unease when Houston nipped my shoulder harshly and without warning. I had no doubt he'd left a mark. Letting my skin go, he placed his lips near my ear.

"I don't want to ask again."

As soon as I took a trembling step forward, Houston let me go. I missed his fingers inside of me even as I felt his eyes watching to make sure I obeyed.

I climbed onto the bed that, until now, I hadn't realized was pretty high, and crawled my way up Jericho's body. As soon as our lips were lined, we met each other halfway for a kiss that rattled my soul.

I loved Jericho's kisses.

They were soft and sweet and slow.

And they smelled like freshly bloomed berries.

Unlike Houston and Loren, he always let me set the pace, and somehow, I still gave him all of me anyway. I trembled once again as a slash of fear sliced me open without warning or cause.

I always assumed he was the safest, but...what if I was wrong?

What if Jericho was the most dangerous of all?

He broke the kiss.

"As much I love your lips, it's your pussy I want to kiss. My face, Braxton. Sit on my face."

Preoccupied by the need in his voice, I stared down into

Jericho's eyes. Those silver pools were like quicksand. You don't know you're screwed until you're already in too deep.

A whimper I hadn't intended slipped out of me, and then I was rising onto my knees. I heard footsteps, and when I peeked over my shoulder, it was in time to see Houston slipping out of the room. Strong hands gripped my ass while I was still frowning at the door, and then Jericho was yanking me forward until I was straddling his head.

Apparently, he'd grown impatient waiting.

My yelp was cut short, a moan replacing it when I felt his felt tongue swipe my slit. Eyes fluttering closed, I lowered myself more as my thighs spread when he began to plant open-mouth kisses on my lower lips.

"Oh, Jericho, fuck," I moaned when he eventually turned to my clit. Those slow teasing licks were going to send me to the looney bin.

Having mercy on me, his attention returned to my entrance, and my mouth fell open at the feeling of his tongue stiffening as he burrowed it inside of me as far as it would go. Pulling free, he repeated the move, and in and out, his tongue darted. I made a sound I didn't recognize as I began winding my hips. I was fucking his face in earnest now, and that was all it took for his easy rhythm to end.

Needing something to hold on to when I felt my control slipping, I fell forward, my hands clutching the sheets as he began alternating between attacking my clit and lapping up every drop of arousal that poured out of me.

Jericho was greedily feasting between my legs as if he hadn't been falling asleep mere moments ago.

The more aggressively he ate me, the wilder my hips moved until I was riding his face with complete abandon. Every so often, I'd wonder if I was hurting him, and then he'd do something with his tongue that made all thoughts, fears, and reasoning flee.

"Jericho, baby, I'm going to come," I screamed.

I couldn't recall if I'd ever been a screamer. I'd cry, I'd moan, I'd whimper, yes…but I'd never been a screamer.

Jericho made a sound of encouragement just before he gripped my ass with both hands, keeping me in place as he attacked my clit like he was a starved man and I was dessert.

I'd never felt anything like it.

When I came, I didn't just lose control of my body.

It felt like I'd left it entirely.

"Jesus," I heard someone swear behind me.

It could have been either Houston or Loren. My ears were ringing too loudly to know for sure. Long heart-thundering moments later, my orgasm subsided, but Jericho was still kissing me there in reverence. I whined when my sensitive pussy protested, so he reluctantly let me go. I didn't go far since my legs were jelly, so I fell onto the bed next to him.

Through my hazy vision, I saw that Houston had returned and was now leaning against the bottom right bedpost with a lazy, lustful look in his eyes.

"We're not done yet," he warned me when it looked like I might fall asleep.

I peeked at Jericho lying next to me and watching me with a similar look as he slowly undid his belt and jeans.

Oh.

His lips were glistening with my juices, and as if just realizing it too, he leaned over and kissed me, making me taste myself.

I moaned greedily as I deepened the kiss.

"We're going to fuck you now, okay?" he whispered after he pulled away slightly.

He shoved his jeans down his legs while Houston undid his own, and I paused as I caught on to his meaning.

"Both of you…a-at the same time?"

Teeth sinking into his bottom lip, gaze hooded, Jericho nodded. I quickly sat up as my heart began thundering in my chest. There were too many smells, too many tastes.

We hadn't tried that yet.

I've had them each alone, and some nights they took turns, but I've never had more than one of them at once.

I've never had more than *anyone* at once.

I felt Jericho's hand grip my thigh as he sat up and kissed my neck.

"It's okay," he gently assured me. "We'll take care of you."

Apparently, it wasn't up for debate.

I glared at Houston, who was naked now, as Jericho continued to attack my neck. I don't know why I liked it so much when we pretended I didn't have a choice.

Their madness evoked and constantly tested my own.

Still kissing my neck, Jericho coaxed me onto my back with sweet nothings while Houston moved to the side of the bed where he set the lube he'd left to get on the nightstand. He then joined us on the bed, and the two of them crowded me until there was nothing but them.

Houston's head lowered, pulling my right nipple between his lips, and I arched my back as I moaned, which drew Jericho away from my neck and to my mouth.

"Where's Loren?" I managed to get out between his kisses.

Houston was the one to answer me as he moved to my other nipple. "Shower."

I was vaguely aware of one of their hands spreading my legs and then long fingers dipping inside of me to check my arousal.

"Jesus, she's soaked," Houston grumbled.

As I sunk deeper into Jericho's kiss, I felt Houston move away. I didn't realize what he was up to until I felt his broad shoulders spreading my legs even wider and then his mouth and fingers continuing what Jericho had started.

Houston was as voracious and relentless as Jericho. I was already on edge, so I came even faster this time while Jericho swallowed my cries.

"I don't think we're going to need the lube," I heard Houston mutter. "She's wet as fuck."

Jericho pulled away from me to look at him while I frowned my confusion at Houston's statement. What did my pussy being wet enough to fuck have to do with my ass? I assumed one of them would be taking me there…

"Use it anyway." Rich's tone brooked no argument, so

Houston nodded and reached for the bottle along with two of the condoms he'd left on the nightstand. The third I assumed was meant for Loren.

The diva who *still* hadn't finished showering.

"Wait," I said just as they started to tear open their condoms. "You don't—" I inhaled and exhaled to clear away the fear and uncertainty creeping in. "You don't need those…unless you really want to." They both paused as they stared at me, and I couldn't tell what they were thinking. "I'm on birth control, and I got tested before we left. If you just wait a sec, I can show you."

I was so happy Griff made me pack my results even though I swore I had no intention of getting laid on this tour.

Or ever again.

I wasn't sure why I even bothered with birth control or getting tested at all. Not doing so just seemed irresponsible despite my nonexistent sex life. Clearly, I was right since here I was. Unexpectedly.

Simultaneously and without much hesitation, Houston and Rich tossed the condoms.

I already knew the three of them were clean since they'd showed me their results a few days after I agreed to be theirs. I just wasn't sure at the time that I was ready to take that next step, so I didn't do anything with the information.

"We trust you," Rich whispered as Houston reached for the lube. "Now, come here."

Kissing me again, he lifted my leg while turning me onto my side so he could spoon me from behind. As soon as I felt his cock prodding my entrance, he slowly pushed inside, letting me feel every inch, and he didn't stop until he was fully seated.

"Have I ever told you how tight and perfect your pussy feels?" he asked me as he leisurely moved inside of me. Whimpering like a wounded animal, I shook my head as I looked at him over my shoulder. Jericho filled me up so thoroughly that I was incapable of words. "No one feels like you, Braxton. No one." Speeding up his pace, I cried out when he hit a spot deep inside of me.

And he hit it again and again with perfect aim.

His hips slammed against my ass while he kept me spread for him with his hand around my thigh and my leg in the air.

He never removed his gaze from mine.

Never once gave away their true intentions.

Not until I came for the third time that night, and he abruptly flipped onto his back, taking me with him.

My body was limp as I now laid with my back on his chest. Eyes closed, I was still fighting to catch my breath when Jericho curved his hands around the back of my thighs, lifted my legs, and spread me open.

It was instinct that persuaded me to open my eyes.

I wasn't prepared for the look in Houston's as he stroked his lubed cock while watching Jericho thrust lazily in and out of me from below. Because it was then that I realized what they meant when they said the two of them would fuck me together.

Houston was suddenly there, his left hand planted by my head and leaning over me as if he'd sensed my apprehension.

I let him kiss me.

I let his fingers when he brought them to my stuffed cunt push inside.

I let him prepare to fill me up too.

"Do you like that?" he whispered as he used his fingers, and Jericho used his cock to stretch me. It shouldn't have been possible, and it shouldn't have felt so damn good. Each time I thought I'd reached my sexual limits, the three of them pushed me further.

"Yes."

"Yeah?" Houston added a third finger, and my eyes threatened to roll back inside my head. "You want more?"

"Please."

He pulled his fingers free and quickly locked his lips with mine. He was still kissing me when I felt his cock at my entrance. Jericho must have felt him too because he stopped moving.

It was only then that I realized the full implication of their cocks being inside of me at the same time.

There would be no barrier to separate them.

No waiting their turn.

It would just be me…and them.

Before Houston could even begin to push inside of me, I was coming again from the anticipation alone. Jericho groaned like he was being tortured at the feel of my walls tightening around him, making Houston chuckle when he realized what was happening.

"I'm starting to think we're going to wear your little pussy out before we're even done with her," he teased.

Still panting from coming again, I couldn't speak, so I nodded. *Me too.*

The moment he pressed forward, my stomach muscles contracted, and I tensed when my vagina immediately began to reject him.

It hurt.

The pressure from taking them both was extraordinary.

Neither of them were small, so "tight fit" would be the understatement of the century. However, with one look in Houston's eyes and hearing the desperate sounds Rich made, I knew.

I'll give them whatever pain they required for their pleasure.

Completely submitting myself to them, I rested my head on Rich's shoulder and turned my face inside the crook of his neck. He smelled so damn good.

It took forever for Houston to get the crown of his cock inside of me, and by then, tears streamed down my face because I wanted them to stop and to keep going all at once. I protested despite my submission, and Houston attempted to soothe me with promises that it would feel good soon.

I didn't want to believe him but…I do.

Reaching behind me, I slipped my fingers through Jericho's black hair. I need something to hold on to, an anchor to keep myself tethered to reality. His eyes are closed, and he's completely still, lost to the feeling of his best friend's cock rubbing against his own.

It was a taboo line my gut told me the two of them had never crossed before.

I never imagined when I joined Bound that I'd ever be this tightly entangled. Through the unlikely event we would ever meet, the mistrust, the hatred, the mockery, and the scorn…we still found our way here.

Together.

Addicted.

Irrevocable.

One.

Houston released a strangle grunt when he was finally balls deep and lodged inside of me. Breathing hard, he held himself there as he strained not to come and end this too soon.

"Okay?" Rich asked me.

In his voice, I could hear that it had taken all of his energy to form those two syllables.

"I-I don't know if I can do this," I told him honestly. It was hard just to breath. "I feel so full."

Jericho wordlessly lifted his head and began kissing my lips. "He's going to move now," he warned me as his hand caressed my thighs. "It's going to feel like you can't handle it, but you're going to take it anyway, aren't you?"

Deciding I liked this forceful side of Jericho as much as the sweet side, I eagerly nodded. "Yes."

"Good girl." After kissing me once more, he dropped his head back on the bed and at an angle that told me how good this all felt.

The moment he did, Houston pulled back only to shove his hips against mine. I could feel their cocks sliding together inside my pussy when he did it again and kept going.

He began pounding me.

With a single-minded intent, he gave and took until the sounds I made became so frantic and wild and irrational that I was outright wailing.

I was saying unintelligible things. I apologized for wrongdoings I hadn't committed yet and made promises I don't know if I would ever be able to keep. I would give Houston anything just to make him understand how mindless he'd driven me.

He kept going.

He didn't stop fucking me as if he'll die without me.

I kept my legs spread and my cunt upright as an offering to the immortal rock god.

My reward was another soul-shattering, back-arching orgasm

that made the two of them gasp and moan as I strangle their cocks together, making an impossibly tight fit even tighter.

"Fuck, I'm going to come," Rich barked, and I could feel his dick begin to swell inside me.

"Come for me," Houston tells him as he picked up his pace.

Because the truth was he was fucking his best friend as much as he was fucking me. There were no degrees of separation, with the two of them stuffed together inside my pussy.

Suddenly, I was overwhelmed by the scent of vanilla and berries. As they mixed and combined, the aroma was almost familiar. However, there was an element missing that kept me from identifying the source and finally uncovering the emotion.

I cried my frustration even as I came again.

Houston showed his appreciation with a hand wrapped around my throat as he lifted my upper body. He hammered my pussy, keeping me in place as he stared down at Rich, who still hadn't come yet.

"Fucking give it to me, Noble."

I felt Rich grip my hair from behind, arching my neck, and no longer still as he joined in and fucked me from below.

I'm caught between the two of them as they try to dominate one another.

Another wave of the berries and vanilla wash over me, and I spread myself wider to let them have their way with me.

"Shit, baby, I—"

Rich didn't get to say more.

His body stiffened as his grip on my hair tightened.

Knowing he'd won also sent Houston over the edge, and together, they flooded my pussy with their cum.

I don't know how long we stayed there, our heavy breathing the only sound in the room before Houston carefully pulled away before dropping to the far side of the bed.

Just as gently, Jericho lifted me off him and placed me between them.

We continued trying to catch our breath for another moment or two before Rich found the strength to leave the bed and the room.

He came back five minutes later with a warm cloth that he used to clean me, something I should have grown used to them doing by now but hadn't.

Houston disappeared next, and when he returned, he was wearing sweats. Picking me up from the bed, he carried me to the bathroom across the dark hall that was pretty impressive for a guest bath. As I peed, I contemplated a shower before deciding that I was much too sore and exhausted to manage it.

I'll do it in the morning.

When we returned to the bedroom, Rich was wearing shorts and lying in bed, waiting. I immediately snuggled next to him with a smile that he rewarded with his tongue and his lips as Houston got into the bed and pressed into me from behind. As soon as Rich was done, Houston turned me over to face him so that he could have his turn kissing me goodnight while Jericho spooned me from behind.

Once again, I was wondering where the hell Loren was as berries and vanilla mixed.

I wouldn't be able to sleep without him here as well, though neither Houston nor Rich seemed to feel the same.

Rich was out first, snoring loudly while Houston's breathing began to slow.

Soon, I'm left alone with my thoughts and the memory of what took place in this bed until ten minutes later, when I finally heard footsteps. The bedroom door opened, and I watched as Loren made his way over to the bed dressed in nothing but black boxer briefs.

Stopping at the foot of the bed, he tilted his head as he scanned me, Houston, and finally, Rich, before his eyes narrowed on me. "Tell me they didn't do what I think they did."

Rich, suddenly awake, lifted his head from my shoulder to grumble a response at Loren. "No one told you to take an hour-long shower the first night we bring our girl home, princess." He then returned his face to my neck while Loren joined us on the bed.

He didn't speak again until he was settled on his back next to Houston with his hands clasped behind his head. "You owe me."

I didn't realize he had directed his statement to me until his eyes cut my way in warning when I didn't immediately agree.

Of course.

Rich had already fallen asleep again, and Houston hadn't stirred.

Untangling myself from between them, I climbed over Houston to straddle Loren's waist. His hands immediately found my ass, and then our lips crashed together.

We kissed like it had been years and we'd crossed an endless ocean, fought bloody battles, and weathered countless storms just to see each other again.

Once again, my senses tried to convince me that I was running through a meadow, so I greedily and purposely inhaled the clean scent of Loren's soap. Recalling that he said he preferred it so that it didn't clash with his cologne, I sighed my unyielding affection.

That was something my bossy brute and persnickety princess had in common. Houston and Loren were both obsessed with details, though for different reasons.

I still hadn't found Rich's flaw yet.

Reaching behind me, I wrestled Loren's cock free of his boxers and began stroking his thick length until his breathing turned heavy, and he was lifting his hips and fucking my fist.

I didn't think twice before positioning him at my swollen entrance.

I was already wet for him.

"I've never met anyone like you, Braxton Fawn."

Loren was gazing up at me in awe while Houston and Rich slept soundly next to us. Slowly sinking down his cock—sore, abused pussy, and all—I held his endless gaze as I rocked my hips and began to ride him.

"And you'll never meet another, so don't blow it."

FIFTY-FIVE

Houston

THE FOUR OF US STOOD ON THE PARAPET JUST BEFORE NOON THE NEXT day. After showing her our home studio, this was the last stop of the tour we'd given Braxton of the house.

At the moment, we were silently, but not quite patiently, waiting for her to break free from her private thoughts. She was admiring one of the creepy-ass gargoyles, a winged-demon with his mouth gaped open, that we kept instead of swapping them out for modern gutters. We'd decided we wanted to keep the integrity of the architecture as well as the rainwater away.

"Did you know that grotesques were used by the clergy in medieval times to inspire fear in their parishioners?" she inquired casually. Learning what we did about her history, I knew there was nothing casual about her question. "I read they were used to remind the people what awaited them if they were sent to hell." Shrugging, she bent over the low wall, bracing her forearms on top of the stone barrier as she gazed out at the forest. I didn't realize I was staring at her ass poked out in those tiny shorts she'd put on for the occasion until she spoke again. "Considering how superstitious everyone was back then, churches had no problem keeping attendance up."

"Want us to remove them?" Loren offered as casually as Braxton pretended to be. The only difference was that he wasn't putting on a show. He'd knock this entire house down with a wrecking ball if she asked him too.

Peeking over her shoulder, probably to gauge if he was serious, she laughed and shook her head when she saw that he was. "No." There was a twinkle in her eye when she turned to face us with her elbows propped on top of the ledge now. "I also read that they ward off evil spirits. I wouldn't want you boys getting spooked all alone in these woods. Los Angeles is too far away for me to come and check under your beds."

As soon as she finished speaking, she was gazing off again as her expression fell.

Fuck.

I could tell that it hadn't dawned on her until now that we lived a thousand miles apart. Eventually, she'd have to go back. Ultimately, we'd have to do without her and try to make an already complicated relationship work long-distance.

The only solution was if she stayed here…with us.

Loren, apparently coming to the same conclusion, brought it up before I, or any of us, could think it over and broach the subject *carefully.*

"So that's what your little history lesson was really about," he teased her. "You want to move in."

Her eyes bucked as she stood up straight. "What? No, that's not what I was saying."

"It's cool, baby fawn. We've got the room."

She frowned at him before rolling her eyes when she realized that it was him leading her into a trap and not the other way around. "I'm not moving in with you, Loren."

He frowned deeply, confirming what I already knew. Loren hadn't been just teasing. "Why not?"

"Because we've been dating for two seconds?"

"You plan on going anywhere?" he asked her quietly, his tone curious but his gaze blank.

Braxton's answer and how carefully she tread would determine how fast this escalated. Rich and I glanced at one another, but for some reason, neither of us felt compelled to step in. He was supposed to be the voice of reason, and whenever that didn't work, I brought the heavy hand and put my foot down. Loren's job usually consisted of finessing the situation—whenever he wasn't causing trouble to begin with.

"There's no harm in taking it slow, Loren. The tour won't be over for *months*. Can't we just talk about it then?" she reasoned.

Unfortunately, Loren wasn't in the mood to be reasonable. Everything she said had gone in one ear and out the other. "Why put off tomorrow what can be done today?"

Nostrils flaring, there was a fire in Braxton's eyes as they searched the ground, and I knew from firsthand experience that she was looking for something to throw at his head.

Rich and I both exhaled our relief when we searched the ground as well and saw no rocks lying around.

When it looked like he wasn't getting his way anytime soon, Loren dug his—our—hole a little deeper. It wouldn't escape her notice that we didn't step in, and eventually, she'd figure out why. "Stop pretending you're not into it too when we all know better," he snapped.

With a mock gasp, Braxton slapped her palm to her forehead. "How could I forget? Naturally, my gender means I'm perpetually confused and don't know my own mind. Have mercy, big man. Tell me what I really want."

Loren threw his head back and made a frustrated sound in his throat. "Are we really going to fight about this again?" he mumbled, referring to her demand to be treated like our equal.

I'm sure we were beyond that now since it started to feel like we worshiped the ground she walked on. Either she couldn't see that because she was stubborn, or we were still shit at this boyfriend thing.

"No, because I'm done talking to you."

She started for the door and the steps that led back inside, and Loren was hot on her heels. Though not as closely, Rich and I followed, and I was once again wondering why neither of us was stopping Loren while he was ahead.

I didn't have to tell him that he could never force Braxton to do something she didn't want to do. He already knew. The problem was that people don't just change overnight, and Loren was too used to getting his way.

Even if Braxton did want to move in, I knew she wasn't sure she could handle that yet. It meant leaving her friends, moving to a strange place, sinking deeper into our web, and abandoning the independence that had taken every ounce of her courage to build in the first place.

"Loren," I called out, making him glance over his shoulder at me.

I knew the moment he read the look in my eyes and realized what he was doing and how bad he was fucking up. His footsteps reluctantly slowed, but by then, Braxton had reached the room we'd given her last night, and we were still right on her heels.

We already shared a house. Obviously, the three of us had never considered or needed to share a room as well, so we each had our own. Until we could think of a better arrangement, it just made sense to give Braxton her own space while she was here.

Thanks to Loren and his "superior" finessing skills, it was already coming in handy.

I could tell Braxton was still pissed when she turned to face us once she was over the threshold. Even during the longer-than-necessary walk that it took to reach her bedroom since she kept getting lost, she hadn't cooled down one bit.

None of us got a chance to say a word or maybe even apologize before she pushed the door shut, making the sound reverberate throughout the house, and we were left staring at the wood we'd painted black.

"Damn," Loren mumbled after he'd turned to face us. "She's been here less than a day, and we're already getting doors slammed in our faces."

There was a loud thump on Braxton's door that came from the inside, telling us that she'd heard him, and I sighed. It was only noon, and I was weary.

"If I don't get laid tonight, I'm making you suck my dick," Rich spat as he turned and walked away.

Loren snorted but didn't say more about it before he went off in a different direction.

I stared at Braxton's door for a moment, but when nothing smart came to mind that would get us back in her good graces, I decided to leave it alone.

For now.

We were sitting in our practice room, attempting to piece together a new song, when she ambled in after spending the last twenty-four hours hiding in her room.

"Oh, shit," Loren whispered once he noticed her. Braxton, wearing a blue spaghetti-strapped dress that only reached her thighs and her hair pinned in a ponytail at her crown, wandered the far edge of the room. She looked over our awards and photos hanging on the red wall as if she hadn't seen them already. "No one make any sudden movements. We don't want to scare her off."

Braxton's head swiveled toward us at that exact moment, and…those two idiots actually froze.

She gave them an exasperated look before her curious gaze met mine. I nodded my head to the empty seat on the leather sofa next to me since Loren and Rich occupied the armchairs on the other side of the black trunk we used as a table.

After only a moment's hesitation, which I still didn't care for, she came.

I'd texted her an hour ago to let her know where we were and what we were up to, hoping she'd come. I had just begun to fear we'd lose another day when she showed up.

It wasn't until she dropped down onto the sofa, and I got a whiff of her brown sugar body wash and saw that her red hair was still damp, that I realized what had held her up. It was still early in the afternoon, so I figured she must have just woken up.

The only time I got her out of bed before noon was when Rich or I coaxed her out of it since Loren was no better. He was worse, actually. Today was the exception, and I had the feeling he'd woken up early in the hopes of catching her roaming instead of knocking on her door and apologizing.

She felt his stare even now and ignored him. Loren was burning a hole in the side of her face, but Braxton kept her gaze steadfast on her purple nails that my back knew were as sharp as they looked, along with the ten silver rings adorning the index, middle, and ring finger of her left hand.

Deciding to break the silence, I handed over the notepad with the current version of one of our new songs scratched onto the paper.

"What do you think?" I asked, watching her closely after she finally took it from me. My heart was pounding as Braxton read over the lyrics, and I didn't have to question why. It seemed like it took an eternity for her to be done even though less than a minute had passed.

"I think finding a melody is going to be tricky."

Damn it.

She'd chosen her tone and expression carefully so that I couldn't tell what she was really thinking. The only evidence that she was feeling anything at all were the subtle cues she gave, like the slight wrinkling of her nose and purse of her lips as if she tasted or smelled something unexpected.

Nodding, I picked up the acoustic next to me, and her brows shot up when I held it out to her. "Would you prefer a keyboard?"

She continued to gape. "You want me to write the melody?"

"No, this is a guitar, and that's my song in your lap," I answered sarcastically. "I thought we'd knit."

Lifting the notepad, it slapped my chest when she tossed it at me as she stood. Jericho caught her, which I'm sure was more of an excuse to touch her after so long than as a favor to me, and kept her from leaving.

"He's sorry, I'm sorry, we're all sorry," he told her sincerely when she was seated next to me again.

Refusing to look at him, she flipped him off, surprising everyone in the room except Braxton. She'd never given him more than her silence, which rarely lasted long when she was upset with him. Loren and I usually bore the brunt of her wrath.

Jericho tried to nix it off, only to end up looking like his dog died. I refrained from laughing since Braxton would no doubt assume it was directed at *her*.

"I'll create the melody," I pretended to concede after picking up the fallen notepad.

I could see in her eyes that she wanted to do it, possibly since the moment she read the first line, but she was too stubborn to let go of her pride. I was starting to wonder if she'd picked up that trait from her conservative upbringing or if she came by it honestly.

Handing her the notepad again, I hid my surprise when she took it. "Sing it how you think it should sound," I requested when she just stared at me.

Braxton had a powerful voice, and even though I should be used to it by now, I was always eager to hear it again.

I waited patiently as she silently read over it again, creating a natural rhythm for the verses, chorus, and bridge in her mind before she began. I listened, hopelessly enthralled, as she tried it a second and third time out loud. She shifted her tone and pitch, speeding up and slowing down her pace when needed until it flowed like water from her lips.

"That was good," I praised as casually as I could manage. Clearing my throat, I lifted the guitar. "Let's try that again. I'll do backup."

She did without argument, singing much slower this time as I tried to find the right chords to match the rhythm she set. We ran through it numerous times until it started to feel cohesive.

"Again," I said the moment we finished our fourth attempt. It almost sounded like a plea. They might have been my words, but the song was always meant for her voice. Braxton didn't hesitate before launching into the song I'd crafted from her pain.

Walking alone in this lonely existence
How much longer can I hide what I feel
There's a wolf in the midst of pious sheep
It rages, can anyone hear me
(Give in to me)

It seems no one understands
No one else but you
You're the vengeance that builds in silence
I'm the demon you wait to free

I can't stop these imminent changes
You send a broken servant; sacrificed, he kneels
Looking into dead eyes, I come alive
Fucked and forsaken, I'm cast aside
(Just give in to me)

Don't let this thing wither
Let my blood run wild
Set the flame and feel it burn
I hear you calling
(Give in to me)

It seems no one understands
No one else but you
You're the vengeance that builds in silence
I'm the demon you wait to free

Just as Braxton was reaching the bridge that led to the fourth verse and the final chorus, Loren's phone started to ring from where it sat on the table. Neither of us stopped. From my peripheral, however, I saw Loren lean over to check it.

I never questioned or understood how I'd become so attuned to my best friends that I could feel their emotions as if they were my own.

My fingers stopped playing.

Only one person inspired the measure of anger and apprehension I felt rippling off Loren in waves.

Braxton waited for me to tell her why I had stopped, but my focus was on Loren, who was lifting his phone from the table.

"Don't answer that," I snapped.

I never even considered if I had the right to come between a father and son. Loren gave me a lazy look like he was bored, but I knew better. He cared about his father calling. And he hated my attempt to strong-arm him into doing what he already knew was best—for everyone.

I didn't know why Orson chose now to reach out, but it couldn't have been because he cared. However, Loren's lack of surprise and the tension radiating off him made me wonder if this wasn't the first time.

It's been six years to my recollection.

What had I missed?

"He's my father," Loren retorted as if that made a difference.

"Then explain why you've only had Rich and me for the past six years?"

"Fuck you, Houston, okay?" He grabbed his phone and stood, making me stand too.

He wasn't answering that fucking call.

Loren might have forgotten how long it took him to stand on his own feet confidently, but I hadn't. Five years and he was still waiting for me to apologize for talking them into signing that deal, but I couldn't.

I just…couldn't.

As much as I regretted Savant, it wasn't even close to how much I would have missed my best friend.

I wouldn't give him up then, and I wouldn't give him up now.

Holding my gaze, Loren pressed the green button.

The moment he tried to speak, I charged the two steps it took to reach him and packed a lot of power into the fist I drove into his stomach. Loren dropped to one knee, and when his phone hit the ground next to him, I quickly scooped it up.

There was frustration and anger written in the look he gave me as he held his stomach and glared up at me. Braxton and Rich also wore deep frowns, but I didn't care. I didn't care if they thought I was being a dick. Frankly, what else was new?

"What the fuck is your problem?" Loren barked once he caught the wind I'd knocked out of him.

"Orson James is my problem. He hasn't changed, and you fucking know it."

The muscle in Loren's jaw ticked. Hitting him and taking away the call with his father hadn't pissed him off nearly as much as his fear that I might be right.

It was more than a possibility, though. It was a fucking fact.

And it was already driving me crazy to think that I might not be there the next time Orson called, and he would. He didn't give up easily, but neither did I.

Standing, Loren didn't break my stare. "What the hell makes you think you're any different?" he spat, calling me out on my shit. I couldn't move. I couldn't do anything other than take it because Loren was right. I wasn't any better than Orson James. "You're still a controlling piece of shit. Nothing's changed."

Bumping me as he passed to leave the room, I almost followed him to…I don't know. Loren shot a look over his shoulder just before he disappeared that warned me off.

Rich jumped on me as soon as the door was closed. "Seriously, Morrow?"

My gaze shot to Braxton for some reason before I quickly looked away. Shame, maybe? I was acting like a lunatic and couldn't explain why. "Drop it."

Braxton silently stood from the couch and slowly walked by me before quietly leaving the room. I had a hunch she was going to check on Loren despite giving him the cold shoulder.

Dropping down into the armchair Loren had vacated and slouching, I leaned my head against the low back and closed my eyes. I'd barely finished exhaling all the air from my lungs and unknotting my fucking stomach before Rich broke the silence.

"I'm meeting with my lawyer tomorrow," he quietly announced. I kept my eyes closed since I was too exhausted to know where he was going with this. "And then I'm going to tell Braxton about Emily."

My eyes shot open at that as I lifted my head.

"No shit?" I couldn't pin a reason on why I frowned when it was immense relief I felt. Perhaps it was because I knew Jericho couldn't have come to this decision easily. "What made you change your mind?"

Rich was forlorn as he stared at the floor for a while before he finally answered. "It's starting to feel like I'm in a hole too deep to climb, and I can't help but hope that I'm wrong. Even if there's a crumb possibility that Braxton will forgive me, I have to hold on to it with both hands, you know?"

I did know.

Because chances were Rich wouldn't be the only one getting dumped when Braxton found out about his wife.

"We'll figure out the rest," I promised him.

Staring at him a little longer, I blew out a breath when that pitiful look in his eyes became even more palpable. I had an inkling of what had held him up from going around Emily and getting his marriage dissolved.

Silently, I waited for the anger and betrayal that never came.

I couldn't bring myself to feel those things because I also knew Rich was giving up the only thing he ever wanted but never got. He might have grown into a man and was beloved by millions now, but to me, Jericho was never far from that sad, lonely kid who'd been denied a single, true attachment. Loren and I had been his first and only until even that had been ripped away by distrust, resentment, and greed.

This time around it was Jericho walking away from that chance for the one his heart decided he needed more. There wasn't a single doubt in my mind that Braxton was worth it, but it wasn't my sacrifice. It was Jericho's.

"Thank you," I heard myself say to him.

Rich finally looked up from the floor, his gaze shocked by my fervent tone and the sincerity in those two words that made his lips tilt at the corner and his silver eyes kindle. "Fuck off, Houston," he spat, making me laugh too. "We crossed swords *once*. Don't make shit weird."

FIFTY-SIX

Braxton

The North American leg of the Bound & Bellicose tour had officially ended. It was mid-afternoon over a week later when my gaze traveled over to the bassist in the partially fogged mirror of his bathroom.

We'd just finished up in his shower, which I actually hadn't minded Loren holding me hostage inside since it was the size of a small closet with black stone walls, a tiled floor to match, and water that rained from the ceiling like a gentle waterfall.

The bamboo bench built into the shower's alcove was pretty sturdy too.

Shifting my feet guiltily, I told myself not to get hung up on how I'd ended up in his bed last night. I wasn't sure I *could* explain since nothing had changed. I was very much scared shitless of his determination to move too fast.

I knew the conversation wasn't over.

It was right there in his eyes that it wasn't far from his mind.

Noticing me watching him, Loren slowed the circular motions his long fingers made as he worked the chemical exfoliant into his skin. It was his third cleanse since he started on his face after the almost painful-to-watch scrupulous flossing, brushing, and rinsing of his teeth.

"What's up?" he asked when I continued to gape.

"Nothing." I tried and failed to hide my smile as I brushed the tangles from my hair. Unlike Loren, I'd already finished with my face and teeth. "It's just that watching you is like using a white towel after a long shower. It's a truly humbling experience."

I felt like I was still dirty even though we'd stayed in the shower until the water turned cold and my skin pruned.

I watched Loren's pearl-white teeth sink into his bottom lip as the heat in his gaze turned up a thousand notches. My poor vagina emphatically protested his thoughts since she was still bearing the brunt of Loren's attention last night, again in the shower, and Houston's visit before the sun was fully up this morning.

Rich was back to being distant again, and I cursed myself for not keeping my word and getting to the bottom of it. I'd been too busy hiding to uncover their secrets.

Now I questioned if I cared anymore.

I wondered if I had the fortitude to chase someone who seemed so unsure about me.

The answer was no. I didn't.

"You have nothing to worry about," Loren said with all the confidence of a man used to getting what he wanted. "When we're old and gray, and I'm struggling to get it up, rest assured there won't be a part of you my tongue hasn't touched." Leaning over from his spot at the double vanity, he placed a sensual kiss on my neck that tasted like cherries and made my knees weak, even as he lewdly groped my ass. It wasn't until he pulled away enough to meet my gaze that I caught his drift. "Not one."

Giving my ass one last pointed squeeze, he resumed his high-maintenance routine.

I returned to my room to dress for the day, and by that time, Loren still wasn't done perfecting his hair, so I tiptoed back out of the room and made my way downstairs. "Black is the Soul" by Korn was blaring, and it led me right to Houston.

I found him sitting at the island in their kitchen that was just as dark, Victorian, and gothic as the rest of their castle and scowling at the laptop in front of him. He was so into his search that he didn't notice me standing next to him until it was too late.

"Are you writing a book?" I asked him when I read the headline of the medical article he was reading.

Quickly shutting the laptop closed, Houston regarded me long and hard. "You're synesthetic."

First, the song he'd written from my point-of-view as if we were one mind and now this. I was starting to feel uncomfortable, though strangely not creeped out, which was disturbing in itself.

No, I was having trouble coming to terms with the fact that I would never be able to hide from Houston Morrow. Never.

Suddenly, I was on the defensive.

"Or maybe everyone else is just doing it wrong, and *you're* synesthetic," I elusively pointed out. "Ever think of that?" My heart thudded as I waited for his answer while Houston waited for mine with all his composure intact.

I sighed when the staring contest ended with me silently accepting that Houston was just as assertive without needing to speak a word.

"I didn't find out until a couple of years ago that not everyone—correction—*no one* I've ever met perceives sound through color."

"Chromesthesia," he said simply for confirmation.

I nodded. "It's not always just color. Sometimes it's shapes and movements too. The only constant seems to be music. Regular sounds like a dog barking or a horn honking have no effect." The faint scent of the ocean warned me of my distress when I wondered if Houston thought I was a basket case now.

"And this?" he asked me, tapping my wriggling nose when I tried to push the emotion away. "What are you feeling right now?"

I took a step back.

My lips parted, but no words came.

He *couldn't* know that.

After three years of searching for articles and conversing with strangers through forums, I hadn't been able to name how or why I *tasted* my emotions or even smelled them. I'd already been scanned, prodded, and tested for tumors and dementia. The closest I'd come to finding an answer was other synesthetes who feel their emotions through colors, temperatures, and spatial sense. But none whose emotions caused them to hallucinate tastes and smells.

Sometimes I wondered if I would have preferred it that way. My emotions, including the good ones, had ruined my ability to appreciate simple things like roses and cinnamon when I actually encountered them.

"What do you mean?" I was back to being elusive.

Houston closed the gap I'd placed between us, making it clear I wouldn't get away with it. "Tell me," he demanded softly, and I found I hated his casual confidence much more than his forcefulness. It was much easier to deny him when he was being a dick.

"Desire tastes like cherries, shame smells like olives, happiness tastes like chocolate, sorrow smells like roses…should I keep going, or do you get the point?"

Houston's hands drifted underneath my sundress, where he placed his hand on my hips before backing and trapping me against the window behind me. "And what about me? What do I smell like?"

My heart skipped a beat as vanilla filled the air.

"How do you know I feel anything at all?"

"The same way I figured out you were a hundred times more complicated than you let on, Braxton Fawn. I haven't stopped paying attention." When he kissed me, he forced my lips to part and my mouth to accept his tongue. I moaned in response. It was a desperate, broken sound. Whatever emotion Houston was responsible for evoking, I was drunk with it by the time he let me up for air. "And I never will," he warned me.

I shivered just as Loren sauntered into the kitchen, fully dressed and brazenly debonair. If there was ever a walking example of perfection, he was it. To my ears, I sounded like a lovedrunk fool, but the way the three of them overwhelmed me, separately and definitely together, it was hard to care about anything other than giving in to them.

"Can you stop groping my girl?" Loren griped. His eyes

weren't even on us. He was focusing on fastening his expensive-looking watch as he stood by the door with a scowl. "We've got somewhere to be."

"She's not just yours," Houston reminded him.

"Keep fighting over me like I'm a chew toy, and I'll dump the three of you for me, myself, and I."

Houston's head swiveled back down to me, and his lips twitched as amusement lit up his eyes. "Damn, baby, Rich isn't even here. He gets dumped too?"

"Yup."

Just not for the reason the two of them believed.

Even now, Jericho was missing-in-action, and my pride wouldn't allow me to ask. I didn't want to know if he was avoiding me again.

Finished fastening his watch, Loren looked up, and then he leaned back with the bottom of his right foot planted against the wall. "What color panties are we wearing today?" he inquired with a smile.

Suddenly, I was standing in a field. There was grass as tall as my waist, and I could almost feel the flower petals slipping between my fingers as I walked. I knew the answer Loren was looking for because I hadn't forgotten the day I became Bound, either.

"Black like my heart."

I saw the pride in Loren's eyes and knew I'd always be theirs.

Jericho still hadn't returned when we left for the hour-long drive to Portland. To make matters more annoying Houston and Loren were pretending not to know where he'd gone or what held him up.

I didn't want to be the kind of girl who didn't ask the important questions because she was too afraid of the answers. Day after day, it seemed that was exactly who I was allowing myself to become. I wouldn't know how to let them go if they forced me to, and it was obvious that Jericho had secrets.

Would we survive them?

My stomach filled with dread when the answer didn't come. My mind couldn't seem to settle on a single theory of what he kept from me because my heart refused to believe any of them. When I realized my hands were actually wringing in my lap, I forced them apart and swallowed past the phantom taste of sour milk.

Fuck this.

Disgusted with myself, I had my phone in my hand and typing before I even knew what I would say.

Where are you?

Green apples burst on my tongue when he answered right away. I hadn't expected that.

Jericho: Home.

I scoffed, which drew Houston's attention to me briefly as he drove with one hand and fiddled with the radio with the other. Finally allowing myself to ask the question that's had my heart trapped in my throat since he first started to pull away, I typed my response.

Are you avoiding me?

My hands shook as I watched those fucking bubbles appear and disappear for what seemed like an eternity. Despite knowing the truth, I wasn't as prepared for it as I thought.

Rich: Yes.

I didn't get to figure out what I should say to that before he sent another text.

Rich: We need to talk.

Loren was saying something. I didn't know whether it was to Houston or me as Houston parked his truck in front of a low stone wall of a small, dirt parking lot. I didn't respond to Loren as I texted Rich instead.

About?

He forced me to watch those bubbles dance long enough to make me fear the worst, only for him to send another cryptic one-word response.

Rich: Later.

I hated him.

Feeling like I was going to vomit, I hurriedly pushed open the front passenger door of Houston's matte gray G-Wagon and climbed out to inhale the fresh air. I could feel their attention, but I couldn't face them yet. They'd know what I was thinking, and they'd make excuses for him.

No, I texted Rich as the smell of embers filled my nose. *I want to talk now.*

Rich: We will, baby. Tonight. I promise.

Fuck you.

My phone had only just confirmed the text was delivered when it started ringing immediately after. I stared at Rich's name on the screen before turning it off completely and shoving my phone in my crossbody.

I didn't want to talk anymore.

I wanted to scream.

I wanted to cry.

I wanted to do both while *murdering* Rich for making me feel this way.

And then I wondered how long before Houston and Loren did the same. How long before they slowly and torturously broke my heart into little pieces too?

I felt heavy arms circle my waist, but I fought them.

They tightened just before the point when breathing would have been impossible, and finally, I relaxed. "It's not what you think," Houston whispered when he felt my surrender. "He's not having second thoughts."

"How do you know that?" I returned flatly. "You're in his head uninvited too?"

Houston squeezed my waist before turning me around to face him. I couldn't handle the intensity of his stare that bid me to trust him, so I dropped my gaze to his feet.

Houston lifted chin right back up.

"I know because there's no such thing as getting over you."

Feeling the butterflies in my belly take flight, I rolled my eyes instead of melting into him like I wanted. I wasn't ready to believe him yet. "Jericho will tell you what he's thinking when he's ready."

"Is this how it will always be?" I snapped as I pulled away from him. "I hurry up when you want, and I wait when you want?"

First, they wouldn't allow me the time to consider the implication of being with all three of them. Now they were keeping secrets and expecting the courtesy of patience—virtues they failed to show me.

Maybe I'm the one who should be having second thoughts.

I was ready to walk away, if only for a moment to breathe and think, as I backed up another step.

I didn't get further than that before Loren, who'd snuck up behind me, kept me trapped between them.

"Something we should know?" he casually inquired while he left me facing Houston. His tone was sinister, like he'd read my thoughts.

Ignoring the metallic smell permeating the air, I lifted my chin, hoping it would be a warning to them.

"You're both dicks?"

Loren's chuckle was quiet as he gently pushed me forward to get me going when Houston stepped away and led us down the forested trail.

"You're not worried about being recognized?" I asked them when we passed people jogging or walking here and there.

Houston shrugged as he kept his gaze fixed ahead and his jaw tight. "It's home."

His meaning became clear when we encountered a few who recognized Houston and Loren—and even me—and welcomed them back before going on their way.

Here in Portland, they didn't have to be gods.

They were able to be the men they were underneath. And I got to enjoy them too.

It was a ten-minute half-a-mile hike to the old stone ruins. I didn't understand why they brought me here since the crumbling structure covered in moss, missing a roof, and had nothing around but woods and more woods wasn't much to look at.

I didn't understand until Loren informed me that Bound's first performance had taken place here. At Witch's Castle. I looked around, feeling my resolve weaken as Loren recounted that night, allowing me to see the face of their humble beginnings with my own eyes. It had been just another high school kegger in front of a crowd of fifty, but it counted.

It counted because I knew despite the secrets they kept that they were *trying*.

Houston, Loren, and Rich were letting me in.

They were stumbling through the dark, but they were determined to find their way. For that promise, as the scent of vanilla and morning dew mixed, I would be patient.

We stayed out for hours as they showed me around the city where they grew up. The sun had long set when Houston drove us through the iron gates that separated the public land from the private hideaway Bound had procured for themselves. They'd left most of it untouched and as wild as they had found it, only carving out what they needed and allowing the rest of the forest to cloak them. The seclusion was terrifying and liberating at the same time.

But I knew it couldn't last.

Eventually, the tour would end, and I'd have to go back to L.A. We still had months before that happened, so I wouldn't dwell on it now.

When their home came into view, the first thing I noticed was Jericho's green and black sport bike parked out front and felt nerves tie my stomach into endless knots.

The house was quiet when we made it inside. Houston and Loren went straight to their rooms to shower off the day while I drifted to the guest bedroom, wondering if Jericho would find me.

I realized he wouldn't have to when I walked into the bedroom and found him in my bed.

His eyes were closed, dark lashes brushing his cheeks, pierced lips subtly parted, and his chest slowly rising up and down while he lay on his side with the muscled arm his head was propped on stretched toward my pillow.

He'd fallen asleep waiting for me.

Waiting to finally have the talk that I fought and failed all day to push from my mind.

He was still fully dressed and entirely in black—plain T-shirt, expensive jeans, and high-top sneakers. The dark color only emphasized his pale skin.

As quietly as I could, I tiptoed back out of the room and to the guest bath across the hall. He hadn't been snoring as usual, which meant he might not have been that deep in his sleep. I didn't want to risk waking him since I knew he'd been having trouble.

I even caught Loren two nights ago forcing him to bed when I woke in the middle of the night to use the bathroom. Neither of them had noticed me standing there watching them. Rich had seemed out of it, which I guess too many sleepless nights in a row would do to you, and Loren had been too focused on his task.

He'd been gentle with Rich, which surprised me at the time and even now. I couldn't forget how softly Loren spoke with his hand on Jericho's back as he coaxed his best friend to bed. That tender moment belied the tension I'd glimpsed in Loren's shoulders just before they disappeared inside Rich's room.

I pondered if the reason Jericho was having trouble sleeping had to do with me as I took my time in the shower. It might not have been super late, but the exhaustion clinging to my bones said otherwise. Whatever Jericho and I needed to talk about, I decided it would have to wait until morning.

Feeling refreshed, I stepped from the bathroom sometime later, wrapped in nothing but a towel, only to freeze in momentary terror when the shadows near my bedroom door moved. My heart didn't stop trying to flee my chest until I finally recognized the tall, slim figure they belonged to.

"Jericho?"

I immediately tensed when those silver eyes seemed to look right through me. To add insult, he walked away without responding, and I frowned as I watched him go.

Something was wrong.

His slow steps were heavy as if he were in a trance. I called his name again when he reached the end of the hall and again received no response. As confusion and alarm battled each other, I debated alerting Houston or Loren.

Rich disappeared as he turned down another hallway, and the fear of leaving him alone decided for me.

I hurried after my drummer, closely trailing him down the

long hallway until we reached the grand staircase leading to the first floor. Every so often, I'd call his name, but I never dared touch him, and I didn't know why.

Still ignoring me, Jericho headed toward the arched doorway and the stairs that led to the tunnels underneath. I quietly followed him down, the stone steps rough and cold beneath my bare feet and my exposed skin chilled by the unrelenting draft. Together, we walked through one of the tunnels partially lit by sconces until we reached the practice room that doubled as their man cave. The rest of the tunnels led all over, but this was the sole entrance into the tower.

Wondering if he'd led me here purposely, I hesitated only a moment before following him inside. If he had, maybe it was to talk. I didn't appreciate his creepy tactics, effective though they were. Words would have worked just fine.

Still so very confused, I stood warily by the door as Jericho walked deeper into the room.

He still hadn't acknowledged me.

Instead, he stopped in the middle of the room, and I watched the back of his head turn as he looked around as if searching for something.

"Jericho," I called, my tone firm and my patience gone.

Apprehension returned with the force of a Mack truck when he strode over to the side table next to the leather sofa, slid open the drawer, and pulled something out. I didn't see what it was until he sat on the sofa with a pen in one hand and a set of papers that looked like they'd been folded and unfolded a hundred times clutched in the other.

His torpid gaze scanned them and the words printed on them. A moment later, Rich became agitated, gripping them hard enough to make them crinkle and ball up at one corner.

I forgot my unease as worry made my feet carry me closer to him. "Talk to me, Rich."

My mind began to turn when he gave no reaction to my desperate plea. None. And then it all clicked into place.

He wasn't ignoring me. He couldn't hear me.

Because Jericho wasn't even awake.

He was sleepwalking.

My suspicions were confirmed when, despite the anger he displayed only a moment ago, he calmly placed the papers on top of the black trunk they used as a coffee table, brought the pen to the material, and began writing. He made slow, lazy loops as he signed what I guessed was his name since he was done rather quickly.

Then…as if nothing had occurred…he stood from the sofa.

Jericho's mind was still on autopilot when he ambled by me. Even though I was worried, I didn't follow or call after him.

I watched him go.

The moment I was alone, my focus shifted to the papers, and I cautiously drifted closer.

One would think they were a bomb, and there were only ten seconds left to detonation. Quietly, I battled with the angel and the devil on my shoulders. I had no right to read what looked suspiciously like legal documents.

But that doesn't mean you shouldn't, the devil draped in red whispered in my ear.

I felt like I was on autopilot, too, when I lifted the papers from the table. The first thing I noticed was Jericho's signature, messier than usual and crammed into the top corner of the page. But it wasn't his name signed in the wrong place that had me frozen in horror and confusion. It was everything that came after.

It was the smell of roses.

It was the emotions that I should have felt but didn't.

Because there was only sorrow.

The grief that gripped me wouldn't allow me to feel anything else. It wouldn't allow me denial or frustration as I read the words again.

I was already looking for a reason to forgive him.

So it didn't allow me anger.

It didn't allow me disgust or guilt or envy.

Because allowing those things would bring me hope that Jericho wasn't lost to me forever and that…my rending heart could not do.

FIFTY-SEVEN

Loren

"Shit." Groaning, I leaned over when my eyes opened on their own. I snatched my phone from the nightstand to check the time.

It was only nine thirty.

Why the *fuck* was I awake?

Tossing my phone back, I relaxed and tried to sleep again, but my mind wouldn't stop sounding the alarm. I must have tried for ten minutes before giving up and rising out of bed. Thankfully, I'd worn pants to bed because I was on a mission when I stormed from my room.

I fully intended to ensure whichever of my friends chose to die at this ungodly hour went painfully. I didn't slow my stride until I passed Rich's room and saw him shuffling out with one eye open and his hair sticking up everywhere.

Houston then.

Tougher to maim, but I'd manage.

I heard Rich following me, only for us both to stop when we reached the stairs. Houston was walking down the short hallway that led to his bedroom, looking just as bewildered when he spotted us.

So…what the fuck?

I didn't have an internal alarm for anyone else. There was no one I gave a shit about that much. No one else except—

I turned away from the stairs and started back the way I had come, back toward Braxton's room, before my mind could even finish that thought. I felt Houston and Rich behind me as I knocked on her door for a minute straight with no answer. The entire time I was rationalizing that Braxton wasn't a morning person either.

She's probably sleeping.

I didn't realize Houston had grown impatient and twisted the knob until my fist connected with air when the door swung open. The three of us stepped inside with matching frowns as we looked around. The bedding was rumpled but still made, which told me she hadn't slept in it last night. The biggest clue that something was wrong, however, was all her missing shit.

Rich was the first to break free of the stupor Braxton had put us in, and I watched him walk over like a skittish kitten to the nightstand on the right side of the bed that Braxton preferred when we weren't making her sleep in the middle.

I hadn't even noticed one of our chef's knives sticking out of the wooden surface handle up.

When Rich just stood there staring at the knife instead of telling us why Braxton murdered our furniture, I walked over with Houston on my heels.

"What's up?" I asked him when I came to stand next to him. Rich was already pale as fuck, but right now, he looked like he'd either seen a ghost or was a ghost.

When he still didn't say shit, I looked at the knife. And then I glanced at the papers pinned underneath, but it was my medallion she'd left as well and the words carved into the wood that held my attention.

Happy Anniversary.

"Happy anniversary?" I mused out loud. Reluctantly, I lifted my medallion from the table and slipped it inside my pocket rather than around my neck. I was annoyed at Braxton's audacity to give it back like we were over, but I wasn't entirely upset. The medallion wasn't what I had in mind for her to wear for me anyway. Braxton deserved something that had meaning and she was going to get it.

"It's September third," Rich mumbled. They were his first words since waking up.

Why did that date sound so familiar?

He looked up, saw the question in my eyes, and said, "My wedding date."

Shit.

My gaze was drawn back to the papers Braxton had skewered directly in the center with Rich's signature in the top right corner for some reason. This time I paid attention long enough to notice what they were.

PETITION FOR DISSOLUTION OF MARRIAGE
In the Matter of the Marriage or Registered Domestic Partnership of:
Jericho Noble (Petitioner)
and
Emily Noble (Respondent)

Date of marriage/domestic partnership: September 3, 2013
Place of marriage/domestic partnership: Multnomah County, Oregon
Date of petition for dissolution:
April 9, 2018

Irreconcilable differences between the parties have caused the irremediable breakdown of their marriage/domestic partnership.

I skipped over the rest of the legal jargon until I reached the part that painted a vivid picture of how thoroughly Rich had fucked us. It wasn't enough for him to stick the knife into Braxton's back, which she had categorically left behind to make her feelings clear.

No.

I blew out a breath.

He had to drive it to the fucking hilt.

He had to make sure we didn't stand a chance of getting her back.

Because Jericho Noble was as much a sadist as he was a masochist.

He buried himself in angst and pain, and when that wasn't enough, he inflicted more.

I shook my head in frustration as I read over the part again, even as I felt the guilt seep into my bones, reminding me that this had been my doing.

Children of the Marriage/Domestic Partnership:
Name: ____________________
Gender: ____________________
Date of Birth: ______________
Age: Three years

"Why the fuck would you include this bullshit?" I exploded anyway. "You don't even know if that's your kid, dipshit! Name, *unknown*. Gender, *unknown*. Date of birth, *un-fucking-known*. Did it ever occur to you that Emily could have been lying? There might not even be a kid."

"She wasn't lying," he assured me, and it made me sick to my stomach to hear him defend that lying, cheating bitch.

"So you've seen her in the last four years? Did she happen to have a kid on her hip?" I yanked the knife from the nightstand and snatched the papers up to study them closer. I just had to know what other dumb shit Jericho's self-flagellating ass had used to screw us over. As soon as I was sure there were no other skeletons in his fucked-up closet, I'd go get my girl.

I wasn't so sure I could do this three-amigos shit anymore.

Jericho had been right about one thing, at least.

If one of us lost her, we all did, which meant the chances of us fucking up were greater with three. I wasn't sure if I could go through losing Braxton a fourth or fifth time. I guess it depended on who was counting.

When I read the same line six times, I gave up and tossed the papers neither Jericho nor Emily had signed, making it crystal clear to Braxton that they were still married.

I couldn't think straight. Each breath felt like it cost me a little more. I wanted to hit something, namely Jericho.

Seeing that wild look in his eyes that mirrored my own, I knew he'd fuck me up just as bad if I tried. In my peripheral, I noticed

Houston sink onto the edge of Braxton's bed with his forearms on his thighs as he stared dejectedly at the floor.

"Now would be a good time for you to tell us what to do," I spat.

He ignored me.

I shoved my fingers through my hair before looking around, trying to convince myself that she was really gone. Braxton had taken everything and left nothing behind. Nothing to confirm that she'd ever really been here at all. I wouldn't be struggling to accept it if I hadn't fallen for her.

Braxton couldn't just settle for being an amazing lay and guitarist. She had to go and fuck with my feelings too.

I was out of the bedroom and back in the hall before I even realized my feet were moving. I heard Rich asking me where I was going, but I ignored him. I couldn't put all of the blame on his shoulders even though I wished I could. I went along with the lie. I kept Braxton in the dark. Now she was gone, and I—

I sent my fist through the wall once I got inside my room and barked a curse when I pulled it away. My hand throbbed and hurt like hell, but the pain wasn't the worst I was feeling at the moment.

Finding my phone and ignoring my hand, I immediately dialed Braxton. Even though I'd hoped, never in my wildest dreams did I imagine she'd answer.

"Yes, Loren?"

My lips parted, but no words came. None that would make it right. When I heard her sigh, however, I knew the small window I'd been given was quickly closing.

"Come back."

"Now, why would I do that?" I pictured her studying her nails and wished she'd stayed to use them on me—to inflict pain rather than give me indifference. I could handle one, but she'd destroy me with the other.

"Because I love you," I told her even though it wasn't even close to what I had planned to say. I could feel her surprise on the other end, but she masked it well with frigid silence. I gulped. "I hate that I waited until now to tell you. I hate that I can't see your face because as much as you want to hate me, you wouldn't be able to hide the truth."

"What's the truth?"

"You love me too." I waited for her to confirm or deny it, but Braxton had returned to giving no reaction at all. I used her silence as the chance to listen to her background and pinpoint her location so I could go fucking get her. It pissed me off that I had zero clue how long ago she'd left because, while she'd been thinking and feeling the worst, I'd been sleeping like a baby. "Please come back," I begged once more. "We'll tell you everything. It's not what you think."

I heard her quiet chuckle, and my head dropped from the weight of holding it up. I knew before she spoke. I knew that I'd lost her.

"It's exactly what I think, Loren. I don't negotiate with liars."

I was still holding the phone to my ear long after she hung up. It was how Houston and Rich found me when they walked into my room. I was still hoping this was all a bad dream, and I'd wake up soon.

"Get out." I didn't look at them after I issued the order. I just pressed my back to the mattress and stared up at the black ceiling.

"We will, but you're coming with us. Tim's on his way," Rich announced, referring to our pilot.

"For what?"

"Braxton was spotted at the airport. It's all over the blogs."

I found myself snorting even though I didn't find a damn thing funny. Our rebel still thought she was a little fish in a big pond, and no one would recognize her. Or maybe she was just that desperate to get away from us. I scrubbed my hands down my face.

"She's going back to Los Angeles." I was so exhausted emotionally and physically that I could barely form the words.

"We can cut her off if you'd get the fuck up," Jericho snapped.

"And then what?" I muttered, still staring at the ceiling.

"I'll explain," he naïvely offered. You'd think we would have learned our lesson about how tightly Braxton held her grudges.

"Tried that."

"We know. We heard," the eavesdropping shits confirmed. I knew if we weren't all secretly losing our shit over Braxton, they'd be snickering like little girls right now.

"So you want me to race a thousand miles across two states to strike out a second time in one day? Pass." Flipping them both off, I rolled onto my stomach, hoping the ache would go away.

"What the hell did you expect, Lo? You wait until your back is against the wall to tell her how you feel, and then you do it over the phone? It was weak."

I was off the bed and in Rich's face, slamming his back against the wall before either of them could blink. He could easily shove me off, but he didn't because he knew this shit was on him.

"Say that again?" I had two inches on him, but at the moment, it felt like two feet.

Apparently feeling the same, Jericho shoved me off, and I cracked my fist across his nose, returning the favor and making him bleed.

Houston stood a couple of feet away, texting as if we weren't two seconds from tearing this house apart. It wouldn't be anything new, so I understood the indifference. Jericho was the only one who acted like the world's fate depended on us getting along every second of the day.

"It's my fault," Rich said as he used his hand to staunch the bleeding. "Now let me make it right."

"She's not going to make it easy," I mumbled, defeated as I stared at the ground. Just getting her to listen, we'd have to wage war—not a battle, *war.*

Houston's head shot up from his phone as if remembering only now that we were here. The look he gave me was a perplexed one as he slipped his phone into his pocket. I guess he'd struck out too.

"Since when has Braxton ever?"

"This is bullshit," I muttered, keeping my voice low in case Braxton heard me. Next to me, Rich continued to bang on the door that looked like it would fall off the hinges at any moment.

That would just make my fucking day, to be honest.

We knew she was here. We watched the cab driver help her carry her luggage inside twenty minutes ago. Houston had suggested hanging back so she wouldn't turn us away on the street, and now here we were. One of her neighbors had already opened the door to openly display his irritation at the noise we were causing like we gave a damn.

Some people.

"If you don't leave now, I'm calling the cops!" the neighbor yelled from down the hall in his ratty, plaid bathrobe.

They must have been the magic words. Braxton's apartment door swung open abruptly, and I could have run to hug and kiss the man whose apartment smelled like fermented cheese and dirty gym socks.

When I saw it was just the insanely hot blonde with green eyes that Braxton had brought to our first two shows, my excitement died a quick but still brutally painful death.

"Hey," I forced myself to greet. "Grendel, right?"

"Griffin."

Whatever. "Nice to see you again," I lied. "Can you get Braxton?" I wasn't about to pretend I didn't know she was here.

Gryffindor crossed her arms as she leaned her shoulder against the jamb. "If she wanted to talk, I wouldn't be answering the door, would I?"

"You would if you were practicing to be a doorman, but I don't know your life. Braxton?"

"Unavailable."

"Can you please just give her a message?" Rich inquired politely.

The way Greta skewered him with her gaze despite his pleasant tone, I knew Braxton had given her friend at least the gist of what he—we'd done. "Sure. The approved words for your message are—piece, shit, married, lying, a, of, I'm." Giving Rich an accommodating smile, she cocked her head to the side, making her blonde hair fall in waves over her shoulder. "Feel free to use them in any order you'd like."

Stepping back, Groot promptly slammed the door in our faces.

"She's so not invited to the wedding," I grumbled as I stared at the blue door with paint chipping off…everywhere. "What do we do now?" I looked to Rich, who now had his back against the wall next to the door and his head tilted back with his eyes closed. Houston was still leaning against the wall across from the door.

"We don't leave L.A. until she talks," Houston said loud enough for Braxton as well as her neighbors eavesdropping from their apartments to overhear. He approached the door as he continued speaking, making sure she heard him loud and clear. "We come back, and we keep coming back. There's no sleep for the wicked, there's no saving the damned, and there's no prayer to be had. We're already ensnared, my little lamb," he said, quoting her song. The same piece that showed us what she was made of and made us want more.

This was her fault, really.

She'd put this monkey on our backs, and there was no knocking it off.

I could hear whispering, mostly Greer talking shit on the other side of the door. When I smiled at the confirmation that Braxton had heard, it wasn't arrogance that drove me to do so. Just utter relief that she had and that she'd been listening all along.

We left Braxton's shitty apartment building and jumped into our rental. Rich drove us to a hotel that erupted in pandemonium the moment we were recognized. We hadn't even considered bringing security, and even if we had, we wouldn't have wasted the precious moments getting to Braxton—even if it had mostly been for nothing.

"How the hell did she find out?" I'd finally asked the question forefront in my mind when we made it inside our suite.

"She obviously found the papers," Houston answered dryly.

"But *how?*"

"I think I had another episode."

Rich was staring at his divorce papers that Braxton had all but destroyed when I turned to him. He knew what she was telling him. He knew they meant absolutely nothing without both signatures and too many secrets attached. Rich pointlessly carried them around still because, as I said before, he liked to punish himself.

"I only remember fragments from last night, but I think Braxton saw me. I remember going to the tower and signing my name, but that's it. She must have followed me and found them after I'd gone back to bed."

"Shit," I muttered.

I wasn't thinking of how badly we fucked up, though. I imagined Braxton and how freaked out she must have been since none of us had bothered to inform her that Rich sleepwalked. He hadn't had an episode in sometime. With everything else, it had been easy to forget. Now, this shit had popped out like 'surprise, motherfucker!' and kicked us in the ass. I should have told her when I found him wandering around in his sleep three nights ago.

There was a lot I should have said.

"So tomorrow then," I decided out loud. If I let my mind linger on things I couldn't change, who knew what would happen. Nothing good. "Operation Stalk the Fuck out of Braxton until She Files a Restraining Order begins."

"What if she doesn't forgive us?" Rich proposed like an ass. He could be so goddamn pessimistic. "We're supposed to be in Europe in three weeks."

"Fuck the tour." There would always be another one, but there was only one of her. If I'd listened when Braxton warned me, we wouldn't be standing here.

"If Carl—"

"*Fuck* Carl Cole." He could take that three-sixty deal and shove it up his ass. He'd already taken everything that mattered and didn't matter. I wasn't letting him take Braxton too. Moving over to the couch, I dropped down onto it and let my head rest against the back as I stared at the ceiling. "We were going to take her to meet Mom today," I reminded them.

My head fell to the side so that I could meet Houston's somber gaze. His grandmother would have loved Braxton, and he knew it.

Rich gave us his back.

The only sign that he'd lost the composure he'd held until now was his shoulders as he walked away.

Jericho's desolation would be a slow descent. His heart breaking wouldn't just sneak up. No, he'd make us feel every splinter. He'd make us watch the pieces wither to dust. The only difference was the girl he'd given his heart to this time had given hers too.

Braxton had offered him everything his lonely soul had been hunting.

And then she took it away.

We kept our word, but Braxton stuck to her guns.

Every day for five days, we tried and failed to get Braxton to let us see her so we could explain. It wasn't until her friends screwed up by getting Braxton to leave their apartment that we got our chance.

We were waiting inside their apartment—it had been way too easy to break in—when the three of them stumbled in after two in the morning. I shook my head. Even in the dark, they should have noticed us occupying their living room by now.

"Oh, shit," one of them drunkenly slurred. Maeko, I think. "I left my bone—I mean phone."

The three of them erupted into laughter that made my ears ring. I think it was Houston that groaned like he was being tortured by nails on a chalkboard. Even though he'd tried to conceal his voice, the apartment fell quiet.

I guess they'd heard him too.

There were more stumbled footsteps, hurried this time, and a moment later, light flooded the room. My gaze caught Braxton's, who was standing by the door with her hand still holding the switch and her full lips slightly parted. I stared at them, lost in the memory of how they felt against mine, until they started moving.

"Are you kidding me right now?"

I smiled at her greeting to silence the roaring in my head. "Hey, baby. Missed you."

"Get out."

Ignoring her request, I turned to Rich, who was slumped in their armchair with the hood of his black sweatshirt pulled so low over his head that I couldn't see his eyes.

I imagined he was staring at Braxton like she was heaven's gate, and he held a one-way ticket to hell.

I was going to fuck him up, though, if he didn't start pleading his case soon.

Sitting up slowly, he pulled his hood back and…yup.

Just as pitiful as I imagined.

He cleared his throat, but his voice was still hoarse when he spoke because he hadn't said a word. Not one goddamn thing since she'd left us. "Can we talk?"

"What is there left to say?"

The moment she asked the question, her friends quietly made themselves scarce, and I thanked God for small favors. It was right there in her tone—the first crack in her armor. Chin in my hand, I kept my focus on Rich because if I looked at Braxton…I'd start pleading my case too.

I would.

Just not now.

Because I knew who she needed to hear from, which meant I had to wait my turn. It was just proving harder than I thought to be patient.

And hope that Rich didn't fuck this up.

"Everything," he said as he stood up. "Starting with the fact that I lied, and there's no excuse for it. I should have told you about Emily. I could tell you that I didn't know what would happen between us, but it would just be another lie. You're the reason those papers existed for you to find."

"So I'm responsible for you wanting to leave your wife?" She rolled her eyes and looked away just as the first tear fell. "That's just great, Rich. Thanks."

I'm sure he could feel my glare, but he paid me no mind as he inched closer to Braxton, who still held up their front door. Houston stood by the window overlooking the street while I sat on their ratty sofa.

"I should have left her a long time ago, but I didn't care about any of that until you. Emily stopped being my wife the moment she fucked Calvin." I saw Braxton's surprise as her shocked gaze darted from Rich to Houston and then me for confirmation. *All my fault.* "If that's not enough to convince you," he continued, "it's been over four years since I've seen or heard from her. I owe her nothing."

"No?" Braxton challenged, suddenly pushing away from the door. She was in his face now, all fire and no mercy, while Rich gazed down at her, pleading for some. "Then what about me? If not the truth, what did I deserve?" Her tears ran freely down her face as she stared up at him. Rich couldn't look away, and neither could I. "You promised you were mine, but you were only pretending."

She broke his restraint, and I tensed when he grabbed her hips and yanked her into him. I relaxed only when he simply pressed their foreheads together.

"If nothing else, Braxton, please believe that I wasn't," he pleaded with his eyes closed. "I haven't always been truthful, but I've been honest about that."

"Why did you lie?" She didn't pull away from him, but her tone made it clear that her guard was still up. I think it was the first time Braxton's ever had it up this high with Jericho. The wall she'd built in seven mere days towered higher than the one she'd been building for seven months. She had only started to let us in.

"I—"

"Don't tell me," she cut in when he tried to speak. "Tell them." My brows dipped when she nodded toward Houston and me. "Tell them the reason why you still hesitated to leave your estranged wife even after you drew up the papers and decided to be with me."

Rich let her go, and her dead gaze followed him as she watched him back away with no emotion. His legs seemed to give out, so he sank onto the arm of the couch with his gaze fixed on the floor. The four of us waited in the heavy silence that followed, and I wondered if they could hear my heart beating out of control.

"I wasn't going to leave her," he eventually whispered so low I almost didn't catch it.

As I sat up, my confused gaze flew to Houston, who gave no obvious reaction. He was pissed, but he didn't seem surprised.

What the hell had I missed?

"Come again?"

Rich looked at me, and I was surprised to see the same plea in his eyes that he'd given Braxton moments ago. "Emily. If her baby was mine, I wasn't going to go through with it. I wasn't going to divorce her."

I can't explain why I suddenly smiled when nothing was funny about what he said. Houston moved away from the window as soon as I stood because he knew what was on my mind. Jericho knew it too, but he didn't move to try to defend himself if it came to that.

He'd let me beat him.

Jericho deserved every broken bone and ounce of blood lost after what he just admitted to, so he'd allow me the pound of flesh.

"Let me make sure I heard you correctly. While Houston and I were risking everything, you were plotting behind our backs to leave us and ride off into the sunset with Emily?"

"Yes."

I stood there in the wake of his confession, waiting to hear him explain or make excuses.

He didn't.

He simply sat there. He let me see his shame. I couldn't hide my hatred or the betrayal I felt, so he welcomed it so that I wouldn't succumb to it.

I was as furious with myself as I was with Jericho. I chose to trust my best friend instead of this very suspicion that had been prickling my mind for months. I'd underestimated him again, but not in the way I could ever respect.

Or forgive.

The truth had been there the entire time. I refused to believe it because I trusted him. Jericho had built enough evidence a long time ago to get a court-ordered dissolution without Emily. She'd run for no fucking reason other than to keep Jericho in her claws. She knew he'd never divorce her without confronting her first. And without knowing if the kid she may or may not have had even belonged to him.

After Braxton, I assumed only the former still held.

I believed he hesitated for the reason his surname implied.

He had to be so goddamn noble.

He had to give Emily the honor of telling her to her face that he should never have married her, that he wasn't in love with her anymore, and that Braxton was the woman he should have fucking waited for but didn't.

Jericho hadn't just been playing Braxton.

He'd been playing us all.

"Fuck you."

I didn't allow myself to say more. I didn't allow myself to look at Braxton, Houston, or even Rich.

When I stormed through the door, I didn't just walk out on our fight. I knew in my heart that I'd just walked out on us.

On Bound.

FIFTY-EIGHT

Houston

THE BOUND & BELLICOSE TOUR HAS BEEN POSTPONED

Sources report difficulties among the band. There are also rumors circulating that Bound's newest guitarist, Braxton Fawn, is dating not one but all three of the band's original members. Could this be the end of Bound?

I CLICKED OUT OF THE ARTICLE AND HIT THE IGNORE BUTTON AS SOON AS Xavier started calling me. I'm sure he wanted to see where my head was, but there was nothing he could do about the answer. Climbing out of my truck, I stared up at the country château that had taken me an hour of driving and pondering to reach.

I still didn't know what I was going to say.

Loren had made us buy and restore that monstrosity in the woods so that he could tell his father that his was bigger.

I hope he got the chance because I wasn't leaving here without him.

It had been three goddamn weeks.

I thought the last six years had been rough, but it was nothing compared to the feeling of actually being without your best friends and losing your girl all in one week.

Braxton had shut down, Loren had run back to Portland, and

Rich…he was a fucking ghost. He wasn't eating, he wasn't sleeping, and he had an episode whenever he did. None of that was what concerned me the most.

Jericho hasn't spoken a single word in twenty-three days.

My fear had reached the point of being irrational. I was afraid he'd forgotten how. I was terrified he'd lost his will—for anything. I was watching our best friend waste away so, yeah. I'd hogtie Loren and drag his ass back if he forced me to.

No, you won't.

Loren's claim that I was no better than his father was a blow I hadn't been expecting. I still hadn't recovered. This insatiable need to control my universe and everyone in it was rooted deep.

All I had left of the source was a newspaper clipping and my grandmother's memories of Susan and Jake Morrow. I'd been left behind to survive on my own in a world too cruel and chaotic to endure. I'd spent the last fifteen years since their deaths trying not to repeat the cycle, so whenever my world began to spiral, I grabbed the reins, and I held on tight. I never paid attention to who I was hurting or stifling. I only cared about my survival.

But what if I had looked beyond myself just once?

Would Rich have trusted me when I warned him not to marry Emily? Would I have convinced my friends to take Savant's deal? Would Loren have pushed aside his pride and come to me rather than ruining our best friend's marriage?

If I hadn't indirectly caused all of the above because of my obsession with control, would Calvin have been able to turn them against me? Besides fucking Emily, all Everill had done was force to light resentment already brewing in the dark. Tearing Loren, Rich, and I apart was how he'd punished us for keeping him out.

Our past was four runaway trains heading to four destinations, only to crash and burn at one intersection.

As much as I was struggling with our turbulent present, my persistent thoughts wouldn't allow me to push away the most important question of all. If our past had played out differently, would we have ever met Braxton?

I hated that the answer wouldn't allow me to regret my

actions fully. I wasn't convinced the universe I fought so hard to rule would have found another way to place her in our path.

The love of our life would have slipped us by, and that would have been my fault too.

Fuck.

Ringing the front doorbell, I crossed my arms as I leaned against the pillar and waited. Here's to hoping Loren still cared enough to come back on his own.

I didn't have to wait long since Orson James insisted on round-the-clock staff. Loren, Rich, and I hired a cleaning service twice a week and someone to handle the landscaping, but other than that, we fended for ourselves.

Out there in the woods, we were able to pretend that we'd carved out a world only the three of us inhabited.

Braxton, when we got her back, would know what that felt like too.

"What do you want?" Loren asked.

He'd taken me by surprise answering the door himself, but it was the beard adorning the lower half of his face and the blond hair covering his forehead and eyes, making him look like a wet dog, that caught me off guard. He wore stained gray sweatpants, a white T-shirt, one sock, and smelled like he hadn't showered in three or four days.

"Loren?"

He didn't bother answering my stupid question. He turned around and shuffled away, leaving the door open, so I followed him inside. The house was mostly quiet since it was mid-morning on a Monday. I was sure Orson was busy running the empire he'd lorded over his son for years. It just showed how little he knew him.

Loren belonged on a stage, not inside a boardroom.

He sure as fuck didn't care about metal fabrication or whatever made his father rich enough to believe his ambitions mattered more than his son's.

"Why are you here?" Loren muttered when I followed him into his childhood bedroom. Unlike my grandmother, his parents hadn't left it alone. They'd converted it into a guest room, completely wiping away everything that helped shape Loren into the man he was today. It was only unusual or unnecessary when you had *nine* other available bedrooms for guests.

He took a seat on the foot of the queen bed before planting his back on the mattress and closing his eyes.

"You know why," I said as I watched him from the doorway. "Come home."

"I am home."

It took everything I *hoped* to be one day not to storm across the room and wring his goddamn neck.

He didn't get to say that shit to me.

When Loren's father threw him out for finally getting his mother to leave him, he had no one else but us. *We* were his family, and it had been that way ever since. Loren thought it had all been in vain when his mother crawled back like a thoroughly whipped dog, but it hadn't. We made sure of it.

I then took that shitty deal with Savant and convinced my friends to do the same.

I couldn't let Loren back under his father's thumb. He'd been close to giving in and ready to accept whatever scraps his father threw for a price much too high when that deal came to the table.

But Savant had only wanted me.

Loren and Jericho had been optional, but I insisted, *begged*, giving Carl Cole the leverage he needed to fuck us. I'd told myself I was helping my best friends. Loren could support himself and Rich would avoid prison. After a while, I couldn't live with that lie anymore.

Some days I felt guilty, others I didn't.

Loren knew, and *that* was why he hated me. It wasn't because I liked taking charge. Frankly, Loren was too lazy for the role. It was because I succeeded where his father had failed. I forced a life on him rather than let him make his own choices. He trusted me, and I used him to feed my addiction.

"You know as well as I do that isn't true."

He didn't respond, but I knew he was listening.

Swallowing my pride, I finally let free the words I should have spoken a long time ago but hadn't. I'd never been afraid that I might actually lose him before. "I'm sorry, Lo." It seemed like I waited an eternity before his eyes slowly opened, and his black gaze met mine. "I'm sorry for breaking your trust in me, I'm sorry for not letting you choose your own path, I'm sorry for making you think we didn't need you, and I'm sorry for not being sorry sooner."

He made me wait.

Loren made the silence stretch as long as he possibly could before he simply said, "Thanks." I was pretty sure my gut couldn't hold any more dread. Clasping his hands underneath his head, Loren closed his eyes again. "You can go now."

I narrowed my gaze on him as if he could see the warning in them. "Don't test me, Lo."

"Or what?"

I casually crossed the room without saying a word. When I reached him, I gripped his collar in my fists and yanked him from the bed until there was no space left between us. He let me. "Or I do everyone a favor, and I make you a bottom."

Loren needed some humility, and one of these days, he was going to push me into giving him some. He made me see the difference between a leader and a dictator, and while I was determined to temper those urges, I would always run this shit. If Loren forced me to make that an undisputed fact, so be it.

We stared at one another for a long while before he swallowed and tried to push me away. I tightened my grip.

"You stink," I informed him. My eyes were starting to water being this close.

He looked away and mumbled, "Back the hell off me then."

Rather than do so, I pushed him toward the en suite until he stumbled inside. "Shower, shave, and get dressed. We have somewhere to be."

"Such as?"

"Braxton's hearing," I informed him, getting back to business. "It's today."

Loren stared at nothing as his mind worked, and he overthought what really should have been crystal clear. "What makes you think she wants us there?"

"Whether she does or not, we will be. We're not letting her do that alone."

I sighed my relief when he didn't argue. While Loren showered, I went downstairs to wait to give him some privacy and figure out my next move. I was so deep in my thoughts as I descended the stairs that I didn't notice the ambush I was walking into until it was too late.

A spitting image of my best friend, though his hair had long turned gray and thinned, Loren's father waited at the bottom of the stairs. I didn't flinch as I held the cold and cunning gaze of Orson James. Loren might have *thought* he hated me, but true hatred was found in his father's eyes. Loren looked to me, he'd given me the respect Orson desired but never bothered to earn, and sometimes Loren even obeyed. For those reasons, Orson James despised me.

"Orson," I forced myself to greet.

Laine Morrow wouldn't care how much contempt I held for the man. My grandmother wouldn't approve of me not showing anyone the proper respect in their own dwelling.

"Get out of my house, Morrow."

"Gladly, but I'll be taking your son with me." My manners only went so far. Fuck him.

"Loren's place is here. He knows that now. That's why he's come home."

My skin crawled hearing the way he talked about Loren, but I forced myself to push past it and keep my composure. "Funny. You didn't seem to think so when you *literally* threw him out in the rain and the street like a dog."

"He was a man. It was time he acted like one."

"Finally, we can agree, but don't think for one second you had anything to do with Loren standing on his own. He didn't do it for you."

"I suppose I have you to thank?" Orson taunted as he straightened the cuff on his blue suit. Someone must have alerted him of my presence if he was here instead of at the office. "Fine. *Thank you*. Now you and that sad, little black-haired shit can watch me reap the rewards."

"That will never happen, but if somehow, I died and let you have him, you'd have Loren to thank, not me." I shoved past him, clipping his shoulder before striding out the door.

An hour had passed when I heard shouting. I was out of my truck and ready to storm back inside when Loren came waltzing out of the door with a sinister smile and looking like himself again. His hair was slicked back, and he wore fitted navy blue pants that hung off his hips and a matching short-sleeve button-up that he'd left undone. The only noticeable difference was the medallion he no longer wore.

My heart was still pounding, however, until I saw the bag with all his shit packed inside and hanging from his shoulder.

Reaching the truck, he climbed inside, and so did I. I could smell the fresh mint from the gum he was chewing and the bergamot in his cologne as he slumped in his seat and got comfortable.

"Let's get the fuck out of here," Lo mumbled without looking at me. He was busy staring through the windshield at his father, who was standing on his massive front porch, fuming and holding Loren's medallion, which hung from his fingers.

Wasting no time, I hit the gas.

I then flipped off Orson James through my lowered window when I sped off with his only son riding shotgun.

I ignored my exhaustion after flying round-trip from Los Angles to Portland in one day as I climbed from the back of the town car Dani had arranged to pick us up. Together, Loren and I walked into the building that held Savant Records, with two of our private security trailing us. Our strides never broke with the knowledge that our girl was thirty floors up fighting Carl's lawyers alone.

That was until we got through the building's security and reached the bank of elevators.

Loren, spotting Rich waiting, stopped in his tracks. "I want to make something clear," he said to me, jaw tight as he glared ahead at Rich, who watched him too but with bleakness in his gaze, "this doesn't change anything. I'm here for Braxton, and that's it. I'm done."

Yeah, we'll see about that.

"You really want to argue about this right now?"

"I'm not arguing. I'm telling you."

"Let's go," I said dismissively. Loren wasn't leaving shit, and it wasn't because I'd make him stay. He couldn't walk away any more than the rest of us. "We're already late."

Rich pushed away from the wall he was leaning against as we approached. For the first time in three weeks, he looked tempted to speak, but then Loren shoved the words back down his throat before he could utter them.

"Save it," he snapped at the drummer. He then walked onto the empty elevator, leaving us no choice but to follow before the doors could close.

The entire way up, Rich stared at Loren from under the cloak of his hood while the bassist stared at the metal doors with no expression and pretended he didn't notice. The tension was stifling, and when the elevator finally stopped and the doors opened, I hurried off before either of them.

We ignored the receptionist when we entered the office suite, and she yelled at our backs that Carl wasn't expecting us.

No fucking shit.

He'd purposely left us out of this meeting.

Everyone in our path parted like the Red Sea when we stormed the hall. It wasn't until we reached our destination and pushed inside the room, uninvited, that the feeling I'd been here before hit me.

Most of the seats at the long table were filled by suited men and women, including Oni Sridhar, and the man I assumed was the arbitrator. He stopped speaking mid-sentence when we entered.

All eyes were on us, but our eyes were for her.

She was seated at the head of the table, furthest away from

the door. The exact spot I'd been standing when I saw her for the first time eight months ago when she burst into this very conference room and interrupted the meeting taking place then too. Even though she was dressed differently, and I knew better now, Braxton still looked as innocent today as she did then.

It was those big, brown eyes, light freckles, and her full mouth that never ceased to make a fool out of me. The only clue of the fire burning underneath was her red hair pinned up to show off her neck.

She was a living flame.

Our eyes met, yet she gave no reaction to us showing up. After what we'd done, just acknowledging our presence even briefly was more than we deserved.

I could only see her top half, but I recognized that sheer, black dress with crystal print and holographic detail. I knew the hem reached her calves. I knew there was a high slit showing off her left leg. I even recognized the black bra she wore underneath and knew she'd paired it with her favorite black boots. I couldn't see her hands, but I knew she wore her rings. Braxton was part goth, part punk, and part boho. She didn't want anyone figuring her out.

On opposite sides of her sat Xavier and her lawyer, who looked way too unsure of himself for my liking. We'd sent someone who stood a chance, of course, but Braxton had refused to accept our help. I was willing to bet she'd ate into most of the paltry advance Savant had given her to hire this amateur and all to prove a point.

At least she hadn't turned away Xavier, not that he would have listened.

Heading in Braxton's direction, I shook his hand as we passed, and then we commandeered the wall behind Braxton before anyone thought to protest.

"What are you three doing here?" Carl spat from the other end of the table. "I made it clear I'd deal with you later."

Loren snorted and smiled. "*Hilarious.* I've been utterly bored these last few weeks. Why don't you deal with us now?"

Rather than get upset, Carl returned his smile as he sat back in his chair and drummed his fingers on the arms. His gaze shifted to each of us before he spoke. "I thought you'd be smarter, knowing what happens to you, yet you're trying to help her anyway." Shrugging, he looked down at the papers in front of him as he shuffled them around. "I guess the rumors are true."

He looked up then to wink at Braxton, and I slammed my arm across Loren's chest to keep him in place before he could even finish stepping forward.

Fucking up Carl would only make things worse for Braxton.

I didn't remove my arm even after Loren relaxed. A calm Loren was just as unpredictable as a homicidal Loren. I glanced at Rich standing on my other side to gauge where his head was and if he'd force me to restrain him too.

He was staring at Braxton like he was stuck in time.

She pretended we weren't even here.

I was pretty certain Jericho hadn't heard a single word spoken since we stepped inside the room, but I could see the wheels in his mind turning. I could see him searching for the right words to say to her. Even if he found them, this was so not the time.

"Not now," I whispered to him. Rich gave no indication that he heard me. Not one.

"What happens to them?" Braxton inquired, drawing my attention from my drummer and Carl's focus back to her.

I heard Rich's subtle but sharp inhale at the sound of her voice and even felt Loren's heart lurch through his chest and underneath my arm. Meanwhile, I was trying to figure out a way to steer Braxton off this course. I'd given Xavier specific instructions, though he hadn't agreed, not to tell her a goddamn thing.

She was always meant to find freedom in darkness.

"Nothing for you to concern yourself with," Carl answered her dismissively. To us, he said, "You see, there was no need for the three of you to ride in on your white steeds. I'm fully prepared to let Braxton out of her contract today. Everyone wins."

And by everyone, he means Braxton and him.

There would be no salvation for us today.

Carl Cole would get what he wanted, and we helped it come to fruition. I should have been angry, but all I felt was relief. I—

"What. Happens. To. Them?" Braxton demanded.

Her forceful tone had yanked me from my thoughts, startling everyone in the room, including Carl. I could feel Xavier's stare. I could hear him silently begging me to tell her.

I ignored him.

It wasn't Braxton's problem. She shouldn't have to pay for our mistakes when she was already hurting from our lies.

Frustrated by Cole's silence, she turned around in her seat to face us.

Just like that, I was catapulted back into her orbit.

I was home.

Braxton's gaze was stern as she waited for one of us to crack and answer her burning question. "Tell me," she demanded when our lips refused to move. That desperate note almost broke me, but I held. We all did.

It didn't matter in the end.

No one, least of all Bound, was prepared for Oni Sridhar to break the weighted silence.

"In exchange for our complete financial support, Savant Records has a vested interest in all streams of revenue earned by Bound, including profits that would normally be denied to us under a traditional deal." She paused when Braxton turned to face her, tempting me to wipe that patronizing smile from her face. "If they so much as sell a pencil with their name on it, dear, we get sixty percent of the profit. That's across the board."

Oni glanced our way, and for the first time, I swore I actually glimpsed guilt in her eyes. I didn't care, though, not when she continued speaking, thwarting our attempt to protect Braxton from the guilt I knew she'd feel when Oni was done.

If Braxton stayed, I needed it to be because she wanted to.

It was her love I was after, not her pity.

"Their contract," Oni continued, "which we locked them in for six years, stipulates that should all monies spent not be recouped, the binding agreement extends until we do. As you're probably aware, Bound's tours gross nine-figure revenues, but to make money, you must first spend it. I assume you can imagine how much this label has already expensed for Bound & Bellicose, a tour that is on the verge of not being completed. Because of you. Tickets will have to be refunded, of course. Unfortunately, the venues, production companies, promoters, etcetera will all still expect to be paid. Your bandmates could simply reimburse the label. However, their lawyers have recently and successfully negotiated the purchase of their masters to include every song recorded during their contract with us."

Oni paused to lean forward, refusing to allow Braxton any give as their gazes remained locked several seats apart. If I didn't hate her before, I certainly did now, especially when she delivered the final nail in Braxton's coffin.

"It bankrupted them." Oni leaned back in her seat, playing the role of a viper to get her point across when she smiled and shrugged. "Since we no longer own the rights to their recorded songs, their only option will be to stay and make us more."

Oni's lips parted like she was ready to say more when Rich suddenly stepped forward and spoke.

"Shut up."

They were his first words in three weeks.

His voice was low and cracked from going so long without it, but it didn't matter because, right now…he commanded the room. He made everyone listen, including Braxton, who was staring at him now.

There was concern, confusion, and sadness in her brown eyes, but his silver gaze was directed at Oni, so he didn't notice. Even if he had, he wouldn't do anything about it. Not while he was a storm ready to crack open the sky.

"Say another word," he warned, "and I will end you, Sridhar."

I glanced at Loren, who noticed and shook his head before his eyes closed even as pride filled them. We both knew it was too late. We knew the kind of woman we fell in love with. She was the kind who took on callous rock stars, public scrutiny, and an unscrupulous label.

All to send a message.

All to inspire.

All to protect one girl's future and save her from a dire fate.

Braxton believed she'd failed her baby sister. She wouldn't allow herself to fail us too. She was bold enough to think she could take on that burden and still keep us from reclaiming her heart.

"Then I'll do it," she said with an unbreakable finality that made my head fall in defeat. I knew the decision coming, but it still hurt the same. "I'll finish the goddamn tour."

FIFTY-NINE

Braxton

"ARE YOU OUT OF YOUR MIND?" GRIFF SCREAMED THE SECOND I was done speaking. "Are their cocks really that amazing?"

I was sitting at the bar above our kitchen sink with an open bottle of wine next to me and my head in my hands while I ignored my best friend's ranting.

Bound was leaving for Europe in three days.

What the hell had I done?

This all felt like déjà vu, except I wasn't in love with my bandmates when it happened before. It had been hours since the meeting with Savant. I half expected my exes—that felt so weird to say—to corner me in the parking lot after, but they didn't. I think Houston, Loren, and Jericho shared my shock that I would finish the tour.

Maybe they were even upset?

I didn't want to dwell on that possibility because it shouldn't matter, and yet I couldn't help being hurt by their rejection. I couldn't erase the last eight months. I couldn't erase my feelings for them. I've been trapped between two realities since walking out on them.

The truth that I'd fallen in love and the fact that we could never be.

I haven't been okay.

I'd forgotten how to be without them, eat without them, sleep without them. I couldn't even remember how to string a fucking chord without them. Trust me—I've tried to write many a sad song in order to purge these unrelenting thoughts inside my head.

Was Jericho still in love with her?

I couldn't help but suspect that I had just been something to pass the time. Or perhaps he thought I could be a replacement for his long-lost love until he realized that I could never measure up. We never did get to have that talk. What if that had been what he wanted to tell me? I wasn't as good as his precious Emily, who had him first, and I never would be.

Jealousy truly was bitter.

I took a sip of my wine to wash away the taste.

"What if Griffin's right? Maybe you shouldn't go," Maeko suggested, pulling me from my spiraling thoughts. It figures she'd take Griff's side since they were a thing now.

They hadn't told me.

In fact, they've been trying to hide it since I returned. I guess they forgot I knew them too well. Griff and Maeko had taken advantage of my absence and set aflame something that had been kindling all along. Now they didn't want to crash my sourpuss party with their happy news even though I *was* happy for them.

On the inside.

Deep down in my darkest depths, the romantic who still believed in love and happy endings but had been stomped to within an inch of her life was over the fucking moon for her best friends.

Yaaaaaay.

I groaned and dropped my forehead on the counter.

I can't do this.

Maeko had been rubbing my back softly when her hand suddenly stopped mid-stroke. "What are you doing, ba—Griff?"

I snorted softly, and since my head was down, they couldn't see my smile. It had been a while since I tasted chocolate.

"I'm sending an email to my boss to tell him that I'm cashing in on my vacation days, and then you're calling yours," Griff said to Maeko. I could hear her laptop keys clicking as she spoke.

"Okay, but why?"

"Because we're not leaving her alone with those liars," she

decided as she continued to type. My head shot up from the bar and turned toward Griff. From here, I could see she was drafting an email from her perch on the couch. "They'll just try to hypnotize her again with their magical penises." I could see her green eyes rolling even though I was staring at the back of her head.

"Have faith much?" I snapped dryly. Maeko's hand immediately resumed rubbing circles on my back.

"Yup," Griff returned unapologetically. "I have absolute faith that you *will* fall for their bullshit again."

The olives lingering in the air told me she wasn't completely off base, which just pissed me off and made the room smell like it was burning. "Get fucked, Griff, 'kay?"

"Thanks, I will." When she turned her head, she wasn't quite looking at me. I felt Maeko's hand pause again briefly, and a rushed breath left her before she started massaging me again.

I was *this* close to calling them out, but then my phone started ringing, and the name on the screen made my heart stop and my head forget everything else. I didn't need the tartness on my tongue to tell me I hadn't been expecting the call, and I didn't need the copper stench that followed to tell me I was scared shitless of answering.

Maybe Griff was right.

I would need backup if just seeing one of their names on my caller ID made me want to weep myself into a puddle. It would be so much easier just to forgive them.

So. Much. Easier.

I'd also despise myself for all of eternity, so maybe not?

I lifted the phone, stood from the barstool, and pressed the green button as I made my way to my room. Maeko had seen who was calling, so I was sure Griffin would know soon too. It was mostly because of them holding my cell phone hostage those first few days that I'd remained strong, and they hadn't let up.

Closing and locking my bedroom door, I went over to my bed, lay down, and stared at the ceiling for a while. I was half expecting him to have hung up when I finally lifted the phone to my ear.

"Hello?"

"You don't have to do this," Rich greeted me. His voice wasn't as rough as it had been earlier, but it still lacked the smoothness I was used to. I wouldn't allow myself to ask him why.

"I'm not doing it for you."

"Then who are you doing it for?" he challenged.

Good question. "Is there a reason why you called, Jericho?"

"She's not my wife anymore."

I jackknifed into a sitting position while all emotions I promised myself I wouldn't feel for him anymore came rushing back at once. He was quiet, and each stretch of silence tore away at the bricks I stacked to keep him out.

I could feel his pain. Could he feel mine?

I had no doubt we'd both be content to let the seconds, minutes, and hours tick by, pretending we weren't silently reaching for each other through the phone. I'd wake up in the morning, and he'd still be there. I'd know because I'd hear his loud snores through the phone.

I almost smiled.

Almost.

"Congratulations," I told him in the driest tone that belied my racing heart.

This changes nothing, you foolish thing.

"Thanks. Braxton?"

"Yes, Jericho?"

"I know you're telling yourself that it doesn't make a difference, but it does. We both know it. You were never a contender for my heart, Braxton Fawn. You were always the motherfucking champ."

I did smile then as the sweet and mouthwatering scent of berries filled my nose. I didn't know if it was luck or misfortune that had Griff pounding on my locked door a moment later, but I was saved from responding.

"Open this door *right now*, Braxton!"

I heard Rich's throaty chuckle, followed by a muffled curse, and then someone's teeth sucking and tasted cherries on my tongue. *Oh, God. Fuck off, vagina.*

"I guess you have to go now?" he asked me.

"Yup. Sorry. Mom isn't letting me talk to boys until I learn how to spot one who's obviously taken."

Cheap shot, but the asshole deserved it.

Rich was quiet again and back to feeling ashamed, which was how it should be. We shouldn't have been flirting.

"Tell me how to fix this," he begged as Griffin continued to pound and shout obscenities through the door. She was quite possibly the most cynical person alive. Even if I forgave them, rest assured she never would.

God speed, Maeko.

"I'm not sure you can." The weight of that truth settled on my shoulders, and I was just glad I was already sitting down. Roses. I smelled roses. "I didn't think I ever could, but I've already forgiven you," I told him honestly. "But I don't know if I can ever trust you again."

He was quiet again and then… "You forgive me?" he whispered. There was relief in his tone and surprise too.

"You have a child that you haven't been allowed to know—a child made in a union that you obviously still cared enough to keep after all this time. I know why you hesitated, and I understand. It's why I can't ask you to turn your back on that. I can't be responsible for anyone else not being who they truly are. Including myself."

"Braxton—"

"You freed me." Closing my eyes, I felt like I could fly right now. "Houston? Loren? I know you're listening." I heard movement in the background and imagined them leaning in closer. "You freed me too," I whispered to them. "But trusting you means asking me to bear that weight again, and…I can't."

I felt the apology on my lips, and I swallowed it.

I wouldn't be sorry.

For a few blissful weeks, they could have asked me to lasso the moon, and I would have told them to hand me the rope.

But they didn't fight for me with the truth.

They chose to lose me with a lie.

There was shuffling in the background as the phone switched hands and then heavy breathing coming through the phone.

Loren.

I knew it was him before he even spoke. I didn't know how. I just knew.

"We hear what you're saying, and I'm telling you it won't be enough," he warned. I could feel him seething even through the phone and clawed the sheets until they were gripped in my fist. "You want to finish the tour? Fine. But know this. It's not over until it's over. You staked your claim with an arrow through our hearts, and now you're going to let us bleed."

He hung up.

SIXTY

Rich

SO THAT WAS HOW SHE WANTED TO PLAY IT.

She was huddled around her friends so that we couldn't get too close. They never left her side. Not once since the moment the three of them showed up at the airport. We assumed her friends had come to see her off until we noticed the luggage. Enough to last them a couple of weeks.

The roaring in my head didn't dull until I started to rationalize.

They'd have to leave Braxton eventually.

It was going to take us over three months to get through Europe alone, and we'd still have four more continents. Each time Braxton's gaze found ours during the twelve-hour flight, I wondered if she'd considered that too.

She couldn't avoid us forever.

And if she wanted us to believe that we didn't stand a chance, she was sending some crazy mixed messages. She was here for no other reason than because she still cared.

Someone should have warned her that if she gave us an inch, we'd take the whole goddamn mile. Maybe her friends had, and that was why they were here.

The only flaw in their plan was that they couldn't stay. We all knew it, but no one dared say a word.

By the time we landed in Berlin around noon, we were all tired and jet-lagged, so we headed straight for the hotel. I knew no one would be sleeping, though.

Houston, Loren, and I were plotting, but so were they.

Tomorrow night we took the stage in front of seventy thousand people at the Olympiastadion, so there would be plenty of time for mischief.

"Wow," Griffin remarked as she looked around the hotel lobby and all its splendor.

"I've never stayed in a place this fancy before," Maeko gushed.

I looked around too as our security escorted the six of us to the elevators, and I tried to see it through the girls' eyes. You'd think an orphan who grew up with nothing, missed a few meals, and wore holes in his clothes until he was twenty-two would never get used to sitting in the lap of luxury.

It had only been six years.

For the first time, I might have identified with Loren, who never seemed impressed by anything with a high price tag. I thought he was just spoiled, which he was, but there was more to it…and to him.

The truth was life got boring fast.

And without what truly mattered, it was easy to stop caring about it at all.

I glanced at Braxton and tried not to stare too hard at her smile. She was telling her friends about the hotels we'd stayed in, a conversation I was sure they'd already had, but I understood. She needed to keep herself distracted from the inevitable.

Dani, who'd met us at the elevator after checking us in, handed over our keys and told us Xavier would be up to talk to us soon. He'd flown in a couple of days ahead, along with the tour manager and the rest of the crew, to make sure everything ran smoothly. The delay had only lasted two weeks, but our drama had still been a huge inconvenience for too many people.

In the wake of the rumors, everyone had decided to blame Braxton, of course.

I wondered if she was privy to it or if she'd been drowning too much in heartache to notice the scrutiny.

My gut told me neither had escaped her attention. I kept

myself from going to her just as Griffin sent me a look to back off. Maybe she'd seen the temptation in my eyes.

As much as I was annoyed by the pitbull, I was just as relieved that Braxton had someone to look out for her after what she'd escaped in Faithful. It was obvious her friends would defend her to their last breath, but so would we.

We just needed Braxton to believe that again.

I just needed her to trust that I would always choose her.

The elevator ride up was awkward as hell. No one spoke until we reached the eleventh floor. The girls got off and immediately turned when we didn't follow.

"Where are you going?" Braxton questioned with a frown. She'd forgotten that she wasn't supposed to care.

The doors were already sliding close when Loren answered. "Penthouse, baby!"

Her friends rolled their eyes while Braxton hid her smile when Loren winked at the last second. I immediately turned to him as soon as the doors were closed. We were only one floor above them, so it would be a short ride.

"Are you ready to talk to me yet?" I asked him.

Loren scoffed while his gaze remained forward. "Nope, and I never will be. You're dead to me, bitch." When the elevator stopped, and the doors slowly slid open, he was the first one off.

Hearing those words and knowing he meant them…

I felt like I'd been backed into a corner.

So I attacked.

It was a good thing we had the floor to ourselves. We never made it inside the suite before Loren and I hit the ground from the force of me tackling him from behind. I didn't care about fair when I sucker-punched him or when he managed to flip onto his back, and I immediately wrapped my hands around his neck. He shoved me off, and I hit the wall next to us, knocking a picture frame from the wall before he punched me and split my lip.

I tasted blood, but it only fueled me.

One way or another, Loren was going to heel.

It was the only way he'd hear me out.

Houston knew it too, which was why he disappeared inside the suite instead of breaking up the fight that was getting more violent and bloody with each blow. There wasn't a spot on me that didn't hurt when I managed to get Loren's head locked inside my elbow. Loren was trying to get me over his shoulder, but I held on like my life depended on it.

Without them, I had nothing.

Again.

So I guess it kind of did.

"Are you ready to listen now?" I taunted in his ear.

He answered me by taking a step back and then another before driving me into the wall behind me hard enough to loosen my hold. Loren whirled on me, but I recovered and grabbed him by the collar of his blue polo shirt.

I yanked him into me.

"You're done ignoring me, Lo. I'm not allowing you another day."

Loren stared down at me blankly since he was taller than me, and I felt my grip loosening under the intensity of his gaze. He didn't take advantage of his chance to break free and walk away, though. His hips were still pressed against mine. I was still breathing in every breath he exhaled.

"Not that it will matter," he eventually said with a curl of his lip, "but fine. Say what you have to say. I need to shower." When I didn't speak for several seconds, his brow rose. "I'm listening."

"I was never going to choose Emily over Braxton. I was never going to choose her over you or Houston. I just needed time to realize that myself, Lo."

"Why should I believe that? You did it the first time."

"Marrying Emily was not choosing her over you, Loren. She was my girlfriend. You were my friend."

"Funny," he retorted while staring at the wall behind me, "since I recall begging you not to."

"I thought you were jealous," I whispered honestly, and he groaned while throwing his head back.

"Seriously?" he spat. "I've busted nuts that lasted longer than my feelings for you. It was a crush, Rich, not a confession of love. I didn't want you to marry Emily because you deserved better, and I didn't mean me. You know she tried to fuck Houston a week after you were married, right? He slapped the shit out of her and then told her to tell you why he did it."

I gaped at him in surprise. Sadly, it wasn't even because Emily tried to fuck my best friend. It was because I was just now hearing about it. "She never told me that."

"Of course, she didn't."

"Why didn't Houston?" I gripped him tighter when a thought occurred to me and brought him closer. I didn't recognize the harshness in my voice when I spoke. "Why didn't you?"

"Because I don't like repeating myself," he told me blandly. "I warned you what she was."

"If you had told me what she tried to do, you wouldn't have needed to convince Calvin and Emily to sleep together. You wouldn't have needed to ruin my marriage to get what you wanted."

Loren sniffed. It was obvious he felt no remorse even after all this time. "I didn't have to convince them of anything, Jericho. It was going to happen whether I left them alone together or not."

"Fuck you."

Loren pressed his forehead against mine and closed his eyes as my grip loosened again. I didn't like how weak he made me. "Don't pretend you don't remember how it was, Rich. I do the fucking, not you."

"Why did you?" I finally asked.

That night had taken a turn neither of us intended, but we never felt the need to do it again. Our resentment for one another wouldn't allow for attraction. Obviously, something had changed since I felt my dick getting harder with each word he spoke.

Loren must not have felt the same since he abruptly stood upright and pushed away. "Why not?" he threw at me.

It was all he said before he disappeared inside the suite.

I lingered in the hall, just staring at the floor, my gaze unseeing and my mind blank, before pushing away from the wall and heading inside the suite. I didn't realize my intention or that I was looking for Loren until I found him.

He was in one of the three bedrooms he'd claimed, pulling his polo over his head. Our bags still hadn't been brought up yet, and he was too high-maintenance to use anything other than his own shit, so I knew I had time.

"I forgave you," I snapped at him. "Why can't you forgive me?"

"Because I did you a fucking favor and because you said it yourself. It's all or nothing with Brax." Shirtless, Loren sat on the edge of the king-bed in his jeans and looked at me. "Do you know how it feels to know that I can never make Braxton truly happy without you? Do you know how it feels knowing I can never be truly happy without you? Yeah, you do," he said before I could answer. "But you were going to leave anyway, so fuck you."

"He wasn't going anywhere," Houston announced after barging inside the room. "A judge was already reviewing his lawyer's request to grant the divorce before Braxton found those papers. Rich had already made his choice. He chose our girl. He chose us. And he didn't do it under duress like you or Braxton think. I'd never say this to her because she doesn't know his past, but you do. Quit whining like you haven't already forgiven him. Stop pretending you don't know why he was conflicted. If that was his kid, he wanted him to have two parents. He was willing to walk through hell so that his child wouldn't walk through life, wondering why he wasn't enough. Emily was never a fucking factor. I don't have to tell you this, though, because you already know. Now kiss and make up so we can focus on what matters—winning our girl back. Again."

Loren stared at Houston, mulling over his words but giving nothing else away before his gaze shot over to me. He kept his expression impassive until he grew bored of watching me sweat and stood.

I forced myself not to start round two of our fight when he calmly disappeared inside the bathroom without a word or indication that we'd gotten through to him.

𝄞

It was still unclear whether Loren actually forgave me since he was the kind who reveled in doing the *opposite* of what he was told. He wasn't shoulder-checking me anymore whenever we were in the same room or glaring at me like my every breath insulted him, so there was that.

The following night, we slipped into Braxton's suite using the extra key card Dani had procured for us without our girl's knowledge. We found them inside the dressing room the size of a large bedroom, "So What" by P!nk on blast. They were posing together in front of the tall, three-paneled mirror and were too busy shifting their bodies to find the right angle to notice they were no longer alone.

"Which one of you is the wannabe actor again?" Loren inquired. The three of them screamed and turned around once he made our presence known. "You'd be perfect for the role of 'girl who dies in the first five minutes.'"

"The correct word you're looking for is aspiring," Griffin informed him.

"Oh, I guess that means I'm talking to your girlfriend then?"

It was obvious Loren had called them out when Griffin and Maeko's eyes nervously darted to Braxton, who unsurprisingly looked unsurprised.

"Is there a reason why you're in our suite?" Braxton asked with a sigh. She didn't bother to acknowledge what Loren had just told her.

"Your suite, babe. We didn't invite them."

Crossing her arms, Braxton shot back, "I did."

Loren gave her a subtle smile before sinking his teeth into his bottom lip while he gazed at her lustfully. "Doubt that."

She wanted to be alone with us too. If we needed to scheme so she could pretend that she had no choice, we were happy to oblige her.

For now.

Eventually, Braxton and her friends would have to come to terms with the fact that we weren't going to let her go.

"Ready?" Houston asked her when her silence became a little too telling. We had the green light we'd been waiting for. Nothing more needed to be said. I just barely resisted smiling smugly at her friends.

"Yes," Braxton answered before slowly walking toward us.

I could feel her gaze on me as I admired her long hair pinned up in a ponytail with a few strands framing her face and neck. I *didn't* appreciate the white, satin slip dress that looked dangerously like lingerie so much. She wore it with a black leather jacket and her combat boots, but she was testing my fucking patience when I once again questioned if she was even wearing panties. I didn't like anyone seeing what was mine unless his name was Houston Morrow or Loren James.

Our show was tonight, and then it was off to Hamburg, Cologne, Mannheim, and Munich. No fucking clue if that was the actual order.

When Braxton tried to pass me, I grabbed her hand. She stopped.

"Panties?" I asked when her gaze met mine.

She pulled her hand away with a smile that was soft but devious. "Is that your concern anymore?"

"It never stopped." I held her gaze so she'd know I was completely serious. "Panties?"

God help her if she made me ask again.

I watched her roll her eyes as she looked away. "Yes, Jericho. Can we go now?"

I don't know what came over me. I pulled her into me, wrapped my hand around her nape, and...I ruined the black lipstick painting her lips.

She let me.

For a while.

And then she remembered the right was no longer mine.

Braxton pulled away, and I immediately began to relive that kiss. I didn't know when I'd be able to steal another. It had been too long since I felt her lips. It felt like I'd been trapped inside a drought. With one kiss, she'd brought me back from the brink of death. At least, that was how it seemed.

We made it to the stadium.

We made it through soundcheck.

We made it onto the stage, and I was still thinking about that kiss.

Braxton's gaze had traveled to mine more than once during the show. She was looking at me now, black lipstick restored, and her gaze wondering *what if.*

What if I kissed her again?

What if she forgave me?

What if I meant every one of the words she still wouldn't allow me to say?

I do, baby. I do.

I know you love me too.

After the show, everyone was wired, so Loren suggested we do something we hadn't done in a while. Celebrate for no fucking reason at all. He made a call, and it was done. The six of us hopped in the black Suburban and drove for thirty minutes.

The club Loren brought us to had one of the strictest door policies ever and was…weirdly obsessed with wearing black? I eyed Braxton's white dress, and so did the bouncer after we bypassed the long line. Either Loren had the pull, or even the formidable guard with tattoos and hella piercings could spot a rebel masquerading as an angel.

We passed through the graffiti-covered door after having the lens on our phone cameras taped over and entered the industrial building that reminded me of a middle-aged cathedral but concealed one of the most secretive and exclusive clubs in the world.

Above the cavernous ground floor bathed in darkness and dancers, loomed ceilings sixty feet high and supported by concrete pillars. The club had loaned us four of their bouncers since they hadn't been generous enough to allow us ours. They cleared a path through the stomping, air-punching crowd of fifteen hundred people dressed in little and some in nothing at all. I even spotted what looked like people openly fucking while others danced around them. As the bouncers pushed aside the revelers, the crowd began to push back when they recognized who had passed them.

I was starting to question whether we should be there until Braxton and her friends started dancing. They didn't stop the entire way up to the DJ's booth on the platform above the dance floor.

As we continued to the far edge of the balcony and the empty corner cloaked in shadows, Loren broke off from our group to embrace and talk to one of the guys standing at the mixer. He was wearing headphones, so I assumed he was the DJ.

"Let's go to the bar!" Maeko shouted to her friends. She and Griffin started to go, but as soon as Braxton moved to go with them, Houston pulled her front into his chest and kept her there with his arms around her waist and his gaze fixed on her friends. "Let our friend go, please."

Houston stared at Maeko before shaking his head at her over Braxton's shoulder. The bouncers had already left, which meant the four of us were stuck here until we were ready to go. Griffin and Maeko could go anywhere they liked.

With a crowd that size and in that state, it was a risk for anyone just being in the building. For Bound, that danger was tenfold. Braxton was staying right here.

"Let me go, Houston," she tried to assert anyway.

I laughed quietly, even though the music drowned me out, as I leaned against the wall next to them. Loren was still standing with the DJ and his entourage, talking with everyone like the social butterfly he was. I didn't miss the furtive glances Houston and Braxton drew our way with their embrace either.

I was sure everyone had heard the rumors by now, and we didn't care to disprove them. Especially considering that, for once, they were true, and we had no intention of hiding Braxton.

"Promise not to make me cause a scene?"

Braxton glared up at him, and taking that as her answer, Houston held her tighter.

No one remarked on the fact that she didn't fight him.

Sighing, she turned her head toward her friends while Houston kissed on the side of her neck she exposed as she told them what drink to bring her. The moment Griffin and Maeko were gone, Braxton shoved away from Houston, and he let her with a smile.

"I think it's time we get shit understood," she started before she was interrupted by Loren, who'd snuck up behind her. Turning her around, he immediately began tonguing her down.

"Tell us, baby," he said between hungry kisses. "Put us in our fucking place so we can put you back in yours."

She pulled away to gawk up at him. "*My place*?"

As "Spastik" by Plastikman began to play, Loren walked her backward until she was sandwiched with her back against Houston's chest, and Loren pressed against her front. He cut his gaze toward me when I hesitated for the brief moment it took me to wonder if I should tread carefully with her.

He still didn't trust me not to bolt.

My divorce had been finalized, and he was still afraid of losing me.

Why the hell did that make *me* feel guilty?

I thought I was in love with Emily when I married her, and I *still* believed it when Loren took it upon himself to rip my marriage apart to prove a point. Anger simmered at his audacity. I hadn't been the only one to hurt my friends, yet he liked to pretend.

I felt the recklessness rise and the need to fuck some shit up.

My gaze fell on Braxton as I moved in to block her only escape.

Perhaps what I truly felt was the desire to take what I wanted and damn the consequences. Forget having patience and waiting for Braxton to forgive me. I could figure it out along the way.

"Any more questions?" Loren inquired once the circle was complete, and we all stared down at her, trapped between us.

Braxton was smaller and shorter, but her brass painted a

different picture. She portrayed a woman destined to make men sit up straight whenever she entered a room.

My toes curled from the anticipation of our rebel pushing back after we reminded her who was in charge. She'd demand respect, and then she'd give us no choice but to give her everything she asked for and more.

I was really looking forward to the latter.

"Yes. Which part of *we're over* was unclear?" She frowned as if she were genuinely confused. "I'm concerned you don't seem to be getting it."

"The part where you agreed to finish the tour to save our asses? The part where you showed up even though you knew what would happen? You came because you were hoping we could convince you to take us back. We will, baby. Just give it time."

"You're off base by a mile," she returned dryly.

Loren's hands slipped beneath her short dress as he stared at her like nothing was amiss. "Then what's with the attitude?" His hands moved up and down as he caressed the back of her thighs.

"Because you lied to me?"

Her gaze cut to me and my stomach twisted sharply. Guilt was the reason I was forcing myself to be a spectator to what Braxton still hadn't realized was unfolding.

"Nah. You said it yourself that you forgave us. You're upset because we're taking too long to earn back your trust." He kissed her tenderly when she looked like she'd sock him. "It's true," he whispered as he pecked her again. "You know it is."

Loren's hands moved up to her ass at the same time Houston shifted his hold to her arms. As smooth as if he were straightening his tie, Loren tore Braxton's panties from her and made her gasp. He smoothly snuck them to me, and I stuffed them in my pocket for later.

"What are you—"

"Have you been touching yourself?" Houston interrupted. She shook her head and then immediately rolled her eyes at herself for answering. "Good girl. Tonight, we take care of your pussy. Tomorrow, we see about your heart."

"Shouldn't it be the other way around?" she muttered bitterly.

Loren's lips quirked. "One's not as stubborn as the other, but rest assured, baby fawn, we'll have them both."

"Someone will see," she pleaded in a last bid to come to her senses. It was too late, though. She'd already given in.

"See what?" he pretended not to know even as he unbuckled his belt.

"You fucking me."

Houston lifted her leg from behind, opening her up for Loren, who was now freeing his dick. "Let them see," Loren whispered as he stroked himself. "Let this happen like we know you will, and we can be done before your friends return." He brought himself to her entrance, and she whimpered from the pleasure when he began pushing inside. I avidly watched every inch he filled her with. "We can be your dirty little secret," he promised as he reached the hilt and began pumping his hips. "Would you like that?"

All she could manage were a few broken sounds.

This close, I could hear over the music how wet Braxton was as Loren moved inside her. There had been no foreplay, no precedent to this moment. There was only the need building inside of us all in the month since we last had her.

Groaning, Loren sped up.

"Make no mistake," Houston said to Braxton as Loren fucked her silly against him. He held her still for our best friend's enjoyment, and Braxton loved every second of it. "We're not going to stop, we're not going away, and we're never giving up. You're Bound. That can never be broken."

"Houston."

The sound of his name on her lips and Loren's groan as she came around him seemed to break Houston's control. "Shit," he said to Loren as he released Braxton's neck and forced his hand between them to undo his jeans. "Speed this up. I can't wait."

Bracing his forearm on the wall next to Houston's head, Loren sped up his thrusts, pounding inside Braxton with no remorse and making their skin slap as she cried out without any thought of keeping her voice down.

"Basiel" by Amelie Lens drowned them out, but the three of us could hear loud and clear along with the small group surrounding the DJ at the booth just fifty feet away.

They couldn't see, but they could hear the remnants of her cries. Even though it was just another night for them and no one bothered to look our way, I made sure my body blocked Braxton and what we were up to as I looked on.

My dick was as hard as a brick, while my gaze couldn't decide where to settle. I watched Braxton's tits bounce under the low cut of her dress since she'd once again gone without a bra. I watched the muscles in Loren's naked ass flex as he pumped inside her. I even watched and listened as Houston whispered dirty threats in her ear. I knew he'd make good on every one of them once Loren was through.

"Today, Lo."

With three more hard pumps and a grunt as he came, Loren obliged Houston without argument. He stayed inside her a few seconds longer, kissing her lips and whispering how much he loved her in between before pulling away.

Braxton didn't react as he knew she wouldn't.

I could see the frustration in Loren's eyes as he fixed his clothes, but he said nothing.

Houston had already turned Braxton around and stolen her attention. He shed her leather jacket, letting it fall to the ground. The thin straps of her dress were next. Houston slipped them off her shoulders and let her dress fall, too, baring her completely as if we weren't in the middle of a fucking club.

"Houston," I scolded, unable to hide my apprehension.

Had we gone too far?

Ignoring me, Houston gripped Braxton's breasts in both of his palms, and together, they moved deeper into the shadows until they were completely shrouded as they kissed.

Not even I could see what they were doing.

I knew the moment he began fucking her, though.

As Loren casually leaned against the wall, I drank in every one of Braxton's incoherent cries and Houston's harsh grunts as he fucked her like it was their last time. He rode her hard, and she took everything he gave.

It seemed to go on forever, and at the same time, not long enough.

"Oh, Houston," she told him.

"Fuck, Braxton," he told her.

Their choked gasps were the last thing Loren and I heard before it stopped. It was a couple more minutes before Houston led Braxton back out of the shadows with a hand on her waist as he kept her upright and steady. Her hair had fallen from her ponytail, and she was already bearing the marks from their attention. I don't know how she expected to hide what she'd done from her friends, but our mission was accomplished.

I could see our victory building in her eyes.

The capitulation.

Her inevitable surrender.

And my permanent undoing.

Almost there.

Loren turned to me and lifted a brow.

"You don't want a turn?" he asked as he lazily chewed a stick of gum.

I saw Braxton shiver at his tone and his question. She only liked being treated like our possession when her clothes were off and her inhibitions were down. If he'd tried it any other time, he'd be on the ground holding his balls.

My throat bobbed as I swallowed the desire that made my mouth water. "Not this time," I whispered as I reached out and brushed her naked nipple with my thumb. "I think we need to have that talk first, right?"

I took my gaze off her breasts for the beauty of her brown eyes.

Braxton nodded eagerly, and I could see her gratitude for my restraint. She wasn't strong enough to turn me down right now, and I didn't want her hating herself in the morning. Regret was not what I needed her to feel whenever she thought of me.

I thought about our kiss earlier, and she must have thought of it too.

Rising on her tiptoes, Braxton planted one on my cheek. "Thank you for understanding," she whispered before settling on her heels again.

I simply nodded as I looked away so she wouldn't see my hidden thoughts.

Enjoy it while it lasts.

SIXTY-ONE

Braxton

PARIS.

I was in Paris.

I inhaled a nervous breath and slowly exhaled the brine. When that didn't work, I started to fidget, adjusting the wig I wore that was long, layered, black with blue ombre, and had side bangs covering my right eye.

Going with the flow, I'd lined my eyes heavily with black liner and clipped the faux silver piercings to my nose and lip. I completed the look picked out for me with fishnet stockings, black jeans with holes in the knees, and a cropped tee.

Seeing my reflection now in one of the seventeen large mirrors made from three hundred and fifty smaller mirrors, I knew without a doubt who'd left the disguise.

The handwritten note asking to meet here and at this time made it clear too. I'd woken up this morning to both waiting for me inside my hotel suite at the foot of my bed that I'd slept in alone.

And now I waited with butterflies in my stomach for him to arrive.

It's been two weeks since Berlin.

Two guilt-ridden weeks since the club and the sex that I wouldn't allow myself to think about, but somehow, I always managed to think *only* about it. Houston and Loren had shamelessly poured their frustration into me while Jericho watched. They made me not just see but *feel* how much they needed me. I needed them too, but it wasn't the same.

This wasn't hiding fear and apprehension behind cruelty like before.

They'd lied to me.

How do we come back from that? How do I learn to trust them again? I keep waiting for some sign that may never come. And if it didn't, what did that mean?

I was afraid to know the answer.

I wasn't ready to accept the truth if it meant being without them.

When my phone pinged, I looked at the screen and frowned at the Twitter notification.

@Em_Anon: You're going to die bitch

I rolled my eyes.

Death threats weren't new to me anymore. I just wished they were more creative. Maybe describe how you plan to kill me?

I don't know.

Just make it worth the tweet.

Peering around the crowded room from my spot inside the arched alcove, I searched for a distraction that shouldn't have been hard to find. Perhaps in the vaulted ceiling painted to depict the history of Louis XIV? Or the chandeliers spanning the two hundred and forty feet length of the hall? There was a lot to marvel at and appreciate inside the famed Hall of Mirrors, the most notable room in the Château de Versailles.

It was kind of annoying. I'd dreamt of seeing this place ever since watching the TV show that had sucked me in only to cancel after three seasons, and now that I was here, my nerves kept me from enjoying it.

It wasn't a coincidence that he'd chosen this place.

I'd made him watch reruns of the show with me after seeing the rants online a couple of months ago regarding rumors of it ending. Any excuse to close the distance he'd put between us at the time.

And now I knew why.

I just needed to understand the rest.

The crowd parted, and as if he'd heard my silent plea, Jericho appeared.

Unlike me, he wasn't wearing a disguise, but everyone was too enraptured by the gilded hall to look past the hood of the sweatshirt shielding the drummer's face and hair from view and the dark shades covering silver eyes. Jericho's mouth set in a grim line, and the ring piercing his bottom lip drew my attention. I didn't have to see his eyes to know that they were haunted.

Longer than I'd known him, he'd never been anything else.

My heart wept for him, even as I kept my expression neutral.

"Hey," he greeted low when he finally reached me. His teeth toyed with his lip ring. Something he only did when he was nervous or deep in thought. At the moment, I was sure it was both. Together, we stood inside the alcove as everyone passed us by. It was a daring move when he removed his shades. I could see his eyes now, and he could stare deeply into mine. "Can we talk now?"

While many emotions assailed me at once, there was only one answer in my mind and heart. It was the one I let fall from my lips. "Sure."

I watched his Adam's apple bob as he swallowed hard and then looked away to search for words in the garden just outside the window.

"Do you still love her?" I blurted when I couldn't take the silence any longer. The answer to that burning question plagued me when I was awake and followed me into my sleep. I had to know. But I wondered if it would change anything.

Jericho's gaze flew to me, and the blatant alarm I saw inside weirdly soothed my aching heart. Slowly, he shook his head, but it wasn't from hesitation. It was disbelief that I would ever think so. "No, Braxton. I don't." He took a tentative step forward, and when his hands found my waist, I let him keep them there. "I love *you*."

"Why? Why me and not her? What did your *wife* do wrong that I did right?"

His eyes narrowed just before his hold on me tightened. It was my only warning before he slammed my back against the wall and trapped me with nothing more than his anger.

Sweet, sad, gentle Jericho was gone.

I was looking at Rich.

The forceful, vengeful reckoning he kept hidden from the world.

One smelled like berries, and the other set me on fire.

"Listen up, and God help you if you make me repeat myself," he cautioned me. "My feelings for you have *nothing* to do with her. I won't compare you because she doesn't compare. You want to know why I love you? Fine. But don't think for a second that I gave you my heart as a fuck you to her. Don't diminish yourself when you set the standard. The girl I fell in love with would know better."

"Rich—"

He shut me up with a harsh grip on my chin. "Have I made myself clear, Braxton?"

My mouth filled with cherries while my pussy throbbed and my stomach warmed and twisted itself. Yes. I understood him. I heard him loud and clear.

Apparently, admitting it to myself wasn't enough, though.

The look he gave me warned me that I'd better speak up soon.

"Yes."

Rich stared down at me for a long while, waiting for even the smallest sign that I was lying. I almost wished that I was when I felt my toes curl at the thought of getting more of what he gave me in Connecticut.

Shaking his head, he leaned in, bracing his forearm on the wall and caging me in. "I want to kiss you," he gently confessed as he brushed my lip with his thumb.

Kiss me.

"But I can't. I need you thinking with a clear head."

"Cocky much?"

He never lost that serious expression when he dropped the hand that held my face to squeeze my ass through my jeans. There was so much possession in that simple gesture. It made me consider how far he'd come from the drummer I'd met nine months ago.

The one who played the background and let his friends call the shots because he didn't like making waves. To my heart, it was now painfully clear why he preferred it that way.

Because the waves Jericho caused were tragic on the soul.

They were one-hundred-foot tsunamis.

"No." He let me go, took a step back, and slid his hands in his jeans as he looked at me. "When I'm not eager to fuck you, all I can process is fear. I've been wracking my brain since the moment I found out you knew about Emily. I didn't think you'd ever forgive me, but then you did, and it gave me hope. I clung to that seed until I realized what I'd truly lost. Trust. You'd given it so easily, and I didn't understand until this moment as I'm fighting for the words to get it back. If I'd known losing you would turn me this inside out, I would have told you about Emily. I would have told you the moment I wished that it had been you I'd given my name. I hadn't even kissed you yet. Did you know that? I wanted to marry you long before I ever kissed you. So much that I filed for divorce the next day."

While Jericho gathered his thoughts and I replayed everything he'd confessed so far, we stared at each other, longing for what could have been.

"I know you feel guilty for me loving you," he said, "but there's no reason for either of us to carry that weight. I stopped wanting Emily long before we met, and she has no one to blame but herself."

His lips set in a grim line, and his brows dipped as he remembered the past.

"We were married for only four months before she cheated and then six before she ran away because I told her if the baby wasn't mine, we were through. I don't know if it was anger that spoke for me, but I know it's been over four years. She won't let me find her because she cares more about her power over me than she does me. She likes knowing that I'm chasing her and doesn't care if it hurts. She doesn't care if I'm driving myself insane over the moments I might be missing with my kid. My heart kept beating when she walked out the door, and now I know the reason. It's because it never belonged to her. It was always meant for you."

Versailles might as well have been a berry field instead of a seventeenth-century palace.

"If she's truly so terrible, kid or no kid, how could you choose to stay with her?" I asked him.

"Because I was an orphan."

I ached for him because he sounded so ashamed. It hadn't been his fault. Didn't he know that?

"I never had a family," he continued. "I never knew what it was like to form a connection that couldn't be broken with the stroke of a pen. Houston and Loren helped fill the gaps, but it was never enough. There was always something missing. Always a need for more. I met Emily, and I was drawn because she was damaged like me"—hesitating, the look in his eyes pleaded for me to understand—"and like you."

I sucked in a breath. Was I just another Emily?

"The only thing she ever gave the world was both of her middle fingers, and I wanted to be right there beside her. I wasn't..." He swallowed. "I wasn't the same after I met her. I was reckless and spiraling too fast to stop on my own. I have memories that keep me awake sometimes because of the things she convinced me to do. Houston and Loren saw what was happening and tried to warn me, but I wouldn't listen. I didn't trust them. They don't know this, but Emily made me hate my best friends long before Calvin, and I was too blind to see it. She'd cry and convince me that they didn't want to see me happy, and I..." He hung his head. "I fucking believed her."

His voice broke on that last, and suddenly, I was transported back to the show in Arizona after I was exiled from their bus and the lyrics I'd foolishly mistaken for Loren's.

I heard Rich sniffle, and then he kept speaking.

"By the time I realized I'd mistaken a carefree spirit for someone who just didn't care at all about anyone, including herself, it was too late." He lifted his head and looked at me. "I'd married her. I thought I loved her, but I knew she didn't love me, and I didn't even care. She was the only one willing to pretend."

"Rich." I couldn't help myself. I went to him. He was slow to wrap his arms around me, but when they did, I wished silently to myself that he would never let go.

"I'm sorry I lied to you," he whispered.

I forced myself to pull away, but only enough to see his face. "Why did you?"

I became so lost in the emotion swimming in his silver eyes that I'd forgotten I'd asked the question until he answered.

"I knew you'd let me go."

"If you had been honest—"

He shook his head before I could finish. "Not what I meant. If I'd told you about my past, I knew you'd sacrifice your heart to let me do what I thought was right. You'd let me walk away, and I couldn't handle that. Years of hoping for a family, and I was suddenly praying that her baby wasn't mine. I was praying I wouldn't have to give you up. I was living in a cloud of shame and confusion, and I didn't know which way was up, much less right." I felt his hand curl around my nape and the other slide through my hair. He'd never held me so tenderly. "But it was *never* my intention to deceive you, Braxton. Hurt you was the last thing I wanted to do."

"But you did," I told him as a tear fell. How could I make him see? My soul reached out for him, but my heart was a different matter. It was afraid of falling again. "After Emily, you should understand how much. Trust is fragile, Jericho. It's rattled often and easily broken. You shattered mine. You can put the pieces back together, but it'll never be as strong. I'll never not see the cracks."

I couldn't describe the range of emotions that flashed in Jericho's eyes in the seconds that followed. God, there were so many. It seemed liked hundreds and then…nothing—only utter defeat. Leaning down, he kissed me. Was that hope I felt? He smashed his lips against mine once, briefly, and then he pulled away.

Why did it feel like the last time?

"It's okay," he whispered to me as he dropped his hands. "It's okay."

"Jericho." I reached for him, but he was already turning away. Desperation forced my voice to rise, and my pride and ego to flee. "Jericho!"

I didn't care about the eyes I'd drawn as he walked away. I didn't care if they looked too long and recognized him or me. I just needed him to turn back around. I needed him to fight for me.

He kept walking away.

If only Griff and Maeko were here to distract me from my heart with wine and angry music. They'd flown back home after our last show in Belgium.

I bet they knew this would happen. I'd known it too.

I stood on the balcony of the penthouse suite, staring at the full view of the Eiffel Tower lighting up the night but unable to appreciate its beauty. I'd banged on Jericho's room door inside the suite the three of them shared for ten minutes, but he wouldn't answer.

Houston and Loren had both sworn that he never came back. Feeling the need to lash out, I'd called them liars before storming out.

That had been five, maybe six hours ago.

I never heard the room door to my suite open, never questioned how he'd gotten the key. When strong arms wrapped around me and the scent of cloves from his soap and vanilla from my warped brain had washed over me, I knew who had intruded on my brooding.

"Is he back?" I inquired softly while staring straight ahead.

Houston's tone was equally gentle and more patient than I'd been hours earlier when he answered, "No."

I closed my eyes and squeezed them tight. "Please tell me where he is."

"I don't know, baby. I swear."

"I'm not your baby," I snapped.

As soon as I said the words, I burst out crying.

This wasn't me. This was *not me*. What the hell had I allowed myself to turn into?

Houston turned me around in his arms and pulled my head

back, using my hair as his handle. The wig I'd worn to meet Jericho this morning had been left discarded on my bed.

"Yes, you are." Houston kissed my lips as if it would prove his claim. I shoved him away, and he yanked me back. When he pressed his mouth against mine again, I kissed him back, and we didn't stop. "Have dinner with me," he proposed after we ran out of air.

"I can't."

His brows dipped. "Why not?"

"I need to be here when Jericho comes back."

"It's being covered," was all he said before forcing me back inside the bedroom whose balcony we'd stood on.

I pretended I didn't, but I liked it very much when Houston didn't take no for an answer. I also liked that he only softened for me. He was only warm and comforting *for me*.

Loren did whatever the hell he wanted and always encouraged me to do the same. That's why he was my breath of fresh air, my ray of sunshine, my earthy spring breeze.

And Rich…oh, Rich. He was pure and sweet and good. Even when he was breaking my heart, he did it with the best of intentions.

Houston pulled me over the bed, and that's when I noticed the red dress.

It was so fine that "gown" might have been a more appropriate term. It was short, silk, with a low-cut bodice and medium width straps. Next to it was a shoebox, and when I opened it, I found gold heels inside.

"You know my size?" I asked without looking at Houston.

Between Jericho ripping me in two and Houston attempting to piece me back together, I was afraid I'd just disintegrate altogether. I silently wondered what plans Loren had up his sleeve for me. Rich thought he'd failed to win me over, but he hadn't.

I was the one who'd failed.

I should have told him the truth.

"I warned you before," Houston said as he lifted my shirt over my head, "I never stop paying attention."

Feeling my belly warm, I let him remove my jeans and stockings and then help me inside the fancy dress. He even pulled my hair into my usual messy top-knot, and I let him do that too. My ass hit the bed when he pushed me down, and then he removed the shoes from the box. I felt like a less innocent version of Cinderella when Houston slipped the first heel on my feet.

"Ready to go?" he asked when, at last, I was dressed for a romantic night with a man who was still my ex but held one-third of my heart in his palm.

I tried not to think about Jericho, who still possessed an equal share.

"Yes."

I grabbed my jacket since fall had come to Paris. As I slipped it on, I noticed Houston's apparel for the first time. His usual jeans, T-shirt, and double leather cords around his wrist were gone. The only familiar thing he wore was the pinky ring. Tonight, he wore dress pants and a white button-up with a gray knit sweater on top. He hadn't gone all out as Loren had on our first date, but I knew he'd tried. For me. I also knew Loren must have helped him.

Security was waiting for us when we stepped from my suite and into the hall. I didn't consider the implications of this date until Houston and I walked through the hotel's front entrance, and the cameras began to flash.

It wouldn't just be a rumor anymore.

With Houston's hand holding mine, the world would know that I was fucking my bandmates. The names they called me and the assumptions they made—there would be no mercy.

And still, all I could think about was Jericho.

Where was he? What was he thinking? How could he just walk away?

Houston and I climbed inside the back of the black Suburban, and we were off with security trailing us in another vehicle behind. Neither of us spoke the five minutes it took to reach our destination.

I sucked in a breath at seeing the Eiffel Tower up close. It commanded your attention during the day, but it was even more breathtaking at night. With the golden lights, how could it not be?

I assumed we'd head straight for the top, but Houston had other plans. He took me to the second floor, where apparently, we had reservations. I didn't have to be an expert to know that a place like this was usually booked weeks or months in advance.

Maybe he'd pulled some strings.

Or maybe he'd always known that he'd bring me here.

Had Houston been biding his time for our first date?

Ignoring the vanilla wafting in the air, I looked at him as he sat next to me in the white curved booth, pretending to peruse the menu. We both ignored the stares we'd drawn from the people who recognized us and even those who didn't. With two guards hovering around, anyone would be curious.

"Why did you bring me here?"

"To eat."

My chest tightened where a heart should no longer be. After all this time, after all I'd been through, I didn't understand why I hadn't just tossed the damn thing away.

"That's it?"

He looked at me then, his somber gaze searching mine, and said, "No."

I waited for him to say more, but he didn't. Our waiter came, and we ordered drinks, our food, and then we ate in silence. Immediately after, we left the restaurant.

We were both too on edge to linger.

It was chaotic as hell, but eventually, we made it to the top of the tower. It was there the tension that had been brewing all through dinner exploded.

He pulled me into his arms and kissed me, and we didn't stop even when we knew we were being photographed and recorded.

"I'm sorry," he whispered against my lips.

"No sweat," I said as I swallowed the cherries. "I think the cat was kind of already out of the bag, you know?"

The look Houston gave me made it clear that I was provoking him. And then he sighed. "Fawn."

"What are you sorry for?" I asked him with an evil smile. I already knew, but I needed to hear him say it.

"I'm sorry for not being a better man to you and a better friend to Rich. It wasn't my place to tell you about Emily, but I should have fought harder to convince him." Houston's jaw tightened as he looked away, over the railing, and out to the city that promised romance beyond. "Even now, I'm conflicted. I chose him over you once, and I won't do it again, but I ca—"

No longer indignant, I felt my legs tremble at the emotion in his voice and the words he couldn't bring himself to say for fear of what they might cost us. Houston looked at me then, meeting my eyes, and I saw the decision not to lie to me again.

One by one, those shards pieced themselves back together.

The cracks were there, but I was no longer afraid of them. Instead, they served as a reminder that love wasn't meant to be a pristine affair. It was meant to be messy and meant to hurt, but it would always mend if it's true.

"I'm in love with you."

It wasn't what Houston had been trying to say.

But it was the truth his heart required.

Before allowing any others, he had to finally let that one free, and now my feet no longer felt like they were touching the ground.

"I need you to know that and for you to believe me. I need it because…I can't pretend I'm not afraid of where he is and what he's thinking. Jericho's lived with this void, and once it has him, it…Loren's looking for him right now, but…"

His fear mounted, making it harder for Houston to finish a thought, so why did I understand everything he was trying to tell me? Was it because I felt it too?

Did I really have to ask?

"Then let's go," I heard myself say to him. "Let's go find Jericho."

Houston's surprise and his relief lasted for only a second before we were rushing hand in hand for the elevator to take us down. It seemed like an eternity passed before we reached the ground. Houston was on his phone checking for an update from Loren, and as we rushed outside and for the car, a new hour must have dawned.

Over my shoulder, I smiled up at the tower we had left behind as twenty thousand bulbs began to sparkle and wish us luck.

SIXTY-TWO

Loren

AFTER READING THE TEXT THAT JUST CAME THROUGH, I QUIETLY exhaled before pocketing my phone.

"So this is your plan then?" I questioned as I made my presence known. The hooded figure sat alone on the green bench, not caring who came along. "You'll get arrested with your record, and she'll take you back?" I snorted. "Think again."

Rich sighed as he continued to sulk at the blue tiled wall in front of him. There was white writing on the dark glossy surface that said the same thing in the few languages I could translate, along with a dozen or so red specks that made no sense to me.

"Fuck off, Lo."

Ignoring him, I frowned as I looked around. "How the hell did you even get in here?"

"I was good at this once, remember?"

Realizing he was referring to who he'd been with Emily, I rolled my eyes before turning to the square's security guard. He was the one who'd found Rich lurking after hours. *"Pouvez-vous nous donner un moment?"* I asked him in rusty French.

The guard hesitated only a moment before nodding and trotting off. Sitting next to Rich on the bench, I got comfortable after looking at the stubborn set of his mouth.

"How did you even find me?" he snapped.

"Night guard's a fan."

I didn't bother to elaborate any further because it didn't

matter how I got here as long as I was here. For the moment, Rich was too much of a jackass to see it.

"Lucky me," he mumbled.

"Would you rather be in jail for trespassing?"

"Yes."

I stared at his hard profile for a moment. "I take it things didn't go well with Braxton this morning?" He didn't bother to respond because I already knew the answer, so I tried a different tactic to keep him talking. Anything to keep him from sinking too deep inside his head where all the fucked-up thoughts resided. There would be too many casualties trying to get him out if he gave into them even once. "So, what now?"

"I'm leaving."

I frowned at his announcement as I sat up. "What the hell are you talking about?"

"Bound." He shook his head as he stared at the ground now. "I can't do this shit anymore."

"Let me guess," I drawled through a smile that felt tight. Wasn't a damn thing funny about what he had said. "You'll run back into Emily's frail-ass arms?"

"Fuck Emily, and fuck you too." He looked at me now, his silver eyes aflame and full of accusation. "After what you did, I wouldn't be surprised if her baby was yours," Rich spat.

Don't slap him, Lo.

"I would have never fucked that bitch with *your* dick. That kid isn't mine, and I'm betting both of my nuts it's not yours either."

"Whatever."

"You're not leaving," I told him immediately. I wasn't going to beat around the bush or beg. The same threat I made Braxton applied to my best friends too. In fact…as Rich and I sat stewing in silence, I fished out my phone and pulled up Amazon. *Damn, I wished I still smoked.* After a few taps, I found the items I needed.

"You can't make me stay," Rich said in a low tone as I concentrated on my task.

Was sixty feet enough?

I ordered three of each before checking out, sending a quick text, and putting my phone away. "Don't be so melodramatic."

"You'd do the same, so don't pretend you'd stay."

"There are a few things I would have done differently, starting with Emily, but I won't beat a dead horse because the shit is starting to stink. Braxton isn't Emily, Rich. You and I both know that no time or distance will change how you feel about her. So she needs you to suffer and grovel for a while. Are you telling me she's not worth it?"

"You weren't there, Lo. She sounded so damn sure that I had no chance."

I absently shrugged as I stared off. "Women."

I could feel his stare after a while and finally met his incredulous gaze.

"Are you supposed to be helping?"

Peering over my shoulder when I saw movement, I felt myself relax. *Fucking finally.* "Nope," I answered him even as I stared at Braxton's sexy ass in that red dress. Suddenly "stunning" seemed like too cheap a word to describe my baby girl. "I'm supposed to be stalling."

Rich frowned until he heard their footsteps and turned his head enough to see them. Forcing myself to look away from Braxton, I watched him rise to his feet slowly and turn, an involuntary movement he probably wasn't even aware of. I couldn't see Rich's face underneath his dark hood, but his emotions belonged to me as much as they did to him. It was all I needed to know.

"You're really going to make me chase you?" Braxton fussed as she approached.

Yeah, I'd snitched. Houston hung back to give them the space to work out their shit properly this time.

"How is that fair, Jericho? You lied to *me*."

"I promise that's not what I'm trying to do. I just wanted to make it right."

"Then stay."

I could tell he'd looked away when she followed his gaze. "I can't."

"Why?"

"Because I can't watch."

"What can't you watch, Jericho?"

"You, them, and not me too. They deserve to be happy. You deserve to be happy."

"And you?" She'd been inching closer the entire time they spoke as if he were a skittish kitten. "What do you deserve? Do you even know?"

"No."

"Don't you want me anymore?" she asked, her voice shaking and making it clear that she was no longer sure. Houston, Rich, and I had nearly identical reactions at almost the same time.

I held back my groan as my eyes closed, and I pinched the bridge of my nose. I was pretty sure I'd murder Rich if he lied to her on some self-sacrificing bullshit. If there was an excuse to be selfish, it was now.

Choose wisely, motherfucker.

"Of course, I do."

"Prove it."

I was proud of the confidence restored in her tone. I didn't want her crying anymore, not over him, not over Houston…not even over me.

"How?" Rich asked her eagerly.

"Stay." He stepped closer to her, and she let him into her space. "I'm not going to make it easy for you," she warned him when his hands gripped her ass, and he pulled her closer. "In fact, I'm going to make it as hard for you as I can."

After pulling his hood back, I finally saw his smile. Seemed like it'd been a while. "You already did," he swore to her.

He was definitely talking about this dick.

Rolling my eyes, I looked away as I slowly stretched and yawned. "Mission accomplished. Everyone's in love. Can we go now?" I snapped as I stared at the wall.

The night was still young, but I'd never been this exhausted.

Now that we had Braxton back, I felt like I could sleep for days.

I must have drawn Braxton's attention to the wall because she broke away from our drummer to stand before it. "What does it say?" she asked no one in particular.

Since I was the only one who knew, I answered her question. "I love you."

She whirled around to look at me and blushed when I held her stare.

Yeah, that's right, baby. I love you.

"All of it?" Her brows rose.

"I can only read a few of them, but that seems to be the gist." I shrugged.

"And the red pieces?" she inquired.

I was silent since I had no fucking clue, but I was curious, so I stood and moved until I stood at the wall next to Braxton. Houston and Rich did the same until we all stood together, staring at "I love you," written in over two-hundred languages.

"It's a heart." Braxton's head swiveled toward Rich. Of course, his angst-riddled ass had to be the one to crack the code. "One heart torn apart by love. Or lack thereof. It could symbolize anything."

"What do you think it means?" Braxton asked him.

Jericho was quiet as he stared at the wall. I'm sure he already knew the answer since he'd been staring at it for hours. "Pain isn't singular. We're not alone, no matter how much it seems that way. Someone out there feels it too, and if we ever meet, we could bring our broken pieces together. We could bind them and form one heart." He looked into her brown eyes. "We could be Bound."

Nice.

Braxton melted, and I smirked.

Rich was good for something, after all.

He looked at me over her head like he'd heard my thoughts. When Braxton turned to me, I made sure to school my expression. We weren't quite out of the dog house yet.

"We can go," our little dictator decided after she'd taken a few pictures of the wall.

I knew she'd post them on her Instagram later, but at least it wouldn't be with some nauseating caption spouting bullshit the person who wrote it didn't even believe.

Braxton was too gangster.

She'd post a heart. Enough said.

We turned to leave, and I scooped her into my arms the moment she took a step forward and winced.

"Thanks," she said with a relieved exhale once she was settled with her arms around my neck. "New heels. I haven't broken them in yet."

"I know." I gazed down at her as the four of us left the garden square to get started on the rest of our lives together. "Can I fuck you in them sometime?"

I was feeling pretty optimistic about our future when she smiled.

SIXTY-THREE

Braxton

TODAY MARKED ONE YEAR SINCE MEETING HOUSTON, LOREN, AND Jericho.

It's been three months since Paris. Three blissful months spent touring Europe. There were no more lies and no more secrets.

Loren told me about being left for dead after convincing his mother to leave her abusive marriage. He told me his father's offer if he quit Bound and came home, and then he made it clear that it wasn't happening now or ever. He even confessed his part in ruining Rich's marriage.

Jericho told me about his time in foster care and group homes. He told me about meeting Emily…and the things she made him do to prove that he loved her. What he *didn't* tell me, but I pieced together on my own, was that she'd taken advantage of his search for an unbreakable bond and used him like her personal puppet.

My heart broke for him.

It broke for that lonely, desperate kid who couldn't see that he'd already found it with Houston and Loren.

Jericho had signed that deal with Savant to give his wife the life she demanded so that he wouldn't have to steal and hurt and destroy anymore. He'd given his soul for Emily, and she ruined him in return.

Even with all that honesty, I was left to wonder what

skeletons Houston was hiding in *his* closet. He didn't seem to have any, but neither had Jericho.

They were tortured, yes.

We all were.

But I was praying there was nothing else waiting to jump out of the bushes and bite us.

That reason and curiosity were why I agreed to meet Houston's grandmother. The three of them had planned for us to meet the first time they brought me home, but I ran away before they could arrange it, so this time, they weren't taking any chances.

It's barely been an hour since we'd returned to Portland, and we were already on our way. The second leg was done, and we had a month before the tour continued until ending for good in May.

I smiled to myself as we quietly rode through the city in the Suburban that had been waiting for us when the private plane landed.

I couldn't wait to get back to their fort.

Or, as Loren called it, the treehouse.

Houston and Rich refused to acknowledge either truth.

I immediately realized where they'd gotten their love for Victorian architecture when we pulled up to the blue two-story on a small hill with white framing the windows and doors and a dark brick roof. The neighborhood was quiet since it was a late Tuesday morning, long after kids had gone to school, and parents had left for work.

It was raining too.

I tried not to take that as an omen as the steady fall washed away the two inches of snow that had fallen recently.

The car stopped, and I looked to Houston, who was already studying me from his seat next to me in the back row.

"Ready?"

Exhaling slowly, I nodded my response while wishing he'd give something away. He was tense too, but I didn't know why since Loren and Rich both seemed excited. They were already hopping out of the truck, and neither waited for us before rushing for the front door and disappearing inside.

Houston kissed my fingers, climbed out, and helped me once he was on his feet. He said something to the driver that I didn't catch because I couldn't hear over my heartbeat.

I'd never done this before.

Houston and Loren weren't the only ones who'd never been in a relationship. Rich was the only one with experience, and considering how well that worked out…yeah, I was nervous.

Rich didn't have parents for me to meet, and Loren's sounded like real tools, so luckily, this might be the only time I'd ever go through this.

What if she didn't like me?

I knew Houston, Loren, and Jericho. It wouldn't change a thing, but…I'd like her to anyway—for them more so than me. I took a deep breath and exhaled once we reached the double front doors. I could hear voices on the other side, and they sounded happy. I just hoped my presence wouldn't change that.

Here goes everything.

@Em_Anon: Watch your back. He's mine.

I snorted at the tweet before tossing my phone back down on the lumpy twin mattress next to me. Lying on my back, I hummed "Light My Fire" by The Doors as I stared at the ceiling and the dead rock star hanging from it. It figured Loren would idolize the most unpredictable rebel of his time and perhaps even ours still.

I was still staring at the poster of the shirtless Jim Morrison with his arms up, palms forward and splayed like he was saying "make way" when my attention was stolen by someone stepping inside the small bedroom.

"There you are."

Loren slowly walked to the foot of his old bed and stopped. He was eating yet another one of the cookies Houston's grandmother, who they all called Mom, had made in the eight hours since we arrived.

No one seemed in a rush to leave, including me, after

learning how open and warm Houston's grandmother turned out to be. She didn't even blink when Houston, Loren, and Jericho told her they were all dating me. Perhaps she'd already heard the rumors, but her lack of reaction had still taken me by surprise. If they hadn't already told me otherwise, I'd think I wasn't the first girl they'd shared before.

Laine Morrow made me miss my own grandmother, who had been my only source of friendship before I lost her to cancer when I was fourteen. In a way, she'd been an outcast too but refused to leave Faithful because she enjoyed making people squirm.

I smiled at the memory of her, even as the room began to smell like roses.

"Here I am." Loren wasted no time crawling onto the bed, and after kissing my lips, he lay beside me. "Interesting choice to hang over your bed," I said, ending the comfortable silence that followed.

In my peripheral, I saw Loren smirk. "Didn't I tell you? I'm not picky about gender."

I turned my head toward him. "Is that your way of telling me you're bi?"

Loren chewed on his lip while staring at the poster. I could tell something was on his mind. "Call it what you want," he answered absently.

I ignored the phantom sweetness filling my mouth and turned on my side until I was spooning Loren's. "Is something wrong?"

"Everything's perfect, actually."

Placing my hand on his chest, I lifted enough to see his face fully. "Then what's the matter?"

Loren met my gaze and held it. As with Houston at the Eiffel Tower, I could sense Loren's indecision before choosing blatant honesty no matter how much it hurt. "I'm just wondering if it will last."

Laying my head over his beating heart, I felt the same sharp chord reality struck every time I was forced to acknowledge it.

"It won't." I heard him suck in a breath at my decision to be brutally honest as well. "Perfection isn't real. There's only us. We'll make each other laugh, and we'll make each other scream. Bad days will find us again. We will be tested, and sometimes we'll falter. We'll wonder if this time we make it through." I lifted my head to look at him. "Love isn't an illusion that requires silence to maintain. It only needs our memory of what it was like without each other."

Loren gently put me on my back before making himself comfortable between my legs. "So we keep fighting anyway?" he questioned as he looked down at me. "Even if it hurts?" There was no doubt in his tone. There was only the need to confirm what he already knew in his heart.

"Yes."

Loren nodded and then looked over his shoulder.

We were no longer alone.

Jericho, also eating another cookie and staring at his phone, wandered over to the other twin bed and sat on the edge. Houston's grandmother had referred to this bedroom as Loren and Rich's when she gave me the tour, so I knew they must have shared it at one point while Houston had his own.

"Where's Houston?" I asked when I was reminded that one of the trio was missing.

"Took his grandmother to the store for groceries," Rich answered as he continued with whatever held his attention on his phone. "We're staying for dinner."

I simply nodded since I had no problem with that. Besides, I was sure it was Laine Morrow's idea and not up for debate. Immediately upon hearing that we were without supervision, a switch in Loren's mind seemed to flip as he turned frisky.

"What are you doing?" Stupid question since I already knew. His hand was now under my dress and pulling my thong down.

"I've been thinking about eating your pussy since we left Dublin," Loren told me. His lips brushed my jawline before reaching my ear. "Can I?"

"We can't," I whined as I caught his wrist just before my

panties could clear my thighs. He could break my hold if he wanted to, but he wouldn't. "Not here." I had to draw the line somewhere, and getting laid in Houston's grandmother's house seemed to be the perfect spot.

"Why?" He chuckled. "You think we haven't brought girls here before?" I didn't respond when I pushed him off of me. "What?" the idiot questioned with a genuinely bewildered look. "What did I say?"

"I don't care about the girls you've fucked, so word of advice," I snapped as I sat up, "don't mention them to me."

Loren scrubbed his hand down his movie-star face before meeting my gaze. "I'm not thinking straight, baby, but can you blame me? It's been three months."

Yup.

That's right.

I haven't allowed them to do more than kiss me since Berlin. For Jericho, it's been longer. Five months to be exact.

I felt the truth of that throbbing between my legs, but I feigned indifference when I shrugged. "Big deal. I went six years without sex." I let my voice soften to a teasing note and hoped they heard the threat underneath. "Remember?"

"That was before *we* fucked you," Rich reminded me. I turned my head in time to see that his attention was no longer on his phone. He was watching me while a threat of his own rose in his eyes.

"Your point?"

Rich smiled like a predator warning off his prey. "You won't last six more days, much less six years.

"Is that a dare?" As soon as the words left my lips, I remembered a forgotten detail, an unfulfilled promise that I intended for them to keep. Turning to Loren, who was now lying on his elbow, I studied him. "There is a solution if you're feeling so hard up."

He perked a brow as he looked up at me.

"You said you're not particular about gender. I said no other women. The three of you made it *extremely* clear that this was a closed relationship when all I did was tell Xavier that blue was his color." Loren was still staring at me, giving me no indication that he was catching my drift. Huffing, I decided to spell it out for him. "We never made rules on what you do with each other."

I could dare Loren since he lost that race in Vancouver, but something told me I wouldn't have to. Loren and Rich had already crossed that line when they kissed. It happened so naturally, I had to wonder if it wasn't their first time.

I watched Loren's lips slowly spread before his attention shot over to Rich.

"Is it me, or was this her plan all along?" He shifted his gaze back to me before Rich could answer. "You didn't have to deprive us of your pussy to get what you want, baby fawn. Even if we hadn't fucked before, right here, in this very bed you're sitting on," he said, dropping more than one bomb without preamble, only pointed pauses, "we still would have given you high doses of whatever the fuck you want. Houston, too, though it's not his thing."

Rising from the bed, Loren took my chin between his fingers once he was on his feet and tilted my head back.

"He already threatened to top me if I don't behave. Did you know that?" he teased.

I shook my head.

"I'm almost excited to see him try if it gets you as wet as I'm sure you are right now."

Loren was right.

I was ruining my panties with each word he spoke.

"Rich, get over here," he ordered without looking away from me.

I couldn't see him with Loren's body blocking my view, but I heard the sheets on the twin bed rustle and his soft footsteps on the wooden floor. A moment later, Jericho stood next to Loren while they both towered over me.

Loren turned his head, meeting Jericho's gaze, and gave him another order. "Kiss me."

Heat enflamed my stomach when neither of them hesitated.

Their lips crashed together with a desperation that wasn't there the first time I witnessed them together. Loren's hand left my face when he used it to pull Rich closer. They weren't shy about using their tongues either or as careful with each other as they were with me.

Loren pulled away first, and the dominance in his gaze sent an excited chill down my spine. Admittedly, I was also a little jealous of Rich. This time he'd get to feel it instead of me.

"You remember how I like it, don't you?"

The drummer nodded at Loren's softly spoken question and slowly reached for his belt. He knew what his best friend wanted and didn't have to be told twice. They started kissing again, teasing each other with their lips as Rich shoved his hand down Loren's jeans.

I knew the moment he wrapped his hand around Loren's cock. The shudder Loren released mingled with my whimper at not being able to see as Rich stroked him inside his jeans.

Loren started to yank the buttons on his crisp, white shirt free while staring coldly at his best friend. "I'm hard, Noble. You can stop toying with my dick like a virgin now and get on your knees. I want that pretty little mouth."

Rich didn't respond as he roughly shoved Loren onto the bed next to me. The bassist was lying on his back and looking at me now, lust clouding his black gaze as Rich dropped to his knees in my peripheral. "Come here, baby."

I went to him without question, and our lips crashed together with a hungry moan from us both. We were still kissing when Loren shuddered moments later and released my lips suddenly with an, "Ah, fuck."

My gaze shot to the edge of the bed where Rich was kneeling between Loren's legs with his mouth full of his best friend's cock.

I'd teased them with the idea but seeing it unfold before me… seeing Loren and Rich gaze into each other's eyes while they gave and took pleasure from one another…

Rich was right.

I wouldn't last six more days.

I wasn't sure I'd make it six more minutes.

"Fuck, I forgot how good you were at this," Loren said with a groan as he tossed his head back.

His abs contracted each time Rich deep throated him—something I hadn't been able to master yet—and each time, I felt my control slip and fought the urge to touch myself or beg one of them to do it. I wanted to fuck, and I wanted to be fucked, but right now, only my need to watch them together mattered.

"Braxton." It was hard forcing myself to look away from Rich's bobbing head and Loren's thrusting hips as he gripped inky black hair and fucked his mouth. "There should be lube in the nightstand," Loren informed me when our eyes finally met. "Get it for me, baby."

Nodding, I crawled to the nightstand between the twin beds. I didn't dare stand. My legs wouldn't support me.

Yanking open the drawer, I found the lube and returned to my boyfriends with it in tow. Loren took the bottle from me and his dick from Rich before sitting up. I didn't miss the regret in Loren's eyes as he brushed the messy black strands from his best friend's forehead while looking down at him.

"I'm sorry," Loren whispered out of the blue.

Rich's lips parted, telling me he was just as surprised as me though maybe not as in the dark. His silver gaze shot over to me, and then he gulped when I saw the guilt in them.

It was then that I knew what Loren meant and why Jericho now look worried about my reaction.

Loren was apologizing for Emily.

He'd sabotaged his best friend's marriage, and until now, he hadn't felt remorse. Rather than anger or jealousy, I felt relief. There was only hope for this next step forward blooming in my chest. I didn't want her hanging over their heads or standing between them anymore.

I smiled at Rich and nodded as a single, happy tear slipped. I was not about this new crying life.

"It's okay," Rich whispered back. "I forgave you a long time ago."

Only now, Loren deserved it.

Rich lifted at the same time that Loren leaned down, and they shared another kiss. This one was tender, making me wonder if there might one day be room for more than just friendship and attraction between them. Neither of them saw my devious smile as they continued to kiss.

They both stood, and I got comfortable on my stomach with my feet up and my chin in my palms as I watched them undress each other. It was like I wasn't even here, and I was okay with that.

I felt like a voyeur.

"We haven't forgotten about you," Rich warned me, bursting my bubble as he sauntered fully naked now over to the bed.

I couldn't even focus on the threat because I was too busy studying every dip and hard ridge that made up his body. He was the leanest of the three, but the natural definition of his muscles and abs was no less impressive.

And then there was that monster between his legs.

What he lacked in muscle, he more than made up for with his cock.

I flooded my panties at the thought of feeling him inside of me again as he lifted me onto my knees and disposed of my dress.

"Rich—"

"Shh. I just want to feel you," he reassured me before his lips quirked. "It's been a while, and I've only done this once. I might need the distraction."

I heard what sounded like a top popping open and looked over his shoulder to see Loren squirting lube into his palm as he stared at Rich with nothing but lust and intent.

Oh.

Well, in that case.

I let Rich undress me until I was as naked as them. He then maneuvered me until I was lying on my side with my back flush against the wall to make as much room on the narrow twin for him and Loren. I was facing him when he joined me on the bed.

"I love you," he whispered to me as we kissed.

I sighed my response, feeling the words on my lips and in my heart but still unsure whether to offer them just yet. I felt the bed dip, and Rich deepened the kiss as I pressed my naked body to his front to distract him from what Loren was about to do.

Jericho's hard cock was pressed against my belly, and I squirmed at the temptation to beg him to put it inside of me. I couldn't. If only for one more night, I couldn't. I didn't want to miss a second of them.

Loren was now spooning Rich from behind, and since I couldn't resist the sight of them pressed together so intimately, I broke the kiss long enough to steal a peek. Loren smiled at me, and I couldn't help but smile back. It wasn't until Rich tensed and groaned in my arms that I realized what Loren was up to.

I hadn't noticed his hand.

Or his long fingers probing the muscled globes of Rich's ass.

The sight transfixed me, my lips parting when I felt Jericho's tongue teasing my nipple as I watched. He wasn't supposed to be touching me, but at this moment, I could deny him whatever he needed no more than my next breath. I could try, but eventually, inevitably, I'd give in or perish.

"Jericho." I sighed.

He couldn't answer me.

His groans were coming more often now as Loren fucked him harder with his fingers. I could hear the sound of him dipping in and out of Rich's ass thanks to the lube and squirmed when the need became too much.

"Would you like me to fuck him now?"

My gaze shot back to Loren, and the wicked gleam in his eye made my toes curl. "Yes, please."

"Of course, baby."

Loren pressed closer to Rich, who was still suckling at my nipple, and produced a condom from…somewhere. He quickly sheathed himself and then pushed his thick cock head between Rich's cheeks.

"Braxton," Rich called to me.

I immediately went to him. Our lips met, and I was his.

But he belonged to Loren now too.

I knew it when Rich practically ran to me to flee Loren when he started pushing into him. I held his face between my hands as I kissed his lips repeatedly to try to distract him from the pain. My eyes opened the tiniest bit, and I could see Loren's hips flexing whenever he worked another inch inside of Rich.

He was staring down at his best friend as he burrowed himself deeper. The lust and desire written on Loren's face were so palpable I clung to Rich in order to keep my fingers from finding my clit.

"Do you remember how it was?" Loren asked as he continued to work himself inside. "Do you remember how good it felt?"

It seemed to take all of Rich's strength to break our kiss and open his eyes. Looking over his shoulder, he met Loren's gaze. "Yes."

"Good." Loren wrapped his arm around Rich's waist. "Me too." It was the drummer's only warning before Loren shoved his cock to the hilt.

"Oh, fuck," Rich barked. He tried to run, but Loren held him still. There was nowhere for him to go sandwiched between us anyway. "Fuck you, man. Fuck you."

Loren's only response was to groan from the feeling of being buried deep inside his best friend. "This ass is mine, Noble."

Resigned to let Loren have his way, Rich's head fell helplessly to the bed. I rubbed his toned arm, trying to soothe him as best as I could while Loren pumped lazily in and out of him.

"How does it feel?" I whispered to Rich.

It was Loren who answered, though. Jericho was too far gone. "You'll find out soon enough."

His daunting tone, coupled with the unyielding look he gave me, made my teeth sink into my bottom lip. Loren began thrusting faster and the sound of his hips meeting Jericho's ass filled the small room as he pounded him.

He held my gaze the entire time he took Jericho from behind.

I was as much a part of this as the two of them.

So much so I forgot to object when Loren yanked my leg over Rich's hip, opening me up for him.

"Finger her pussy," he ordered Jericho.

Eyes still closed while Loren used him, Rich blindly obeyed. His fingers fumbled around before finding my soaked entrance and immediately plunging two of them inside.

"Yes," I cried out as he fucked me while Loren fucked him.

Soon after, my eyes drifted closed against my will, and I was left with only the feeling of Rich's fingers, the sound of Loren's grunts and Jericho's groans, the taste of cherries on my tongue, and the smell of morning dew and berries.

The small bed rocked beneath us, making the headboard bang the wall relentlessly as we found the perfect rhythm and rode it. I briefly worried it might break, but then Jericho's thumb began circling my clit, and the only thing that mattered was the orgasm cresting. I felt what must have been Loren's hand push between us and then him stroking Rich's cock.

"You're going to come for me," he said to Rich. There was a pause and then, "Open your eyes."

The way my body responded told me that the second command was meant for me. Letting my eyes slowly open, I found them both watching me, waiting for me to come even as they fucked each other. My breasts were smashed against Jericho's chest as Loren's thrusts became so forceful our bodies moved together as if the three of us were one.

I was the first to come.

I didn't think to temper my cries.

I couldn't think of anything else but the shock wave seizing my body. It took some time, an eternity it seemed, and then, I was finally spent.

Rich splintered apart with a choked sound, and I felt his warm seed splashing my belly as I stared into his gray eyes.

Loren wasn't far behind.

His movements became less and less controlled until he shoved inside Rich one last time and filled the condom with a groan.

There was only our heavy breathing after he was done. That... and the sound of the front door slamming shut.

Houston and his grandmother had returned.

𝄞

Could Houston hear my heart pounding?

I felt like I was sweating bullets each time he studied me closely. Loren, Rich, and I had rushed to clean up, get dressed, and make our way to the front of the house as if nothing had happened. Laine was too busy starting dinner to notice the tension and our ruffled appearance, but Houston was right on our trail.

I *knew* he wouldn't appreciate me having sex in his grandmother's house the first time he brought me over. Or ever.

Yup.

Never having sex here would have been better.

I couldn't even blame anyone but myself since it had been my idea to goad Loren and Rich into having sex.

Unable to take the heat, I got the hell out of the kitchen and made my way to the bathroom. I splashed water on my face and once again tried fixing my hair. Once I accepted that it wouldn't get any better, I finally left the bathroom only to run into Houston waiting for me. He was leaning against the wall across the hall with his hands in his pockets.

"Have fun?"

I fidgeted on the threshold. "I-I um—"

He walked toward me, and I stopped speaking immediately. I stared up at him while he towered over me, but I refused to cower even when I was in the wrong.

"You wait until I'm gone to end the hiatus? Tell me why I shouldn't be pissed."

"Wait…*that's* what you're upset about?"

"What else would I be upset about?"

"This is your grandmother's house, Houston."

"You do realize I was raised here, right? I spent my teenage years in this house. You didn't do anything I haven't done a million times. Besides, she wasn't here." He then glowered at me. "Neither was I."

"We didn't have sex." I paused. "Well, *I* didn't." I paused again when I remembered that I wasn't entirely innocent. "It was my idea, though."

Houston's brows rose, but he didn't comment on what I'd told him. Loren and Rich fucking wasn't news to him. Houston simply took my hand and then led me down the hall to his bedroom. I immediately looked around even though I saw it briefly during the tour hours ago. Unlike Loren and Rich, Houston had a queen bed situated between two windows. He also had a desk that I tried to picture him sitting at while studying for a test or writing a school paper.

"Have a seat," he ordered after closing the door.

Instead of doing so, I watched him walk over to the dresser and pull open the top drawer. He then looked over his shoulder, and when he saw me still standing, he stared.

Hearing his silent command, I walked over to the bed and sat on the edge.

Why had he brought me in here?

It wasn't that I minded being alone with him in his childhood bedroom. It was just that I couldn't help noticing the tension lining his shoulders and back.

Maybe this was when the other shoe dropped, and he told me he had a wife and kid too. I didn't know what I'd do then, but I knew it wouldn't be good.

Have faith, the angel on my shoulder whispered.

Unfortunately, the devil who was never far away still felt a little raw and wasn't in the mood today. *Shut. The fuck. Up.*

Houston quickly found what he was looking for and came to join me on the bed. I frowned when I realized what he held and even more when he handed it to me. I hesitated only until I glimpsed the words printed in bold at the top of the newspaper clipping.

DOUBLE SUICIDE PARALYZES PORTLAND
March 9, 2004 / The Portland Pioneer

Married couple Jake Morrow, 32, and Susan Morrow, 31, were pronounced dead yesterday afternoon. The famed duo died from an overdose on antidepressants, which sources report had been prescribed to both victims. It is also rumored but has not been confirmed that the two were found in their home by their thirteen-year-old son, Houston Morrow.

I stopped reading.

It took a few deep breaths before I could bring myself to look at him. Houston was staring at the cut-out portion of the newspaper with no expression. I knew better, though. I was inside his head like he was in mine. It seemed he needed to gather his emotions, too, before meeting my gaze.

"You found them?"

Slowly, he nodded before looking away like he was ashamed. He was reliving it, and he didn't want me to see. Standing from the bed, I stood between his legs and brought his eyes back to me.

"I'm sorry."

"Me too."

"Wh—why did they…" I gulped when I couldn't bring myself to ask why his parents killed themselves. What had been so terrible? They had to know Houston would be the one to find them, but it wasn't enough to make them stay.

I didn't want to hate his parents. I wanted to find solace that at least they were no longer in pain, and yet, looking at Houston, seeing his struggle to forgive them, I couldn't stop the burning smell plaguing my senses.

No.

Houston was the only one who had the right to be angry. Regardless of my feelings for their son, I had no right to judge them. I was only allowed sorrow—for them and Houston.

"I don't know," he answered, guessing at the question I was struggling to ask. "I feel like I never knew them at all. I can't remember them not smiling. Not even once. They were always laughing and finding reasons to sing and dance. Everyone knew them. Everyone. They were contagious. The wild parties they threw were popular in Portland." Houston shook his head before resting it against my belly. I ran my fingers through his brown hair. "All along, they were just distracting themselves, making sure they were never alone for long, even with each other. They kept themselves surrounded to keep from giving in to the pain, and I'll never know what caused it. No one will."

Because Jake and Susan were like so many others, both living and dead. They were the kind who never let anyone see that they were sad. Not until it was too late. Not until they were gone.

"It hasn't stopped me from trying to figure it out, though," he admitted after a while. "I wanted to know why so I could understand, but I've only been left with fears and assumptions. Had too much happened? Did they lose control and let the bad outweigh the good? They were so young when they had me. Maybe I was the reason their life didn't turn out how they hoped. Maybe I pushed them to do it."

I quickly climbed into his lap so that we were eye level and held his face in my hands so that he couldn't look away. "Houston, *no*. Your parents chose to leave you with memories of them happy because those were the ones they wanted you to have. *They loved you*. I wish that it had been enough, but you were the reason they held on as long as they could. I know it like I know the last thing they want is for you to blame yourself."

I was sucked in by the vortex his gaze created. His eyes were so green, and I wondered if it was because he stored all of his emotions there, hiding them in plain sight. I've called him an overbearing brute and controlling asshole, and I was almost sorry for it now that I knew the reason. He didn't want to end up like his parents. He didn't want the people he cared about to either. Now Houston would have to figure out a way to overcome that fear, and I was more than ready to help him. I knew Loren and Rich were too.

"You don't have to forgive them today," I told him when he seemed to struggle with words, "or even tomorrow. But one day, when you're ready, I think your parents would like that. I think you would like it too."

Houston mulled it over for a moment before simply nodding. He was quiet when he fell back on the mattress and took me with him. He held me on his chest and in his arms while I listened to his complicated heart beat. We didn't speak a word for the rest of the night, and we didn't leave his room. Eventually, we fell asleep together, missing the dinner his grandmother had no doubt slaved over. Laine, Loren, and Rich must have known because no one had the heart to knock on the door.

SIXTY-FOUR

Braxton

HOUSTON WAS TWENTY-NINE TODAY.

For that reason alone, I was awake before dawn. I was planning to bake his favorite cake with Laine's help, and I wanted it to be ready and back before he was up.

Birthday cake for breakfast sounded like a good way to start any Sunday.

We'd only been back in Portland for a few days, and it was eerie how quickly I'd adjusted to their surroundings. I wouldn't dare say that out loud, though, and risk the conversation of me moving in returning.

They'd forgotten it for now, but I knew better than to think it wouldn't come up again. We'd only been together six months and already had one break up under our belt.

I think my point had been made that it was too soon.

They wouldn't care, though, so yeah…I was bracing myself for that argument again.

After kissing Houston's lips gently, I carefully untangled myself from his arms.

He didn't stir.

Last night, I had an ulterior motive when I broke my ban on sex. I knew they'd take all of their frustrations out on me. I knew they'd wear themselves out in the process. Even I had to fight my sore muscles and the fatigue begging me for a few hours more when I crawled out of bed. I was pressed for time, but when

I stood, I couldn't help but lean against one of the bedposts to watch them sleep.

My bad boy.

My vain princess.

My sad emo.

The three of them slept soundly. Loren had his face buried in Jericho's neck as he spooned him from behind with a strong arm curled around his naked waist. It wasn't how they'd gone to sleep, so the two of them must have found each other at some point.

I smiled.

Loren claimed he wasn't one to cuddle.

Jericho and I had both proven him wrong.

After looking my fill at the three of them in all their naked glory, I turned to shower and dress as quietly as I could. I then tiptoed downstairs, lifted Houston's car keys from the foyer's entry table, and made my way to the detached garage.

As I was climbing inside his G-Wagon, I admired Jericho's green and black bike. Maybe I'd convince him to teach me one day. I also put it on my mental checklist to ask why Loren didn't have a car and why Houston and Rich never let him drive. To be fair, he never offered, and they seemed to be fine with that.

I plugged his grandmother's address into my phone's GPS since I didn't know my way around yet before pulling out. The device attached to the visor opened both the garage doors and the front gate, so I was on the road just a few minutes later, and nearly an hour later, I'd arrived.

The street was quiet, and the sun wasn't fully up yet when I climbed out of the SUV with my phone unlocked and in my hand.

Hoping Laine hadn't forgotten that I was coming this early, I was debating whether to call or simply knock on her door when I heard my name softly spoken.

Apprehension rippled through me before I could even turn to face the person who'd posed my name like a question. I didn't recognize the petite girl now standing in the driveway.

Where had she come from?

Even in the semi-dark, I could see that she was a few years

older even though she looked young. And her hair wasn't just platinum. It was stark white, a color that could only be accomplished with dye. She had pale skin and piercings in her nose and lips, but what gave me pause wasn't that I didn't know her.

It was yesterday's eyeliner.

I knew because even though she'd applied it with a heavy hand, it had smudged and was starting to fade.

I couldn't help my frown or care how it would be perceived.

Had she been here all night?

The dark hood she wore over her head didn't conceal the evil intent in her eyes even as she smiled up at me with her hands behind her back.

"You're Braxton Fawn, right?"

Only then did I realize I'd never responded.

"Who wants to know?"

She brought her thin arms around, showing me the bat she carried. I backed up a step, but it was too late.

"Emily," she cheerily supplied. She barely finished speaking her name before she brought the bat up and swung.

The first thing I lost was my feet when the bat connected with my head. I hit the ground with a cry, and that was the last thing I heard when my hearing went next.

I could feel the first crack in my skull and my blood running down my forehead, though. She hit me again and my cheek connected with the concrete with a hard smack. I didn't question how I could turn my head and see that her lips were still spread.

Emily's smile never wavered.

It was also the last thing I saw when she took my vision with her third swing. The bat connected and I finally, mercifully, lost consciousness too.

SIXTY-FIVE

Rich

IT SOUNDED LIKE FIREWORKS OR A CAR BACKFIRING.

I almost went back to sleep with an annoyed exhale until I remembered we lived too deep in the woods. Whatever made that sound had been too loud and too close.

"What was that?" Houston asked. He'd woken up too.

"I don't know," I answered with a tired shake of my head. My eyes were still closed.

"Then how about you both go back to sleep before you wake Braxton?" Loren grumbled in my neck as he hugged me tighter from behind. I could feel his morning wood, but sex was the last thing on my mind.

If Loren was awake, that means he'd heard it too.

Houston and I weren't imagining things.

My eyes drifted open for the first time to see if Braxton was awake and wondering the same thing.

The spot where she'd slept between Houston and me was empty.

"She's not here," I said more to myself than to them as my heart began to race.

Having noticed, too, Houston was already up, grabbing his phone, and heading for the door. "Get the fuck up," he barked at us both.

I threw Loren's arm from around my waist, got up, and snatched a pair of pants—I didn't care whose—from the floor as I went. Loren was right behind me, though he'd settled for the sheet wrapped around his waist.

Houston was already coming out of the bathroom when we stepped into the hall. For the first time, I cursed the size of this house. There was no sound now to tell us where to look next, and there were too many options to choose from.

"Braxton!" I shouted when I couldn't think clearly enough to figure out where she would go. Our exhaustion had made it too hard to sense before, but now we were all too painfully aware.

Something was wrong.

Why was Braxton even up this early?

As soon as my mind formed the question, I remembered.

Today was Houston's birthday.

She'd wanted to bake a cake.

My limbs were getting heavier, too heavy, as we raced down the stairs. I was nothing more than a block of ice by the time we reached the ground floor. Or maybe I was trapped inside of one.

Maybe she hadn't left yet.

We rushed into the kitchen to check there first and came to a dead halt. The last person we expected to see was sitting on the island, swinging her short legs while she waited.

"Baby!" she squealed when our eyes connected.

I closed mine a second later.

How the *hell* was she here?

We didn't buy this place until long after she'd disappeared. Emily wouldn't know where to find us, much less how to get inside the gates. She'd need the code or the device, which she had neither.

"What the fuck kind of fatal attraction, soap opera, *Days of our Lives* bullshit are you on?" Loren snapped. "I don't even want to know how you found us or why you're here. Just get the hell out."

My eyes opened when I heard what sounded like Emily's feet hitting the ground. She was thinner than I remembered, and where there had once been mischief in her eyes, there was now only malice.

"You chased me for years," she pointed out while ignoring

Loren. "Now that I'm here, you want me to go? Sorry, I don't think so."

"Where's his kid?" Houston asked her. "Since you're well aware that's who he was looking for."

Emily glowered at him before turning to me. "You're still letting them speak for you, I see."

"What do you want?" I demanded, speaking up for the first time. I still hadn't recovered from seeing Emily and finding her in our house.

Where the hell was Braxton?

"I want to give us another chance," she answered as she kept coming closer, "and I know you do too. I know you still love me."

Loren snorted.

"It's too late for that, Em. I—we—we're divorced."

"Why do you think she's here?" Loren mused out loud. "She knows that already." The asshole couldn't mind his business for two goddamn minutes.

"Yeah, but so what?" Emily challenged. "He still loves me."

To fuck with Loren, she reached up and wrapped her thin arms around my neck. I saw my best friend stiffen out of the corner of my eye. I knew if I didn't push her away soon, he'd fling her ass across the room.

It wouldn't just be for Braxton, though.

It'd be for him too.

Loren was jealous of Emily then, despite his claims, and he was still jealous of her now.

I removed her arms from around my neck and took a step back. "Leave," I told her. "And don't come back unless it's with my kid."

"If there even is a kid," Loren couldn't help adding.

I gave him a look to shut the fuck up already. I could handle Emily all on my own. Loren made sure to sigh as loud as he could before closing his goddamn mouth. Finally.

"Can we talk in private?" Emily requested.

"It's been five years. You had the chance to talk and work things out, but you chose to run away. I'm not interested in what you have to say anymore. Not unless it's about my kid." I searched her eyes. "Where is he?" Or her. I didn't care as long as I got to be in their life. I didn't want to miss another day.

"Jericho," she said while letting the tear she'd drummed up teeter on her lower lash before rolling down her cheek. I was immune to them now, but she didn't know that, so I let her play her little mind games. "It was very hard when I left. I was scared of what you might do if the baby wasn't yours. I didn't want to lose you, so I..."

"You what," I snapped. I could barely hear my voice or thoughts over the roaring in my head.

"I didn't have it." She shifted on her feet as she looked everywhere but at me. "I-I got an abortion."

"Then tell me," I started as I backed her into the island behind her. I could feel my control slip to the point of no return. It was her body, so it was her decision, but I was pissed as hell that she let me chase her all that time for no reason at all. I stopped wanting Emily the second I found out she cheated. My only reason to stay had been my kid. "Why *the fuck* are you are here?"

"Because I lo—"

"You used me!" I exploded before she could finish. I didn't want to hear those words from her. It only reminded me that I was still waiting to hear them from Braxton. I knew she felt it, but she wasn't done making us sorry. I once told her if she wanted our respect she'd have to make us listen. She was *literally* taking my advice to heart. "You preyed on my weaknesses to get what you wanted, and then you threw me away when I got a damn clue. How the hell is that love?"

"Is that what they told you?" she snapped, referring to Houston and Loren.

I chuckled as I looked off. After five years of hunting her down, it was amazing how little I gave a shit now. All I wanted was to get Emily out of my sight so that I could find Braxton.

I didn't care.

I just...I didn't give a damn.

None of it mattered anymore.

Emily didn't matter anymore.

There was no baby, which would have been my only tie to her. I was equally relieved and disappointed. I didn't know how to feel about not being a father, after all. I just knew that as far as Emily was concerned...I was free.

I wanted to find Braxton and celebrate. Maybe put a baby in her instead.

Yeah...

I liked that idea so much more.

"Thanks for stopping by, Emily. Let me show you the door." I turned away to do just that.

"Show me the—wait...are you kidding me?" she screeched, forcing me to face her again. "That's it? You're kicking me out?"

"Yup," Houston and Loren said at the same time. "See ya."

She curled her lip at them. I couldn't believe I once thought she was beautiful. She was attractive still, but I wasn't attracted. Honestly, I didn't understand how she ever got my dick hard in the first place.

My ex-wife was evil as fuck.

"Jericho—"

"Not interested," I cut her off.

"Well, I'm not leaving."

I sighed and looked at my friends, dismissing Emily altogether. I didn't even care enough to force her out. "Have either of you tried calling Braxton?"

I knew she must have been at Laine's by now, but Emily being here had me paranoid and on edge. We never did figure out the noise that woke us or how Emily had found us or even gotten through the gate.

Wordlessly, Houston lifted his phone. He'd been the only one smart enough to grab his.

I started to pace as he dialed Braxton. Emily didn't say a word, and surprisingly, neither did Loren. I was still walking back and forth when my gaze caught the damage on the wall near the entrance.

Was that a hole?

Just as I headed toward it to inspect it closer, the sound of a phone ringing filled the room.

It sounded like Braxton's.

"What the fuck?" Loren barked.

Turning to face them, I found Emily holding Loren at gunpoint while waving Braxton's phone in the air.

"As I was saying," she taunted, "I'm not going anywhere."

The look Loren gave me told me he was more annoyed at the inconvenience than afraid for his life. "I told you not to marry her."

"Shut up! Just shut up!" Emily screamed. "This is all your fault! You ruined everything!" She walked up to him with a vicious smile. "So how about I kill you first? You can join your little slut and rest in pieces."

The irritation left's Loren's face until there was nothing left.

Only the sheet of ice that seemed to cover the room.

"Where is she? What did you do?" Houston asked her calmly.

I knew he was anything but calm. We were all just biding our time. The problem with Emily was that she was too damn sure she already had the upper hand. Gun or no gun, there were three of us and one of her. She'd turned her back on me, and now we already had her surrounded.

Loren would take that bullet if he had to.

For Braxton.

For us.

I just prayed it didn't come to that.

"In hell by now, I suppose. I bashed her skull in and left her bleeding."

I felt my knees buckle at her announcement.

The breath that rushed out of my chest caused me to tremble violently.

What Emily was telling us couldn't be true. No way Braxton was dead. It wasn't possible. My heart wouldn't continue to beat even for a moment after hers stopped. I believed it so much I held on to that irrational hope.

"Sweet ride she was driving too," Emily continued to taunt.

"I'm sure she wouldn't mind that I borrowed it considering she's dead and all."

"Emily," Loren said with a humorless chuckle. He smiled at the ceiling, and I knew he was close to losing it. "Pull that trigger right now, and hope you kill me."

I knew it wasn't simply a threat.

He wanted to die.

If Braxton were truly dead, neither of us would live longer than it took to get our revenge.

"You should kill us all," I told her. She turned to face me like I knew she would. The gun was no longer on Loren. It was pointed at me where it belonged. "If you don't, there will be nowhere you can run. You thought I was relentless before? I won't stop, I won't rest, and I won't eat until I've buried you, bitch."

"Tell us where she is," Houston advised her. "Give yourself a head start."

"I don't believe you," she told me while ignoring my friends. "You won't let them hurt me over *her*. It's obvious you love me more."

I tilted my head to the side. There wasn't anger in my tone when I spoke. Just genuine bafflement and curiosity. "Why is that?"

"Because you would have never shared me with them. I make you jealous. She doesn't."

"Yet he wouldn't hesitate to push you in front of a train," Loren deadpanned.

"Not to mention," Houston added, "I would rather stick my dick in a garbage disposal."

She switched her aim to Houston, who didn't flinch, but I did. I didn't want my friends to be hurt over my mistakes. I might have already lost Braxton. I couldn't handle losing them too.

"I didn't love you." Emily kept her gun trained on Houston as she cut her gaze toward me. "I was in love with filling a void, and you were the only one willing. You used me, but I used you too," I said, recalling Braxton's confession about Jacob Fried. I now understood why she wasn't convinced she was wholly innocent. Emily and I had destroyed each other in vain, searching for what was never there. "I lied, I stole, and I hurt people for you, but it was never enough because I wasn't enough. There were limits to what I would do for you, and you were too empty to fill my cup."

Emily's hand shook when she aimed the gun my way again. I gave Houston and Loren a look not to say another goddamn word. I couldn't risk them. I wouldn't.

"And you think Braxton will complete you?" She scoffed with a sardonic laugh.

"She already has."

That made her smile drop.

I could see the hysteria in her eyes rising even as she fought to retain control. "You gave me limits, but how far are you willing to go for her, Jericho? Are you willing to die?"

She thought she was taunting me, testing me, and putting me in my place. Emily truly didn't know me anymore.

"Yes." There was no hesitation. "Tell them where to find her. Let them go, and then pull the trigger."

I kept my gaze on Emily, but I could see Houston and Loren shift. I knew they were looking at each other and silently forming a plan. Because they hadn't given in to the inevitable yet—the truth that there was only one way we were getting to Braxton.

One of us would have to go down.

"I cannot believe you," Emily said as tears, real tears, fell. "*I* was there for you! She wasn't! You were supposed to love me."

"That's not her fault, Em. It's mine. I should have waited. Braxton was out there, but I was too busy pretending with you."

"Pretending? Oh, yeah? Well, she's dead now, so you can go be with that bitch."

I wasn't looking at Emily when she aimed for my heart. I was staring at my friends and memorizing their faces as they rushed to stop Emily before she could pull the trigger.

Too late.

SIXTY-SIX

Braxton

WHERE WAS I?

Everything hurt. Everything.

I slowly lifted my hand and whimpered my frustration when it seemed to take all of my energy and concentration too.

Had it always been this hard?

I didn't think so.

My eyes were still closed, and I didn't want to open them. I couldn't be sure of what I'd find. I was slowly becoming aware of all the telltale signs—the beeping machines, the antiseptic, the bed underneath me, the bandaging my stiff fingers found wrapped around my head, and the sensor clamped on my finger.

Hospital.

I was in a hospital.

And I couldn't remember why.

I searched for my name. Another sound of distress, louder now, ripped from me when I couldn't find it.

"Baby?" a voice croaked. It was masculine, cultured, and full of disbelief. Or was that hope? He sounded a little groggy, too, like he'd been sleeping. Had I woken him?

I know you.

But I didn't know me.

I recognized his voice, but I couldn't remember his name.

Or mine.

"Braxton?" This voice was different—melodious and strong. I recognized him too. He'd make a wonderful vocalist.

And now I knew my name.

Braxton.

I was Braxton.

How did I get here?

Why was I here?

I listened to the chairs scrape the floor when they hurriedly rose, and then their soft footfalls coming closer as I waited for the answer that never came. I fell asleep before they could reach me, and I welcomed the darkness.

Being awake was just too hard.

A baby was crying.

I frowned and flinched when the sound reached a high-pitch. It pierced my bruised skull and already aching brain. I couldn't stop my groan.

"Why don't you take Braxen out into the hall until he settles?" my mother suggested immediately after.

My heart started racing at the sound of her voice. I quickly grabbed for her name and rejoiced when it came. Amelia Fawn.

My mother's name was Amelia, and she was here.

"Okay," my sister said with a reluctant sigh. I heard her stand and quickly leave with her baby.

Rosalie.

My baby sister had come. She'd had her son a few months ago, and she named him after me.

I remembered.

Or at least…I was starting to.

I still didn't know why or how long I'd been here.

My lips quivered at the possibilities. My muscles tensed, ice crept up my fingertips, goose bumps peppered my skin, and my heart pounded so hard it made my chest hurt.

I couldn't be sure of what any of it meant, though.

Because the phantom smell of copper that always told me

when I was afraid was missing. Nothing lingered in the air as my body tried to warn me of my rising panic.

Nothing at all.

So I passed out again.

"Braxton?" my mother called out to me. She was still here, and I was once again wondering how long it had been.

I didn't answer right away.

I was too busy trying to recall basic motor functions like opening my eyes.

They'd never felt so heavy.

Eventually, I managed to force my lids to part, only to snap them shut again to shield them from the bright light.

"I'll get the doctor," my father announced before leaving the room.

He was here too? I thought he hated me. I didn't know how I felt about his presence because there were no tastes or smells to tell me.

I whimpered.

I didn't understand this new reality, but I also wasn't sure if I wanted to go back. It was too soon to tell.

One step at a time.

I forced my eyes open again and kept them pried.

Who died?

It was my first thought when I looked around the room.

There were flowers.

Everywhere.

All different kinds.

No roses, though, thank God.

The hospital room looked like a florist shop. What the hell? My mother smiled down at me, unaware of where my attention was fixed and the confusion marring my brow.

"Welcome back, Braxton."

"W—" I swallowed when I found speech difficult. Why was

my mouth so dry? As soon as I lifted my head, the room began to spin, so I forced it back onto the pillow, closed my eyes, and waited for the dizziness to pass.

"It's okay. Take your time," my mother coaxed. "You've been out of it since yesterday morning."

Hearing that I'd only lost a day helped a little, but it wasn't enough. I still couldn't remember what happened or why. All I had to go on was how much it hurt.

So much, I wondered how I was still alive.

"You were attacked," Mom finally told me. I looked into her brown eyes and saw the tear that fell. "Someone found you and brought you here."

Those words immediately sparked a memory.

A flash of white hair, a bat, the smiling face of a stranger, and a name I knew but couldn't recall.

I tried to sit up.

Fuck. Too fast.

It felt like my brain was pushing against my broken skull. I cried out in pain before lying back down.

"Braxton, you have to take it easy," my mother scolded. "You almost died." When my eyes slowly opened once more, I took in my mother in her Sunday finest. "I almost lost you."

It sounded like a plea to not scare her again, and I paused.

She actually cared?

It was a cruel thought, but a true one. I honestly didn't believe she would.

"I'm…sorry."

It was the best I could do so soon after gaining consciousness.

I also couldn't think of a response that wouldn't hurt her the way she'd hurt me or disappoint her, as I'd done countless times before.

Amelia and I weren't just different.

We were opposing ends of an unbreakable spectrum.

Neither of us would budge.

"I know what you're thinking," she said as she rearranged

the bouquet on my bedside table. It was an excuse not to meet my eyes. "But you *are* my daughter, Braxton."

Just not the one you wanted.

I couldn't even nod without hurting my head, so I gave no reaction at all.

"You were too young to remember, but these were your favorite," she casually informed me. I watched her toy with the short, purple petals on the long stems. "We took you to so many doctors, heard so many opinions. No one could figure out what was wrong. Phantosmia was the best diagnosis they could give, but they couldn't figure out what was causing the symptom. We tried therapy, and they swore it was just a phase you'd grow out of someday, but you never did. We spent most of your childhood afraid we'd lose you, and we wouldn't know why." She looked at me briefly before she started to rearrange the stems again. "We're still afraid."

It was on my lips to tell her that she had no reason to be, but she kept talking, and I…I wanted to listen. Call me needy or vain, but I wanted to hear more of my mother as she admitted that she cared for me and always had despite our differences.

"It wore on you too," she told me. "You were always so frustrated, so confused. You stopped eating and couldn't bear to smell anything, real or imagined, pleasant or bad. Sometimes you'd cry, and sometimes you'd get angry. There were even times your blood pressure would skyrocket until you passed out." She took a deep breath before shaking her head and started rearranging those stems again. There were at least thirty more bouquets in the room, but she was focused on *this one*. "And then, one day, you vanished. We searched for hours, but you were simply gone. After a while, you gave us no choice but to think you ran away, harmed yourself, or worse…someone had taken you." Bringing one of the stems up, she sniffed the petals and smiled. "It was another day before we found you." She turned to me with an admonishing look. "You were sleeping in a field not far away as if nothing were amiss." She looked at the bouquet again. "A field full of these."

My eyebrows rose because I didn't remember that.

At all.

"You looked so still after so many restless nights that for a moment, I thought…" She loudly sighed when she struggled to find the words. "I thought you were dead, Braxton."

I winced at the weariness in her voice even now.

"We took you home," she continued. "But the next day, it started all over again—the crying and the fits. Whenever you were overwhelmed, afraid, confused, or hurting, you ran to that field. Even during the rare times that you were happy, you still went back. You always found a reason because you were never truly at peace unless surrounded by these. Sometimes we'd find you sleeping again. Other times you'd be singing, crying, dancing, or laughing for no reason at all. Your father didn't understand. He got so fed up that he threatened to send it up in flames. The last time he dragged you out of there, you begged and promised not to go back, but his mind was made up." She hesitated to tell me what I already knew. "He destroyed it."

I frowned, wishing I could manage more than that. I wanted to stand up. I wanted to scream. I wanted to rage. "If you knew," I struggled to get out, "what it meant to me… why didn't you… stop him?"

"It was his decision to make, Braxton, and you were so young. Anything could have happened to you."

I didn't react to my mother justifying her being too subservient to stop her husband from taking away my only solace because it inconvenienced him. I didn't react because I didn't have the energy for anger.

And because it wasn't new information.

"You told me why…after," she offered. I didn't care anymore, but I didn't have the heart to tell her, so I let her keep going. "You told me why you kept going back."

I didn't ask for the reason.

I didn't say anything at all.

I quietly waited for her to tell me on her own.

"Long before this all started, you fell in love with that field.

Sometimes, you'd beg us to drive by just so you could see it." She paused. "I suppose it makes sense that it was the only thing you could tolerate during such a terrible time."

She plucked one of the stems from the clear vase, but instead of putting it in a different spot to start her rearranging all over again, my mother came to stand by the bed with it clutched between her fingers.

"I'm guessing you don't remember how they smell?" she asked me.

I shook my head and immediately cursed the blinding pain that followed. My head started to pound, and I wanted to cry. Noticing my agony, my mother calmly waited, flower in hand, for it to pass.

Thanks to the garden in my room, I knew that I hadn't lost my sense of smell. Only the ability to feel my emotions through it. The scents from the different flowers blended together, however, making it impossible to separate and identify each one.

I wondered who had sent them.

I didn't think to ask a moment later when my mother stuck a stem from this particular flower under my nose, and I drew in its scent.

Earthy.

With a strong aroma like it had been plucked fresh from the meadow I had once loved but couldn't remember. I inhaled the breath of fresh air it inspired, but instead of drawing forth the forgotten memory of that field, I saw a face.

Regal lines, opaque eyes, perfect blond hair…and an arrogant tilt of his lips.

It faded too soon.

Before I could even remember his name.

Desperate, I used what little strength I had to snatch the stem from my mother who, honest to God, clutched the cross at her neck. I greedily inhaled the flower yet again, only this time, it summoned a different smell and another image.

Vanilla.

Rustic, mouthwatering, and warm when it wanted to be.

The face it conjured had a strong jaw, rigid mouth, brown hair, and intense green stare.

Just like before, I inhaled again.

Just like before, it gave me something different.

Berries.

Sweet, nourishing, and addicting.

I couldn't get enough once I had a taste.

It came with sad silver eyes, shaggy black hair, and the pinkest lips pierced.

Jericho.

My heart sighed his name, and the others immediately followed.

Houston.

Loren.

How could I have forgotten them? It may have only been a day, but even a moment was too long. I'd never forgive myself. I was even more desperate to see them now that I knew.

Lilac.

Love smells like lilac.

Love *is* lilac.

My head may have forgotten that field, but my heart hadn't. It had been trying to tell me all along. I'd found my haven all over again in three broken rock gods. When the world wrote off my pain, I could run to them and forget. They'd be my shelter, my peace, and my solace. I could sing, I could sleep, I could laugh, I could cry. In their arms, I could just be.

All I needed to know was why they weren't here now.

"Mom—"

The door opened, interrupting me before I could ask her about them. I felt my belly tighten and warm. Was it them?

"Ms. Fawn, you had quite the ordeal," the doctor greeted when he walked in with my father.

Sighing, I deflated against the mound of pillows before staring at the lilac stem in my hand.

Yeah.

No kidding.

SIXTY-SEVEN

Houston

IT WAS THIRTY-EIGHT DEGREES OUTSIDE, AND MY BALLS WERE FREEZING, but I stayed put out in the open and the blowing wind. I wanted to be sure we were the first thing Braxton saw when she was wheeled from the hospital.

It had been ten days since she ripped my heart from my chest. Her parents had kicked us out when they arrived, and there was nothing we could do when they forbade us from seeing her.

Braxton, always the merciless mind-fucker, kept her expression neutral as I took her in. She had bruising under her eyes and on her cheeks that were beginning to fade and wore the change of clothes we had Dani deliver thanks to Rosalie tipping us off that today was her sister's discharge date.

Eventually, Braxton tore her gaze away and lifted her head to say something to her mother.

When Mrs. Fawn immediately started to argue, we started forward. Amelia had no power outside of that hospital, and we weren't leaving here without her daughter.

Our only relief was the amusement in Braxton's gaze as her mother became more and more upset by the syllable. We were close enough now to clearly make out their conversation.

"They didn't have to tell me you banned them from seeing me, Mother. How would they? I know you. Better still, I know them."

"Braxton, I did what was best for you, and I will not apologize."

"No. You did what was best for *you*. If it had been about me, the support I needed, however much, would have outweighed your comfort."

It was clear whatever common ground the two had found over the last week and a half had ended.

"You've made it clear how you feel about my choices, Braxton, but if you don't have to apologize for who you are, why should I?"

Braxton nodded her agreement and then raised one truth with another. "Exactly. It was your choice. I've never tried to force my ideas on you, and I've never ostracized you for thinking differently than me."

"Is that what you call raising and protecting you?"

"I'm an adult now, Mom. What's your excuse?" Braxton asked her dryly.

"You told your sister to murder an innocent life when it goes against everything we've taught you both. *That's* my excuse."

"Mom." Braxton closed her eyes and kept them shut. "For the last time, I *never* told Rosalie to abort her baby. She knew what she wanted before she came to me. I didn't put those thoughts in her head or the words in her mouth. She spoke them all on her own. My only crime was offering to stand by her no matter what." Her eyes opened, and they met her mother's. "Something we both knew you'd fail to do."

"Rosalie's a child. She didn't know what she was saying."

"I considered that," Braxton told her while nodding again. "So I made sure I didn't sugarcoat a damn thing, and guess what, Mom? Rosalie never wavered. Not even once. Because she didn't want to be a wife and mother. She wanted to stay a kid. She wanted to grow up on her time. She wanted the chance to find herself." My baby gave her mother a withering look. "Clearly, the repercussions of having an abortion didn't scare her nearly as much as you."

Braxton stood from the wheelchair on shaky legs, but when we started forward to help her, she gave us a look to back the hell off. Loren and I held up our hands in surrender as we did just that.

"So congratulations, Mother. Your personal opinions just cost Rosalie her dreams, her childhood, the chance at true love, and the next eighteen years of her life. But as you pointed out, you made your choice, so why not make your daughter's too."

Braxton shrugged as if it didn't matter, but her eyes told a different story.

"I'm her mother. That is my job."

"No. It's your job to provide her safety, love, and support. And yes, help her find a direction. It is not your job to choose who she is, what she believes in, or how her future gets to be. That was always meant for Rosalie to decide when the time came." Braxton started to limp toward us when she stopped and turned back to her mother. "Spoiler alert—it's not at thirteen."

Loren had snuck up on Braxton when she turned toward us again and lifted her in his arms before she could object. She smiled at him, and it felt like a punch to the gut.

I'd missed that sight.

Braxton didn't bother to say goodbye to her mother when we turned to go, but clearly, Amelia wasn't done.

"You should take some responsibility, Braxton. This isn't all on your father and me. If you weren't such a whore despite all we've done to teach you, none of this would have happened to your sister. She looked up to you, and look where it got her."

Loren slowly turned with Braxton in his arms. I did too. She put her finger to his lips before he could say anything and then kissed them.

"Take me home," was all she said before laying her head on his chest.

Despite her cruel words, it didn't change the fact that Amelia had come to her daughter's side when she needed her most. Braxton would never forget that. At the moment, she was repaying her mother's short-lived kindness by protecting her from our wrath.

Loren started for my truck with her while I took one last look at Amelia Fawn. It was foolish to hope I would never see her ass again, but I couldn't help myself.

"Where's Jericho?" Braxton asked once we reached the G-Wagon.

Loren and I looked at each other, but neither of us said a word as he helped her into the back, and I climbed into the driver's seat. Braxton's gaze switched back and forth between us as she waited for the answer that we couldn't bring ourselves to give.

"Loren…"

He leaned down to gently kiss her lips before closing the door in her face. I made sure to keep my gaze forward as Loren climbed in the front seat, and then I peeled off out of the parking lot, heading toward home.

"You guys are both jerks."

It was all Braxton managed to get out before Jericho grabbed her and started tonguing her down with a groan right there in the doorway. "I missed you," he said to her, "and I'm so fucking sorry. So goddamn sorry."

Emily's aim hadn't been true.

She'd been so wrapped up in her misplaced anger and scorn that she ended up putting a bullet in the wall rather than his heart. Loren had wrestled the gun from her and kept her ass in check long enough for the cops to come. By then, my grandmother had called to tell us what had become of Braxton. Emily had been lucky the cops had already arrived, or she'd be buried out back rather than sitting in a jail cell.

I once threatened Braxton with the same, but back then, it had been just another mind game. I hadn't meant a word of it.

I couldn't say the same for Emily.

Loren and I left Jericho and Braxton where they were as we entered the house and looked around, taking in the banner, streamers, food, and drinks.

Jericho had stayed behind to oversee and finish setting up Braxton's welcome home party. The guest list was short, but it was more than we'd ever allowed inside our home before. We'd even invited Oni, who'd quit Savant recently and mysteriously, and was currently looking like a fish out of water while ensuring Xavier stayed on the far side of the room from her.

"Excuse me, but you're not the only one who was worried and missed Braxton," Griffin bitched as usual as she approached them.

"Why did we invite her again?" Loren whispered to me with his eyes on them.

I shrugged because I honestly didn't know. She was Braxton's best friend so…whatever. Maeko was busy chatting up Xavier while Griffin tried and failed to free Braxton from Jericho. The more she pulled, the harder he clung.

"Hey, cut that shit out," I finally barked when I had enough of their tug-of-war. Braxton had just been released from the hospital an hour ago. "Not so fucking rough with her."

Jericho finally let our girl go with a few last pecks and walked away. Braxton blushed and flashed me a quick smile before finally turning to Griffin.

While they talked, I found Loren and Rich in the kitchen standing on opposite sides of the island.

Loren was stuffing his face while Jericho peered into a brown box with Amazon tape. Dani, who must have checked the locker we used for our mail, had brought it with her when she showed up for the party.

"What the hell is this, Lo?"

Rich pulled out duct tape and rope, holding one in each hand as he stared at Loren.

"Oh, hey, it came!" With a mouth full of cupcake, Loren smiled wide as his opaque eyes glittered.

"What do you need two-hundred feet of tape and rope for?" I asked him after peering into the box and seeing more.

Loren was nonchalant now as he brushed his hands free of crumbs, leaving them on the counter instead. "Hopefully, you won't find out." While Rich and I gaped at him, Loren swiftly changed topics. "So, are you planning to tell Braxton about that shit you tried to pull?" he asked Jericho.

"I was thinking I'd let her enjoy her party and being home

first," Rich sniped sarcastically. He threw the tape and rope back into the box and pushed it toward me.

I knew all the best hiding spots.

"Right...*the party*. You just don't want her knowing you're as stupid as you look."

"I'm dumb," Rich returned with a sneer, "but you were sucking my dick two hours ago. Make it make sense, Lo."

Loren shrugged as he licked icing off his thumb while staring at our best friend. "I was excited and feeling generous because Braxton was coming home. Sue me."

Rich glowered at him while Loren flirted with his eyes.

Braxton ambled in a moment later, and our attention was stolen. The moment she was close enough, I lifted her and set her on the counter.

"How are you feeling?" I felt like a sap as I skimmed her cheek with my lips. I didn't care. She made me not care.

"Sore," she admitted on a mumble. "Weak. Mostly confused."

I lifted my head. "Confused?"

"I can't...I can't tell what I'm feeling." She looked at Loren, Rich, and then back at me. "Or if I'm feeling anything at all."

My hands found her thighs, and I began to caress her through her jeans, hoping to soothe when she started to shake. "What do you mean?"

"I can't tell when I'm scared or when I'm happy or excited. There are no smells or tastes to tell me. I've never learned how to identify my emotions without them. What if I've lost the ability to feel anything at all? I'm afraid—"

"Right there," I told her, cutting her off. "You're afraid. How do you know?"

"I..." She shook her head with a frustrated frown. "I don't know."

"Your emotions were never just a neurological response. It's also been about instinct. What's in your gut and what's in your heart. You don't have to think." I lifted her chin when she lowered her gaze. There was nothing for her down there. "You just have to feel. Your brain gave you an extra advantage that you've relied on until now, but you've always been a quick learner, Braxton. You'll figure this one out too." I kissed her. "We'll help you," I told her as Loren and Rich closed in.

They stole her attention, and she took her time kissing each of them before leaning back on her hands and smiling at us.

"Good, because I have something to tell you."

"What?" the three of us asked a little too eagerly.

She shook her head, and damn that teasing smile. It already did unspeakable things to me without the added suspense. "Later."

"You know, I've been thinking," Loren said.

Braxton, Rich, and I groaned before he had the chance to say more.

Loren thinking was never a good thing since it usually involved him igniting the flame and setting the world on fire.

"What's up?" Rich reluctantly asked him.

"First of all, fuck you." He paused long enough to wink at Braxton. "I've been thinking about that fight with your mom," he said to her. "And baby sis."

In an instant, Braxton's brown eyes were sad, and she didn't bother to hide the emotion or push it aside. She let us see. "What about them?"

"You said it was too late for Rosalie. Why does it have to be?"

"Because she's Faithful's now," Braxton answered, her tone leaving no room for argument. She knew that town and its people better than we did.

Loren, however, was just as stubborn. "You joined Bound to send a message." His eyes flickered to me for some reason before returning to her. "Maybe you just weren't loud enough."

"But Braxen's here now," she reminded Loren, referring to her nephew. "And I don't regret him. Neither does Rosalie." Braxton grimaced suddenly. "I just wish I could say the same about her husband, Pete. Apparently, my sister's talking to the atheist she met online again."

"That's kind of my point, babe." Loren flashed her a patient smile. "Baby sis hasn't made up her mind yet. You can still get through to her."

Braxton stiffened. I could see the struggle not to hope in her eyes. "How?" she eventually asked him anyway.

Loren's eyes returned to me, and this time, they held. It only took a moment for me to read his mind.

It took even less time for me to decide.

SIXTY-EIGHT

Braxton

A DOOR SLAMMED BEHIND ME, AND I FLINCHED FROM THE UNEXPECTED sound as keys scraped inside the lock before I heard the click from it turning.

"How long do we have?" Houston asked cryptically. I knew it was him that took my arm a moment later and began steering me forward.

"Not long," Loren muttered. It was his birthday today, and for his present, he asked me to wear a blindfold.

I drew in a nervous breath.

Hopefully, today wouldn't be a repeat of Houston's birthday two and a half months ago. We had to delay the tour again while my brain healed, and it wasn't scheduled to resume until the end of summer—pending my doctor's approval, of course.

I was already back to feeling normal. Mostly.

There were still no phantom smells or tastes, but as promised, I was adjusting. I was learning how to identify my emotions without my superpowers, as Loren dubbed them. Emily's attack had changed us all, but it wouldn't define what we became.

Suddenly, my brows dipped, but not from that memory. From another.

Why did this place smell so familiar?

I recognized that sweet, warm, and woodsy incense. It only grew stronger as the wooden floor creaked underneath my feet. I was being led…somewhere.

I still wasn't allowed to see.

We'd flown three hours to get here, drove for thirty minutes once we landed, and the entire time I kept my blindfold on for them.

Houston, Loren, and Rich.

The four of us rarely separated for longer than a couple of hours since I was released from the hospital. Where one went, we all went.

"Careful."

I was slowly led up three short steps.

"Do I get to see now?" I asked once we finally stopped.

The floor was softer here. I could feel the thick carpeting underneath my feet, and for whatever reason, my mind conjured red fibers.

"Not yet," Rich whispered.

And then the buttons keeping my dress together were slowly being undone.

I knew by the clove soap that Houston was the one who came up behind me and peeled the tight dress from my shoulders once Rich had finished with the buttons.

Appreciative groans echoed around the room.

"I take it you like it?" I asked them with a small smile. I may not have known what they were up to or where they'd taken me, but I knew where the day would eventually lead.

Houston's hands fell on my hips—I knew because his fingers were softy teasing the light purple lace between my thigh and center—and then he kissed my shoulder. "Yes."

"And we're going to show you how much in a minute," Rich warned.

My legs trembled even as my head swiveled as if I could actually see through the pitch-black cloth. It only heightened my other senses. "Where's Loren?"

"Over here, baby." My head turned in the direction we'd come from—toward the smile in his voice. The birthday boy wasn't standing as close as Houston and Rich, and I wondered why. "They're going to play with you first," he announced, reading my mind. "I want you ready for me."

I drew in a sharp breath. Ready for what exactly?

Unfortunately, I was too tempted by the unknown to ask.

Houston removed the corset pushing my breasts damn near to my chin while Rich disposed of my boots, garter, and panties.

As usual, they left the socks that reached my thighs.

Rich, who must have been kneeling, kissed and sucked on the skin there while Houston palmed my bare breasts with both hands from behind. I could feel his erection against my spine. Eager to get his thick cock inside me, I moaned as I turned my head toward him.

He didn't need much more convincing to kiss me.

Feeling the pad of Jericho's fingers push between my lips below, I began to squirm in Houston's arms. Jericho caressed me—my clit, my entrance—no part of my pussy went untouched. I was dripping now as Houston tweaked my nipples and swallowed the sounds I made.

I heard wood creak a few feet away and imagined Loren shifting in his seat.

Why was I picturing him on a long, wooden bench? Was his cock in his hand? Was he stroking himself as he looked on?

My thoughts were stolen by Jericho's fingers when he pushed them inside of me and pressed until he was knuckle-deep. He gave me his tongue next, flicking my clit and fucking me hard with his fingers simultaneously. It didn't take long at all for me to come. Either he was that fucking good or my feelings for him were just too strong. My gut told me it was both.

Houston's hands left me once I stopped shaking, and he stepped back.

And then Jericho was pulling me down to the floor with him.

My knees dug into the thick carpet with my hands planted on Jericho's chest as he hurriedly undid his belt. I listened to his clothes rustle as he shoved his jeans and boxers down enough to free his cock. Even the coarse hair peppering his thighs turned me on when he brought me down. I almost came a second time when I felt the thick head of his cock brushing me as he searched for my entrance. Finding it, his hands gripped my hips, and then he pushed me down, burying himself inside me without a word.

Only a groan that mixed with my whimper at his size.

He was so long and thick and unrelenting that each time was like the first time.

I almost understood why Emily had been willing to kill me over him, why she had been ready to kill Jericho than let me have him.

I cried out at the unexpected and harsh slap on my ass as if Jericho had heard my thoughts and wanted to punish me for them.

"Ride me."

Smiling, I dug my nails into his chest, making him grunt as I did just that. And as I blindly bounced on Jericho's cock, I vaguely heard the sound of something popping open.

I paused.

"What was that?"

"Nothing," the three of them said at the same time.

My stomach burned with anticipation because I knew they were lying. I also knew I'd enjoy whatever they had up their sleeves.

"Come here." With an unforgiving grip on my hair, Jericho brought my top half down until my naked breasts were pressed against his chest, still covered by his T-shirt. "Did I tell you to stop?" he asked me. I could feel his lips moving against my neck when he spoke.

"No."

"Then why aren't you moving?"

"Jericho…" There were no words left to be said once I flooded his dick.

The hand that had been holding my hip slapped my ass once more when I didn't move fast enough. Still pressed against his chest with his hand in my hair, I raised and lowered my bottom half, letting him split me open.

"Fuck," I heard either Houston or Loren groan from behind.

Bent over like this, I knew they could see Jericho's monster dick tunneling into me over and over again. The only sound Jericho made was the little puffs of air he released, telling me he was holding himself back from coming.

Even with the blindfold, my eyes were closed.

The feeling was just too good.

I heard soft footfalls and felt the rush of air and clove soap wafting the air when Houston crouched behind me. I stiffened, and as soon as my hips began to slow, Jericho slapped my ass again to keep me moving.

I wasn't allowed to stop. Not until he was good and ready.

Houston waited patiently.

The three of them quietly listened to my cries echoing around the mysterious room, and I knew it was because they were also enjoying the sound of my sopping pussy being abused.

They didn't relent until I came hard a second time, and then...

Jericho gripped my hips with both hands.

He didn't take over fucking me, though.

No.

I was kept seated to the hilt on his dick that was still very much hard.

Wet fingers skimmed my butt cheeks, and I knew they belonged to Houston. I also pieced together what he intended to do just before they pushed between. He circled the entrance to my ass, building up the anticipation until I began to shake in Jericho's arms before he pushed the tip of his digit inside.

Immediately tensing when he continued pressing, I whimpered Houston's name, and Jericho soothed me with soft kisses.

"Relax," he implored me. I shook my head even as I tried to do just that. "You want it to feel good, don't you?" I placed my head on his shoulder as he rubbed my thighs before nodding weakly. "Then let Houston take care of you, baby. He loves you. We all do."

Houston placed a kiss on my back, punctuating Rich's claim as he continued to open me up, slowly, with one finger, and then with two.

God, it was so tight.

There was so much pressure.

If I tried to imagine for a second how his dick would feel, I might not let myself go through with it. So I took my head out of the equation and let my heart and body reign free.

Once Houston worked both of his fingers inside, Jericho began to fuck me from below.

My lips parted at the sensation.

It wasn't as intense as when they were both inside my pussy at the same time. At least, not yet. Houston stretched me by tunneling in and out, and soon, I was eagerly anticipating each press of his fingers.

Yes. Fuck yes.

I was starting to wonder how I ever lived without this and them when it all came to a halt. Houston had abruptly pulled his fingers free and moved away. Lifting my head, I started to beg him when Jericho stopped fucking me too and spoke.

"Do you trust us?"

I gulped when I realized I didn't have to think about the answer. That frightened me. After what we'd gone through to get here, it should. Where they once made room for doubt, they now worked overtime to fill that space.

"Yes."

Jericho's grip tightened briefly from surprise. He hadn't been expecting my answer either. I heard the relieved exhale that left him and knew that I would find gratitude in his silver eyes…if only I could see them.

Suddenly, there was a tug on my blindfold as the knot was loosened, and then the cloth was pulled away.

It was dark in here too.

I blinked down at Jericho's handsome face, which gave nothing away, and then I looked up. My gut-punch reaction told me it was a huge mistake before my brain could catch up.

Wordlessly, I gaped at the wooden planks forming a cross and nailed high near the ceiling. Guilt made my gaze shoot away.

It landed on the altar Houston was casually leaning against just a few feet away.

The very same altar I stood before for three days without food and water while the rest of the town stared and whispered "whore" as they passed by.

It wasn't just any church Houston, Loren, and Jericho had chosen to fuck me in.

This was Angels of Purity & Faith.

We were in Faithful.

I sucked in a breath just as my jaw was seized from behind, and teeth nipped my cheek. "Ready to give me the rest of my present now?"

Loren.

I listened as he stroked his cock while he waited. The wet sound as he distributed the lube over every inch told me he already knew what my answer would be.

"I shouldn't be surprised, so why am I surprised?"

"Because you're complicated," Loren told me as he pushed me forward. My breasts were now pressed against Rich's chest again as his hands kept my ass displayed like an offering for his best friend. "It's what we love most about you."

I didn't get to respond because his dick was there in the next moment, pressing forward and making my lips part.

I'd been prepared for it to hurt, but not like this.

Not like this.

"Loren."

"I know, baby." He continued to work his crown inside of me. "We've got you." There was a pause, and then, "Distract her."

I assumed he was talking to Rich, but then Houston was pushing away from the altar where he'd been silent.

My gaze rose from watching his feet carry him forward to watching him undo his belt with pure intent in his green eyes. By the time Houston reached me, his cock was out. I lifted my top half and eagerly swallowed as much of Houston as I could, bobbing my head and losing myself in the taste of him.

Taking advantage, Loren chose that moment to push past that initial resistance with a groan that, with the help of Houston's dick down my throat, drowned out my cry.

"Fuck, I don't know what's tighter," Loren remarked, his voice strained as he held himself still, "your pussy or your ass."

I had a few things to say about that.

They were all forgotten when he and Jericho began to move.

Slowly, carefully, the three of them worked together to replace the memories I had of this place and this town. And they didn't stop until they made themselves clear.

They were my home now.

And I could be as wild as my illicit heart desired.

But first…I had to free it.

Houston came first, then Rich, and finally Loren. Before we could even catch our breath, calm our racing hearts, and let the sweat on our skin dry, I met each of their gazes and they were already watching mine.

"Lilac."

EPILOGUE

Braxton

Four Years Later

"THAT WAS A RED LIGHT!"

"Oh, was it?" my husband teased.

Yes.

We'd gotten married.

The four of us—to each other.

I wore a dress, we had the ceremony, and we exchanged the rings—the whole nine. And I didn't just wear their ring or they mine.

No.

Houston, Loren, and Rich also wore rings from each other—a symbolism of their devotion to each other and to me.

The law didn't recognize it—or God, according to my parents—but our souls had accepted the bond, and that was all that mattered.

Loren kept his cool and his smile as he continued to steer the rented GranTurismo. He now wore his hair with the sides shaved, creating a sexy blond faux hawk. Paired with the large tattoo he'd gotten to cover the entire right side of his neck, the pretty boy now had a dose of ruggedness that made my thighs quiver whenever I stared too long.

Shaking my head at him, I gripped the "oh shit" handle above me. He'd just taken another turn on two wheels, making me close my eyes and pray. I hadn't done the latter in a while, but it was my fault.

Houston and Rich warned me.

They told me to never get in the car with this fucking maniac. There was a reason they never let him drive. I felt like my stomach was in my throat by the time the car finally stopped, and Loren killed the engine. I snatched the keys from the ignition before climbing out of the black sports coupe. I heard his chuckle, but he didn't object.

The security that trailed us in a separate car caught up, and moments later, we were escorted through the busy grounds.

People who should have been too preoccupied to notice our presence stopped and stared. Some took pictures from afar, but more than a few were brave enough to approach for an autograph or selfie.

Of course, we stopped, and we stayed until the crowd became too big for two hair-trigger guards to handle safely.

Another five minutes, and we finally reached the building and the room we sought. The door flew open after only one knock from Loren, revealing the excited face of my baby sister.

"You came!"

"Of course we did," I told her as she stepped aside to let us in.

She talked our ears off while I looked around the small room. I felt emotions, too many to name, welling inside. Loren's thumb swept back and forth over the back of my hand since he was still holding it as he talked with Rosalie.

I couldn't bring myself to.

My heart was in my throat as I took in the twin bed with purple bedding and too many pillows, the small desk at the end already loaded with textbooks, the pictures of Braxen who was a few weeks shy of five pinned on the wall, and her trusty bible waiting on the nightstand.

She'd done it.

Rosalie had forged her own path.

And she did it while keeping her faith.

Something my parents had been convinced was mutually exclusive.

Loren was right about me not being loud enough, but I wouldn't credit myself.

This was all her.

She wouldn't have heard me if she hadn't wanted to listen. I'd only spoken out loud what she'd hidden in her heart.

Rosalie was starting her freshman year at Berkeley while Braxen stayed in Faithful with our parents. It was their only concession after Rosalie divorced Pete. To Amelia and David, their youngest daughter had committed a sin worse than murder and wanted nothing to do with her beyond their grandson.

I didn't relish that.

I didn't feel victorious or satisfied.

I wished more than anything that my baby sister could have it all—her dreams, her faith, her son, our parents, and true love.

But she had me, and she had Braxen whenever she needed family.

Houston, Loren, and Rich too.

"You're missing two," Rosalie pointed out. "Why didn't Houston and Rich come?"

I absolutely knew the three of them had spoiled my sister rotten when she actually pouted at their absence. They doted on her. The word no was never an option, no matter how much I warned them.

"Next time," I promised her. "You know they're good for it."

Rosalie gave us the tour of her dorm and the campus, and a few hours later, Loren had to pry us apart when it was time to go.

Loren was eager to get back, and so was I for the same reason Houston and Rich had elected to stay behind.

The flight home was short. Our day trip quickly came to an end when we finally reached our path, our woods surrounding it, and our castle hidden within.

Even though I had been reluctant to move in and determined to wait during the first year of our relationship, I couldn't seem to find a reason to leave—only ever excuses to stay until the three of them had put their foot down and hijacked my address. I've been living with them ever since and never looked back despite Loren's refusal to help with chores, Houston stealing my leftovers, and Rich hogging the TV.

The only real downside was that I didn't get to see Griff and Maeko, who were now married, as much.

A shirtless Houston, wearing only basketball shorts, was waiting underneath the carriage porch when the car pulled up. I knew if he turned around, I'd see the tattoo on his strong back, but he never took his gaze away from me. Even though I was eager to be in his arms and feel his lips, I stopped to smell the flowers.

Literally.

Rich, on his hands and knees, had planted a small meadow in the middle of our drive that had once been just a grassy island.

Lilacs.

He'd given me lilacs.

Finally reaching Houston, he lifted me, wrapped my legs around his waist, and kissed me deeply as if it had been days instead of hours. Our lips were still attached when he carried me inside while Loren trailed us.

"Any change?" I asked him as we moved through the house.

"Temperature's dropped two degrees."

Loren rushed past us at hearing that news, and we followed him into one of the bedrooms a few seconds later. Rich, also shirtless and wearing jeans, was sleeping in the rocking chair with his head back and mouth open as he snored like a bear. Like Loren, he'd made some changes too. His hair was no longer shaggy but cut short, and his eyes were no longer sad but filled with the confidence of someone who'd found their place in the world.

The drummer was completely oblivious to our presence after being up all night.

"Da-da."

It was all the permission Loren, who was standing over the crib, needed. He reached inside and lifted our son from his bed. He started bouncing his chunky butt excitedly in his father's arms despite his fever that forced our trip to be quick.

"Missed you too, tough guy."

Finally spotting me, our baby started squealing, which startled his father out of his sleep. Rich shot to his feet before realizing we were in the room and relaxing but only slightly. Houston set me down, and I went to him.

"Sorry to wake you."

"It's okay," he told me in a groggy voice. After scrubbing his eyes, he grabbed me and kissed me briefly before turning to our son, who was babbling excitedly at the four of us. "Coda, what are you doing awake, man? We had an agreement."

Coda.

The beginning of the final passage.

Or, in our case, the start of our happily ever after. I didn't think it was possible to feel any more complete until his arrival a year ago.

He definitely hadn't been planned.

Too much time on the road hadn't allowed me to remember birth control.

Red hair.

Brown eyes.

Moody as hell.

Without a DNA test, I couldn't be sure who'd fathered him. I didn't care, and neither did Houston, Loren, and Jericho. Coda would always have three fathers.

Our son reached out, and Jericho carefully took him in his tattooed hands. He'd gotten the piece at the same time Loren and Houston had gotten theirs.

Whatever had been responsible for me smelling and tasting my emotions never returned, and maybe it never would.

So Houston, Loren, and Jericho had tattooed themselves and filled every hall and room of our home with lilacs so that I never forget what love smells like.

The house lights lowered, and the roar was deafening.

Backstage at The Forum, I waited with them.

"Okay?"

I met each of their gazes—green, opaque, and silver.

Once I nodded, they smiled and pushed forward. I watched them take their places on stage. I listened to Houston's song through my eyes—red, blue, and purple shapes lighting up the arena—as they roused the crowd.

This was always meant to be.

It was what they'd told me four years ago, and I'd believed them.

I still do.

Free from Savant, they could do whatever they wanted.

We could do whatever we wanted.

Smiling, I put one foot in front of the other until the spotlight bathed me with the loves of my life standing behind me.

And then I, Bound's new front man, lifted my mic.

You crept in like the dawn
You showed me a new day
But instead of bringing light
You followed me into darkness
Belligerent, bellicose, broken, bound
We painted our r*evol*ution backward
Eventually, we found love

AUTHOR'S NOTE

Lilac is what happens when you color outside the lines. It's such a freeing experience. This story certainly taught me how to live a little. It turned out to be so much more complex than I intended. These characters gave and gave and it took me by surprise. I couldn't walk away. When I first thought of Braxton, Houston, Loren, and Jericho, they were college students, but after being in the When Rivals Play series for three years, I needed to get away from all that teenage angst and turn up the heat a little. Thank you so much for taking a chance on Lilac. If you loved them, stick around. I'm a sucker for bonus scenes.

ACKNOWLEDGMENTS

This book, while so much fun to write, also had its moments where I thought I'd go insane. Tijuana, you were with me every step of the way—for the good writing days and the bad. Thank you for letting me ramble, vent, and absolutely lose my marbles whenever I needed. Sunny, we are truly the blind leading the blind. Lilac is done thanks to you cheering me on. Now, let's see about getting yours written this century. I've got my pom-poms and bullhorn ready. Amanda, the first six thousand drinks are on me, one for every ludicrous idea I thought of and you made happen. Rogena and Colleen, my fearsome duo, no one does dedication and patience like you two. I also swear I don't sit and think of ways to break your back each book. Somehow, I manage anyway. Jamie, thank you so much for holding the fort down when I'm offline. It's hard to think it's been six years since we found each other through Fear Me. Stacey, I'm keeping my fingers crossed that we get to grab lunch one of these times I'm in Florida. Bring the pecan pie! Nina, and her amazing team at Valentine PR, thank you for your wisdom, expertise, versatility, and care. Thank you to my faithful, loyal readers who I would not be here without. Now that we've met ...onward! Mom...yes, I know. You were cut for me. You'll always be at the top of my list even when you're at the bottom. Love you.

CONTACT THE AUTHOR

Follow me on Facebook
www.facebook.com/authorbbreid

Join Reiderville on Facebook
www.facebook.com/groups/reiderville

Follow me on Twitter
www.twitter.com/_BBREID

Follow me on Instagram
www.instagram.com/_bbreid

Subscribe to my newsletter
www.bbreid.com/news

Visit my website
www.bbreid.com

Text REIDER to 474747 for new release alerts
(US only)

ABOUT B.B. REID

B.B. Reid is the author of several novels including the hit enemies-to-lovers, *Fear Me*. She grew up the only daughter and middle child in a small town in North Carolina. After graduating with a Bachelors in Finance, she started her career at an investment research firm while continuing to serve in the National Guard. She currently resides in Charlotte with her moody cat and enjoys collecting Chuck Taylors and binge-eating chocolate.

Made in the USA
Middletown, DE
26 September 2023